DAVID L. ROBBINS

TRANS-MONGOLIAN EXPRESS

For Katharine Sands

Inspired by the Warren Adler Novel
Trans-Siberian Express

The wolf could not count. She knew only few and many, different from none.

She understood cold and heat but did not think of either unless they were extreme. Even then, she knew what to do, curl in a place out of the wind or the light, or move.

She knew living from dead, and living meant hunger. Hunger drove her to everything. She was raised in a pack and left them because of hunger. She was the largest of them, the best hunter, but too often, even when the kill was hers, she had to fight the others to eat her fill. She fought wolves more and more, until she began to understand hate. Then she bit an old one in the throat and with a bloody muzzle she wandered away.

She did not know time or distance, only the wander. She put her tail to the place where the sun rose, her teeth to the place where it fell, and walked. Now she was few.

She did not turn back because she found food as she walked.

She leaped on rodents in the grasses, dug for bugs, snapped her jaws on birds before they could take wing, and trod in shallow waters where she nabbed fish. She swam wider waters to new shores and found game she could outrun.

Sometimes she searched for signs of another pack but nothing of her kind crossed her nose or tongue. She wandered more, following her hunger.

Under her paws the grasslands turned to barren rock, then great reaches of sand. She entered an expanse so vast, so blank she could see and hear everything, air she could taste. Food was easy to find with fewer places for it to hide. Scaly quick things made her meals. Their blood was her water. Larger beasts crossed her path, but she would need a pack to bring them down.

She lived and hunted in the Gobi, though she knew not its name. She learned, indeed, to count to one.

Wandering behind her hunger, she did not know time, but light and dark, and now. In a now, she chased a hare.

The hare sprinted but she gained on it. Then it leaped over something in the sand. She let the hare run off, her senses alerted. She stopped to let the thing in the sand slither away to hide from her. When it did not, she dropped low. Everything hid from her.

Slowly, sniffing, she approached the rail, though not by its name. Bravely she touched it with the pad of a paw. It was harder than any bone, warmer than the sand. It vibrated. She knew life from death, and this was life. She ran to the top of a sand hill to watch down on it.

Soon, a monster, though not the name, but a monster with an immense back and a rumbling roar raced over it. The monster came from the end of the sand and rushed away to the end. She stayed on the hill, smelling fire.

She remembered something from the pack. To be afraid.

She waited more while hunger set in harder. The sun peaked, then began to plummet. Then another monster passed like lightning and thunder, but not the words.

The monsters had no pack. They wandered alone, like her. She howled at this one.

Below her hill, under her keen eyes, this one lost a small

piece of itself. The piece flew off to hit the sand and roll until it came still.

Like the other monster, this one chuffed away, far to the end. In dimming light she crept down from the sand hill.

She crawled close to sniff the piece. She did not know the scent, but she knew life from death. This was dead.

She turned away from the path of the monsters. She would not cross it. She was hungry but not so much that she had any hunger for this flesh. This belonged to the monsters, and they could keep it.

Russia and Afghanistan

1982

1

LARA

September 8
Moscow

Inside the sack over her head, Lara's adrenaline-hard breathing sounded like a freight train. She couldn't hear what was being said.

The car rattled around a corner. She swayed against the man on her left, then straightened up into the meaty shoulder of the one on her right. She couldn't calm herself.

The burlap bag itched; in her fight to hold back mania, this felt intolerable. Lara was forced to sit on her roped-up hands, so she blew up at her nose to scratch it. One of the men scratched her nose for her. Lara corralled enough breath to say, "*Spasibo.*" The one on her right leaned close to mutter, "*Zatknis.*" Shut up. The men laughed loud enough for her to count four of them.

The ride lasted ten to twelve minutes. Not long enough to leave the limits of Moscow. The car didn't careen, the driver wanted to draw no attention. But they hadn't made Lara lean over, didn't push her blinded head across one of their laps for

7

another laugh. Nor were they worried about being spotted driving in Moscow with a hooded woman in the backseat.

The car eased to a stop. Lara gained control of herself enough to catch the crunch of gravel under the tires, the bawl of bad brakes. The door squeaked when it opened. This was a shitty car and these were low-level thugs.

The shoulders of the men on both sides disappeared, leaving Lara alone in the backseat. She turned her head fast like an owl to grab at more sounds. Then a mild hand guided her out of the car, nudging her head down to keep her from bumping the frame. The hand cupped Lara's elbow to walk her away on the gravel. The crunching stopped and became a sidewalk. High heels clicked.

A woman's voice said in accented English, "Don't be frightened."

Lara answered in Russian. "*Ya net.*" I'm not.

The woman laughed like the men in the car.

———

Lara was lowered into a chair. Her wrists were cut free. The woman in heels pinched the top of the sack to sweep it off like the reveal of a magic trick, tousling Lara's hair; she tried to clear the brown curtain from her eyes but her hands had gone to sleep and felt like clay. She rubbed at her eyes with the backs of her wrists until the woman behind her cleared her face and said, "*Nu, dorogaya.*" There, darling.

A heavyset man behind a metal desk waited for Lara to gather herself. His pink forearms on the desktop were slabs, his shaved pate capped a big head; a snowy beard tumbled down his linen *vyshyvanka* shirt. His eyes were onyx. He looked like the old Russian writers Lara had grown up on: Tolstoy, Dostoevsky, Turgenev.

Mint-hued cinderblock walls squared the small room. The concrete floor had a drain. This was a basement. A lone bulb in a table lamp lit the rotund and looming man in sallow, pustulant light.

Some sibilant draw of steel hissed close to Lara's ear. The woman behind her stroked the back of Lara's neck, then saw herself out on her heels.

On the other side of the desk, the big man said, "Luba Mikhailovna Dilkova." His voice matched his girth.

Lara drew one deep breath. She let it go smoothly, the way she'd been taught to shoot.

In Russian, she asked, "Who are you?"

He wagged a sausage-sized finger.

"Oh, you know who I am."

"Why'd you kidnap me?"

He wagged again. "You know why."

The returning blood flooded needles into Lara's hands. She rubbed them away.

"What do you want?"

"I want to decide whether to kill you." He drew his arms off the table to sit back. He blew out through rubbery lips. "I probably won't. But."

Lara's lungs tried to quicken again. She flattened a hand over her breast to feel her chest rise and fall, and breathed through her nose to hear every rushing in and out.

The bearded mobster sat forward. "Are you having a heart attack?"

Lara expelled one deep breath, then lowered her hand.

She had no more questions. There'd be no rescue. She gazed straight at the heavy man who knit fingers across the big ball of his belly.

"No."

"Good, Luba Mikhailovna. So. You are Russian."

"I was born Russian."

"This argues in your favor."

"You haven't shown any hesitation about killing Russians."

"Only for business. Tell me. Why do you not use your

beautiful Russian name? Luba. Is Slavic." The fat man aimed his voice over Lara's head, to someone behind her. "Rugo? What does it mean?"

A grating voice, the man in the car who'd told her to shut up, answered.

"Love."

"You see? Love. And your father, the policeman. Mikhail."

Lara said, "Michael."

The mobster batted this away. "His name should live on in you. Mikhailovna."

"Don't worry about him."

"Listen. This American name you use, Lara Dill. This sounds like a pill. A laxative. Laradil. Take a laradil for a good crap."

Rugo's chortle was a wheeze. If Lara's number was up in this basement, Rugo would do it. When he was done snickering behind her, Rugo coughed. It sounded deep, damaged.

Without turning, Lara asked, "Speaking of which. Rugo?"

Behind the desk, the big mobster's gaze flitted above Lara's head. Rugo was asking if he might respond. The mob boss nodded.

Rugo said, "Yeah."

Lara asked, "Have you had diarrhea lately?"

"What the fuck?"

"Anything swollen? Your throat maybe? A hand?"

Rugo said something that sounded like Czech, then a spit.

Lara asked the big, bearded man, "Did he handle any of the plutonium?"

"Yes."

"He could be sick."

"Sick?"

"There might've been a leak in the container."

Rugo said, "Fuck you."

The big mobster pawed the air. "No, no, listen to her. This

is a doctor. An expert." He leaned across his desk as if to speak conspiratorially. "He *has* been shitting a lot."

Rugo said, "Fuck you, too." The effort raised another gurgling hack.

Lara said, "Have him see someone. Any others who were with him."

"Yes, okay. Thank you."

Still leaning over his desk, the mobster twisted an index finger on the metal top.

"Now. Do I kill you?"

"No."

"Okay, alright. I see your position. I will make other argument."

He sat back to pet his white beard.

"You know a great deal about my operation. You blew a whistle at the American embassy."

"I'm the science attaché. It's my job."

"If you knew how much money the Afghan mujahideen were paying me for radioactive material, you'd bring it to me yourself."

"You're stealing uranium, plutonium, cesium. You don't know how to handle these things."

"No, we do not. So work for me."

"The mujahideen are going to make dirty bombs out of what you sell them. They'll kill Russian soldiers. Your own people."

"My own people are getting killed in Afghanistan anyway. It's a fucking war. Why not make money?"

"Is that a serious question?"

"Yes. Work for me. Or I think I may have to kill you."

Lara leashed everything running wild in her head and chest, and led it all down to the one finger she tapped on the chair arm.

"No."

The bearded mobster raised his gaze again above Lara, to

Rugo. He slapped the table and leveled his gaze at her.

"You have balls."

"No I don't."

His laugh fueled a small nod of his bald, bearded head.

"Alright, Luba Mikhailovna. Alright."

The big mobster's chair squawked as he sat back. Lara imagined bits of herself going down that drain in the concrete floor. Again she flattened a hand over her heart.

The mobster continued: "Let me ask. Did you notice after you blew your whistle, nothing happened? No one was fired, no one arrested? Your report disappeared like a pebble in a lake."

Lara nodded.

He circled a digit in front of his beard. "What does that tell you?"

"That you don't run this operation."

"I do not. Other very powerful people do. Some of them want you dead."

The mobster snapped his fingers. Rugo came forward to pin back Lara's forearms; she didn't resist while a fresh rope lashed her wrists. The bald mobster inclined his hairless brow in farewell. Rugo swept the burlap sack over Lara's head.

The chair behind the desk squeaked a last time. The big mobster lumbered close. His voice spilled down on her from overhead, a deep tone that tolled through the sawing rasps of her breathing inside the sack.

"However, now that we have met, I find I am not one of them."

Lara's head dropped as though a noose had been cut. The high heels re-entered the basement.

The mobster said, "Goodbye, Luba Mikhailovna. It would not be wise to mention that you and I have met."

A heavy mitt landed on her shoulder. It stayed a moment, to tell Lara the weight of it would remain long after the hand was gone.

2

ANTON

Trainee Nikolai beckoned Anton to a window.

Young Nikolai didn't have to point. Above Unit 1, a pillar of steam twisted high out of the vent stack. From his perch in the third-floor Turbine Department between reactors 1 and 2, Anton checked the stack of Unit 2. The tall, scaffolded chimney remained stoic and silent. No venting had been scheduled for today, nor for this week.

Trainee Nikolai peered at Anton, not the reactor.

Anton asked, "Tell me what you think?"

The heavyset assistant displayed certainty when he said, "An accident."

Certainty was a good trait for a nuclear engineer. To a point.

"Perhaps. What sort?"

"A broken water pipe inside the reactor. Or worse."

A pale plume eddied toward a tufted sky. Rain was expected at sunset. If Nikolai was correct, and he was, whatever radioactive nuclides were twirling out of Unit 1's vent would fall back to earth inside the raindrops.

Anton left the assistant at the window. The situation had moved beyond a trainee.

He dialed Unit 1's Control Room. Anton let the phone ring for a long time, set down the receiver, and dialed again. He waited more tolling minutes until someone answered.

"Control Room One."

Anton said, "This is Chief Engineer Epstein in Turbines."

"Yes, Comrade Chief Engineer."

"Are you the shift supervisor?"

"I am."

"Please see to it that someone in your Control Room answers the phone at all times."

"Yes, Comrade Chief Engineer."

"Have you had an accident in the reactor?"

The shift supervisor paused to compose his lie.

"Not an accident, no. Nothing of consequence."

"What happened?"

"It was very small."

"That's not what I asked."

"We're very busy fixing the problem right now, Comrade Chief Engineer. Another few hours or so. Anything else?"

Anton didn't know this shift supervisor, the man may have been new. He sounded new, protective. Anton gave him another chance to ask for help.

"Has there been a radiation release?"

"No, Comrade. There's no emergency. Nothing to concern yourself with."

"You need to shut down the reactor. My team and I will head your way to take a look."

"Shut down? No, absolutely not. There's no reason to shut down."

"I can see the reason coming out of your vent. Shut down."

The line went dead.

————

Without a formal request from Unit 1, Anton could do nothing. Each team at Chernobyl was expected to be excellent on its own.

Anton assembled his four engineers and the trainee. He instructed them to prepare their hazard suits. They gathered and tested the team's three Geiger counters to measure alpha and beta particles, plus a handheld ionization chamber for gamma rays. Then they waited.

As scheduled, the rain began at sundown. It fell softly, as if careful. After an hour, sensing nothing untoward, the rain came down in earnest. The cloudburst scissored the rising steam into puffs that scattered on the swirling winds.

With endless coffee, Anton sat by the phone. He stayed apart from his team to let them deal hands of *Durak,* or nap.

After five hours, Unit 1's vent continued to fume. Anton called a half-dozen times but the phone in the Control Room was not answered again. At midnight Anton freed his team to go home. Alone he waited another hour. Ringlets of blinking lights lit the seething stack.

He drove to Pripyat through the rain. In his apartment, dark and after hours, Anton could not sleep. He could only stand at his dim window watching the raindrops, and the KGB teams arriving in black mackintoshes and brimmed hats. At intersections and corners they secured Pripyat's streets and stopped the few cars moving. The agents sent anyone outdoors back into the buildings of the atomic city.

Several dozen bulky trucks bearing great yellow barrels on their backs rumbled onto the boulevard below. The vehicles dispersed into Pripyat. A pair worked up and down Anton's street. Both opened great faucets in their cisterns to sluice the road in ankle-deep water that washed away into the storm drains.

Anton emptied a pickle jar into the kitchen sink. He boiled the jar in a pot, let it cool, then tucked it into his raincoat.

Downstairs, outside, he approached a KGB man. The droplets had not eased predawn. The agent moved toward him, not waiting.

"Go inside, Comrade. It's just a scheduled street cleaning."

"I'm a senior engineer at the plant. I want to know what's going on."

The agent smiled but it was not a smile.

"Then, Senior Engineer, you should know that there can be no panic-mongering, no provocative rumors. No negative manifestations."

The KGB man's hands had not left his pockets. A little rivulet dribbled off his brim.

Anton said, "Of course," and turned around.

Heading back to his apartment, he held the open pickle jar at his waist where the KGB man could not see. Anton walked as slowly as he might, collecting the rain.

3

LARA

The boy arrived at the bench with arms full. He juggled down to Lara one stuffed blini wrapped in yellow wax paper and a Styrofoam cup of kvass. He kept the same for himself.

Zach sat beside her. He nestled his cup of bread wine between his thighs, risking a spill on his suit pants. Lara pressed her cup between her legs, too, but she wore blue jeans. She was not going to the office.

She said, "Thanks for meeting me."

Lara didn't look at Zach but out across the elevated view of Moscow five miles north. A summery sky gleamed on the city's black glass skyline, above the Olympic stadium, and on the Moskva River. The Lenin Hills had once been the Sparrow Hills under the monarchs, but the Soviets coveted everything, even beauty. Kiosks sold cheap food to tourists who came for the view. An old vendor leading a horse and cart tapped a keg of the bread-brewed kvass wine. Moscow,

17

the greenest of any world capitol, waved goodbye to Lara on boughs of apple, spruce, and oak.

Zach had been waiting to bite into his blini, some show of politeness or support, maybe pecking order. Lara took a nibble of the ham and cream cheese crepe. This released Zach; the boy tucked in, young and inelegant. He chewed and slurped the kvass. Any semblance of sympathy from him evaporated.

She asked, "How bad is it?"

Zach chuckled as though he was already telling the story over beers with his fellow gofers from the embassy.

"Bad enough they sent me. Who'd you piss off?"

She looked down from the trees and sunshine. Though she would not answer, Zach waved her off.

"It's a rhetorical question."

He licked cream cheese off fingertips before he plucked an unfastened envelope from his suit jacket and handed it over.

"Last paycheck."

From another pocket, Zach produced a second envelope, also unsealed.

She asked, "What's this?"

He said, "Plane ticket. To Beijing. One way."

Lara muttered, "Goddammit."

Zach shifted on the bench to face her. Annoyance flashed into his posture and face.

He said, "Christ, what do you want me to do?"

The boy was twenty years her junior. Zach was a low-level factotum at the U.S. embassy, he fetched coffee and stamps, he was somebody's nephew.

She asked, "Why the fuck would you think I want you to do anything?"

Zach balled up the blini's yellow wax paper and tossed the dregs of the kvass into the grass. He shot off the bench like she'd jilted him.

"Alright, fine. Here's the deal. Your flight out is Sunday. Pack up your flat tomorrow, whatever you want forwarded to

Beijing. I'll make sure it gets there. Get a taxi to the airport, okay? Don't go back to the embassy, not your lab, nothing. You won't get past security. Someone from the Beijing office will meet you when you land."

Zach handed Lara one more envelope, a small one, like a thank-you card. This one had been glued shut.

The boy knifed the air with both hands. He said, "That's it," and walked off. Then he turned back.

"By the way. I know who you pissed off, Lara. Everyone."

Zach stamped away on the brick path, down the emerald Lenin Hills.

She turned over the envelope. Handwritten on it was her name.

Luba Mikhailovna Dilkova.

With her thumbnail Lara sliced open the envelope. Her hands trembled to unfold the white page. The note, too, was a handwritten scrawl.

Ne vozvrashchaysya v Rossiya. Do not come back to Russia.

4

TIMUR

The last stone bit was dulling fast. Timur had already gone through three.

The next bit wouldn't come for another week or two. But the blast needed twenty-four holes, a clockface pattern of channels in the rock wall. This hole was the twenty-fourth.

Timur shoved all his weight behind the big pneumatic drill. He did not swipe the sweat off his brow or the rock dust from his lips. Around the corner in the tunnel, a diesel generator strained, pushing the drill with everything it had, too.

Timur's muscles raced with the rock to see which would quit first. He'd been unlucky in this section of the tunnel; he'd run out of the softer sedimentary limestone into igneous veins of granite.

His arms shook on the drill with a fury that would take hours to fade once he was done; his hands would buzz like there were bees in them. Timur couldn't turn the work over to any of the watching mujahideen, they were all rail-thin men; the impact drill weighed half as much as some of them. The twenty Russian prisoners couldn't be trusted.

Timur growled at the rock face. The angled shothole, only a quarter of a meter deep, drooled ghosts of dust. Timur screamed at it. Then he stopped and left the hole too shallow by half.

He staggered back; the impact drill protruded from the wall like a knife that hit bone. Timur leaned his spine against the rock face and slid down. He spit between his knees into the mound of granite dust.

Five mujahideen crept up through the haze Timur hadn't noticed he'd raised. The drill hadn't been cutting the rock, just scorching it. He used the sweat on his fingertips to clean his lips.

In Arabic, Timur said to the approaching Afghans, "*Tafaḍḍulu.*" Go ahead.

———

He didn't wire the dynamite, his hands trembled too much. Timur bent over at the wall to keep from bumping his head. A queasy little *mujāhid* slid the two dozen sticks into the circle of shotholes, each with a prayer.

The last stick didn't slip fully into its channel but stuck out like a red button in the rock. The little Afghan looked to Timur, who shrugged.

Timur showed the nervous *muj* how to attach a blasting cap to each explosive, then safely insert ignition wires into the caps. The small man worked cautiously, and his hands shook almost as much as Timur's.

Once the dynamite was wired, Timur unpooled thirty meters of fuse cable along the tunnel floor. The Afghan hustled past him to duck around the bend in the shaft.

Timur rounded the corner with the wire, to squat beside

the initiator box. Fresh air from a ventilation duct fifty meters away traipsed across his damp back. The draft smelled like rain. Timur couldn't guess the time; none of the Afghans owned a watch and he'd broken his own. Inside the tunnel, like in the mines of Siberia, it was always night.

He snipped the det wire, then held up the severed end for another little mujāhid to attach to the initiator. Though Timur's hands had quit vibrating, his fingers hummed too much to feel the smallness of the task.

When everything was ready, the five Afghans retreated up the shaft. Behind Timur stood a beardless boy, a rifle strapped to his back. Timur beckoned the boy forward. Tiptoeing past the older men, the boy moved furtively; he seemed accustomed to sneaking. He stood over Timur who, on his haunches, came eye to eye with him.

Timur asked, "How old are you, *fata*?"

"Fourteen."

"What's your name?"

"Ismail."

"What are you doing here, Ismail?"

"I want to see the explosion."

"Have you not seen too many already?"

Ismail seemed not to understand.

Timur said, "Alright. Kneel here, Ismail."

The boy leaned his hunting rifle against the tunnel wall, then got on his knees in pebbles beside Timur.

Timur showed him how to twist the hand crank that would rotate the magneto inside the detonator. An electric current would rush a spark down the wire to the blasting caps.

Ismail drew a deep breath over the crank. He paused to take some mental photo of himself, doing this momentous thing at Tora Bora.

Timur said, "Now."

"*Na'am, Almarid.*" Yes, Giant.

Ismail left smiling, dynamite smoke at his back. Quickly he returned with twenty Russian prisoners, guarded by himself and four mujahideen. The Afghans were not boys like Ismail but craggy, oleo-eyed men with knotty hands holding scarred Kalashnikovs. They'd all been selected as guards because each had lost family members to the Russians. They called the Russians *shavki*. Dogs.

The prisoners drudged past. Timur stayed in a crouch; he couldn't straighten to his full height in the shaft. The captured Soviets bore on their shoulders sledges, picks, and shovels.

Ismail grinned at Timur when he walked by. The boy had no beard; everyone else did, even the Soviets. Timur's own beard was patchy and sparse, a legacy from his Chinese grandfather.

The explosion had flung debris all the way to the bend in the shaft where Timur and the Afghans had taken cover. The Russians were given no commands; they knew what to do, another captive day for them in the tunnels of the mujahideen. Wooden carts squealed from the cave mouth, prisoners pushing wagons loaded with hewn beams to support the roof of the new shaft. The rubble would be carted outside to build more defensive positions and watchtowers around Tora Bora.

The prisoners hammered at the larger rocks to break them into moveable sizes. Each wallop clanged in the tunnel like a ricocheted bullet. Too many blasts for a decade had left Timur's hearing raw. He got headaches. He suffered rashes in summer heat, his eyes didn't like the sun. His graying hair, gathered with a leather thong, had once been black. He could no longer tan. The mines had made him a pale, cold creature.

Timur and most of the mujahideen wore lungee turbans. A few wore pakol hats. The Russians worked bareheaded, scalps shaved to limit lice. In lanternlight, Timur walked past

Ismail and the guards. He moved among the shavki smacking the blasted boulders or shoveling pulverized debris into the carts. Timur had no worry that one of the Russians might drive a pickax into his heart or brain him with a shovel. The prisoners of Tora Bora knew every one of them would be gunned down if a single mujahideen were harmed. More Russian soldiers would be captured in their place.

Timur's turban scraped the ceiling as he approached the remains of the blast wall. Tools striking on all sides made him wince. He spider-walked his fingers along the ceiling as he swept a flashlight side-to-side, feeling for faults in the stone, for fissures, pressure.

He halted at the rockpile. The two dozen dynamite sticks blowing at the same instant should have formed a shaped charge funneling the power of the blast into the mountain, scooping out another two or three meters. Timur looked for evidence whether the one shallow shothole might have upset the balance of the pattern. He aimed his torch above the rubble into the newly carved-out portion. The ragged shaft looked to have advanced another three meters, as it should have. Three Russians with a cart gathered behind Timur, waiting to clear the debris.

He clambered over the broken, blackened rocks. Timur poked his head and the torch through an opening, peering farther into the fresh wound in the mountain. The flashlight illuminated a thin shadow, a razor slit across the limestone roof. Timur scrambled over more shifting rocks, barking his knees until he could wedge his chest and arms inside the fresh chamber.

Reaching up, Timur flattened a palm over the fissure. The crack crawled from under his hand, like the black that spreads in a poisoned vein.

The mountain shivered.

He tried to chase the fault with his fingers, but it outran him. The fracture spread above his head; Timur swiveled the

24

light to follow. The crack raced above the rubble pile, then split into bolts. Before he could blink, the crevice spread into the roof over the heads of the waiting Afghans and the Russians.

Timur yanked his head and shoulders out of the chamber. He skidded down the rubble until his boots hit the stone floor. The prisoners with the cart gestured to him: Do we start?

Forgetting himself, Timur spoke in Arabic, "*Ālhurūbi.*"

Run.

None of the prisoners understood, but by then Timur had hurried past and did not turn back to repeat himself in Russian.

Hunched over, he couldn't go full out. Timur shouldered through another ten prisoners. He didn't glance behind him to see if the fissures in the ceiling were quicker than him. His turban bumped the uneven roof and fell away. The Russians didn't stop pounding rocks or hefting them into the carts.

Galloping at Ismail, Timur swept the boy off his feet. Ismail dropped his hunting rifle. Timur put the squealing boy under one arm and ran.

The cave-in shook everything. The floor shifted, pinballing Timur off the sharp-edged walls. He dropped the boy to let him run and save himself. Dust stormed around them as they sprinted out of the mountain's throat. A thick gray cloud caught them five meters from the tunnel mouth. The shock-wave arched their backs, blew them off their feet, then spit them out under a blue sky.

Timur lay faceup, head spinning. The sun hung low in the east, morning. His hands burned from cuts. One of his knees was gashed.

Woozily, Timur sat up. The tunnel mouth rang like a gong. The Afghans coughed, most of them hurt. Little Ismail's cheek had been cut. The cave-in had coated Timur and all of them in dust, white as bakers.

Timur was first to his feet. The boy came to stand with

him. The nervous Afghans looked about to see that all ten had escaped and they congratulated each other. They combed fingers through their beards, paddled one another's robes and doffed their pakols and turbans to knock the debris out of them.

Timur limped away. Ismail walked with him, bleeding down his cheek. The mujahideen lingered to gaze back at the fuming tunnel. One by one, they followed Timur and the boy. No one mentioned the Russians.

5

ANTON

OCTOBER 15
PRIPYAT
UKRAINE

Anton plucked a fat red Estonian apple off the top of a pyramid of apples. From a bin he picked a Cuban pineapple. Then two Kazakh peaches. He filled a paper bag with strawberries from Azerbaijan. He popped a Mekong Delta blueberry into his mouth to see that it wasn't bitter, then bought a hundred grams for his oatmeal tomorrow. The Soviet Socialist republics grew fine fruit.

Into his mesh bag, Anton dropped a can of Czech ratatouille, then added a Chinese marshmallow bar. A bottle of Caucasian white from Sochi on the Black Sea, and he headed to the checkout counter.

The bespectacled young clerk said, "Comrade Engineer Epstein."

"Comrade Sergei Sergeyevich. How are your studies?"

"Very good, thank you."

Anton unloaded the contents of his string sack onto the counter for Sergei Sergeyevich to tote up. The boy said, "I'm

27

pleased to see you. I've had news. I moved up to third in thermal hydraulics."

Anton nodded. Next year, if the lad pushed his grades to second, or first like Anton had as a Volgograd schoolboy, he might get admitted to the Moscow Power Energy Institute. Pripyat's Nuclear Pioneer School was an excellent training ground, but only the best could climb to the next level, become an *atomschiki*, one of the elite Soviet nuclear engineers. Anton wondered if he ought to add an East German chocolate bar.

Sergei Sergeyevich asked, "Have you been to Moscow lately?"

"Why do you ask?"

The young clerk held up Anton's string shopping bag, the *avoska* that all Muscovites carried should they stumble onto a store with a sudden surplus of things they might want, like toilet paper, sugar, canned peas. None of those shortages plagued Pripyat. Here, the twenty thousand workers at the Chernobyl power complex and their families were provided with all they needed. The avoska was a giveaway that Anton had been to Moscow.

Sergei Sergeyevich adjusted his glasses as he finished adding up Anton's groceries. The boy tore off a small green sheet with the items totaled. He stuffed the fruit, cans, bottle, and marshmallow bar into the sack.

Anton said, "I was in Moscow, yes. I was scheduled to lecture today at the Institute."

"You didn't?"

"No."

"Why not?"

Anton hefted the bag. It held enough for Anton's day and evening, and there would be blueberries for his morning oatmeal.

"I was called back."

―――――

Anton pushed open the door to the offices of the Third Directorate, punctual for his 1 p.m. meeting.

A secretary half his age ushered him down a hall made bright by October sun. A row of windows gazed into the white face of Reactor 1, the first of the four goliaths to rise at Chernobyl.

Chief Pavel rose behind his desk at Anton's entry. The two shook hands and said each other's name without the patronymics. Pavel came to sit with Anton.

"I'm sorry I had to bring you back from Moscow."

Pavel straightened his Italian tie, shot his cuffs, and crossed his legs at the knee. He'd grown thicker than Anton over the years, the desk had done that to him. He dressed very well. Anton wore a burgundy cable-knit sweater from Romania.

For moments, the two looked out through Pavel's picture window, at what they'd shared over a decade. The massive nuclear facility, a square kilometer of walls, pipes, cranes, sheds, chimneys, transmission wires, fences, all of it seemed to have erupted out of the ground. The azure expanse of the cooling pond and the faultless sky made the vista idyllic even as it was marvelously technological.

Anton and Pavel had arrived at Chernobyl together in 1971. Theirs had been some of the hands which raised the reactors, the power, from the earth. Anton had been a fresh-eyed *atomschiki*, Pavel worked in logistics. Today Anton headed the Turbine Department for Units 1 and 2. Pavel managed Security for 1 and 2. They'd become old men at the plant; presently the average age in Pripyat was twenty-seven. Chernobyl was nothing, just grass and marshland when they'd arrived.

They spoke a bit about their recent lives; they'd not seen as much of each other outside work the way they'd once done. No more tennis. Promotions and bringing the new No. 4

reactor critical and online had overshadowed the past few years. Neither had found a hobby or a wife, neither had tried very hard.

Pavel said, "Alright. Tell me what happened."

Anton indicated the file on Pavel's desk. "It's in there."

"I want to hear what's not in there. In your own words."

"Why?"

"Because I have to make a decision. You understand this."

"I figured it would fall on you. I'm sorry."

"Go ahead."

Anton walked to the picture window. Unit 1 was the first in the line of monoliths. The four RBMK reactors at Chernobyl were each the largest on the planet, each one ten stories high. This had been the mandate when designing and building them, to make them colossuses, make them Soviet.

"Pavel, there's a coverup."

"Is there?"

"The night of the incident at Unit 1, I collected a rain sample outside my flat. I tested it."

"You used equipment belonging to the state to do this test?"

"Of course."

"With permission?"

"I'm a senior engineer, Pavel."

"Continue."

"I found traces of iodine 131. Fragments of uranium dioxide fuel. Iodine and cesium. Hot particles of zinc 65 and zirconium-niobium 95. Xenon 33. Strontium 90. Particles of irradiated graphite."

"What was your conclusion?"

"Where else would I find irradiated graphite? There's been a partial meltdown of Unit 1's reactor core."

Pavel lifted Anton's report from his desk. He set it in his lap without uncrossing his legs. He covered the file with both hands as if to muzzle it.

"There was no meltdown in Reactor 1."

Anton came back from the window to sit beside his old friend. Pavel was a scientist. He would rely on facts.

"The wind that night was northwest. The next morning I drove five kilometers to Chistogalovka."

"And what did you find in Chistogalovka?"

"Levels of radiation four hundred times normal."

Pavel pushed a finger into the report on his thigh. "What else?"

Anton said, "Bulldozers worked for two weeks turning over the ground in the forest around the plant."

"Simple maintenance."

"In the middle of Pripyat, Lenina Prospeckt was repaved."

"More maintenance, Anton. Stop it."

Pavel raised the report. He held it with fingertips to show Anton how light it was, and how toxic.

"You've claimed that the RBMK reactors have flaws."

"They need to be shut down."

"You're one of the engineers who built them."

Anton had arrived at the meeting with Pavel prepared to defend himself, his report, his facts and conclusions. But Pavel's challenge took him back a decade, to the dream they'd all shared, that the USSR would build a network of nuclear plants from the Gulf of Finland to the Caspian. While the United States dithered with flying to the moon, the Soviet Union would make itself a modern wonder of productivity and power on earth. They'd both gotten swept up in that vision. Anton clung to it across all the years that followed; that was why he'd written the report.

"I am."

"Then why do you make this claim now? For twenty years, since you were a student, you've been studying the RBMK. You know as well as anyone, we've been handicapped all that time. Bureaucracy. Bungling and inefficiencies. Now, *now* we are underway. Now we are on the cusp. We can build the ideal of Communism, you and me and those like us. We can bring power to the worker, the state, we can unlock the potentials of economic development. Think of it, Anton. We can manufacture nuclear reactors like tractors. Atomic power will irrigate deserts, bring warmth to the Arctic. We can correct the mistakes of nature. *We* can do this. These are the facts. So, why now, Anton?"

"Because I believe in my nation. I believe in science and the ways it can serve humankind. I also know the ways science can destroy humankind."

"A fine answer."

"Why, particularly?"

"You mentioned your nation first."

Anton relied on facts, too, and they were gathering fast. The sum was clear: He was not going to reach Pavel. Pavel had lied. The decision to silence Anton was made before Anton was recalled from Moscow. And it was not made by Pavel.

Anton had dug his own hole with the report on the RBMK. There would be consequences. But he was very senior at Chernobyl. He could weather this. And Pavel was, after all, his friend. Anton decided to dig a bit deeper, to see what he might find.

"May I ask you a question?"

With a flick of the wrist, Pavel tossed Anton's report back on his desk.

"Yes."

"You and I both know of more accidents at Chernobyl. In the last ten years, how many?"

"I can't say."

"I know of at least a dozen, in Units 1 and 2 alone. Probably twice that in the whole plant. All of them were small, nothing we couldn't chalk up to a learning curve. My team and I wrote them up. I assume others have done the same. We've made recommendations, asked for changes. Tell me,

Pavel, before you tell me what you've decided. Did any of those reports leave this office?"

"I'm your friend, Anton."

"I know. Is that your answer?"

"It is. And as your friend, I will say this." Pavel raised a manicured finger between them. "This is bigger than you and me and a thousand of us. The Soviet Union is the greatest nuclear power on earth. You and I cannot alter that. We should not try."

"I don't want to alter it. I want to make it true."

"Walk away."

"I've walked away for eleven years."

"Make it twelve. Why are you so selfish?"

"You think this is about me?"

"I think that when we first came to Chernobyl, we were gods. Now the plant has grown beyond even what we imagined. An entire city has cropped up around it. We're no longer young nor are we gods. Just workers for the state. I think this report is about a lonely man who still wants significance."

In the early days of Chernobyl, when the plant and Pripyat were both taking shape, a statue of a god, Prometheus, was erected in front of the city's movie house. Naked beneath a windblown robe, Prometheus held high above his head tongues of fire stolen from Olympus. Prometheus brought flame to Earth to give mankind light, heat, civilization. This was the message of the statue to Pripyat's young atomschiki, just as Pavel said: You are gods. And they were, Anton and Pavel and all of them. But they'd ignored the terrible ending of the fable, how Zeus became angry at the theft of his most powerful secret. In punishment, Zeus shackled Prometheus to a rock where a giant eagle came every day for eternity to peck out his liver.

Anton said, "It seems we don't know each other anymore. But that doesn't matter. Nothing changes the truth."

"What is the truth, Anton?"

"The RBMK is dangerous. It's a time bomb and it's been trying to tell us. We're fools if we don't listen. You're not a fool, Pavel. So you're a puppet."

Now that it was out, now that Anton had perhaps chased his tongue off a cliff, he rose to speak what might prove to be his final words as an atomschiki, standing.

He pointed at his report on Pavel's desk. Inside the folder were schematics, tables, calculations, forecasts, warnings, the best work of Anton's life.

"I beg you. Show that to the energy commission."

"The *Soyuzatomenergo* has already seen it."

A last pride flickered in Anton's chest. At least this report, his opus, had made it out of Pavel's office. That was something.

Pavel stood, too. He shook Anton's hand with little grip. When Pavel let go, his arms fell to his sides as if the strings had been cut.

"Do you insist on pursuing this matter? These false claims?"

"There's no other course. Anything else is criminal. Because the claims are not false."

"What do you intend to do?"

"I don't know yet. But I won't let this be ignored. Pavel, there were bits of the reactor core in the goddam rain. Iodine in the streets."

"Then I regret to inform you that you will be arrested."

"*Gospodi.*" Good God.

"It seems so."

Anton's jaw went slack, he felt himself leaning backward. He righted his balance or he might have fallen over. Anton cleared his throat, knowing that he'd made a weak show just now in front of Pavel. He worked his jaw left and right to shake off the blow.

He said, "Arrested. For a report."

"Not the report. For refusing to leave it in the hands of the proper authority."

"They'll do nothing with it."

"As is within their power. All nuclear incident reports are property of the state. You know this."

"When will they come?"

"Soon."

"Can't you do something?"

"Anton. I've done it."

"You're sending me to prison?"

"You're sending yourself if you won't let this go."

"You know I'm right."

"What we both might know is irrelevant. For the last time, let it go. You've been heard. What more do you want? To be martyred?"

Anton turned his hands palm up between them, as if there were blood on them.

"I just want to make energy. For our people. But we'll kill them if we do nothing. I can't live every day afraid of the next accident, the terrible one I know is coming. We can stop it."

"You don't know it's coming."

"I fucking *do*."

"Then you'll take your clean conscience to prison."

Anton could only, finally, laugh. He turned for the door. Pavel's hand stopped him.

Pavel moved closer, as if to step away from one version of himself and quietly, secretly, into another.

He whispered, "There is an option."

Anton grasped Pavel's upper arms. Hushed, too, he said, "What is it?"

"Leave."

"Leave Pripyat?"

"Leave Russia."

Anton's legs wanted to buckle. He propped himself on the back of a chair.

He stammered when he spoke. "I...I can't disown the report, Pavel. Everything, everything I wrote is true. I can't live like that, knowing we could prevent a tragedy, knowing we won't."

"We once had the power to build it, Anton. We never had the power to stop it."

"But leave Russia?"

"There's no other way."

Pavel shook his head to forestall any more objection.

Anton said, "Alright. Alright. How soon?"

"Tomorrow should keep you ahead of the KGB."

"Tomorrow? Pavel, tomorrow?"

Pavel only winced, as if there were a bright light in his face.

Anton said, "I have no travel papers."

"I can prepare them. You'll go to Beijing."

"What? Why on earth Beijing?"

"There's a conference on hydraulics starting Monday. I'm sending you."

"Send me somewhere else. Pavel. Beijing?"

"I can't. You understand, if I let you go away without a reason, I'll be seen as abetting your escape. I can, however, tell the KGB that you have renounced this." Pavel indicated the file on his desk. "Then I can say I sent you to a conference in China as a reward."

"What will I do in Beijing?"

Pavel smiled for the first time. "You're a senior engineer of the Vladimir Lenin Nuclear Power Plant. You'll find something."

Anton's gaze tumbled into the short space between their chests, Pavel's silk tie and his own cotton sweater. "I can't believe this."

"Stay quiet. Make no mention of this incident or any other at Chernobyl. Dispose of all copies of your report. Put your head down and get on with your life."

Pavel retreated to his desk. He sat, slid open a drawer, grabbed a pen, and seemed to get on with the business of sending Anton into exile.

"Goodbye, Antosh."

Anton headed for the door, feeling stupid at every step for hoping Pavel might speak again, might at the last moment announce some other solution.

With his hand on the doorknob, Pavel's voice made him turn.

"Anton. As your friend."

"Yes?"

Anton's report on the RBMK was already missing from Pavel's desk.

"Don't come back to Russia."

CHINA

1986

6

TIMUR

Timur pressed his forehead to a dead man's prayer rug.

He whispered the *sujud* three times: "Glory be to God, the highest."

Kneeling in tandem with Shah Barat beside him, Timur sat up, legs folded under him, hands in his lap. He gave himself over to reflection.

He'd landed in Beijing last night after forty hours of rickety Soviet airplanes and dusty airports, man-pulled rickshaws and tuk-tuk taxis. After arriving, after washing, alone in his lavish guestroom before bed, Timur's *isha* prayer had been for Allah to renew his strength. Now before sunrise, in the *fajr* prayer, Timur asked Allah to inspire the wealthy young Uyghur worshipping beside him to give him money for guns.

Together, they muttered in Arabic the sujud three more times.

Timur raised one finger to declare his devotion. The young man pressed a fist between his shut eyes.

Timur waited. When Shah Barat opened his almond eyes, he dropped his hand and turned his handsome nutbrown face to Timur.

Still in Arabic, he said, "Peace be upon you, and the blessings and mercy of Allah. Timur Makhdi."

Timur touched his own lips, then his heart. "And upon you. Shah Barat."

Shah Barat unfolded easily from his prayer rug. Timur had a much larger, older frame to lift off the mat. Reaching his bare feet, he towered over Shah Barat. The young Uyghur wore silk morning clothes, Timur a red tracksuit.

Shah Barat spread his hands as a way to offer all that he had to Timur. He switched to the language of Timur's grandfather—the tongue of Beijing, Mandarin.

"You are welcome in my home. Thank you for joining me for morning prayer."

Shah Barat's spacious study opened onto a marble veranda made to face southwest, to the *qibla* eight thousand kilometers away in Mecca.

Beyond the open double doors, Beijing's business district honked itself awake. The stink of diesel crawled up twelve floors to drift in Shah Barat's penthouse study. A servant set a tea service on a table of elephant ivory.

Shah Barat motioned Timur to a leather chair beside the white table.

"I'm sorry I could not greet you last night. Business. How was your travel?"

"Miserable."

"Tea?"

Timur nodded. Shah Barat poured with lean, smooth hands.

"Thirty years ago, the National Minority Hotel was the first modern structure Mao approved to compete with the height of Beijing's old temples. Twelve stories. In a few more years, this will be one of the shortest buildings in the city."

Shah Barat was small of stature himself, though he effused the kind of strength that came with prosperity. A man did not need to strike mightily if he could not be struck. Shah Barat's brother had different hands.

Shah Barat presented Timur a warm china teacup on a cool saucer. The tea was Moroccan mint that chased the diesel smell out the open French doors. Shah Barat nodded while he poured his own cup.

Timur said, "You have no beard. Even so, you look a great deal like him."

"I saw Gul in the mirror every day. So I shaved it."

"I understand."

"When is your flight out?"

"I return to Peshawar at midnight."

Timur's schedule out, like the timetable in, was misery. Shah Barat, now the eldest son of Barat Construction of Asia, had little taste for discomfort, judging by his silk and his home. Gul, the brother, had not been this stamp of a man.

Shah Barat said, "Stay a few days. Rest, sleep. I'll take care of your ticket when you're ready. Enjoy Beijing."

"May I decide after we talk?"

"Would you like that talk to be now?"

"I would."

Timur set down the tea without sipping, without waiting for Shah Barat to agree.

Shah Barat brought his teacup beneath his nose to live in the mint for another moment. He sipped, almost as a rebuke to Timur. He set the tea on the ivory table.

Shah Barat asked, "Is it as bad as you make it seem?"

"Yes. But we are winning."

"Were you with Gul when he died?"

"No."

From a pocket of his tracksuit, Timur withdrew a note. On it were scrawled longitude and latitude coordinates in Paktika province, the burial site of remains that were not Shah

Barat's brother. A Russian tank shell had left little of Gul
Barat to bury, but if Shah Barat ever sent to Afghanistan for
his brother's body, he would at least get some pieces.

Timur dug into his other pocket to hand Shah Barat a
gold signet ring. The symbol on the ring was the dove that
flew an olive branch to Noah, the Barat family crest,
connoting redemption through building anew.

Shah Barat clutched this memento of his older brother.
He pressed the fist again to his forehead. When he lowered his
hand to the arm of the chair he did not open his fingers.

"I am told you're a miner, Timur Makhdi."

"I was made one by the Russians."

"How long?"

"Four years."

"I'm sorry."

"I cannot feel sorrow anymore, Shah Barat."

The young Uyghur kissed his knuckles around his brother's ring.

"I understand. What do you want?"

"Uyghur money. Moslem fighters."

Shah Barat's head swayed, not to say 'No' but to worm his
way into the core of a thought.

"How much money?"

"Three million American dollars. The CIA gives the
Afghans weapons but never enough. We need to buy on the
open market."

"That will be difficult."

"Shah Barat. With respect, now that your older brother is
gone, I know your family will call you back to Xinjiang from
Beijing."

"Who told you this?"

"We fight the Soviets with every tool available. Knowledge
is one of them. Because the United States takes the side of the
Afghans against the Soviets, we have access to a great deal of

information. The CIA has told me you will take over your family's company soon. So I believe it will happen."

Shah Barat's gaze bounced from one fine thing in his splendid office to another, like a bird out of its cage. This small brown man had won construction projects for his family around the Pacific Rim from his base here in China. He had been the junior son. The Russians changed that.

Shah Barat smiled, just a trace, transparent as dew. He would bribe Allah to pay for the opportunity.

"You may have three million dollars."

Timur said, "And fighters."

"That will be harder than money."

"The Russians are trying to stamp out Islam in Afghanistan. When they are done, they will turn on Chechnya's Moslems. If the Russians are not stopped, the Chinese will consider themselves free to do the same to the Uyghurs in China. You will fight, Shah Barat, I promise you. Today beside us in Afghanistan. Or tomorrow in Xinyuan alone."

The young Uyghur rose. He glided in his silk robe behind an ornate desk of teak carved into tiny scenes of Buddhas on donkeys. Shah Barat left his brother's ring on the tabletop. He strode to the center of the open French doors, facing Beijing's wealth tangled with hovels, temples and towers, and Mecca far away.

"I won't send fighters. Money we can hide from our investors. But men will return from jihad and tell stories."

"I see. You do business with the Russians."

"We do business, Timur Makhdi."

Timur rose to shake Shah Barat's hand. He'd gotten three million dollars.

Shah Barat gestured to the rest of his condominium, two stories, so spacious he and Timur would not need to see each other again.

"Stay a few days. Rest. The war will not end without you."

Shah Barat's handshake was not firm like Gul's had been. "I will stay a day or two."

7

LARA

L ara blocked a punch to the head. Björn was going easy on her. She repaid him with a short, solid fist to the sternum.

The Swede backed off, stung. He put a hand to his chest, then mock-checked his fingers for blood. Lara bounced on her toes; the Swede nodded, then spit into his wrapped hands.

He put them up, Lara hers, and they waded back into close quarters. Both had white towels taped around their heads, midsections, shins, forearms, and hands. They looked like bandaged people fighting.

Lara popped a swift jab. She meant only to draw a defensive response, got it, then sideslipped to deliver a lightning judo backfist to his ear. Her knuckles tapped his sideburn; Björn surged in but Lara stopped his advance with a roundhouse kick to the ribs. Again, she only tapped him, but Björn knew she'd scored. He tackled her.

Björn landed on top of Lara in the tall grass. The muscle-bound Swede needed only seconds to swarm her, wrap her like an anaconda, squeeze a few joints, and make her tap out. When he reached to help her up she slapped away his hand. Neither had noticed the llamas and leather-faced shepherd come down from the wooded hill across the road to watch.

Using Björn's Swiss Army knife, they cut away the tape and towels. They balled everything into a backpack, sat cross-legged in the grass, and shared a thermos of water and strips of jerky for breakfast. The grasses wavered under a salty breeze that carried the nip of rivets and sparks. Lara stood first to help Björn to his feet. They tramped across the field to their sky-blue United Nations van parked beside the tall chain-link fence. They talked of how bored they were.

———

Björn leaned on the horn until Lara worried about draining the van's battery. Through the fence she watched a hundred Chinese workers weld metal beams two and three stories up, cranes swing rusty girders into place, several earth movers hawk out diesel smoke, and hard-hatted men tightrope-walk the steel framework high in the air.

Blue-veined and pallid as a glacier, Björn had little Nordic cool. He'd run out of patience; he started the van's motor and spit, *"Helvitisk säck av skit."* Lara spoke no Swedish but after two days with Björn driving south from Beijing over potholed streets, slowing every few miles for oxen in the road, or chickens, children, bicycles, mopeds, or funerals, and after a sketchy hotel and unsanitary meals taken at rural eateries served outdoors squeezing into small plastic chairs to eat among hordes of squabbling villagers, she'd learned that when Björn cursed in Swedish, she could easily interpret him. Björn said what it sounded like he was saying.

He scootched the van up to the chain link fence, close

enough to where Lara could not open her door. Björn shut off the engine, leaped out of the driver's side and jumped up on the bumper, the windshield, then the van's roof. Lara clambered out the driver's door.

Björn climbed over the fence, then clambered down. Stamping away over bare dirt, he shouted, "Stay here in case this doesn't go well."

She called through the fence, "You're supposed to be a diplomat."

"*Skruva på det.*"

Björn stomped off, UN credentials in hand. He made a beeline toward the men and machines that were ignoring him.

Qinshan would be China's first nuclear reactor. The project was in its earliest phases, just framing and excavation. The construction site was a manmade promontory protruding into Hangzhou Bay in the Yangtze River delta. The bay surrounded the project on three sides, making it seem a fortress.

Qinshan wasn't planned to go critical for another six years. The completed reactor would be small by the world's fast-growing standards of nuclear power, generating only a thousand megawatts, enough to light two hundred Chinese homes. Still, Qinshan was the beginning of power modernity in China, a Great Leap Forward.

China was only dipping its ancient toe into the pool of modern commercial nuclear power. But Qinshan was designed to be a breeder reactor; it would create more fissile material than it consumed. Once online, the reactor would generate uranium-238 as waste. That uranium could be re-utilized to fuel the reactor, or to create plutonium-239 which could then be fashioned into a nuclear weapon. The nascent Chinese nuclear program was casting global ripples that the UN and the International Atomic Energy Agency wanted to keep close tabs on.

Björn worked for the IAEA office in Beijing; Lara was the

US embassy's Beijing science official and an IAEA fellow. The UN had sent them both to Qinshan to show the flag early in the reactor's creation. Their mission this morning was to observe progress and report, not provoke. But Björn was out of earshot too fast for Lara to remind him.

She curled fingers around the chain links to wait for his return.

Björn came back an hour later, marched at the business end of four Chinese rifles.

———

Björn offered to climb back over the fence. His pantomimes were plain, but the Chinese soldiers forced him to sit against the chain links. Björn muttered "*Fan.*" The guards wouldn't let Lara speak to him.

She clambered on top of the van with binoculars and a notepad. The guards motioned for her to get down, but Lara told them to go *fan* themselves.

They were all waiting for something or someone.

Lara scribbled notes. She estimated the scope of the construction site, counted sheds, bulldozers, cranes, cement trucks, guessed at the size of the workforce. After thirty minutes, two of the soldiers strolled away; the pair who remained relaxed and lit cigarettes. Björn nodded off, his chin fell to his chest. Lara tossed the packet of jerky down to the guards, gestured for them to take some and give the rest to Björn.

Ten minutes later, a sedan hurried up the dirt lane toward the gate. The guards tossed away their smokes. Lara climbed down and Björn got to his feet.

The boxy car, a luxury Hongqi, flew China's red five-star flag on its bumpers. The sedan drove urgently over the corduroy road.

When the Hongqi stopped at the gate, its rooster tail

caught up to it and blew past. The driver, a short fellow under a chauffeur's cap, exited before the dust had cleared, it made him cough.

The driver jogged around the chrome grill to open the rear passenger door. A tall woman sparkled as she emerged. Pomade slicked her short platinum hair, cufflinks glittered when she shot the sleeves of her black pants suit, gold rings winked on both pinkies.

She sliced one polished fingernail through the air as she approached; one of the soldiers jumped to unlock the fence. Björn knocked his trousers clean of grit, then walked through the gate. He extended a hand, saying said, "*Xiè xie.*" Thank you.

The tall, shining woman did not accept Björn's hand, only offered her card. She barked an order to the second soldier who dashed the short distance from the fence to the blue UN van. He poked his head inside the driver's window, reached, then yanked out the keys from the ignition. He dangled them for the tall woman who snapped another order. The soldier opened the van door.

Lara surged forward. "No, no, no."

Björn said, "Lara, stop."

The soldier got in and started the van.

Björn said, "Get our backpacks out."

"What's going on?"

Björn held up the calling card as if it explained things.

The soldier let her retrieve the backpacks which held their passports, money, and clean underwear. When she was clear of the van, he drove off.

"What's going on?"

Björn handed Lara the calling card. The silvery woman tapped a folded white page in her palm. The chauffeur stayed with the idling Hongqi, but had opened both rear doors.

The card read:

Zhang Yang
China National Nuclear Corporation Commission of
Science, Technology, and Industry for National Defense
Shanghai Office

In unaccented English, Zhang said, "Dr. Lindberg. Dr. Dill. You were not expected until tomorrow."

Lara answered. "We're scheduled for this morning."

"No one makes the drive from Beijing in two days. The schedule is meant to be flexible."

When neither Lara nor Björn replied, Zhang nodded at their diligence.

"We will return your van to the IAEA offices in Beijing. You will take my car." Zhang motioned regally to the Hongqi. Her chauffeur made a slight bow.

Lara asked, "Take your car where?"

"An official plane is waiting for you at Pudong in Shanghai. A courtesy from China to your governments."

"A plane to where?"

"You have been recalled to Beijing. With urgency."

"What's happened?"

Zhang indicated Björn. "Fallout has been detected over your country."

The Swede took a step toward Zhang.

"What is it? Has there been a bomb?"

"The earliest reports are that Sweden is being contaminated by a nuclear accident somewhere abroad."

"Where?"

"Initial indications are the Soviet Union."

After a fast round of thanks, Lara and Björn hustled to the Hongqi. The chauffeur tried to close the doors after them but Lara shooed him off to the driver's seat.

"*Kuài dian!*" Go, fast.

8

ANTON

Anton almost knocked over a table lamp reaching for the phone. He snared the tilting base, rebalanced it, then snatched up the receiver. The student who'd delivered the note to his office hadn't left.

Anton made a backward broom with his free hand. "*Guān mén.*" Close the door.

The student, a bucktoothed boy with intellectual promise but little else to distinguish him, spun on the door, closed it behind him, and remained inside.

Anton didn't want to admonish the student, a good lad with connections, his father taught in the chemistry department. Anton gave him seconds to see if any instincts might arise. They did not.

He pointed at the door. "*Zài wài miàn.*" Outside.

The boy nodded so fast his glasses went to the tip of his nose. He left Anton's office pushing up his spectacles.

Anton stabbed a button to open an outside line. Then his finger halted. Who would he call?

53

Pavel, to find out what happened? No, not after four years of exile. Anton remembered the numbers for the Control Rooms of Units 1 and 2, they dredged up in him with the pang of old lovers. He couldn't phone the Control Rooms, he was a stranger, and if he wasn't, he was worse, a myth, a deserter.

He re-read the small news item the bucktoothed student had brought to his office: Nuclear fallout detected over Sweden and Finland. A reactor accident in Ukraine was suspected. No further information was forthcoming from the Soviet Union.

It had to be Chernobyl.

What if Anton called the president of the Beijing Science and Technology University? He might indicate to the president that he had specific knowledge and experience with the nuclear power stations in Ukraine. Could there be some role for their midlevel university to play? What would the university do? At worst, silence him, at best, politicize him. Anton was an assistant professor of hydraulics, a Russian. China and the USSR were only nominal allies; their competition for dominance was intense. Anton would be made a pawn, and his work—if it even saw the light of day—would be taken from his control, used only to further China's status against his homeland.

He could visit the Beijing offices of *Pravda* or *Tass*. Tell the Soviet newspapers what he knew about the RBMK reactor, its flaws and history, the potential dangers that may or may not have become real. He could hand over to the Russian press his study of the RBMK, the report that took him his four years in Beijing to reconstruct from memory. But what would *Pravda* do? Suppress the report again? What Soviet journalist would take the risk of facing-off against the KGB or the Politburo? Even if Anton found an editor brave enough, would it be fair to ask that?

What of the Americans or the British in Beijing? The *New*

York Times, the BBC. Hand them the report. Maybe give it to a Western consulate. Then stand aside while the West pilloried Russia with written proof from a former senior Chernobyl engineer that the USSR had hidden the truth that it was a technological hazard on a global scale and had been for years. Stand mute while the Allies blamed his old colleagues, even Pavel who'd saved him but sent him away. Turn Anton into a traitor.

He held the receiver away from the cradle, stretching the coiled cord. Anton could not hang up, that would be the beginning of helplessness. While he held the receiver, while he gritted his teeth as the dial tone wailed like a little siren, rummaging furiously in his head, Anton might still do something.

9

LARA

L ara didn't knock. She twisted the knob on her boss's
carved and enameled door, then pushed her way in.

Rutherford Poats waited behind his polished desk, ten strides
of Oriental carpet from the door. Lara covered it in seven.

She folded into a wing chair. She'd been traveling twelve
hours straight since Qinshan: in the limo to Shanghai's
airport, on a Chinese government plane to Beijing, in a van to
the embassy, past armed US Marines, down the decorative
halls to this leather chair. She tapped her heels like a runner in
the blocks and drummed her fingers.

She said, "Rudd."

The American embassy's Director for Science and Health
wore shirtsleeves, no need for a suit coat at one in the morning. He kept his tie up tight, sleeves buttoned, mustache
groomed, but his eyes were as twitchy as Lara's feet.

He curled in his lips and steepled his fingers. This was a
purposeful pause. Diplomats did not blurt.

56

"Lara."

"Tell me what happened."

"We think there's been a nuclear accident in the Soviet Union."

"You think?"

"We don't know."

"Where?"

"Looks like Ukraine."

"That would mean Chernobyl."

"Probably."

"You have any reports on how it happened?"

"Nothing. You know the Soviets, they keep a lid on everything. Except their reactors. That's a joke."

"I'm laughing. How bad is it?"

"Can't be sure. The Scandinavians tell us they're monitoring levels of radiation like what they used to see after Russian nuclear missile tests in the Arctic."

"So they're finding iodine, uranium, plutonium, cesium…"

"All of it." Rudd waved tired fingers, "All of it consistent with a fuel melt."

"Are there casualties?"

"You figure a containment breach pumping this much radioactivity into the air, there's got to be a lot of dead and wounded on site."

"Expect more."

"If the rems are ten times what they ought to be seven hundred miles away in Stockholm, I can't guess what it's like ten miles from the reactor."

"What about the politics?"

"Sweden, Denmark, Finland, Norway, they're already demanding the Soviets open up their entire civilian nuclear program to inspection."

"That's not going to happen."

"Maybe, maybe not. The new guy Gorbachev's been making noises like he wants to raise the Iron Curtain a little."

Lara said, *"Glasnost."* This was the new First Secretary of the Communist Party's watchword for transparency between the USSR and the world. It would be a daring, unprecedented approach, if he could pull it off.

Rudd said, "The Soviet Affairs wonks are waiting for the Reds to issue a statement. So far the Russians have just said there's no information on any kind of nuclear accident inside the USSR."

"It's hard to hide a radioactive plume over northern Europe. What's our position?"

"The US agrees with the Scandinavians, but we're on the sidelines. It's the Swedes' ballgame right now. The cloud's over their heads. We don't know where it's going next."

"Can it hit the US?"

"Can't be sure. The EPA says if the plume reaches the polar cap, it can be over the West Coast in three days. Depends on the winds aloft, but they can blow a hundred miles an hour. And on how fast the Soviets can shut this goddam thing down. We won't know more until we can get our own readings and some eyes on close up."

Lara braced hands on her knees and pushed off to stand.

"No."

"Sit down, Lara."

"Get me a plane back to Qinshan."

"I'm sending you to Russia."

"I'm not going."

Rudd rubbed a hand over his scalp as if his thoughts were on his head instead of inside.

"Look, I know something happened with you and the Russians."

Lara leaned both palms on her boss's desk. Before speaking she peered down at her reflection in the sheen, like into a pond. Her image was diffuse, ghostly.

She said, "Yeah. Something."

"Sit down and tell me."

Lara didn't sit.

"They grabbed me off a street corner. Stuck a sack over my head, tied my hands, and dragged me to some basement in front of a fat man in a white shirt. He could've had me killed with a snap of his fingers. And he wasn't even the big boss. I can't go back there. I was told in very clear language not to."

"Why am I hearing this for the first time?"

"I didn't report it."

"Why not?"

"Are you out of your mind? I caught the Russian mob stealing radioactive material to sell to the mujahideen in Afghanistan. I'm pretty sure they had American help. I'm talking about higher-ups in *our* military, *our* government."

"Did you get names?"

"No. I only managed to backtrack some plutonium that turned up in Kandahar. It led back to a reactor in Balakovo. I did some digging and found some discrepancies at the plant's fuel storage facility. I wrote it up, turned it in, and the next thing I know there's a bag over my head. The report got buried and I got transferred to China the next day. No way the mob could've done that on their own. No way. So I'm pretty sure reporting my kidnapping would have gotten me buried next. Get someone else."

"Will you sit?"

Lara withdrew her hands from Rudd's shiny desktop. She left a pair of smudges; she hadn't washed since Qinshan.

He said, "All I knew was that you got sideways with some mafia types in Moscow. Sorry you went through that. But I got a call from State telling me to send you."

"Me?"

"You. By name."

"To do what, collect soil samples? Send a dosimetrist. Send a kid with a shovel."

"Listen to me. The soil sampling is just a cover. This Ukraine accident is big and getting bigger. We don't know what's going on or what's going to happen. We need you close. If we can get you back in Moscow, even into Ukraine, maybe you can get us some reliable intel. Get in touch with some of your old contacts in the Russian scientific community, see what's what. Otherwise, we'll have to swallow whatever the Soviets feed us."

"What about whoever's in my old job in Moscow?"

"They didn't replace you."

"Figures."

"While you were in the air from Shanghai, the security folks at the Moscow embassy reached out to some underworld connections."

"Oh my God. Are you serious?"

"We got assurances. You're good to go. The mob's cool so long as you report only on the Ukraine situation, then get back to Beijing."

"That's what you got. Assurances. So I can go be your spy."

"You're not spying." Rudd spread his hands to show they were empty of all else. "Alright, it's spying."

In the middle of her chuckle, Lara muttered, "Oh, man." Then she asked, "Why me?"

"Don't fish for compliments."

Of course her. The circumstances called exactly for her. PhD in Radiation Health Physics. Fluent in Russian. Long experience with Soviet bureaucracy. Probably still had connections among the good guys in the Soviet hierarchy. Ten years as a cop in Boston.

"You promise, I'm okay? I mean you trust this, Rudd?"

"We have their word. You know better than me whether

that's worth anything. But there's no one else in Asia with your credentials we can send."

Lara tugged her hair into a ponytail. She made a twist as if she were about to get into the shower, but let it fall loose again. A shower wasn't in her immediate future.

"You know I'm scared, right?"

"You're not stupid."

"What do you need me to do?"

"The radiation seems to be moving north and northwest. We can't trust the Soviets to give us accurate readings. They tell us what direction the plume's heading, but what if it turns back toward the Urals and Siberia? What if it drifts as far as Mongolia, or heads over the polar cap? The Reds won't tell us straight, and if they do it won't be in time to take any precautions. We can't rely on them. The Chinese have made it clear privately that they can't, either. Go to Moscow. Dig around. We'll share what you find with the Chinese. It'll help us with Beijing."

"What about glasnost?"

"Fuck glasnost."

"Am I going alone?"

"The Swedes are sending one of theirs. He's former Swedish Special Forces."

"Name Lindberg?"

"Björn Lindberg."

"*Jäveln.*"

"What's that mean?"

"It's Swedish for son of a bitch."

"Because?"

"He forgot to mention he was SFS. When do I leave?"

"Dawn."

"That's in four hours." Lara stood. "I'll run home and pack."

"No time. I'll send someone to your flat. I need you in the

lab. Pack up an ionization chamber, dosimeters, soil sample kits, hazmat gear, you know the drill."

"That's a lot to take on a plane."

"You're not going on a plane."

"I'm not what?"

"All the air routes over Russia have been shut down because of the plume."

"Then how do I get from Beijing to Moscow?"

Rudd handed Lara an envelope.

"Here's your ticket."

"To what?"

"The Trans-Mongolian Express."

10

TIMUR

Timur answered a soft knock at his door.

One of Shah Barat's old housekeepers held a fist beside her ear. She shook the fist and pointed her other hand at Timur. A phone call.

He followed her downstairs to the kitchen. The maid picked up the receiver to hand it to him in a servile gesture, then went out of the kitchen with dragging steps.

To be safe, he spoke first in Russian. "*Privet.*"

"*Salam.*"

Timur switched to Pashto.

"What do you want?"

"Something has happened inside the Soviet Union."

"What."

"There is the suggestion of an accident. At a nuclear plant, in Ukraine."

"What do you want from me? I'm in China."

"The Soviets have put out an emergency call for miners and subway workers. Six hundred of them."

"That's a lot. For what?"

"We don't know. But there may be some chance here. Go find out."

Timur lowered the phone, imagining his next few days without rest.

"I'll fly to Kyiv tomorrow."

"The planes are not flying. There's radioactivity in the air."

"How will I get there?"

"You must take a train to Moscow. Then another into Ukraine."

"A train? It's seven thousand kilometers to Moscow."

"Eight, Timur Makhdi. Go. *Mashallah.*"

What God has willed, has happened.

———

Timur stuffed clothes and toiletries into his soft sports bag. He dressed in his red track suit and buckled on his fanny pack where he kept his passports, the mujahideen's money, plus a roll of cash from Shah Barat. He carried his black boots down the hall. In stocking feet, Timur opened and closed the doors on his way out like a mouse, not to wake Shah Barat.

He put on his boots in the elevator.

———

A light rain had passed in the early morning. The flagstones of the plaza reflected the train station's twin pagoda clocktowers. In puddles, the clocks seemed to reach out for Timur.

Taxis and sleepy people crowded the streets and station entry. Tuktuks shunted to the front like piglets to deliver their fares; none of the drivers yelled or shook fists when they cut each other off, this was just the pre-dawn tournament at the train station. Timur dodged a motorcyclist dropping off his sweetheart. The girl carried two suitcases on the back of his bike even as she held on. The boy did not get off the bike when he kissed her goodbye, then puttered away into dark Beijing. Timur shouldered his travel bag.

Beijing's train station had been designed for grand welcomes and farewells. In stories-high murals, statuary carved into granite pillars, portraits and exclamatory lettering on every wall and open space, the station blared China's imperial past and socialist future. Mao always wore fatigue green, Deng in coat and tie, ancient emperors in silk robes, soldiers in khaki, all gazed over the heads of Timur and the early crowd. Every image pointed somewhere, up at the many chandeliers, or to tomorrow. Vintage battles were depicted in primitive style, crimson banners bruited the CCP's hammer and sickle, immense murals portrayed blue skies, streaming clouds, fertile fields, factory smoke, omnipresent laborers. Visitors to China were promised that they'd arrived in a dynamic and inevitable land. Departing passengers were reminded to go forth and tell the world what they'd seen.

The currency exchange kiosk was a tall wooden box like a casket on end. Timur turned Shah Barat's money into rubles. At the ticket booths, he was early and first in line. The people flowing into the pre-dawn station were mostly locals traveling inside the country. The line that formed behind Timur to go west out of China were sour-smelling Tatars, Uzbeks, Ukrainians, Buryats, Mongols, Chuvashs, Udmurts, Russians. All shuffled into the queue behind Timur with faces turned down, common folk, their luggage showing heavy use. The men wore block-cut business suits and the cloth hats of the working class. Women waited in pastel headscarves, ankle-length floral skirts, and velour coats. The young men wore plastic jackets. Elsewhere in the station, wealthier travelers in better-tailored clothes strode ahead of porters wheeling their bags on carts.

Finally, an elderly ticket clerk raised the steel grate of her booth. Her cheeks made Timur think of cherries. She beckoned him with both hands, curling her fingers to say to Timur: Come forward. Where may I send you?

———

At the top of the steel steps into the second-class carriage, a rack of brochures offered pamphlets about Maoist doctrine on agriculture, China's Five-Year Plan for economic growth, and Marxist philosophies on the laborer in a worker's state. Timur's compartment was at the other end of the car down a narrow companionway, the next-to-last door.

He had to duck to enter his cabin. The cot was neatly made, a blue wool blanket tucked around white linen. The compartment was spotless, walls and ceiling of gray. A folding tabletop separated the two cots above a strip of red carpet like that in the corridor. A sheer curtain on a rod obscured the lower half of a dingy window. One light fixture was centered in the ceiling, each cot had a small gooseneck lamp in the wall. A water carafe waited on the table to be filled from the hot water samovar at the other end of the carriage. Two hand towels were folded on his cot. The compartment smelled dank; the heat had not yet been turned on from the coal-fired furnace in the corridor behind the samovar. Timur raised the tabletop out of the way, tossed the hand towels under the berth, snatched a starchy pillow off a shelf, and lay down.

He didn't open his eyes when the train lurched. Timur rolled over to face the shuddering wall. He'd left Shah Barat's apartment in the early morning with no sleep and missed the *fajr* prayer. He'd do penance with an extra *ishraq* later and list his sins.

When Timur awoke, he lay on his back. He'd not taken off his boots, his heels touched the wall. He bent his knees; Timur's height was too much for the cot. Sun flooded the window, sharp on the ceiling, unbroken by cityscape. The Trans-Mongolian had left Beijing.

He turned his head before sitting up and did not react to the man seated across from him.

The man did not uncross his legs when he said, "*Dobroye utro.*" Good morning.

Timur lowered his feet to the floor. Alone in the little compartment he'd not felt so large. Faced with a standard man, he sensed his own size.

Timur answered. "Good morning."

"You speak Russian."

"I am Chechen."

"I hear it's a beautiful land. I've never been. I hope I didn't wake you."

"No."

The man wore a burgundy cable sweater with roll collar, khaki slacks, slip-on loafers, black socks. He was slender, may once have been an athlete. The man's hands were smooth, but his temples were shot with gray in a handsome way. He looked to be around fifty. In the mines where coal dust filled the wrinkles and every face was smooth, a man was old at fifty.

Timur lowered his brow but did not touch his forehead and heart. This was not another Moslem across from him, but a Russian.

A briefcase stood beside the man's ankle. The man said, "Anton Epstein."

"Timur Makhdi."

Neither reached out. As strangers, they'd been assigned the same soft-class apartment by some clerk. Timur nodded to Anton. They would wait a bit to shake hands. Timur crossed his legs like the Russian and watched China ease past.

The rails out of Beijing canted west. The morning sun fell on the Trans-Mongolian's back. Timur had slept through the last populated parts of the vast capitol; now the land rose in cliffs and fell sharply into densely green ravines.

With a suddenness that made Timur tense, the view vanished. A smeared collage whooshed past like an out-ofphase film. The compartment was shaken and the air vacuumed out, his ears pressured in a hummingbird beat. All other sound vanished beneath the long crescendo of wheels and rushing train cars going in the opposite direction.

Like the snap of fingers, the rattling quit. Anton never uncrossed his legs. Timur let go his breath and relaxed his grip on his own knees.

The Russian asked, "First train ride?"

"First one in China."

"The Trans-Mongolian's tracks are thirty years old and close together. When they were laid, the trains didn't go so fast."

Timur had shown himself badly to this Soviet. He folded his arms and sat back, trying to appear comfortable and surly.

Anton said, "There'll be a lot of trains going the other direction. You'll get used to it."

"You're going to Moscow?"

"Yes. You?"

Timur said, "Yes."

"Then I suppose we're here for the next five days, Timur Makhdi."

The compartment door slid aside. A corpulent Chinese in an olive uniform with red piping filled the portal. His hat rode on the back of his large head as if he were already tired of the journey.

"*Mén piào.*"

Anton produced his train ticket from a coat pocket. Timur dug his out from his football bag. Together they handed their papers to the porter. The large railroad man checked them against a clipboard that touched the orb of his belly.

The porter first returned Anton his ticket.

He returned Timur's ticket. The porter waggled a chubby finger between the two of them, then removed his hat to smile and bat his eyes. "*Dān chéng piào.*"

Anton said, "*Nǐ cuò le.*"

The porter pouted before he capped his big head, nodded away some loss, and slid the door shut behind him.

Timur asked, "What was that?"

"We both have one-way tickets to Moscow. He thought we were a couple. I told him he was mistaken."

Timur shook his head. Anton did, too.

Timur said, "I have no idea what to say."

The Russian laughed first.

He asked, "Do you live in Moscow?"

"No. Do you?"

"No."

Another eastbound train surged past on to the too-close tracks. The compartment shivered as if it were afraid. Timur and Anton could not speak while the two speeding trains roiled the air between them. Timur crossed his arms and legs, to show the Russian he was in control of himself and five days of this would not bother him again.

When the last car whizzed by and the Trans-Mongolian steadied itself, Timur and the Russian faced each other from their benches without a word.

This Russian had a one-way ticket to Moscow. So they both had secrets.

11

LARA

KILOMETER 100

The Trans-Mongolian's shock absorbers were excellent. Lara's coffee and cream didn't ripple, her soft egg yolks did not jiggle.

She sliced a pork egg roll; her knife rang nicely on the white porcelain. She ate, then dabbed her mouth with a well-ironed napkin. The dining car could have been any intimate, red-decked restaurant in Beijing except for the passing scenery and the lack of customers.

Lara gazed out the window. During her four years in China, she'd traveled much of the country's eastern half, always on highways and UN airplanes, always bound for cities: Shanghai, Chongqing, Hunan, Wuhan, places where health crises effected sufficient millions for the UN and the US to take interest. Or like yesterday in Qinshan, to keep an eye on China's baby steps into nuclear power.

The vista from the train rose to spiky sharp peaks, dove into ravines, whitewater rivers, forests so dense they seemed painted on the mountains. Rural China dared humans to come out here and take their best shot.

There the humans were. Villages nestled in small patches of even ground. Smoke, the banner of civilization, rose above hollows. Here and there, roads and paths in crazy switchbacks climbed the face of the unwilling earth. Humanity was hard to hold at bay.

The railroad itself told the same urgings of mankind. This morning out of Beijing, Lara had already covered a hundred miles of steel track and wooden ties; every jangling minute of her breakfast covered another mile. Steel rails and wooden ties had been carted into these highlands, rivers crossed before there were bridges, mountains beaten down or tunneled, made to submit to the Trans-Mongolian. The railroad asked what else man could do if they could do this?

"May I join you?"

The pink-patterned bowtie snagged Lara's attention first. A lanky young English-speaker in a blue seersucker sport coat asked to sit. He was young, stringy, with a reddish cast to his skin and a receding hairline.

He swept a hand elegantly at the rest of the empty dining car. "It's so full. There's nowhere else. May I?"

Lara said, "Grab a seat."

"Ah." The man pulled out a chair. "American."

"That was fast."

"No one else 'grabs' a seat. It's charming."

Lara's new companion lifted a hand before she could respond. He reached over Lara's coffee and eggs for a handshake.

"Sinjin Alonso. My first name is spelled like the saint, pronounced like the devil. My grandmother used to tell me that."

"Lara Dill."

She returned to her breakfast. Sinjin peered out the window at China sliding by.

He broke his silence. "Do forgive me."

"For what?"

"You're a beautiful woman. A bit older than I."

Sinjin raised a finger, asking to complete his thought.

"What I mean is, it's intimidating. I don't meet people well. I can be a bit of a jabbermouth."

"Alright, Sinjin. What were you doing in Beijing?"

"I live there."

"What do you do?"

"I'm a diplomat."

Lara set down her fork with a clink onto the plate. She covered her mouth to stifle a laugh. "A diplomat?"

"You see the dilemma."

Behind her hand, she nodded.

"My parents, you see, are quite well connected in White-hall. My father was an ambassador. My mother a doyenne in economics at Cambridge."

"So they sent you to Beijing?"

"After a bit. First, they packed me off to boarding school. Then St. Andrews. Following that, four years with the Cold-stream Guards. Then to Beijing where I am currently employed at Her Majesty's Chinese embassy."

"What do you do there?"

"I don't exactly know. But whatever it is, I'm on holiday."

Lara called the attention of a waiter.

Sinjin said, "I'll be getting off at Novosibirsk. I intend to spend two weeks collecting mushrooms in the Ural forests."

"You like the outdoors?"

"I love the outdoors."

"Do you know how to set up a tent?"

"Goodness no."

A waiter approached. Lara said, "*Fuwuyuan, ta yao dian cai.*" Waiter, he would like to order.

In immaculate Mandarin, Sinjin ordered eggrolls, orange juice, tea, three eggs, and blackbread toast.

When the waiter was gone, Sinjin turned again to the

window. The landscape, dramatic, serrated, emerald, and bald, dazzled him. It seemed to set him yearning.

Lara said, "Thank you for the compliment."

"Did I?"

"You said I was beautiful."

"Yes, I did."

"How old are you, Sinjin?"

"Twenty-seven. And don't fear. I've no intention of asking your age. I have that much sense, at a minimum." Sinjin tapped his noggin, to imply he'd gotten the point.

He said, "I'm in the compartment to your left in second class. I see you don't have a roommate."

"Sinjin."

"Ah." He raised both palms in submission. "Ah, no. No, no. I meant to imply nothing."

"Then what did you mean?"

"*I* don't have a cabinmate. I thought perhaps it might be something curious we had in common. For conversation."

"Why don't you have a roommate?"

"I purchased both tickets. As I said, I'm on holiday." Sinjin waggled both raised palms as though erasing the notion of other people.

Lara said, "I've got my own cabin because the other rack is filled with my equipment."

"Smashing. I'm a bit of a shutterbug. I have several cameras along. So, Lara. If I may?"

"We'll see. Give it a try."

Sinjin cleared his throat and straightened his pink bowtie.

"Who do you work for, such that your second berth is covered in equipment? What sort of equipment? And are you a spy? Yes, that last bit was a joke. Aha."

Lara tapped the back of his hand.

"*Zuò de hǎo.*" Well done.

Sinjin's tea arrived. He waited with mitts in his lap, smiling while the waiter poured. Sinjin was good at being served.

Others would set up his tents, surely. Lara watched him savor the tea, something an Englishman could do very well.

She said, "I'm the health science liaison for the American embassy in Beijing. I also work for the International Atomic Energy Agency. My field is the health effects of ionizing radiation."

"And the equipment?"

"For radiological testing. I'll be taking readings along the train route west."

Sinjin held the teacup beneath his nose.

She asked, "What do the British know about the accident in Ukraine?"

"As I say, I don't have much in the way of duties at the embassy. I wander about." He set down his tea. "What I did catch in bits and pieces is that something awful has happened. People are being sickened, some are dying. There's a radioactive plume heading northwest of Kiev. The Scandinavians are in a fit. Do you know more?"

"The Soviets are being tightlipped."

Sinjin said, "I suppose you're headed towards it."

"I am."

"I suspect it may prove to be a pleasure to have met you, Dr. Lara Dill."

His breakfast appeared and Sinjin tucked in.

12

ANTON

KILOMETER 287

Outside the cabin door, a woman's voice said in English, "Oh my God."

A young man added, "Incredible."

Timur the big Chechen asked, "What's going on?"

Anton rose off his berth, Timur followed. For the last hour, Anton had lost sight of the Chechen's size while they'd both gazed out the window at misty gorges or rested with eyes closed.

Timur left the cabin first. The companionway ran the length of the six soft-class compartments with the corridor's windows facing south. Three passengers stood on the wine-dark carpet, hands pressed to the panes. All marveled at the Great Wall of China.

The nearest passenger was a tall, lissome woman, dark-haired. Anton stepped beside her; when she smiled her eyes gleamed green like an old growth forest. Her face was oval, Slavic. She greeted him with "*Zdravstvuye.*"

Next to her stood a well-built, straw-haired fellow, perhaps a Scandinavian. Anton returned this man's friendly nod. He and Timur seemed to take the measure of each other.

At the other end of the gawkers, a gangly young fop in a summer suit and rosy bowtie operated an expensive-looking camera. His Adam's apple bobbed in excitement. He tried to lower the sooty window for his photography. The window would not budge, and he made a racket of attempting to lower it.

The door to the first compartment slid aside. The fleshy Chinese porter emerged, hat cockeyed. He surveyed his flock, then approached to slap down the fop's wrists from wrestling with the window. Out of his open door came a breeze carrying the odors of diesel and ozone; he'd managed to open his own window. Then the big conductor ambled back inside and closed his door. The fop returned to snapping photos through the spotty glass.

Two hundred meters away and a hundred overhead, the Great Wall snaked along a razorback crest. Anton, an engineer, couldn't fathom so many stones, carried up these emerald wastes to build such a remarkable thing as the wall. The human capital alone was boggling; it said something miraculous, even frightening, not just about the Chinese but man himself.

Anton addressed the woman. "My name is Anton. This is Timur."

Timur dipped his brow.

"I'm Lara. This is Björn. The one with the camera is Sinjin."

For another ten kilometers the railroad tiptoed along wild ledges running parallel to the Great Wall. The tracks took a sudden bend then surged unexpectedly over a short bridge, across the Wall itself. In that rumbling moment Anton glimpsed down a hundred-meter length of the stone parapet; his imagination manned the battlements for a thousand years with armored warriors, archers, and signalmen who spoke to each other across the distances in dots of smoke.

In Russian, Sinjin said, "This part of the Wall west of Beijing was built in the fourth century, during the Northern Wei Dynasty. Some parts along the Gobi Desert date back to the fifth century BC. Taken altogether, the Great Wall of China is 13,000 miles. Give or take."

Sinjin turned a bit red, like his bowtie. Björn the Swede required a translation. Sinjin gave it in silky English which sounded more like the young man's native tongue.

Anton and the others thanked Sinjin for his knowledge. Timur pivoted first from the windows, which seemed to break the Wall's spell. Then everyone turned away.

In their cabin, Timur sat on his berth, Anton on his. The tracks began their descent out of the highlands.

Timur asked, "Did you notice anything?"

"Such as?"

"That Englishman."

"What about him?"

"Did you see he was the only one who knew anything about the Wall."

"Yes. And?"

"He knew the train would go near it."

"Probably he read up on it."

"Precisely. I didn't. Did you?"

"I did not."

"Why not?"

Anton said, "I left Beijing in bit of a hurry."

"As did I."

The giant stroked his gray beard while his eyes narrowed.

He said, "So the woman. The Swede. They left Beijing in a hurry, too."

13

GANG

The drive from Baoding to Datong took three hours. Gang had allowed five.

He parked in a shaded neighborhood in a northern *Xiàn* of the city. He selected a middling street and a small house. Sea-green ginkgo trees muffled the pleasant lane, plum blossoms bloomed with the red of lips. For minutes, Gang studied the little home and tidy street; he decided to say this was where he lived. He left the sedan at the curb with the key in it. The car would disappear. He stopped wondering about that years back.

Gang had two hours to waste. With only a shoulder bag, he rode a bus into the business district where a million workers began their day. This was nothing compared to Baoding where ten million citizens bustled daily to their jobs. He strolled to Datong's walled old city, past a dozen pagodas and temples built a millennia ago, to the Nine Dragon Wall, into and out of the spring perfume of cherries. At a tourist center Gang read brochures about Datong's Buddhist grottoes, stone carvings from the fourth century, her history of coal mines, and the steppe weather.

At noon he paid a female rickshaw bicyclist double to ferry him to the train station. Fresh flowers ringed the woman's carriage. Gang rode like a king for a couple of kilometers.

A half-hour later, the train announced itself with a faraway tweet. The whistle tumbled down out of the northeast mountains, forlorn and echoing in the foothills.

From a vendor Gang bought a paper sack of walnuts grilled on a brazier. He purchased an orange fizzy at a kiosk and put a straw in the bottle so he wouldn't have to tip his head to drink and break with his surroundings. He slung his cloth bag over his shoulder; it held one change of clothes. He waited at platform nine for the Trans-Mongolian Express.

The engine arrived with a husky smoothness. The engine and all the cars were painted pea green with crimson accents; on the locomotive's nose was embossed the red star of communism. The train radiated power; every cog and lever moved like clockwork. The Trans-Mongolian eased along the track, slowing to a halt. The locomotive wore a jade coat like Mao; it exhaled, a leviathan coming to rest, then began to hum, deep-throated and satisfied. Fifteen passenger carriages and twenty cargo cars stopped in front of Gang. Arriving passengers got off with bags while those who would board stood aside on the platform.

Gang didn't have to wait long. She stepped off the train from the same soft-class car where his compartment was booked. She carried a bright yellow metal box the size and shape of a lunch pail. She moved fast, the train would only pause in Datong for minutes. The concrete platform had neither grass nor soil, only a row of Mandarin lilacs planted in tree wells. She made a beeline for them. Gang's black sneakers made no sound on the platform when he followed.

She darted through the crowd, across the platform to the lilacs. Kneeling at the trunk of one, she stabbed a trowel into the dirt, lifted some soil, then sealed it in a glass vial. When she got to her feet, Gang was five strides away. She did not startle.

The American woman was pretty, shorter than him, a red cast to her brown hair, a liveliness in her eyes. She was supple and striking.

Gang said in English, "Hello."

She dropped the soil sample into a backpack, then shouldered the pack. The trowel remained in her hand.

"Can I help you?"

He touched his own chest. "I'm Gang."

He waited as if she was supposed to recognize the name.

"I'm the Chinese rad tech. You should've been told about me."

"I wasn't." She walked forward, hand outstretched. "Lara Dill."

He said, "Dr. Dill." When he accepted her hand, Gang let her squeeze harder than him.

She said, "Lara."

Together they turned from the lilacs, headed across the platform to the track. The locomotive snorted steam. Around them, families, spouses, girlfriends, boyfriends, chauffeurs holding Chinese signs, all greeted travelers to Datong or waved goodbye to the ones going west on the Trans-Mongolian. Another train arrived on a separate track, chiming like a cowbell.

Lara indicated Gang's soft bag.

"Is that all you've brought? It's a five-day trip."

"I'll be getting off at the Russian border."

"No equipment?"

"I found out an hour ago I was getting on a train. There wasn't time to grab anything. I was told to ask if you'd mind sharing your findings?"

"Of course not."

Gang indicated the yellow box she carried. "You brought an ionization chamber."

At the train, a rotund conductor stood on the steps. He glanced left and right as if he might have some power over the train. He climbed down to let Lara Dill board, Gang behind her.

Lara asked, "You're in this car?"

"I am."

Gang followed Lara Dill down the narrow companionway. He stopped at a door.

"I'm right here."

She moved on a few steps, then gripped a door handle. With a nod, Lara Dill entered the cabin next to his.

14

LARA

KILOMETER 390

The rails ran north out of Datong, alongside a puny river between sparse hills. Then the river was dammed and widened from a ravine to a great shining lake.

Lara labeled the first soil sample *Datong, China*, adding the date and time of collection. She slid the glass vial into a foam slot in a steel locking case. Testing the soil would have to wait until her old lab at the US Moscow embassy. The spectrometer would reveal the levels of gamma radiation in the samples she'd collect over the next five days.

Lara checked the dosimeter, the size of a playing card, she'd clipped to her backpack; the small device would record her cumulative radiation dose for the six-thousand-mile journey. The meter displayed only ten microrems, just background rad. A Geiger counter, big as half a cinderblock, lay on the unused cot.

The ionization chamber showed only trace amounts in the soil sample of cesium at 662 kiloelectron volts. This was consistent with the fact that Datong lay a thousand miles east of China's nuclear bomb testing site at the Lop Nur salt lake.

The last atmospheric test explosion had been six years ago in 1980.

What was happening in Ukraine? How fast was the plume of radionuclides growing, how high did it reach, what direction was it drifting? How major was the reactor accident? What caused it? The Soviets owed the world a lot of answers. Lara had no shortage of questions.

The next station was Erlyan on the Mongolian border, five hundred kilometers north. Six more hours. Sunset.

A knock came at her door.

"Who is it?"

"Gang."

The rad tech? What did he want? Probably to see what other equipment she'd brought. Gang had a job to do, too. They were going to spend the next few days doing it together at their governments' request. Gang mentioned he might be leaving the Trans-Mongolian at the Russian border. He seemed pleasant enough. They were about the same age. She had a doctorate, he was a lab tech.

"Come in."

Gang opened the door. The next instant, night swallowed him.

All the light stripped away, the screech of wheels and tracks tripled like sirens. Gang entered, moving his hands in small circles so she could track him in the dark, a shadow unstaked. He slid the door shut.

"Tunnel."

He moved the big Geiger counter aside on the berth across from her. Gang sat, a black figure against blackness. Lara's hand flattened on her breast, then she lowered her hand to say, "Hello, Gang."

He did not reply. The screaming of steel inside the tunnel was so loud, any conversation would have been forced.

Suddenly, the blackness and clatter swept away. Daylight

flooded in, perhaps before Gang was ready; Lara caught him grinning.

The train continued north between sere hills, beside the lake. After the inky tunnel, the water glinted so sharply that Lara had to look away.

Gang said, "I'm sorry."

"For what?"

He hooked a thumb over his shoulder. "That was weird timing. Going into the tunnel like that. I think I scared you."

"It's fine."

"You sure?"

"Yes."

"Okay. Cool." He picked up the Geiger counter, a clumsy big unit. "This thing is useless."

"Is it?"

"It lacks the sensitivity for atmospheric gamma this far out. Why'd you bring it?"

"Same as you. I had no time to figure out what to bring, so I just grabbed things. Gang, if you don't mind my asking."

"Sure."

"Your accent is perfect American. Where are you from?"

"Datong."

"Then how?"

"I went to high school in Baltimore. A little Catholic school that took exchange students. You're from Boston."

"And how did you know that?"

Gang shrugged with his hands, a way of telling her: "I work for a paranoid communist government."

"Now can I ask you something?"

She said, "Shoot."

"How did a Boston cop become a doctor of health sciences with a specialty in radioactive isotopes?"

"You did your homework."

"Someone did. I just read the files."

"What if I just say it's none of your business?"

"Then that'll end up in a file somewhere."

"Funny."

"I wasn't trying to be. But, hey, Lara. If I can call you that."

"You can. So far. What."

"It's seven thousand kilometers to Moscow. Seriously. You're going to need to talk to someone. Me, too."

Gang stood. "Or I'll just go and we can both find someone else. But that's not fucking friendly."

She waved him down, laughing a little at his bluff.

"Alright, sit. You're pitiful."

"So you've read my file."

He returned to the berth opposite her. Gang wasn't without some charm. He knew his way around a Geiger counter and a curse. And seven thousand kilometers on a train was a long goddam way.

She said, "Alright."

Gang sat back, legs and arms crossed. He made himself cozy. He may have been popular in that Baltimore high school.

"My family's from Russia. My father was a mechanical engineer in Leningrad. When the war came, he fought the Germans on the Eastern Front. He was a tanker at Kursk. He got captured and spent two years in Germany working in a munitions factory. When the war ended, he went back to Leningrad. Stalin didn't trust anyone who'd been in the hands of the Nazis, especially someone who'd been in the German camps. Before they could arrest him, he made it across the border to Finland. He met my mother in Helsinki."

Lara paused. It would be polite now to ask him for some of his story. But Gang, folded on the opposite berth, seemed focused on her. He listened like he was deciding something.

She continued. "They got married in Helsinki. They had me pretty quick. My dad couldn't find work in Finland, the Finns didn't love Russians. So they got visas to the US, wound up in Boston because it was the closest they could find to Russian weather. My dad had been a soldier on the Eastern Front, so he made a good Boston cop."

In the window, the gleaming lake had dulled to a skinny river. The train rushed through a village of clay tile roofs. Barefoot children chased a chicken. A man carried water buckets hung from a yoke across his shoulders. The hills looked stripped.

Gang said, "Coal mining country."

Then the village was gone. The hills flushed green again.

Gang said, "Tell me about your mom."

"She was from Stalingrad. A nurse. She got wounded in the battle there in 1942 and was captured. She spent six months in a German field hospital. When the Red Army surrounded the Germans outside Stalingrad, they found my mom working as a nurse for the enemy. They arrested her and sent her to a gulag in Novosibirsk. Two years later, a week before the war was over, she escaped and made it to Finland."

He said, "That's badass."

"She was that."

"Are your folks alive?"

"Dad's in Boston, stayed a cop 'til he was in his sixties. Mom died when I was a kid. Cancer."

"I'm sorry."

"Volgograd was a factory city. The Germans blew it to pieces. A lot of industrial chemicals were spilled all over the place. She wallowed in that for months. It came back ten years later to bite her."

"So you joined the police like your dad."

"He raised me. The whole precinct raised me. A Southie cop's kid becomes a Southie cop."

"Did you like it?"

"We cracked a few heads."

"That's the part you liked?"

Lara chuckled. Gang uncrossed his arms and laughed along.

He said, "Then Johns Hopkins for a PhD."

"Fun."

"So you became a cop for your father. Then a health specialist for your mom."

Lara leaned toward Gang, one finger raised. She wanted to point at him, to call him out; his knowledge of her ran deeper than it ought to for a stranger, even one with a file. But she didn't want to argue or shift the mood in the cabin, so she shook the finger instead, to issue a soft warning.

He showed both palms. "I just read the files."

The train knifed through another village, no different from the hamlet two minutes prior, more clay roofs and raven-haired children in the hills of China. Nothing to keep her eyes away from Gang.

He asked, "You got kids?"

"Nope."

"Married?"

"Nope."

"Why not?"

"Nope."

Gang dipped his head, agreeable, a little charming.

Lara said, "You now."

He rested elbows on his knees. Lara sat back, arms and legs crossed. She caught herself mimicking Gang's pose.

He said, "Pretty much the same as you, really. Raised mostly by one parent. Both were in the war."

"Tell me about your mom."

She asked this first because good boys loved their moms.

"My mother grew up in a little town in Manchuria, called Fouzhou, three hundred miles inland from Taiwan. She was eighteen when my father walked up her street bleeding."

"What?"

Gang mixed his hands in the air. "I sort of need to tell them together. My folks."

Lara nestled more into her berth.

He asked, "You know about Doolittle's Raid on Tokyo?"

"I've got no files on you. Just talk."

Gang seemed to like that, Lara's cop voice.

"A couple months after Pearl Harbor, the US decided to show Japan that their home islands were fair game. Sixteen B-25 bombers were put on a Navy carrier and sent to go bomb Tokyo. The mission was supposed to take off six hundred miles from Tokyo, but the carrier group got spotted by a Japanese picket ship eight hundred miles out. That was too far out for the bombers to make the raid on Tokyo, then fly back to the carriers. So Jimmy Doolittle led the mission over Tokyo, the B-25s dropped their bombs, then they flew west, across the East China Sea into Manchuria. The idea was to go until they were over areas controlled by Chiang Kai-shek's Nationalist Army. Then the crews would bail out and crash the bombers into mountains so the Japanese couldn't re-use them. Hopefully, the local Chinese would find the Americans first and hide them from the Japanese until Chiang's army could show up and send them home. Seventy-three out of eighty fliers made it."

"You're telling me your father was one of Doolittle's Raiders."

"Radioman."

"Oh, my god, let me guess. Your mother was a nurse."

"She was."

"She took care of him and they fell in love."

Gang flipflopped a hand.

"Half right. She took care of him. But she was the only one who fell in love."

"Uh oh."

"He left before I was born."

Again the light was torn from the cabin when the train

raced into another tunnel. Anything Lara or Gang could say would be shouted down, so they sat mirroring each other, arms and legs folded for two miles through a mountain.

When daylight flooded in, the cacophony was sucked out. Gang did not go on with his story but sat closed like a jack-knife, staring at Lara, pensive. She let him continue when he was ready. Gang cleared his throat.

"My mother never told me his name. We lived a tough life. I was a half-breed, she was an outcast. She died when I was fifteen. One of the forty million Mao starved in the Great Famine."

Lara moved to sit upright, as if at a funeral.

"You went to a Catholic orphanage."

"I did."

"You did well in school."

"I did."

"And they sent you to America."

"You sure you don't have a file on me?"

"Just a cop. Go on."

"I asked to be sent to Baltimore. The nuns came up with a school there that would take me as an exchange student."

"Why Baltimore?"

"After my mother died, I found a letter from my father. His name was Hulsey. He wrote her when I was ten. One letter, that was all. The address was in Baltimore."

"What did it say?"

"He was sorry. He hoped she was well. That I was well."

"So you went to find Hulsey."

"I did."

"Gang?"

"Yeah."

"Tell me when you've said enough. I don't want to pry."

"Yes you do."

"It's your call."

"Ask me."

"Did you find your father in Baltimore?"

"I did."

"How'd it go?"

Gang looked out the window at nothing notable. China rippled past in hills and rows of crops, villages made small by the speed of the train, people made common.

Gang brought his gaze back to Lara.

"I killed him."

15

GANG

H e'd only told Lara Dill one lie, that he was from Datong. He hadn't even needed to mention the little house and the shady street.

Lara's mother was a nurse, so was his. Her father a tanker, his a pilot. She'd been the child of Russians in Boston. He'd been half-American in a rural village. Lara had been raised by one parent, too. She'd been the law. He'd been lawless.

The closeness of Lara Dill's truths to his own was a little awesome and seemed like a bridge. She made it feel like one, the way she listened.

But her reaction to the news that he'd killed Hulsey in Baltimore. That amazed him.

She heard it like a cop.

Lara winced as if to clear something from her eyes.

"How did you do that?"

Not why. No judgment. Only how.

"I was a kid. But I figured out the perfect way."

"Did you."

"I found him easy enough."

"You followed him for a while."

"Good guess."

"It's not a guess."

Lara stayed impassive, as if scribbling notes.

"He was a factory worker. A drunk. One time I saw a woman run out of his apartment with a bloody nose. Another came out with her dress torn almost off, screaming. He got in bar fights. He called people shitty things. He was a racist."

Lara said, "He didn't do any of these things to you."

"No."

"That's not why you hated him."

"No."

"Keep going."

Gang said, "I never approached him, never met him. I watched for three months. Then one night I broke into his apartment while he was at some pub in his neighborhood. I stole his car keys. Waited for him to leave the bar. At midnight, he came out. He crossed the street and I ran him down in his own pickup. Turned around and ran over him again. I left the truck in an alley and rode my bike back to school."

"Hit-and-run with his own vehicle."

Gang nodded. "Dead end for the cops."

"No one knew his Chinese son was in Baltimore."

"No one. Ever."

"Just me."

"Just you."

"I think you might be a dangerous man."

"I have been."

"You're not a radiological lab tech."

"I've got a really good memory. All I have to do is read something."

"The files."

"Yeah, Lara. The files."

"Who are you?"

The train flew into another tunnel. Daylight swiped away, left to right. The din flooded the compartment, and in the rattling dark Gang was careful not to flinch while Lara's question hung unanswered.

Inside the tunnel, a southbound train raced down the other track. The locomotive and cars rushing in the other direction seemed to put hands on the Trans-Mongolian and shake it the way one might force another to speak the truth. The vortex between trains made the air in Lara's cabin box Gang's ears.

This tunnel was quick, the train righted itself. Emerging into daylight felt like only a page had been turned, a black page.

He said, "Please."

"Please what?"

"I need you to listen to me."

"I have been. You murdered your father when you were a kid because he abandoned you. I want to know who you are right now. Then get the fuck out of my cabin."

"I'm a man who's done things for survival. And money."

"Are you doing it now?"

"Yes."

"What do you want with me?"

Gang leaned at the waist to whisper when he did not have to.

"You need to get off this train before the Russian border."

Lara Dill made no sudden move. Slowly, she pushed away from him until her back was against the bulkhead. She brought in her legs in case she needed to kick at him.

"How do you know that?"

"I'll get off with you. I'll make sure you get back safe to Beijing."

She asked again, less controlled, "How do you know that?"

Gang straightened. "That's not what matters."

In the afternoon sun the river kept pace with the train. Gang turned his back to Lara Dill, a show of trust before he left her cabin.

16

TIMUR

I f hell was sitting with a Russian, at least this Russian was
quiet.

The man read with glasses perched on the tip of his nose.
He'd removed a narrow file in a green cardboard binder from
his briefcase, spread it over his crossed knees, and settled in.
Every so often he peered above his spectacles at China drib-
bling past. In the tunnels when he could not read, he took off
the glasses to rub between his eyes.

Russian Anton must have known Timur was watching.
Timur had nothing in his lap, nothing outside to watch but the
same impoverished, red-roofed village over and over, and the
measly river running up to the tracks, then away like a puppy.

Anton only read and gazed. He did not chat or doze;
always he returned to the file after looking up. He read each
page for a long time. He appeared to be memorizing, readying
himself for something.

The Russian didn't clear his throat or fidget. He made
himself purposefully unobtrusive. Timur's size could have that
effect, make him appear something not to be roused. Or

perhaps it was snobbery; the man was plainly a scholar of some sort. Perhaps Timur's Chechen accent made the Russian consider him an inferior.

Might as well find out. It was hell anyway.

"Why don't you talk?"

Anton didn't lift his head at Timur's growl until he'd finished something on the page.

He looked up. "You don't seem to want to."

Anton took down his glasses. He twiddled them between his fingers. "We're strangers on a train. Here for a few days. We likely will not see each other again. Would you like to talk?"

Timur put hands on his own knees, big hands. He gazed down at his scuffed boots, a quarter larger than the Russian's brown shoes.

Anton said, "You're quite a large fellow. Do you do something with it? Are you in a physical trade?"

Timur worked his jaw, champing side to side, mad at himself because now they were talking.

"Miner. I'm a miner."

Anton pointed with his folded glasses. "Ah, I've been in a few mines. Extraordinary places. Uranium in the Urals. What an incredible feat, to dig so deep into the earth. And perilous, at that. I'll tell you, the whole world runs on what you lot bring up out of the ground. There's not an industry I can think of that doesn't use some bit of carbon, gem, or metal. Good for you. I imagine you're marvelous at it."

"Why?"

"You're strong, yes? Isn't that good for a miner?"

"I stoop a lot."

"I suppose that would be a disadvantage. Even so, Timur, well done."

"Anton."

"Yes?"

"You don't have to."

"Have to what?"

"Talk so much all of a sudden. You don't have to make up for the last five hours."

The Russian chuckled. He seemed to look inward and saw himself foolish.

He said, "I apologize."

"For what?"

"I've been told that asking what someone does for a living is a very American thing to do. It's not a Socialist question."

"You took five hours to do it. It's fine."

The train made a pleasant rocking, the rails muttered.

Timur said, "You're a scientist."

"I am."

"Something with nuclear power."

"And how did you know that?"

"You're not a miner. You're no prison guard. You don't look like an apparatchik. You would have no other reason to go into a uranium mine."

"Excellent. Correct."

The Russian lifted the folder off his lap. He left it open on the bench beside him. "And you, my friend. Have you been in prison?"

Anton left his legs crossed and folded his arms. He let his head loll a little to suggest that a game had begun between them.

Timur asked, "Because?"

"Who mentions guards in a mine? Only someone who's been guarded."

"In some of the mines, there were prisoners working alongside us."

"I see."

Timur ran fingers over his lips. He asked, "What were you doing in Beijing?"

"I have a teaching position at a small university."

"But not a teaching position at a big university in Moscow."

"No. I do not."

Timur indicated the slender report open next to Anton, a hundred or so pages.

"Because of that."

"Excellent again."

Timur said, "And you have no woman in Beijing."

"Because?"

Timur smiled. He was doing well in the game.

"You have no basket of snacks. No extra blanket. No thermos."

Anton tapped his temple, then pointed at Timur. "Correct."

Timur pointed back. "And I think you are going to Moscow to make trouble."

"Am I?"

"The way you read that file. Like you will be answering questions."

"I am impressed."

"And your one-way ticket."

"Like yours."

"We both left Beijing without snacks."

Anton chuckled, "That is what I regret most."

"So tell me, Anton Epstein. Why is a Russian Jew scientist with no woman who is memorizing a file going back to Russia to make trouble?"

Anton took down his glasses, creased them into one hand, then waved them in the air as if erasing something.

"You first."

"Me. Why?"

"Because if I go first, you'll tire of listening. Then you'll stop speaking and won't answer. You'll know my story but I'll have to wait for yours. That's not fair."

"Fair."

"That matters, doesn't it?"

Timur nodded. "You are some Russian."

Anton said, "Then, if you please."

The train took a long curve around a contour of the gently climbing land. The terrain had grown shrubby and sandy, with the occasional outcropping of rock. Shadows shifted in the cabin as the train rounded a hill.

Timur said, "It's late in the afternoon."

"Would you like to pray?"

"Why do you ask?"

"You don't seem like the sort of chap who says, 'It's late in the afternoon. I'm hungry.' You're a Chechen. I took a guess that it's time for a Muslim to pray."

"I think you will make a good amount of trouble."

"Ample praise."

"Yes, I would like to pray. Do you mind?"

"Not at all."

Timur rose off his berth. He had no prayer carpet and no way to face Mecca on a winding railroad. He got on his knees on the carpet between the beds.

Anton asked, "May I stay?"

"Why would you?"

"I should like to pray, too."

Timur raised his hands beside his head to greet Allah with praise. With no water to wash, he imitated the act of ablution of his hands and face. Anton stayed seated. He crossed his wrists at his chest, then set to leaning back and forth, tapping his breast in the tempo of the train.

17

LARA

Kilometer 598

For an hour, Lara gazed out her east-facing window at the stiletto shadows of telephone poles. When she wasn't watching the sepia plain redden, she stared at her locked door.

In one hand she squeezed enough *yuan* to make a phone call at the next station, Erlyan, the last stop inside China, on the Mongolian border. That would be in two hours, at sundown. In the other hand she gripped the trowel, the only item available which might make a serviceable weapon.

In Erlyan she was going to call Rudd. She'd try not to scream that he'd promised she was safe. That the sons of bitches who'd almost killed her four years ago had okayed her return. Rudd had told her, straight up, that she was permitted to step on Russian soil just this once, do this important job, then go back to Beijing. He had assurances.

Instead, the mob had sent Gang to threaten her.

She would, in fact, scream at Rudd. This was not *safe*.

Who was Gang? Just a messenger? A warning shot? Or was he the mob's enforcer to carry out the threat if she ignored it?

Who was Gang behind all that? What sort of man was shaped by the cheerless short life of a mother? By a hero and bastard for a father? Abandoned in China, heartbroken in Baltimore, the killer boy in a stolen truck?

Gang said he'd done things for money and to stay alive. Maybe the Russians were holding something over him? Had he been forced onto the Trans-Mongolian? Was he also under some threat, too? Or was he a bastard like his old man?

Whatever else, one thing was for sure. Gang was a killer. A patricide.

She wanted to call her father a world away. Ask him about the many young Boston killers he'd arrested. How many reformed in later life, how many second chances made good? How many of the bad kids got worse?

Who was Gang? What was Gang?

She wanted to ask her father, though he wouldn't know the answer: Why did she care?

———

A ruckus came through the wall from the compartment shared by Björn and Gang, like the whoops and excitement of gambling.

Lara stuffed her Chinese phone money in a pocket and tightened her grip on the trowel. She unlocked the cabin door to look out into the back of Sinjin's seersucker suit outside Björn's door.

Lara moved into the passageway to tap the English boy on the shoulder. He turned, red-faced and pleased about something. Sinjin turned sideways to let her by; the corridor was so narrow she had to rub against him. Sinjin cast his eyes to the ceiling like a gentleman.

She squeezed through the doorframe into Björn's cabin where she came up against the breadth of the big Chechen Timur. She poked him in the back.

"Izvinite." Excuse me.

With little room to pivot, Timur glanced over his shoulder; he retreated a stride to vacate his spot. She maneuvered around him, then halted behind the shorter Soviet scientist. Lara had forgotten his name. Timur loomed over her head from behind.

The Russian wore a burgundy cardigan. He looked comfy with hands in his pockets, smelling a bit musty up close, maybe a pipe or books.

Seated before him were cabinmates Björn on the left bench, Gang on the right, slap-fighting.

Both held open palms before their faces, wavering as if to hypnotize each other, like cobras. Suddenly Björn struck, so quick his white arm blurred.

Gang blocked Björn's flashing touch an inch from his cheek. Gang struck back, his hands a blur in the short space between him and Björn. The Swede countered, the two men's forearms collided. Around Lara, the little crowd of second-class passengers gasped at the pinwheel speed of both.

Björn's and Gang's fingers wriggled like worms. Hands probed, bobbed, weaved. Lara wanted to stop them but couldn't say why and had no mandate to do so. She bit her lip and hoped Björn would knock Gang off the bench.

Gang snapped a backhand at Björn and clipped his ear. Björn nodded. He feinted a straight-on assault of his own, Gang parried, then Björn used Gang's move against him and swept in, a knuckle-rap against Gang's sideburn. Gang nodded. In the corridor, Sinjin shouted that he had to run to get his camera and for no one to stop until he got back.

Gang and Björn sat bolt upright, spines locked, clashing faster than Lara's eye could follow, flickers of motion. Gang or Björn would turn a paddled cheek, then nod.

Sinjin returned in short order. The clicks of his camera joined the clack of the wheels and the smacks of skin.

Lara said, "That's enough."

Björn glanced at her and dropped his hands. Gang gently slapped him.

"I didn't agree."

Lara expected another Swedish curse, but Björn brought up his hands. The contest went into a higher gear.

Björn didn't lay another hand on Gang, who had another level Björn did not. Gang hissed with each swift blow, "*ish, ish, ish*..." He seemed to know every flick of Björn's arms before Björn did. Gang blocked and struck in a single motion; Björn's head seemed to twitch from the cuffing Gang gave him.

Gang, point made, said, "That's enough." Then he spotted the trowel in Lara's hand.

"Give me that."

"No."

Björn ran fingers over his chin like a man checking the quality of a shave.

"Give it to him."

Above Lara's head, Timur's voice rumbled. "Give it."

Lara gave Gang the trowel. He offered it to Björn.

The Swede was the larger man, forty more pounds of muscle. He was dexterous and powerful. But Gang was nimble, flowing, so fleet he could disappear into motion like a propeller.

Neither man stood, they stayed arm's length apart. Björn held the trowel like a dagger, scribing circles in the air. Gang waited, hands on guard, motionless. Sinjin stopped taking photos, Lara leaned against the back of the Russian, the giant leaned in behind her.

Björn couldn't decide how to attack. Gang waited, locked in.

Gang said, "Go ahead. It's okay."

Björn thrust the sharp trowel straight at Gang's heart. Gang reacted but the move was a feint by Björn. Gang was left blocking air. Björn yanked back and instantly went for Gang's eyes.

Lara saw only a flinch on Gang's face, Björn's white teeth clamped in pain, and the trowel falling.

The tool rolled on the cabin floor. When Lara looked up from it, Gang had Björn's knife hand bent backwards. Gang's other hand was clamped around Björn's throat. Björn choked between his teeth. Gang let him go.

Björn coughed to put his windpipe back in place.

"*För tusan.*"

From the hallway, Sinjin sang out, "That's 'goddamit' in Swedish."

Gang reached across to rub Björn's upper arms. "You all right, buddy?"

The Swede blew out his cheeks. "*Kristus*, you're fast."

To Lara, a little breathless, he said, "He's fast."

Gang plucked the trowel off the carpet. He offered it, handle first, to Lara.

She spun around to stomp off; the mass of the giant blocked her way. The Chechen was slow to move aside in the small cabin. Lara looked up into his scraggly chin, expecting him to make himself a gate and let her pass.

Timur grinned down. "Incredible."

She said in English, "Get the living fuck out of my way."

Timur didn't seem to understand, but he let Lara go by. She hastened the short distance to her cabin. Behind her in the passageway, Sinjin loudly interpreted into Russian what she'd just said.

18

ANTON

Kilometer 640

R eturning from the fascinating duel in the next cabin, Anton closed the report he'd left open on his berth. He tucked it into his briefcase to tell Timur he was done reading for a while. They could go back to talking, or silence.

He let Timur choose. The big man elected to face the window.

The train worked its way north. The landscape shrugged off the industry of humans, not a trace of civilization reared its head on a grassland mesa so vast it might have been the sky turned upside down and green. Not a tree, not a hill, nothing broke the horizon where the east bruised to dusk.

Timur leaned the side of his head against the bulkhead, arms crossed. It was the pose of a lonely man. He surveyed the passing world and did not blink.

Beside the rails, the stretching shadow of the train traipsed over ground conquered a millennia ago by Genghis Khan. This was Inner Mongolia, still a frontier, too expansive even for China to know what to do with it. Anton kept an eye on

Timur watching it roll by and wondered what Timur dreamed of.

The big man said, "All right. I will go first."

Timur pivoted from the window. He put both boots on the red carpet, covered his knees with his hands. Timur's knuckles were so great his hands seemed bolted together.

Anton said, "Please do."

Timur ran a finger and thumb around his opened mouth, choosing words.

"I am Chechen."

"Yes, you've said that."

"Stop talking."

Anton raised a palm in submission.

Timur said, "For five hundred years there have been wars between your country and mine. Every time, Chechnya wants independence. Every time, Russia throws Chechnya under her heel. One tsar, then another. Then Lenin, then Stalin. This will go on, another war is coming, you wait. Russia will never let Chechnya stand on her own. There have been ethnic cleansings. Deportations. My father fought in the Red Army. After the war he was a voice for Chechen Muslims. Stalin's little bastard Beria sent him to Kirghizia to freeze to death."

Anton tapped the air lightly as though rapping on a window. "You know I am sorry about that. You understand I agree these are terrible things."

Timur said, "I do not need your agreement. But it is appreciated."

"Please, continue."

"You have not asked what I was doing in Beijing."

"May I?"

"I was raising money."

"For Chechnya?"

"For Chechens, Afghans, Mongols, all Muslims. In Beijing I was informed of an accident in Ukraine. A nuclear reactor.

Something happened. You are a scientist. Is this true, this accident?"

"A reactor core may have melted down. Or it might be worse."

"Worse?"

"A reactor may actually have exploded. If it did, I believe I know which one."

"Yes?"

"Chernobyl."

"How do you know?"

"I was a chief engineer at the plant."

"A scientist. Good. Your turn in a moment."

"Of course."

"Ukraine has put out a call for Soviet miners and subway builders to come. They have called an emergency. Six hundred. Why? Why do they need miners for a reactor?"

"If there has, in fact, been a core meltdown, and if the core has breached containment, the fissile material may actually be burning down into the earth. They will ask miners to dig a tunnel under the reactor."

"Why?"

"To stop it."

"With what?"

"A concrete pad."

"Will this work?"

"I don't know, Timur. There's never been an incident like this."

"How long will such a tunnel beneath your reactor be?"

"At least a hundred fifty meters."

Timur asked, "Why do they need so many miners?"

"It tells me they'll be digging by hand. No heavy equipment. They don't want to disturb the ground under the foundation. Probably it's already fractured by the explosion."

"That sounds right."

"Timur, can you guess how long it might take to dig a tunnel like that?"

"How deep under the reactor?"

"Again, I'm guessing. To protect the miners from radiation, ten to twelve meters."

"Digging without machines? Four weeks, maybe five. If the work goes day and night."

Timur pointed at Anton, now a question for him, they were volleying Chernobyl back and forth. Timur's interest was keen.

The Chechen asked, "Will there be enough time? How fast does a core burn through the earth?"

"It will be a close-run thing, but there should be enough time. Understand, creating the tunnel will be only half the battle."

"What more is needed?"

"There will have to be some sort of heat exchanger inside the concrete. Something to cool the core as it burns through the cement. Piped-in liquid nitrogen, maybe, or a graphite plate."

"That will stop it?"

"It's impossible to know. All these are guesses. At best, something could work, yes. At worst, it might delay the lava by one or two months. That's all."

Timur asked, "Is that what is in your file? The exploding reactor?"

"The possibility of it, yes."

"What will happen if the concrete does not stop the core?"

"Something terrible."

Timur's attention turned almost icy. The great Chechen had sat forward while Anton described the tunnel and concrete pad, hands on knees or stroking his beard. Now that the talk had swung to the consequences of failure, Timur tilted back against the vibrating wall. He watched the passing land, his inner eye looking elsewhere.

After moments, he leaned over his knees at Anton. "What is below the reactor?"

"Timur, that's not something I should discuss."

"Listen to me." The Chechen leaned closer; his head almost bridged the distance between them. "I am going to Chernobyl. Are you?"

"No."

"Then between the two of us, I should know."

"That's fair."

"And fair matters, so you have said."

"Groundwater. There's an aquifer under the Chernobyl reactors."

Timur recoiled. "I am no scientist and even I know this is madness. Who builds a nuclear reactor on top of water?"

"Apparently we do."

Timur angled in again, hungry for more about the dangers of an exploded reactor. "What will happen if the core reaches the water?"

"First, let me ask. Why are you going? You seem to hate Russia. And Russians."

"The Quran tells me to go."

"Truly? What does it say?"

"'O my son. Keep up prayer and enjoin the good and forbid the evil, and bear patiently that which befalls you.' It is my faith that calls me to the tunnel. Not Russia."

He should tell Timur not to go to Chernobyl. If an RBMK had burst open, that was the last place any human should go near. But warning him away was an intimacy they did not have.

Instead, Anton asked, "Do you know how a nuclear reactor works?"

Timur's chest shook in a small, leviathan laugh. "Doesn't everyone?"

"If you let me tell you, you'll understand better what's happening. It will help you decide what to do. Alright?"

Timur held out a platter of a palm. "As you wish. We have four days."

———

"Thirty years ago, the Soviet Union connected the world's first commercial reactor to the Moscow grid. The Oblinsk reactor was small, it generated only five megawatts. It had been designed only to power a submarine. Also, to make fuel for a plutonium bomb. The choice had been made. The Soviet Union would rise out of the wreckage of the Great Patriotic War to lead the world in nuclear power."

Timur said, "Stalin. May he rot."

"Actually, it was Khrushchev who drove the idea the hardest. He needed to find ways to compete with the United States. While the Americans were busy going to the moon, the Soviet Union started a crash program to build a fleet of nuclear subs based on the little Oblinsk reactor. But the plant proved too unstable. So it was repurposed for civilian use."

"Wait. The reactor was shit for the military? So they gave it to the people?"

"Yes."

Timur collapsed his hands to his lap. "Russians."

"Do you wish me to continue?"

"I wish for many things."

The Chechen's splayed legs and girth filled the cabin. Timur's spurts of intellect and disgust, his wide and rare smiles, light and dark moods, all made him a chiaroscuro, like the moon. His raw size gave him a gravity that pulled Anton in. Anton found the Chechen pleasant enough company.

"With typical Soviet gigantism, we designed our civilian reactors to be the biggest in the world. The first RBMK we built at Chernobyl was twenty times the size of any reactor in the West. It generated a thousand megawatts, enough for a million homes."

"So how did your big reactor at Chernobyl manage to explode?"

"It appears a flaw in the little Oblinsk reactor came back to haunt it. The submarine reactor was too small for the error to manifest. It was only present in theory, that's where I first spotted it. But once the RBMK was scaled up to enormity, the flaw grew in size. Do you want to hear something amazing?"

"I will tell you when I am amazed. Go on."

"The activity inside a reactor is almost impossible to imagine. In order to generate a single watt of electricity, there must be thirty billion neutron fissions every second. Ninety-nine percent of uranium neutrons travel at such incredible speeds, they can't be controlled by a reactor. These are called prompt neutrons."

"What speed?"

"Twenty thousand kilometers per second. That's so fast that the instant one neutron is about to hit another, they're both literally somewhere else. It's called neutron flux. Neutron flux is not very useful for power generation which requires the heat of collisions. But."

Anton paused for effect. Timur, mildly annoyed, echoed, "But?"

"Less than one percent of the neutrons flashing about during fission go much more slowly. Their movement is actually measurable in seconds, even minutes. These slow neutrons can be managed. They are what make a nuclear reactor possible."

Anton sat forth, growing eager. He bumped knees with Timur.

"Fission, the colliding of those slow neutrons inside a nuclear reactor, is controlled by inserting rods made of neutron-absorbing elements. Cadmium, for example, or boron. Both act like sponges to trap the neutrons and stop them from triggering more fissions. It's a very delicate balance. You pull out the rods to increase fission. Insert the rods to slow it. Push them in too fast, you stop the fission entirely. With-draw them too fast, or pull out too many, and the neutrons can overtake the reactor, causing an uncontrolled spike of energy."

"And?"

"And that could melt the core."

Timur said, "Or make it explode."

"Yes."

Timur nodded, slow as a great bough under snow.

"You mentioned a flaw in the little reactor. The one that got too big to be theory."

"Yes."

"You will tell me."

"Alright."

The Chechen rose to his feet. He yawned but could not raise his arms for the ceiling.

"Not now."

"Why not?"

Timur said, "You were wrong about me, Russian."

"Was I?"

"Yes."

"How so?"

"I am hungry."

19

GANG

G ang led Björn through five juddering carriages to the restaurant car in the direction of the locomotive. In Chinese and Russian, he excused their way past a hundred travelers milling in the corridors.

Theirs was the only soft-class carriage in the train. The first three cars they passed through contained four-berth cabins; in the following two, open bunks lined the walls like dormitories. Snorers and the bored filled the bunk beds.

Small children zoomed about in the narrow passageways. Their parents left them unchecked, figuring the kids couldn't get too far or into too much trouble on a train. Soviet sailors in blousy white uniforms and blue-and-white tunics staggered past, already drunk. Russian soldiers in greatcoats shouldered between rooms clutching armfuls of beer. The doors in the four-berth cabins were left open to the corridors for ventilation since the windows would not open. Inside each compartment, sturdy matrons—Chinese, Mongol, or Russian—set out meats, cooked cabbage, and spongy breads to be torn by hand, all from baskets, then set out on the fold-down tables. Husbands, brothers, and strangers gathered on the lower cots to smoke, laugh, and argue before the meal. Old men in striped pajamas ready for their sundown bedtime shuttled to the bathrooms at each end of the cars, some with pajama bottoms opened in unfortunate ways. Gang and Björn slipped among the passengers who spotted them as foreigners and let them by with a kind of humility.

In each car, the Trans-Mongolian's conductors cared for their carriages. Coal furnaces were stoked in advance of the cool night ahead in the Mongolian highlands. Water was added to samovars for tea and face-washing. The conductors bulldozed down the corridors behind vacuums, bumping any feet slow to move out of their way. On the platform just before the restaurant car, a Chinese girl squatted, peeling potatoes. She let the skins fall onto the rushing tracks.

Gang slid aside the portal to the diner. He stepped inside, the big Swede on his heels. Gang felt secure with Björn behind him; the Swede would not be easy to get through. Björn wanted to learn some of the moves Gang had used in their little bout. He'd asked where Gang had learned them. Gang said, "Fighting since I was eight."

The dining car resembled a Chinese tearoom, crimson splashed everywhere, on the wallpaper, carpet, tablecloths. Embossed into the leather-padded back of every booth was the communist gold star. A framed sickle and hammer logo hung above each door beside a portrait of a farseeing Mao.

The tabletops were set in white porcelain and linen. Wine goblets chimed against water glasses where they'd been put close together.

Only one table was occupied. Gang hesitated in the doorway. Björn pressed past him, saying, "Come on." The Swede moved into the aisle between tables to join the lanky Englishman in his pretty suit and pink bowtie, who waved for Gang and Björn to join him and Lara.

Björn took the booth beside the Englishman, leaving the

seat next to Lara open. Gang sidled up to the table but did not slide in until she nodded.

The Englishman introduced himself as Sinjin and extended a hand first to Björn, then Gang. As they said "Hello" and clasped above the table, Sinjin extolled that he was something or other with the British embassy in Beijing. He was a photographer also, and on his way to gather mushrooms in the Urals. He thought the clash in their cabin had been a remarkable display. He'd taken many photos and even when he developed the film did not expect to be able to see their hands.

A waiter appeared, a Chinese boy with silver teeth. In English, the Swede ordered beer; Sinjin translated and ordered a beer for himself. The waiter stammered there was no beer onboard, no alcohol at all except Chinese champagne. Sinjin, whose Mandarin was excellent, ordered two bottles for the table on his tab. The price per bottle was half a yuan. Five rubles. Eight American cents.

Sinjin considered himself the major-domo of the table. He asked after Gang's background that made him such a marvel. The Englishman rested his chin in one palm.

He said, "My goodness."

Gang repeated the one lie he'd told Lara, that he was from Datong. Then he unpacked all the other untruths he'd not fed her, wondering as he did why he had not? He claimed his father was a businessman, his mother an English teacher. During the Japanese occupation of Manchuria, both worked for Chiang's Nationalist resistance. The Japanese police, the *Kuomintang*, found them out and executed them. Gang was raised in an orphanage where he learned to fight to survive the older boys. He went to a technical school in Nanjing, was fascinated by the atomic bomb over Hiroshima, studied radiological health, learned all he could about ionizing radiation, got a government position in Datong that had lasted fifteen years, got a call last night, and here he was on the Trans-Mongolian.

During his lies, Lara fixed him with a stern gaze. He smiled glancingly at her. Gang lied in front of her to show her, as he'd done when he'd choked the Swede, the truth of who he was. For her to take him seriously. To understand that he was a man to believe when he told her to get off the train before Russia.

The restaurant car placed one window at every table. The time-etched glass beside Gang faced a falling sun. The last rays shined on a gray-brown panorama where every shadow lay sharp and dark. The Trans-Mongolian coursed across a cloudless pan that in another hour would go untouched by light or sound until dawn, or until another train flew down these rails.

As Gang told his last lie, Sinjin spoke up in sympathy. He, too, had been in boarding schools his whole childhood. He knew the cruelty of boys, and he knew fighting.

The waiter returned with two surprisingly chilled bottles of rosy champagne. The Swede handled the chore of opening them. Sinjin poured, saying with each glass of bubbly, "And for you."

Before they drank, Sinjin lifted his glass. "A toast?"

Gang raised his champagne flute. The others joined, Lara last, still glaring.

The Englishman said, "I would rather drink with you all than with the finest people on earth."

He giggled, Björn sang out, "Agreed." Gang put his glass in front of Lara to see if she would clink it. She muttered, "Fuck," and did. Gang touched his glass to no one else's and drank.

The door to the restaurant car slid open. The massive Chechen ducked under the doorframe. He wore black slacks, a light wool jacket over an olive T-shirt, and scuffed boots. He stepped among the tables set with china and fragile glass. He seemed unfazed by the dining car's small spaces. A sparse beard and blunt face gave him a hint of the Asiatic. In his imagination, Gang fought him. Gang lost.

Behind the giant, almost out of sight, came the Russian in his maroon sweater. He was well-groomed, a strut in his walk. Gang figured him for somewhat of a peacock, perhaps vain. If not vain, then frightened.

Sinjin waved as he'd done at Gang and the Swede. He grabbed two chairs and two more champagne flutes from a neighboring table. Sinjin told Lara and Gang to scooch in.

The Russian settled beside Lara. The giant folded at a neighboring table where he blocked the aisle with his legs.

Sinjin poured another round for all.

The waiter arrived, even more jumpy at the sight of Timur. Sinjin made suggestions off the Chinese menu, then translated everyone's orders to the young waiter. He purchased two more bottles of champagne.

No passengers filled the seven other tables. Everyone in the lower-class cars ate tonight out of baskets, pockets, or purses. They supped with family, friends, fellow travelers, and beer.

The young Englishman continued to play ringmaster, a sort of fugue state of amiability. In his patrician British accent, fingertips on his own starched shirt and buttons, he described himself first for the giant and the Russian, the last arrivals to the table. Sinjin zeroed in on Timur, as if the man's size made him someone to appease. He asked about Timur's home, his family and work.

Timur told his story in a tolling voice that recalled a freighter at sea, her great motor, shaft and blade, all her muted roar beneath the surface. The giant's size, high cheeks, small eyes, and wide brow made it easy to think him uncomplicated. But Timur picked his way carefully through his words, listened with a quick, avian attentiveness. He had a gathering intellect, he was a wary man. Timur was a Chechen, a miner, with no family. Gang addressed him in fluent Russian, raising Lara's eyebrows. Gang shrugged, to remind her that all he had to do was read a book.

Björn, Gang's cabinmate, grew up privileged in Stockholm. An attractive man, he'd been trained by the military, refined by university, he was made powerful by good fortune. The luxuries of his life had made him kind and indulgent. He said he enjoyed being this man and had drunk more champagne than the others at the table. Gang would never lose to him.

Russian Anton said little. He laughed where he ought, sipped from his flute, and left his chin in his palm like a professor with students. He was not showy, but his modesty was the deliberate kind. He had much to say but would wait to let it be pulled out of him.

Sinjin let Lara go last at the table. It wasn't chivalry but to showcase her, the beautiful American scientist, the best of them all.

She lied.

The lies were little, only for Gang to catch. Her father was not a tanker on the Eastern Front but a sniper. He'd met her mother in Budapest, not Helsinki. He wasn't a cop in Boston but a fireman. She'd become a firefighter, too. Not Johns Hopkins for her doctorate, but Virginia.

Lara smiled at Gang as she lied and drifted her smile around to the others. Big Timur was taken with her when she made up a story about a fifth-floor rescue on a firetruck ladder. Björn, tipsy, appeared confused; likely he'd heard different stories. While she spoke, Sinjin sputtered "No you didn't," and "My stars." Anton the scientist watched it all as if from above, allowing Lara her moment, waiting for his.

Lara lied to tell Gang he was nothing special. He was not a mystery, just a liar, and she could do it, too. She wasn't afraid of him.

The meal arrived. On the giant's plate a thin overcooked steak crowded a scoop of jasmine rice with scallions and cashews. The big man chewed with displeasure but at his size he wasn't likely to be a connoisseur. Sinjin's selection was a steaming plate of Szechuan chicken which he drowned in soy sauce. Björn accepted a salad of iceberg lettuce topped by a nearly raw filet of salmon that looked congealed. Gang purposely ordered the same meal as Lara, plain Chinese noodles with herbs and freshwater mussels fried in peanut oil. Anton ordered goose pâte with white toast. His meal seemed a judgment on the others; while Timur struggled to cut his steak and the others tucked in, Anton only nibbled.

The food caused gaps in Sinjin's chatter; the conversation wilted. The young Britisher may have realized he'd overdone the role of host, so he ran silent for a bit. Silverware clicked on the porcelain, they all swilled more champagne ordered by Björn. The Swede maintained his lead and grew so affable he quietly hugged Timur. Gang sensed the alcohol pooling in his own blood. He tried to slow down but Lara poured and drank another glass with him.

Anton finished his meal first. He stopped spreading goose on toast and set down his butter knife, eased back, fingers laced over the waist of his sweater, to gaze out at the immense Chinese night. No one at the table knew one another. Events had jumbled them together on the Trans-Mongolian, and without Sinjin's cajoling they fell to eating alone, shoulder-to-shoulder.

When everyone had finished, Timur was the one to restart the conversation. He laid his knife and fork over the fatty detritus on his plate. He leaned back, meshing his mammoth knobby hands across his waist. Timur tipped his chin at Anton.

"He knows why Chernobyl blew up."

Piqued, all heads turned to the Chechen. They dabbed their mouths on cloth napkins. Lara slurped the last entrails of noodles, then cleaned her lips on the back of her wrist.

She asked Anton, "What does he mean, blew up?"

"I think the reactor core did not simply melt. It may have exploded."

Flummoxed, Sinjin asked, "What does that mean? That sounds worse. You mean like pieces-of-it-on-the-ground kind of exploded?"

Sinjin spun on Björn beside him, put a hand on the Swede's arm, but Björn had slumped and closed his eyes.

Timur said to Anton, "Tell them about the flaw."

Lara perked up more. "What flaw?"

Anton asked, "Dr. Dill? May I ask what you know about the negative void coefficient?"

"I know enough."

"Would you explain it to the table?"

Lara hesitated. She considered Gang beside her, privately sharing her annoyance to be quizzed by the Russian.

Gang put a hand close to Lara's arm, not touching her.

"I'd like to hear."

Timur said, "Please," so the explanation would not be left to Anton.

"Alright." Lara poked Björn to wake him. The Swede folded his arms, muttered "*Fan*," and sagged further into the booth.

Lara rubbed her palms as if to warm them. If she was going to be quizzed, she was going to ace it.

"Every element except hydrogen has neutrons in the nucleus. Fission is the collision of neutrons. Those collisions produce heat. A reactor creates heat that turns water into steam that drives turbines to make electricity. The element of choice for nuclear reactors is uranium."

Sinjin asked, "Why?"

Without lifting his head, Björn mumbled, "Uranium-235 has ninety-two protons and a hundred forty-three neutrons."

Sinjin stroked Björn's shoulder to tell him to go back to sleep. Lara pressed on.

"Uranium has too many neutrons, which makes it basically unstable. When a U-235 atom absorbs just one more neutron, the atom splits apart. That split releases a burst of energy and more neutrons. Those neutrons collide with other uranium atoms in the reactor and split them. More neutrons are set loose and so on until you get a chain reaction."

Timur said, "There are two kinds of neutrons."

Lara said, "Tell us, Timur."

"Prompt and slow."

Anton hoisted a finger to Lara, indicating that he, not she, was schooling the giant. Anton told Timur, "The slow ones are called delayed neutrons."

Timur nodded.

Lara continued: "Ninety-nine percent of neutrons in fission are prompt. The problem is they move at a tenth the speed of light. They're so fast they miss each other. In order to get enough collisions to create fission, the neutrons have to be slowed. That's done with a moderator."

Björn snorted and sat up. "Where are we?"

Sinjin said, "Moderators."

The Swede smoothed both hands over his blond head as if waking in a bed. "Okay." He cleared his throat while getting his bearings.

"Yes, alright. A moderator absorbs prompt neutrons. This slows the neutrons enough to create fission at a speed that can be controlled."

Anton said, "Thank you. Would you like to go on?"

From slapping him many times, Gang knew the big Swede had no temper. The man was a happy drunk; he did his best to stumble out a reply.

"In the West, we use water as a moderator in our nuclear

reactors. When water heats, it makes steam. Steam creates air bubbles. Bubbles are gaps in the water. The hotter the water gets, the more bubbles. The more bubbles there are, the fewer neutrons get slowed. That means a drop in collisions, and reactivity falls. If it falls enough, fission stops and the reactor shuts down."

Björn made a small bow to the table. He turned a bottle upside down to dribble the last champagne into his glass. He downed it, then addressed the bottle, a little slurred: "The negative void coefficient."

Anton steepled his fingertips. He said to Lara, "Doctor? Please describe the positive void coefficient."

Lara badly masked a glare but complied.

"Another neutron moderator is graphite. Most developed nations are building water-moderated reactors. Only a few use graphite. The Soviets are the only ones on the planet to use graphite and water moderators in the same reactor."

Anton said, "That is correct."

"In water-moderated reactors, the negative void coefficient works like a fail-safe, a sort of dead man's switch. If the fission gets out of hand, it'll make too much steam and shut down the reactor. In a water-graphite reactor, the opposite happens. As the water heats and more turns to steam, fewer neutrons get slowed. But the graphite keeps doing its job, absorbing neutrons, countering the effect of the steam. So instead of reducing fission, graphite keeps the chain reaction going. That lets more water turn to steam, more heat and pressure build up inside the reactor. There's no fail-safe, no shutdown, so the fission continues until it overwhelms the reactor."

Lara raised her hands off the table in a gesture to mimic an explosion.

"That's the RBMK. Theoretically."

Anton said, "Correct again, Doctor."

She said, "Tell me something."

"If I can."

"Why use both?"

"The RBMK generates more power. That has always been the Soviet goal. But in truth, it is not the principal reason."

"Then why?"

"The RBMK, the largest reactor on earth, is also the cheapest to build and run."

Lara didn't back off. "You know what else makes it cheap?"

"Perhaps, Doctor. But tell me."

"When we build a reactor in the West, we construct a containment building around it."

Sinjin asked for an explanation.

Lara said, "It's a thick concrete hood or a cap to stop radioactive contamination in case there's an accident. But Anton's RBMKs are so fucking big that adding a containment structure would double the cost of every unit. So the Soviet Union makes do without them."

Gang expected the Russian scientist to take Lara's tone and words as accusations. But he only nodded sagely and said, "There is more."

She abided. "The RBMK's so big that inside the core there can actually be different regions of reactivity. The operators have to make dozens of adjustments every minute. Handles and switches wear out all the time and need replacing."

Timur shook his head. "It sounds like war. Exhausting."

Lara said, "Mistakes are bound to happen."

Sinjin asked Anton, "Do you think this happened at Chernobyl? Someone made a mistake?"

The scientist made a scale of his hands, tipping neither left nor right.

"Human error played a role, certainly. But the causes of the explosion were born into the reactor from the start."

Anton held out a palm to Lara, to ask if she had more to

add about the faults of his reactor or his nation. When she did not for the moment, he continued, not as a confession, not embarrassed, but as if reciting a passionless alphabet.

"In an emergency, every Soviet reactor control room has a 'scram' button. When an operator hits it, a special bank of boron carbide rods is driven down into the core. In addition to that, every control rod not already fully inserted into the reactor comes down. Boron is a neutron poison, it slows the uranium neutrons to a speed where fission is no longer possible. These rods should shut down the reaction. But the designers of the RBMK didn't want to be able to stop the reactor immediately."

Timur tapped his own skull, then asked, "Why not? This is absurd." He seemed the most provoked at the table. Gang set this aside as its own mystery.

Anton answered. "A sudden cut in power to the Soviet grid is something to be avoided. Somebody's head will be on the block if there is a drop in electricity. So the RBMK's scram rods have been designed to take twenty seconds before they fully enter the core. In a runaway reactor, that is an infinity. And."

The Chechen cast about the table for someone else to demand these answers. But Gang and all of them had delegated the inquiry to Timur's unexplained verve.

Timur shrugged, chosen. He asked, "And? There is more? Unbelievable."

Anton smiled as though proud of his giant roommate.

"When fully withdrawn from the reactor, the tips of the scram rods hang just inside the core. Because the rods are boron, even that little bit touching the core causes a small but constant drag. So, to make the RBMK more economical, the decision was taken that the scram rods would be tipped with graphite, a neutron moderator that increases reactivity. This means that, in an emergency, when the operator hits the scram button, the boron rods lower slowly into the core. And on their way down, the graphite tips encourage fission rather than reduce it. Now the operator, who is already in the midst of an emergency, must make more adjustments. If he can't regain control of the reactor, there's no more he can do but hope."

Timur, flabbergasted, fluttered his great hands at the others around the table, for someone to join him in his dismay with the Soviets.

Lara reached out to push down his arm. She would take it from here.

She said, "A graphite reactor can't blow up, but it will burn. A water reactor won't burn but can explode. By combining them, the Soviets run the risks of both. So Anton?"

"Yes?"

"What the fuck?"

The Chechen fixed his gaze on Anton as if to say: Well, answer her.

The Russian gently applauded, a drawing room clap.

"I am pleased, Doctor. Beyond words."

"Pleased? For what?"

"To hear what you've just said. A Westerner. You *know*."

"It's only a theory."

"I once thought that."

Lara said, "Wait a minute." She aimed a finger at the Russian. "Are you saying you saw Chernobyl coming?"

"I did, yes."

Timur cut in. "He has written a report. The bastards ignored it, then he wrote it again in China. Now he goes back to Moscow. To make them listen. To tell the world."

The Chechen lay a hand on the shoulder of Anton's burgundy sweater. Timur said, "Hero."

Anton excused himself from the table. He pressed a hand on Timur's big shoulder as he passed. The Russian left the restaurant car to stand in the cool night on the little platform between carriages.

Sinjin checked his watch. "We should be at the Mongolian border in an hour."

Lara stood. "Gentlemen, excuse me. I've got to get my travel papers in order. Sinjin, thank you for the champagne."

Sinjin looked kindly down on the passed-out Björn. "Your friend's wallet is in his front pocket. He'll be glad to pay for our dinners. Then I'll make sure he gets back to his cabin."

Gang rose. He said to Lara, "I'll walk you back."

"I'll be fine."

Gang moved in front of Lara. "I know. Come on."

20

TIMUR

The American woman and the Chinese had some private contest going on as they left the restaurant. The drunken Swede was passed out; the Englishman rifled through his jacket for a wallet, found plenty of yuan, and paid for everyone's meal.

While Sinjin bundled the Swede to his feet, Timur rose. Standing, he bumped the table behind him, upsetting a glass. It fell over with a tink.

Timur opened the portal to the platform between cars where Anton stood in the diesel-tainted wind.

An unlit cigarette was stuck in the Russian's lips. Firing it up out here between cars would have been impossible. Anton stashed the cigarette in the breast pocket of his coat.

Timur stepped onto the platform but not beside the scientist. He let Anton have his own view to the east, of a gibbous moon low over the last kilometers of China. Timur took the darker side, the west. They stood like this together between cars, facing away from each other.

Anton would not come back from Moscow. Everyone at

127

the table knew that now. Anton was going to speak to the world, but the world would not save him. Russia would kill Anton at worst, imprison him at best. The only flip of the coin was where his body might rest, in a prison or an unmarked grave.

Unspoiled steppe scrolled by, speedy up close, amber below the train's windows, motionless and gray in the distance. Only the absence of stars marked the black horizon. In the open air near the locomotive, the Trans-Mongolian, with strength and squeals and grunts, carried Timur and Anton to Russia.

21

LARA

G ang led the way through the hard-class carriages. He glanced back many times, and if she fell too far behind, he slowed. Once he reached for her hand. She did not reach back.

The dinner hour in the hard classes had ended, but the cooking aromas lingered on. Lara had grown up on boiled cabbage and lamb, and in the cabins of the humble hundreds she saw the face of her father, smelled him in his Boston kitchen. The Mongolian border approached in the night. In the four-berth compartments, women stowed their utensils and plates in woven baskets. Men smoked and assembled the transit papers for their families. Older siblings corralled the young ones. In the open-dorm cars, sixty bunks gave off the odors of food and feet, clothes hung on rails.

Gang opened the door out of the last hard-class car. He stepped onto the platform before their carriage. Lara followed; the door slid shut behind her. Gang turned.

He took one stride toward her on the small steel platform. Lara had room to backpedal but held her ground. Gang

129

raised a hand between them and snapped his fingers like a flamenco dancer. The next moment, a train zoomed by the other way. In the strobing light, Gang twinkled.

The eastbound train shuffled the air, Lara's hair flogged her face. In ten seconds the train was gone. She straightened her hair with a headshake.

He said, "I could feel it coming."

"What do you want?"

"I want you to be safe."

"Why? You don't know me."

"I ask myself that."

Lara moved to slip around him, to open the door into her carriage, to her locked door. Gang stepped in her way.

He started to speak. Lara held up a full-hand stop sign.

"Don't."

"Don't what?"

"Don't tell me to get off the train before Russia."

"You have to."

"No. I have permission. I've been told I could do my job and go home. I don't know who sent you, but you need to check with your bosses."

Gang moved aside. Lara reached for the handle that would get her off this rattling platform with him.

"Who do you think sent me?"

She reeled in her hand.

"Big man. Bald mafia guy in Moscow."

"The one who kidnapped you."

"The fact that you know that bothers me."

"Fatso."

"Seriously."

"Nickname. These guys call themselves Fingers and No Nose, whatever. His was Fatso. He's dead."

Hearing this shoved Lara onto a back foot. The mobster who'd let her live was dead.

"When?"

"After he said you could come back to Moscow."

Lara pushed Gang aside. She bolted through the opening and jarred her elbow. Gang stayed in her wake down the narrow companionway. No one else had returned from dinner; the corridor was vacant save for the porter in the cocked hat vacuuming his carpet one more time before Mongolia.

Lara made it to her cabin. She dove in, then slammed the door on Gang's arm. From the hallway he said, "Ow."

Gang entered. In the compartment she got as far away as she could. She flung herself onto her berth, knees pressed to her chest. Lara pointed the trowel at Gang. On the opposite couchette, he pushed aside the yellow Geiger counter, sat, and rubbed his arm.

"You've been set up."

She jabbed the trowel once. "By who?"

"I don't know. Probably someone in your report."

"But it got buried, four years ago."

"Not deep enough."

"I didn't get any names. I was just told it was higher-ups. That's all I reported."

"Let's figure it's somebody really high up."

"Why won't they let it go?"

"Whoever it is wants to stay unnamed. It's a smart move."

"How the fuck is this smart?"

"You went back to Russia. You broke the rule. No one's fault but yours."

"But he said I could come back."

"No one knows that but you and Fatso. And Fatso's dead. That's the smart part."

Gang patted the air, calming.

"I'm just saying, in that world where they eat their own dead, it's smart. Put that down."

She didn't lower the trowel. "Who called you?"

Gang spun a finger beside his head, a little whirlwind.

"Some guy who got a call from some guy who got a call. It doesn't matter. Point is, you've got to get off this train before Russia. Put that down. I told you, you're safe."

Gang flicked his wrist and the trowel was in his grasp. Lara barely felt his touch.

"I don't like being threatened any more than you do." He tossed the tool into a corner of the instrument-strewn berth. "Sit up. Talk to me like a person."

Gang sounded annoyed at being considered the bad guy here.

Lara sat upright. "What if I don't?"

"Don't what?"

"Get off the train before Russia. Will you do it?"

Gang turned to consult some invisible pal, to ask, Can you believe her?

"No."

"So, you were just sent to warn me."

"No."

Lara didn't flinch. She was done with the fear that made her curl up, and now felt only the fear that made her careful.

"So you'll kill me."

"No. For fuck..." Gang lifted his hands again, palms inward to himself, and blew a breath to expel exasperation. "No. I will not kill you."

"Why not?"

"Because I will drag you off this train if you don't walk off on your own."

At the head of the train, the locomotive issued a doleful whistle. For those moments, Lara imagined herself a wolf or whatever creature was out there roaming the wastes. From a hill she watched the long beast with many yellow eyes gallop across the night plain. In those few seconds Lara knew nothing of what was going on inside the Trans-Mongolian, or that it was even a train.

"Gang."

Saying his name seemed to soothe him.

"Yes."

"How many have you killed?"

Gang didn't turn to his imaginary ally this time, but sucked in his lower lip. He despised the question.

She said, "I'd like an honest answer."

Gang crossed his arms. The train slowed into the station of Erlyan, the border city.

"I have a lot of money, Lara. I live in a big house. I don't have to do this anymore."

"How many?"

"Over twenty-five years? Enough to live in a big house and not have to do this."

"Why are you reluctant to tell me?"

Gang laughed and checked again with his invisible buddy. Then he said to Lara, "I think it's obvious. I want you to trust me. I'm not sure a body count is the best way to do that."

"Gang. How many? Let's get it out of the way."

"I'll tell you. Then we don't talk about it again."

"Tell me or don't. But if you don't, I'll never trust you. As in, never."

"A dozen, that's all."

"That's all."

"Over twenty-five years, yeah, it's not that many."

"No?"

"No."

Lara tried having an imaginary friend. She turned sideways to check with her and found her friend was a cop.

She said, "Tell me. All of them."

Gang waved this away. When Lara folded her arms and sat back, he said, "You're serious?"

"I am."

Gang sat back, too.

He said, "Some of them."

The first was a local thug in Dezhou who got so greedy the

Triad noticed. Gang, a good pickpocket, slipped a castor bean pill into his bubble tea at a public market. The man died two days later, and Gang bought a house. The fifth was a gem dealer in Shanghai who put too heavy a thumb on the scale. Nostalgically, Gang ran the man over in his own car. Gang invested in a commercial garage. The ninth was a dirty policeman in Tianjin who took a bribe but didn't keep his word. The cop left a suicide note, typed by Gang, saying he'd seen too much violence in his work, before he stepped off a roof. Gang speculated in gold. The last was an inebriate politician who claimed he intended to clamp down on the Triad in Chongqing. Gang hired some toughs to rough him up, but the drunk old man mouthed off and got himself knifed. Gang didn't feel he could charge for this one. He'd used poison, cars, his hands, and other men to do his work, never gun or blade. With every job, the target was someone of increasing importance, and the Triad paid Gang more. Lara was considered a major target; a large down payment had already hit his Hong Kong account. Before Lara, Gang hadn't received an assignment in three years, so the call came as a surprise. He'd hoped the phone would never ring again. If it hadn't for maybe one more year, he would have cashed out, left the city for some piece of earth under this same speckled sky above the tracks, perhaps a yurt and a camel herd out here on the Mongolian range.

"Like I said. The mob eats its dead. Every job I ever took was to take out an asshole worse than the asshole giving me the job. It's the life these guys sign on for. It's the rules. I'm just a consequence."

"So that makes it alright?"

"No. It makes it my life."

"What about Fatso?"

"Okay, in that instance, the bigger asshole won out."

"How've you stayed alive this long?"

"Because I'm anonymous. I'm way down the food chain. I

don't know anyone or anything but the job. I don't squawk and I don't walk."

"What is that, some kind of professional slogan?"

Lara referred one more time to her fantasy cop friend. Her friend had a question for Gang. Lara asked it.

"So it pays well."

"Yeah."

"Did I pay well?"

"Somebody thinks you're a big fish. I made it a condition that you'd be my last job. The guy who called the guy who called me called his guy. *His* guy agreed."

"After me, you're out."

"Out."

"So I'm worth a lot."

"A lot."

"Should I be flattered?"

"Please be flattered."

"Are you fucking kidding me?"

"What?"

"You want me to *like* you? What are we, in fucking high school?"

Gang said, "No," a little sheepishly.

"Good. Because in high school, you killed your father."

Gang's hands went up as if Lara were being unfair.

She said, "Say what you want. But you're still an assassin."

"As soon as you walk off this train, I won't be anymore."

The Trans-Mongolian tiptoed into Erlyan. The little city was a gateway to the Gobi Desert. The tracks entered through an industrial district of oil tanks, warehouses, corrugated-roofed garages, loose dogs, and chain fences. Streetlamps tinted the place a sallow shade of isolation, like candlelight. Hundreds of cargo cars and flatbeds waited on side rails to leave Erlyan.

Lara asked, "Do I have to leave here? This is the middle

of nowhere. If I have to wait for a train back I'd rather get off in a real city. And I'd like to do my job as long as I can."

Gang shook his head.

"The deal you made was you wouldn't return to Russia. You're good in Mongolia. It's seven hundred kilometers to Ulaanbaatar. Around dusk tomorrow."

The industrial clutter and sad lighting of the railyard vanished. Lara leaned to the window; the entire train had been swallowed inside an immense high-ceilinged shed. The Trans-Mongolian slowed, then creaked to a stop.

In the corridor, the Chinese porter made an announcement:

"This is Erlyan. The train will stop for four hours. The bogey wheels will be changed to fit the wider Russian tracks. You may stay in the car or you may debark. This is Erlyan."

Gang stood. "Want to hit the town?"

Lara stayed put. "Find a dark little alley in the last town in China. I disappear. You get paid."

"I only get paid in Russia. I'm going to find a beer. I bet I can find two."

Gang extended a hand. Lara let it hang there.

"Was your father really one of Doolittle's Raiders?"

"He was."

"That's all true?"

"You know as much about me at this point as anyone on the planet. Come have a beer. Bring your trowel. You can brain me with it when I turn my back."

She took his fingers in hers, let him tug her standing, then let him go.

Gang added, "Which I won't."

"One last question."

"Yeah."

"What happens to you if I don't get off the train, and you don't kill me?"

"We've been over this. You're not going to Russia."

"I know. But just answer this one."

Gang drew a breath deep enough to outline the muscles in his neck. Out in the huge shed, loudspeakers played exotic orchestral music. A hundred passengers from the hard-class carriages filed off the train, most with luggage, some only to stretch their legs. A dozen Soviet soldiers in greatcoats marched into Erlyan.

Lara repeated. "What happens?"

"Then it's me who broke the rules."

Gang moved close. He spoke low, as if someone might have an ear to the door.

"From this point on, you stay in one of two places. In here behind a locked door. Or with me."

Up close his eyes were not so pitch black.

Lara asked, "Why?"

"Because I guarantee you. I'm not alone on this train."

22

ANTON

With the train motionless in the great shed after a long day of moving, Anton felt oddly out of balance. When Timur stepped into the corridor, Anton joined him. The majority of their time had been seated across from each other. Standing beside Timur reminded Anton just how imposing the Chechen was.

Through the windows they watched Chinese and Mongol passengers file off the train into the border city. The tannoy system inside the shed broadcast a version of *O Solo Mio* played on Chinese instruments. Gang walked away with Lara Dill. They strode with the same athletic grace and seemed well matched. The Swede Björn snored loudly in his room. The rotund Chinese porter left the soft-class car carrying a lunch pail, his hat, as always, askew.

Timur crossed his arms, hands on his biceps. Several knuckles bore scars.

Once those travelers leaving the train had done so, a drove of Chinese workers in yellow hardhats and white gloves flooded across the clean white-marble tile floor.

Timur did not unfold his arms or glance from the window. Anton gazed up the side of him. The Chechen's hair covered his ears and touched his collar. His beard was thin enough to see the long jaw beneath.

In the shed, the music quit, not intended for the workers. The building rang with hammer blows and the yelps of straining metal. The second-class car jolted, rolled several meters, then jarred to a halt. The carriage shuddered again.

An orange-painted screw jack at the front of the car was edged into position, another at the rear. An identical pair of jacks was put into play on the opposite side. The big screws inside the lifts whined, the jacks hoisted into the belly of the carriage. Smoothly, level, the car was elevated.

Anton went out to the platform for a better view. He was careful not to step off: the third-class car that had been attached had been uncoupled and rolled three meters away, raised now on its own quartet of jacks. The carriage hovered without wheels, a big green box risen above the steel wagon that had carried it from Beijing. All the train cars, cargo or passenger, were being lifted off their wheels. Legions of workers scrambled around and under each chassis, banging about with tools and twisting rods. The lighting in the vast shed was fluorescent and harsh.

Anton returned inside beside Timur. "Do you know what's going on?"

Timur tapped the window. His fingertip was the width of a ten-kopek coin.

"We're getting wider wheels before the Soviet Union."

"Why?"

"The Chinese tracks are four feet eight inches apart. Soviet rails are five feet."

"Why don't China and the Soviet Union use the same gauge rails?"

"The Russian tracks are a hundred years older."

Anton gestured to the commotion outside the window. "It

doesn't make sense. Using the same rails has to be better than doing this for every train that runs between them."

"No one wants to be invaded on his own railroad."

"How do you know these things?"

"I have some experience with Soviet trains."

"Ah, of course. You said you were a miner."

"Not what you think."

"Would you like to tell me?"

"I spent four years in Siberia. Loading Russian coal trains."

Timur gazed without rancor out the window. Anton had the urge to apologize again for Russia but nothing about Timur seemed to ask for that.

Anton asked, "What did you do?"

"To get my apprenticeship as a miner?"

"No. You'll tell me that when you're ready. What did you do before? Were you a soldier?"

"A welder."

"Is that how you got the scars on your knuckles?"

"Yes." Timur displayed the etched backs of his hands. "These are from goddam bicycles."

"Beg pardon?"

"I bought a bicycle shop in Grozny. I thought I could build them, weld them. Damn those things. Everything so small. Little chains, spokes, little frames. I tossed the shop keys to my cousin."

Anton imagined a circus bear on a bike. Timur grimaced as if he'd read the thought.

The Chechen turned, not slowly or sadly. He bent a little to fit inside the doorway to their cabin. Inside, he sat hard on his berth. With Anton seated across from him, Timur slapped his own thighs.

"How did this happen?"

"How did what happen?"

"Chernobyl. This reactor, this accident. You are scientists. How could you do this? No one else in the world builds these monster reactors. Putting graphite and water together, even I understand this. No one puts a reactor above an aquifer. Alone in the world, you have made these mistakes."

"We are Soviet scientists. Just as you say, we are alone in the world. We are not allowed to read Western scientific journals. We can't attend Western conferences or consult with Western scientists. We built the RBMK in darkness and we've kept it there. We can't even learn from ourselves. The KGB treats every reactor incident as a state secret, so we know nothing of each other's mistakes."

"But you, Antosh." Timur indicated the report in Anton's briefcase. "You wrote that."

"Yes. And I was censored for it. This was taken from me. I was shipped off to Beijing, one step ahead of the KGB."

"Right now, only one country in the world has ever reported a major nuclear accident. America. It was called Three Mile Island. I remember, we laughed at them. We thought it was humiliating. That would never happen to us. We didn't know we were next because we weren't allowed to believe it. Chernobyl will change that. It has to."

"You. *You* will change that."

"I will try. But the entire Soviet nuclear industry lacks even the most basic safety precautions. We have relied on operators to behave like robots day after day, with a precision they cannot achieve. They are driven to beat deadlines and over-perform. This has made a disregard for safety inevitable. Chernobyl did not need to happen. I will try to see that does not happen again."

The carriage shivered. All four heavy jackscrews eased the carriage chassis down onto its new, wider bogey wheels. Workers waved white-gloved hands downward as though fluffing pillows. The jackscrews whined, the hard-hatted men shouted, everything echoed off the marble floor and the ceiling beams. The carriage quaked, then settled on top of its new wheels for the long ride west. Workers scurried beneath to secure the joining.

Timur sat back, arms folded again.

"Why?"

"You mean, why me?"

"I do not want to put it that way. But yes. Why you, Antosh?"

Anton dug into his case for the report. He handed it to Timur. The Chechen accepted it with both hands, hefting it to appreciate the weight.

Anton said, "Your four years in Siberia?"

"Yes."

"This is my four years."

Timur handed the report back, gingerly. "You know you are going to die in Moscow."

Anton slid the report back into his briefcase.

Timur asked, "Do you want to die?"

"Of course not."

"Then what are you doing on this train?"

"The new First Secretary of the Communist Party, Mikhail Gorbachev, he talks about reform. Transparency. *Perestroika*. Soviet dissidents are speaking out louder than ever. Sakharov, Solzhenitsyn, Bukovsky, Medvedev. Some are returning to Russia."

"You think you are Solzhenitsyn?"

"No."

"Maybe Sakharov?"

Anton stood. "I don't have to listen to this."

Timur motioned Anton down. "Sit, sit. You called me friend, so we are friends. Sit, Antosh."

Anton returned to his berth, his back off the wall.

Timur spread a hand over his own breast. "May I speak a bit more?"

"Yes. I apologize."

"Fah. Nothing." Timur struck his breastbone with the flat of his hand, twice. "Listen to me. Those people, those dissidents. You say they are speaking out. Good. About what? Their *lives*? How the Soviet state has *mistreated* them? How unfair, how wrong? Anton, that is not what you are going to do."

Timur shot a hand at the briefcase.

"That report is not about unfairness. That is no argument about rights and liberty. That, you very stupid man, is a condemnation in *fact*. You have numbers, physics, examples. There is nothing in your report to be argued over. Chernobyl has *happened*. Four years ago you warned them. They shut you up and sent you away. Now you go back to Moscow while their reactor is killing the world. You are no dissident. You will not condemn them with a speech or a book about the gulag, not a show trial or your exile. You will denounce them with science. Fucking Gorbachev will not allow you to do that, Anton. No."

Timur put his elbows on his knees, laced his fingers between them, and leaned in.

"So you are going to die in Russia."

"I certainly hope not."

"Eh. They have not killed Solzhenitsyn yet. Either way, good for you."

"What about you, Timur?"

"Probably Ukraine."

The Chechen locked eyes with Anton. There was something of the locomotive about the man, not only his uncommon size but his quiet urging, his pull.

Timur said, "The Quran commands you to go, as well."

"How so?"

"If a man would right a wrong, there are three ways. He may use his heart, or his tongue, or his hands. But the heart is the weakest way."

143

"So you are the hands."

"Yes. And you, Antosh, are the tongue."

Anton sat with this for a moment.

He said, "I need to get off the train. Let's go for a drink."

"Moslem. I do not drink."

"Russian. I do."

23

GANG

E rlyan was a small, meager city on the steppe, at the border between two empires, astride an ancient trade route. It was built in wind and dust and no amount of concrete or seed could hide that. Erlyan was known for the number of dinosaur bones found nearby.

On the street in front of the train station, Lara and Gang passed Sinjin wandering with his camera, capturing the mélange of Mongol and Chinese in the place's architecture and people.

Six blocks away from the station, Gang chose a restaurant hawking dishes of sheep, yak, goat, and horse. Bistro tables lined the sidewalk; Gang took a seat in a red plastic chair while Lara went to a tree well to dig up soil. She bagged the dirt, then came to the table. She scribbled a label, stuck it on the bag, and stored it in her pack. Lara had left the yellow Geiger counter and the ionizing chamber on the train. The only scientific equipment she brought was a black dosimeter button on her lapel and the trowel.

The Mongolian waiter, a beefy man in a messy apron, had

a moony face and a smile that pushed his cheeks up into his eyes. He owned the restaurant and came to serve them personally when he saw a pretty Western woman take a seat. Lara gave him her best smile, better than any she'd given Gang.

In passable Mandarin, Lara said, "He'll order for me. May I use your telephone? It will be a call to Beijing, but I will reverse the charges."

The owner escorted her into his little establishment, then returned to the table. Gang ordered for himself *shǒu bā yángròu*, hand-stripped mutton. For Lara, he requested *shāo hǎn bí*, roast deer noses. The owner approved with a meaty nod. Gang looked forward to lying to Lara about it.

When she returned, Gang had a cold Tsingtao waiting. She guzzled half the beer.

Gang asked, "What'd you find out?"

"I called my boss. I told him he was an asshole and I'm getting off the train at Sukhbaatar."

"What'd he say?"

"He said no I wasn't. That he'd take care of it."

"He can't take care of it."

"That's where the asshole part came in. Then he gave me the latest on Chernobyl."

"How bad is it?"

Lara finished her beer. "Get us two more."

Gang poked his head inside the restaurant to call for another round. When he returned to his plastic chair, Lara had finished his beer, too.

Gang asked, "That bad?"

"The Soviets are circling the wagons on Chernobyl, everybody expected that. The Swedes and the Norwegians are pushing hard. We'll know more when they do. Here's what we can figure so far. There's two thousand tons of graphite blocks in an RBMK reactor. Graphite burns at a thousand degrees Centigrade. Pretty soon that heat is going to melt the zirconium casings around a hundred tons of uranium dioxide fuel pellets. Once the casings are gone, the uranium will start to burn. When that happens, a whole lot more radioactive material is going to be thrown into that fire."

"But the Russians are going to put it out, right? They've got to have a fire department there."

"A nuclear blaze can't be put out by a fire department. All they have is water and foam, and both of those will just evaporate before they get anywhere near the flames. At the temperatures of fission, you've got to worry the water might split into hydrogen and oxygen atoms. Then you've got the risk of an even bigger explosion. Even if that doesn't happen, water on the core adds more steam to lift the fallout into the air. This isn't a fire. This is a star."

"Holy shit."

"Yep."

"What if they can't put it out?"

"Then let's hope there's enough beer."

The merry owner arrived to set fresh bottles on the table. He cleared the four empties. Gang held out his Tsingtao to Lara to touch spouts, but she tipped hers straight up again. With her head back, the owner walked away glowering at Gang, to have done something at his restaurant to make such a good-looking woman angry.

When she lowered the bottle, Lara's eyeballs pitched up and rightward, calculating. She drank slowly for the first time, then licked her lips, then changed her mind and finished the beer.

She said, "Let's assume the graphite blocks burn one ton per hour. If the Reds let the core burn itself out, Chernobyl can burn for two months. The radionuclide cloud from that will circle the planet for ten years. Most of the Soviet bloc and a third of Europe will be uninhabitable for a hundred years."

"So the Russians have to put it out."

"It's going to kill a lot of folks to do it."

147

"What would you do? If you were there, if you were in charge?"

"After I punched a bunch of people out?"

"Absolutely."

"Boron."

"Okay. Why?"

"Boron's a proton absorber. If somehow they can cover the core with boron, it'll stop more chain reactions in the uranium. Then they'll need to dump sand on it to starve the fire of oxygen. We're talking hundreds of tons of both. Problem is, there's bound to be so much gamma radiation pumping out of that reactor that no one can survive getting close enough."

"So how?"

"Swear to God, I don't know."

Lara eyed his untouched Tsingtao. Gang slid it her way.

24

TIMUR

Timur had forgotten it was Sunday.

Old folks and young lovers strolled after dinner along streets with little traffic. A grassland breeze rustled the larch trees of a park where youths played football beneath an out-of-round moon. A fountain trickled in a public space where teenagers smoked. Under a streetlight, Sinjin angled his camera to capture the moon above the prairie city. Timur dragged Anton around a corner to avoid him.

Anton said, "I miss Russia. How long have you been away from Chechnya?"

"Six years."

"Did you keep in touch with your family? How is the bike shop?"

"I don't know."

"You don't? Why not?"

"My family believes I am dead."

Anton tugged Timur's arm to stop.

"How can this be?"

"While I was in prison, the Russians sent word I was killed in Afghanistan."

"Why on earth?"

"They did this so no Chechen would look for me. No Chechen would write me. No Chechen would work to free me."

"This is terrible."

"That is what it is like to be jailed by the Russians. Solzhenitsyn was right."

"How did you get out?"

Timur shrugged. "One day they gave me back my boots and said 'Timur, go away.'"

"Where did you go?"

"Back to Afghanistan."

"And you told no one at home?"

"No."

"Why not?"

"I did not want them to see me die twice."

Timur raised his hands, then flapped them against his pockets. "Why do you ask so many questions?"

"I know nothing about these things. I'm sorry, Timur."

"You are sorry about Chernobyl. Sorry about me." Timur poked Anton so hard he put the scientist on his heels. "You are no Russian."

Anton indicated a neon light farther up the block; chairs and tables on the sidewalk marked a restaurant.

"I think they will have something to drink there."

Timur said, "Likely."

"Come. Then decide if I am Russian."

25

LARA

Timur tried to sit in one of the plastic chairs but it buckled under him. The pleasant restaurant owner brought out his personal metal office chair. Anton and Lara discussed their shared affinity for Russian authors; Anton favored Nabokov. Gang asked Timur to stand and outstretch one arm, then did pull-ups on it. Timur's laugh was like a landslide. The big Chechen taught them about the intricacies of bicycle repair. Lara told of a time in Boston she had to pry a six-hundred-pound woman out of a bathtub. No one mentioned Chernobyl or dying.

Timur and Anton ordered meals. They all shared off each other's plates, though Gang would not touch Lara's plate of Mongolian meatballs. Without Sinjin to play host and pour, or Björn to order bottle after bottle, Lara limited herself to one more beer. Anton knocked down a half-dozen shots of Chinese yellow rice vodka; after each shot he turned the glass upside down in front of Timur. The table rang with the high chatter of strangers dispelling their differences. Lara mentioned nothing about leaving the train tomorrow night.

Anton and Timur wondered aloud about the next four

days' journey. The two seemed excited to be doing it together. Timur called it an adventure. Lara smiled to hear them.

Gang ticked off what lay ahead for them on the Trans-Mongolian: the Gobi Desert, followed by Ulaanbaatar, the coldest capital of any nation on earth, then Lake Baikal, the largest freshwater body on earth. The expanses of Siberia, Russia's grain belt as well as her prison. Next, the Ural Mountains, the boundary between Europe and Asia. Yekaterinburg where the communists executed the royal Romanovs by gun, bayonet, and club. Then several industrial cities. Then Moscow.

When the meal was over, Timur produced a wad of Chinese currency. He paid the whole bill, exchanging bows with the owner. The rice vodka didn't hit Anton until he stood. Gang kept him from listing. He propped Anton with a shoulder for the walk back to the station. Timur sidled up beside Lara.

"Doctor, I have enjoyed your company."

"And I, yours, Timur. May I ask a question. About Anton?"

"Perhaps you should ask him."

"It's something you said. That he's going back to Moscow to make the Soviets listen about Chernobyl."

"Yes."

"I know the Russian scientific community. They won't listen. They can't. And if he goes public, they'll try to hurt him."

"He knows this. He thinks he is a dissident."

"Is that why he was in Beijing? He was exiled?"

"I like you, Doctor. You ask questions."

"Anton's a courageous man."

"I think he is a wounded man. I think he wants revenge for his wound. He wants them to know his name."

"You called him a hero."

"Have you been in a war, Doctor?"

"No."

"A hero is not who a person is. No one is so good. Heroes are only what they have done. Do you understand?"

"I believe so."

"Now, may I ask you a question?"

"Of course."

"About the reactor."

"I see Anton has you interested in it."

"I am going to Chernobyl."

Lara graced fingertips against the giant's swinging forearm.

"You are?"

"Yes."

"Oh, Timur, why?"

"I will work in the tunnel underneath it. They say there is no other way to stop the core from burning into the ground. A call has gone out for hundreds of miners."

Lara knew so little about this colossus. Her heart broke anyway, because she did know so much of what could happen to him at Chernobyl. She wanted to tell him not to go, but that was not her place. It was someone else's. Whoever that person was had not convinced Timur. Or there was no one.

"What can I tell you?"

"Anton says there is a water table under the reactor. What will happen if the melted core reaches it?"

Lara halted. Again she put a hand on Timur's arm to bring him to a stop; she saw how fruitless the effort would have been had this giant not wanted to be stopped.

"Timur. Are you afraid to go? Because if you are, what I have to tell you isn't going to help."

He bent at the waist, putting his head almost over hers. Timur smiled inside his meager beard, patient as though she were ignorant.

"Of course I am afraid, Doctor. I have reasons to live. But I also have reasons for knowing. I will ask you to respect that they are my private concerns. Now, if I have not been insulting, please tell me. What will happen if the melted core reaches the groundwater?"

"If the lava hits the aquifer, the water will superheat, vaporize, and expand. There'll be a thermal explosion."

"How big?"

"Very big. Two to four megatons."

Timur blinked. His face went blank. His mouth opened, then froze open as if he might stutter.

Lara nodded, because the fireball Timur was envisioning was correct.

She said, "That's four million tons of TNT. Two hundred and fifty times bigger than the atomic bomb dropped on Hiroshima. It would be the single worst disaster in the history of mankind."

Timur rattled his head as if shaking himself awake. He eased a palm into the small of Lara's back to usher her into walking again toward the station.

"This is what you do? This is what you study?"

"It is."

"Then what you say is true."

"I'm sorry to say it is."

"Tell me what four megatons at Chernobyl would do."

"The blast would level everything inside fifty kilometers. That includes the three other reactors at Chernobyl. All the radioactive material in their cores will be ejected into the atmosphere. The shock wave will carry the particles two or three hundred kilometers in every direction. That will kill the populations of Kiev and Minsk. Five million people. Timur, that will include you."

Timur watched himself tread on his own moon shadow. They slowed their gait to keep from catching up to Gang and drunk Anton.

The Chechen stuffed hands in his pockets and asked more. What about the radiation, where else would it go? Who would it affect, how badly? What about the groundwater, how contaminated would it be? Timur had admitted he was afraid but showed nothing of it. He inquired and listened without expression, his questions lacked inflection. He seemed without awe or shock, neither eager nor repelled. His calm struck Lara as eerie, like a hurricane's eye.

Ukraine and Belarus would be uninhabitable for at least a century. The prevailing winds would sling severe levels of radiation across Latvia, Belarus, and Lithuania, plus most of central Europe, including Poland, Czechoslovakia, Hungary, and East Germany. With a slight shift in the winds, the fallout could turn on Moscow.

The water beneath the reactor fed into the Pripyat River. The Pripyat flowed into the Dnieper. The Dnieper opened into the Black Sea; radionuclides in the Black Sea would poison the water supply for a hundred million people, devastating agriculture and livestock. For decades, there would be steep increases in the rates of cancer and birth defects.

Ahead, Sinjin arrived out of a side street. He added his arm to Gang's to propel the wobbly Anton.

Lara said, "It would be an apocalypse."

The giant halted. Lara passed him and turned back. Timur tipped back his great head for a deep breath of the night. He searched high for the moon and stars but the street-lamps close to the station blotted them all out.

"Will it reach Chechnya?"

"Chechnya's a thousand miles southeast. No, I don't think so."

"Then it would be an apocalypse for the Soviet Union. Go on to the train. I will be behind you."

They stood too far apart for her to reach to him. He made no gesture her way. She'd told Timur that his homeland would probably survive Chernobyl. He would not. Then he thanked her. He had his own reasons, as he said.

Lara walked alone across the plaza. Ahead, Gang, Sinjin, and Anton plowed on toward the station. Behind her, Timur stood under the stark light of streetlamps. Hands in his coat pockets, he gazed upward as if trying to sense the direction of the wind.

MONGOLIA

26

ANTON

KILOMETER 843

Anton woke into a gauzy half-sleep. His berth lurched as the loudspeakers in the shed struck up the love theme to *The Godfather*.

Anton's shoes were still on. He tried to kick them off, but his feet floundered and failed. He cozied again into the berth, drunk and thinking he had done well.

Not long after, or so it seemed, a hand shook him. Anton didn't know how long he'd dozed but being wakened again felt unfair. He ignored the hand until it became a tap between his shoulder blades.

Anton said into his pillow, "Go away, Timur."

"Time to sit up, comrade." The voice was not the earthquake, the rockfall that was Timur. The words were higher pitched.

"Comrade. You have to get up." With each syllable the tap insisted in Anton's back, like a telegraph.

Anton grunted. He had to urinate. He rolled his shod feet off the mattress to sit up on the edge of the cot.

A woman had jostled him. Anton's vision began at her

159

shoes, a pair of sharp-toed blue heels, then up to a gray-blue skirt. Before he got to her waistline he knew she was tall and curvy. She wore a gray waistcoat over a white blouse; a name-plate let his eyes linger a moment at her breast. Natalya. Above broad shoulders and a long smooth neck she was thin-lipped and blue-eyed. Butter-blonde hair framed an angular jaw. Her train porter's uniform showed no wrinkles and her face had only a few. Anton hadn't been touched by a woman in years, even before Beijing.

He said the name on the tag. "Natalya."

"Comrade Epstein."

Anton licked his lips while he blinked away a haze. He wanted to rise in her presence. Natalya stepped back in the small cabin to allow him; she took up less space than Timur, but her figure required room. Once on his feet, Anton realized the train was not moving. His watch told him the time was just past midnight.

"Where are we?"

"Across the border in Mongolia. The Dzamiin Üüd station. Passengers on the *Rossiya* must present their travel documents inside. Bring your luggage. If you please."

"The *Rossiya*?"

"A locomotive of the Soviet Union now pulls this train. You are on the *Rossiya*."

"Of course." Anton cleared his throat. "Of course."

Natalya left the compartment, wounding Anton a bit. Her heels dotted the carpet in the corridor fading from him.

Anton sighed, to have been so dowdy in his slept-in sweater and shoes, vodka on his breath, invisible. He grabbed his travel documents, valise, and briefcase. In the companion-way, Anton found he was the only one left in second class. This hurt his feelings a little, too. The Swede had been drunk, but they'd roused him.

At the doorway to the train, the brochure rack had been refreshed. It brimmed with pamphlets in Cyrillic on Lenin's theories of capitalism's failure, the USSR's ten-year economic plan, socialism as the engine of history, and Marx-Engels' doctrines on corn.

Anton stepped down off the train. Buzzing lights lit a few hundred people milling about a paved mall behind the station. A desert night's chill crept across the concrete to make every Mongol and Russian bundle beneath a scarf or fur hat. The station itself featured a four-sided steeple attached to a squat windowless structure of columns, an unbalanced design under a peppered sky.

Anton might have been the last to climb off the *Rossiya*. He passed Natalya who guarded the lowered stairs with a flashlight like a half-dozen other porters patrolling the steps to their own carriages. Natalya did not acknowledge him. A new locomotive grumbled at the head of the train, another pea green goliath.

Anton followed painted arrows for Immigration Control. Under more humming lights he submitted his passport which allowed him, a Soviet citizen, to travel through Mongolia. A burly border agent waved him away sleepily without going through his briefcase.

At a cola vending machine, Anton approached the Englishman Sinjin, camera around his neck.

Anton asked, "How long has the train been here?"

"An hour."

"Why did everyone leave me?"

"Beg pardon?"

"I woke up on the train alone."

Sinjin smiled warmly. He rested an unexpected hand on Anton's shoulder.

"No one left you, mate."

Anton wanted his grievance heard and cared not that it was small.

"Of course you did."

Sinjin pointed to a sitting area where a hundred passengers waited in long vests and woven caps, children's heads rested in the laps of colorful skirts, men in poorly tailored suits, black shoes and battered luggage hunkered in hard plastic chairs mounted on chrome rails. The others from the soft-class carriage sat together, with two seats preserved.

Sinjin said, "That big bastard over there? He stayed with you to the last minute, just so you could get some extra sleep. Until the new porter ran him off."

Sinjin waggled a hand as if to shake something off it. He whistled.

"Did you *see* her?"

Anton bridged his own arm onto the young man's shoulder. Timur had sat a vigil beside him. The others were saving him a place.

If Anton was invisible to Natalya, then *k chertu yeye*. Screw her. She was invisible.

"I did not."

27

GANG

At each end of the second-class carriage was a lavatory. Gang and Björn waited to go last, since it would have been unseemly to go before Lara, unwise before Timur, Anton looked wan after his drinking bout, and Sinjin got to one of the loos first and took a long time.

The bathroom was cleaner than Gang had anticipated. He credited this to the few apparent duties the porter had: vacuum, make announcements, maintain the hot water samovar, keep the washroom tidy, and stay behind a closed door. The taps were hard to turn on and off, spurting either freezing or scalding water but never at the same time. A pink bar of soap, rounded now that it had been shared, rested on the silver sink. When flushed, the metal toilet opened onto the tracks.

In their shared cabin, Gang and the Swede sat on the facing berths, both in long pants and T-shirts. They clicked off the gooseneck lamps to view the black desert without reflection on the window. No fires except stars lit the world, and the

Trans-Mongolian streaking like a comet on a single track through Mongolia.

Gang said, "I've lived in cities too long. I forgot what this looks like."

The Swede lifted his chin to the Milky Way. The cosmic glow on the Gobi spilled over his white face.

"I served in the Arctic. This takes me back."

A soft knock sounded at the door. Björn asked, "Yes?"

The door slid aside to reveal a comely blonde in exotic green eyeshadow. Her conductress's uniform strained to contain her powerful physique. In veined hands she bore a tray of hot tea. The clear glasses were inside metal holders embossed with images of cosmonauts, Sputnik satellites, Russian warships, and wedding-cake skyscrapers. The conductress's name tag read Natalya.

The glasses of tea were free, but Natalya charged four kopeks for a scoop of sugar. Gang bought a one-ruble chocolate bar, Björn a cake for twenty kopecks. Natalya didn't smile when making change for the handsome Swede.

Before taking her leave, she stopped in the doorway. One tea glass remained on her tray. She addressed only Björn.

"You are wanted in the dining car."

"It's 2:00 in the morning."

"The time is 9:00 p.m. Moscow."

"What?"

Natalya fluttered her green-tainted eyes to find patience.

"The train has entered Mongolia. We are now on Moscow time. All schedules will be in Moscow time for the duration of the trip. It is 9:00 p.m."

Björn asked Gang, "Did you know about this?"

"Why would anyone know about this?"

Natalya repeated, "Please go to the restaurant car."

Björn asked, "Why?"

"The Intourist Agency has sent a guide."

"I didn't ask for a guide."

Natalya cocked her head to make it plain that in her world, the world of the Trans-Mongolian, one got what one got.

Björn, a scientist, did not question the unquestionable. He pulled on a sweater. The conductress gave Gang, her fellow communist, a mannequin's grin.

"You need not come."

"I will anyway."

Natalya shrugged. She had nothing more, only instructions and tea.

Gang zipped on his waist jacket. He and Björn stepped into their loafers and headed into the companionway. Natalya had disappeared into her cabin; she'd already made the rounds to Sinjin and Lara, both of whom shuffled into the corridor looking lost. Sinjin wore a terry robe and leather shoes without socks. Lara was bundled in black pants and blouse, a leather jacket, and had combed her hair.

She asked Gang, "Did you know it was 9:00?"

The door to Timur's and Anton's compartment stayed shut. They'd not been summoned.

Gang told Sinjin to lead the way through the five passenger cars to the restaurant. Sleepily, the Englishman did as he was told. Gang sandwiched Lara between himself and the Swede.

All the doors in the third-class carriages were closed; the open bunks in fourth class snuffled and snored. Sinjin, Björn, Lara, and Gang met no one else heading for the meeting.

The restaurant car had been swapped out in Erlyan, the blood-red Chinese décor exchanged for an earth-tone Mongolian motif. Carved bas-relief images of horsemen and camel riders lined the walls; satin tassels and wooden replicas of Mongol shields hung beside a dozen padded booths set with linens and cutlery.

In the booth at the far end of the dining car, a young man of Gang's height arose. He was not muscular like Björn or ropy as Gang but cut of a softer cloth. A black sweater vest covered a white button-down shirt, he wore khaki pants and trainers, all comfortable traveling clothes.

Greeting them in Russian, the man motioned Gang and Björn to join him in the booth. His eyes were blue, and his hair cropped short. The table held no food nor tea. He shook hands. "My name is Maxim Sprygin. Please, sit. This won't take long."

Gang took the booth across the aisle, Timur's accustomed spot. Lara sat across from the stranger, Sinjin collapsed across from Björn.

The dozy Englishman put his chin in his palm to prop up his head as if it were on a stake. Björn, who could not be less than pleasant, sat attentively. Lara leaned back, skeptical.

Maxim said, "Thank you all for coming. I am a representative of the Intourist Travel Agency."

Björn turned quizzically to Lara. She said, "He's our watchdog."

Maxim raised one finger, not to refute but explain.

"The Agency is charged with escorting all foreign tourists through the Soviet Union, to make certain your travels are organized and fruitful. We want you to return to your homes with glowing opinions."

Lara made little circles in the air with a finger like she was winding a clock.

"We're diplomats. We don't require an escort."

"Ah," cheered Maxim, "of course. And you are correct, so long as you are conducting the affairs of your governments. As I understand it, you, Doctor Dill, and you, Dr. Landsee, are on official business of your respective governments." Maxim inclined his head at Sinjin. "Mr. Alonso, you are not. If I am correct, you are on vacation."

Without lifting his chin off his hand, Sinjin asked Lara, "Is he KGB?"

"KGB light."

Maxim blinked as if he didn't understand. But he did.

Sinjin said to him, "Well, I'm getting off at Novosibirsk."

Maxim clapped and kept his hands pressed.

"Excellent. You will find the Ural forests breathtaking. Even so, I will be with the train for the entire journey to Moscow."

Sinjin glanced at Lara through slatted eyes. "Sorry, mate."

Maxim addressed Gang. "And you, sir, are a citizen of the Chinese Soviet Republic. And a Russian speaker, I see."

"What I am is none of your concern."

The Agency man smiled buoyantly as if over a brandy.

Maxim said, "Exactly right."

Lara asked, "And this ridiculousness with the clock?"

"The time difference will become less intrusive as we continue west. Now that you are pulled by a Russian locomotive, the train's name is the *Rossiya*. The *Rossiya* will cross five time zones. It's the Russian way of helping you acclimate."

"Sleep," Sinjin groused, jaw clamped, "is how the English acclimate."

Maxim tapped fingertips on the tabletop. "And so you shall. I simply wanted to introduce myself. And provide you with some guidelines for your trip."

The Agency man lifted a plastic binder onto the table. He opened it with a brio that drew a grunt from Sinjin. The man was cheery and emotionless all at once.

"Over the next five days, the Trans-Mongolian will stop several times. Please understand that many of these stops will be short. Or they may be off-limits to foreigners. You may not be permitted to leave the train."

Lara wiped this notion out of the air between her and the Agency man.

"I'll be getting off to collect soil samples. At *every* stop. That's on direct orders from my government. With the permission of yours."

"I have been made aware, Dr. Dill. I will accompany you."

Gang said, "And I'll accompany *you*."

Maxim's smile didn't reach his eyes.

"The Trans-Siberian and the Trans-Mongolian are the two greatest railways on earth. We will cover thirteen hundred kilometers per day. As passengers, you will witness the remarkable diversity of Soviet lands and economic development. In return, we simply ask that, as foreign citizens, you respect our concerns for national security."

The speech was a practiced preamble to something. No one spoke or nodded until Sinjin muttered, "Sure."

"Excellent. Here are a few policies for you to follow."

Maxim handed out a thin Intourist pamphlet. Gang read over Lara's shoulder. The brochure was titled *Rules for Cine-Camera Fans and Photographers*:

> *It is forbidden to photograph, film or make drawings of all kinds of military weapons and equipment and objects of a military nature, seaports, large hydroelectric engineering installations, railway junctions, tunnels, railway and highway bridges, industrial plants, research institutes, design bureaus, laboratories, power stations, radio beacons and radio stations. It is forbidden to photograph or draw pictures of industrial cities on a large scale, or to take pictures and make sketches within 25 kilometers of the border. It is also forbidden to take photographs of any railway station, or photographs from trains, as it is to take photographs of any factory or government office, or of anyone in service uniform, without special permission. Intourist hopes that you will take home many interesting photos and films of your visit to the Soviet Union.*

As he read, Björn said, "A few?"

Sinjin grew more awake and agitated. Finished, he slid the pamphlet across the table to Maxim.

He said, "It seems, old son, you and I will get to know each other."

The Agency man stood, the folder tucked under an arm. He left Sinjin's brochure on the table as if he were being generous.

"I look forward to that. Enjoy the rest of your evening. I will see you all in the morning."

The Agency man took his leave with a sharp turn. Lara, Sinjin, and Björn watched him depart. Sinjin said, "Well, he's a prig, isn't he?"

Heading back to second class, Sinjin led the way again with Lara sandwiched between Björn and Gang. At Lara's cabin, Gang held her door open for her. She paused in the doorway, maybe to say something. Then Lara stepped back and closed the door.

Gang said, "Lock it."

28

TIMUR

APRIL 28
KILOMETER 1107

At seven in the morning, Anton was gone from the cabin. The scientist had been a quiet sleeper, he'd not snored in the night, but that may have been the champagne.

The train barreled over a grassy lowland limited only by a sunny horizon. The emerald emptiness would dwarf anything man could build on it, so history had chosen not to try. Timur set his bare feet on the rug, his face to the bright window to warm.

He took his dopp kit into the corridor, to the lavatory. Timur sat on the toilet, a wide metal platform with footpads left and right for those who preferred to stand. He peeled off his tunic to wash his torso and face. When he stood upright, his head touched the roof.

Back in the cabin, Timur made neat his berth and changed shirts. He pulled his hair into a ponytail and tied it with a lace. Timur sat again to be alone a bit longer. Mongolia glided past, verdant, cloudless.

When his cheeks had soaked up enough sun, Timur

170

headed for the dining car. He did not have to push a path through the lower-class carriages; everyone who saw him stepped aside.

The Chinese diner had been exchanged for a Mongolian-themed car, decked with carvings and cheap souvenirs of a steppe culture. The restaurant was empty save for Anton and a young man. They sat in a booth facing each other in a box of sunshine. Anton's report lay open on the table, no breakfast. Both turned at Timur's approach.

He stopped beside them. Anton wore his shawl collar cardigan, the stranger a blue wool pullover.

Timur asked Anton, "Who is this?"

Anton craned his neck up. "Good morning. Sit."

"Who is this?"

The other man got to his feet. He stood no taller than Anton. He was tightly groomed, auburn hair barbered short, pressed trousers, starched white collar. His brown eyes were nothing special.

"My name is Maxim. I'm with the Intourist Agency."

Timur took the Agency man's hand for a shake.

"Timur."

"Yes. The Chechen."

Maxim retook his seat in the booth. "Will you join us?"

"Why is there no breakfast?"

"It's too early."

"No it's not."

Anton said, "Sit down, Timur. I'll explain."

Timur sat in the booth across from them and left his legs in the aisle.

He indicated Anton's open report. "Why is that here?"

Anton said, "Maxim is interested in the Chernobyl situation. I was explaining what I believe happened."

"Why are you doing that?"

Anton pulled back his head, far enough to express his surprise.

Timur addressed the Agency man. "You got on the train at the border."

"I have the cabin next to the samovar in your carriage."

Anton said, "Maxim will be going with us to Moscow."

The young Agency man raised a palm to Timur, to fend off an objection, expecting one.

"You and Dr. Epstein are citizens of the Soviet Republic. I am not assigned to you. You have nothing to worry about."

Timur asked, "Should someone worry?"

Maxim chuckled, treating this as a joke between citizens.

Anton said, "Maxim is a guide for foreign tourists."

"He is an agent."

Anton's mouth opened to respond, but the Agency man, without looking to Anton, raised a finger to hold him at bay.

"It's alright. Timur is correct. The foreigners I assist are citizens of the Soviet Union's political adversaries. It is, in fact, my job to be certain those who visit do nothing to erode our security while they're here."

Timur said, "You were Red Army."

"Yes. How did you know?"

"You are around thirty."

"Twenty-nine."

"There is conscription in Russia. Everyone serves unless you are the son of a rich man or a politician. You are not."

"I am not."

Anton shifted, gathering himself again to intercede. In a quiet voice as if Maxim might not hear, the scientist said, "Timur, this is not a game."

Timur ignored him. "Where did you serve?"

"The 103rd Regiment."

"Airborne."

"You know the 103rd?"

"Well enough. What years?"

"1980 through '83."

Timur said, "Afghanistan."

"Afghanistan."

Timur leaned elbows onto the table. He flipped shut Anton's report that had foreseen the tragedy of Chernobyl and would likely get Anton killed.

The Agency man asked, "Were you there, Timur Makhdi? Afghanistan?"

Timur brought his face closer.

Anton said, warningly, "Timur."

Again Timur ignored him. He said to Maxim, "I was."

"What unit?"

"I was a sapper."

"Ah. Fortifications, demolitions. Dangerous work."

"For some."

Maxim asked, "Where?"

"Tora Bora. The Khyber."

"Hard fighting there. You and I may have much to talk about over the next few days."

Timur rose. He looked down on Anton.

"Perhaps. Good morning. Anton, a word."

Timur turned away, expecting the scientist to follow. He exited the diner to wait on the clacking platform above the tracks. Still inside the diner, Anton made what apologies were needed.

The steel under Timur shimmied so much he had to grip the rail. He looked out over the limitlessness of Mongolia. In the distance a round white yurt floated on jade grasses. Timur could not imagine a nomad's life, a slow, peaceful, free life, wandering with sheep.

Maxim came out of the diner, Anton behind him, carrying the report.

The Agency man said to Timur, "We are on Moscow time now. Breakfast will be in six hours." Then he disappeared into the next carriage.

Timur said, "You cannot speak with that man."

"I don't see …"

173

"You don't know his kind."

"What kind is that?"

"He is part of the machine you are trying to wreck."

"I'm not trying to wreck anything."

"You are, and don't pretend to be a fool about it. You are going to Moscow to tear the lid off what the bastards did at Chernobyl. They shut you up, they banished you, they lied and let it happen. When they *knew*. You are going to spill their secrets. That man, your new friend Maxim, may not be KGB but he fucking reports to them. He is an enforcer of secrets. Anton, he is your enemy. And he is mine."

"Timur, you told me you weren't a soldier."

"I wasn't."

"You said to Maxim you were in Afghanistan."

Timur nodded. "I did not fight for Russia."

Anton backed away. "Oh, my God."

The Russian cast about his gaze as if he might leap off the train. He retreated more until his back bumped against the restaurant car's door. He fumbled behind him for the latch, eyes wide on Timur.

"You were mujahideen."

"I am not going to hurt you. I am trying to protect you."

"Leave me alone."

Timur took a step to bring Anton within arm's reach. He rested a hand on the scientist's shoulder, framing Anton's throat between his thumb and forefinger.

"I'm afraid I can't."

Gently as he could, Timur led Anton back to their compartment.

———

In the cabin, they sat squared off at each other until Anton spoke.

"So, I'm your prisoner now?"

"Of course not."

"But you will prevent me from talking to Maxim."

"Until I get off the train."

"You're leaving?"

"Once we are inside Russia. Tonight at Sukhbaatar. I'll make my way from there. If you want to tell that apparatchik everything you plan to do in Moscow with your report, go ahead. It's your head. If you want to tell him I fought on the side of the Afghans, I don't care. But you'll wait until I'm gone."

Cloud shadows scudded across the grassland. Timur fixed on one gray patch until it disappeared behind the train, then another, as if they were stepping stones. He wondered which of Allah's seven heavens he would be assigned to? If heaven looked like this plain, might he have a tent of his own?

"I am ready."

Anton exhaled. "For what?"

"You said I would tell you when I was ready."

"About?"

"Afghanistan."

"Timur, I don't think I want to get to know you anymore."

Anton had changed in this, but Timur hadn't. He still admired Anton for his commitment to truth, science, even to his country. Anton was Russian, and Timur intended to ruin everything Russian. He could not save the man any more than he could save himself. To Timur that felt like a bond. So he ignored Anton's protest.

"Six years ago the Russians invaded Afghanistan. I knew then what I know now. If they are not stopped, every Moslem under their thumb will suffer. As I said, I gave the bicycle shop to my cousin and traveled to Pakistan. Then into Afghanistan."

"Where you became a terrorist."

"No. That comes later."

Anton turned to the window.

Timur said, "I will not speak to the side of your head."

The scientist returned his face. He surprised Timur by saying, "Go on, then."

"I had a Russian wife."

"Indeed."

"She was a Volga Tatar. Marisa. When she was eighteen, the Russian Orthodox church gave her family's lands to Christian settlers. That was an easier way to get the Moslems out of Kazan than to kill them. Her father took the family to the Urals. Marisa refused to go. She went instead to the Hindu Kush."

"That's where you met."

"Outside Kabul. She saved me after I took a bullet." Timur poked a finger into his midriff.

"She was a nurse?"

"Marisa? No. No nurse. A fighter. Better than me. Kalashnikov, rocket launcher, mortar, knife, any weapon. Any hole in the ground, any cave, she would crawl in and wait for a Russian, a tank, anything Soviet to come her way. The mujahideen were not happy at first to have a woman fighting among them. Then they saw her fight."

"What happened?"

"Anton, thank you."

"Don't thank me. I'm not playing games anymore. I'm trapped in here with you."

"As you say. On that day I was wounded, she knelt by me and drove the Russians away. I married her that week. A year passed, until another day, another firefight, she was hurt. I did for her as she did for me. I stayed. But I could not get her away before the Russians surrounded us. We were captured.

Marisa got sent to a different prison than me. I went to Siberia. She went to the Pul-e-Charkhi in Kabul."

"What happened?"

"A person like Maria, what do you think? She didn't last long. The Russians made the Pul-e-Charkhi a famous place."

"Famous for what?"

"Torture."

"Did you have a Moslem wedding?"

"An interesting question. Why do you ask?"

"Because I wonder if you've ever been happy."

"Do you judge me?"

"Yes."

"We said our vows in a valley of the Kush. The sky in Afghanistan is the widest in the world. We told each other that the sky and the mountains could never be conquered. That is what we swore. Marisa was the sky. I was the mountains. We believed it as we promised."

"After prison?"

"I was too old and broken to be a fighter any longer. The Afghans are part goat, I could not climb with them. So I turned what the Soviets taught me in the mines against them. I became a tunneler. I dig bunkers, storage, and headquarters inside mountains. I do this for the Afghans and the CIA. And I recruit Moslems for *jihad*."

"Timur."

"Yes."

"I have one more question."

"What is it?"

"What are you going to do in Chernobyl?"

Timur stroked his beard. He could silence Anton. But to do that would be to silence Anton's damning report. So he would not harm the scientist.

Timur traveled with three passports provided by the Americans. He had Shah Barat's money in his pocket. He knew how to move without detection into Pakistan, China,

Afghanistan, among the Tajiks, and in India. He had vanished before.

Timur said, "I am going to sabotage the tunnel."

The scientist went expressionless. His head fell to the side, almost a twitch.

"Under the reactor?"

"Yes."

"Is that what you've been planning?"

"I had no plan, until this train. Then I spoke with you, and with the American woman. You gave me the idea."

"If you do that, the core could reach the aquifer."

"*Mashallah*." If Allah wills it.

Anton the scientist stayed calmer than Timur would have believed. It seemed as if he could conceive only in numbers what Timur intended to do.

Anton asked, "Do you understand what will happen?"

"A thermal explosion."

"A massive one."

The Russian turned to the window, the empty emerald plain. He stared and nodded to himself, like the land was a slate where he'd ciphered out the answer.

"You're trying to destroy Russia."

"Do not forget. That is not my piece of shit reactor." Timur pointed. "Yours."

"You want to kill millions."

The words hung between them. Anton meant them to be terrifying, but they were not. Timur leaned into them.

"How many has Russia already killed? How many *kulaks* did Stalin starve? Twenty million, I think. How many citizens were in the gulag? Ask your Solzhenitsyn. How many of my people will die if Russia invades Chechnya? Ask the Afghans how many of theirs lie dead? How many millions are under the Soviet boot today? Ask the Poles, East Germans, Hungarians, Ukrainians. How many in the world will perish if Russia starts a shooting war with the West? Ask yourself, Anton. Your reactors will make the fuel for Soviet warheads."

Timur sat back hard against the wall, causing it to shudder.

"Yes, it will kill millions. It will make half the Soviet Union uninhabitable. What is left will be a pariah in the world. I will save more lives by wiping Russia from the earth than letting it exist."

Anton said, "You can't save Marisa."

"No. But I can keep my promise to her."

"Why are you telling me this?"

"Because we are going to Russia for the same reason. To ruin it."

Anton spoke behind a raised finger. "I am not."

"Yes, yes, you say you're going to help. But Antosh, be honest with yourself. You want to make them pay for what they did to you. To show how wrong they were not to listen. I want you to do this."

"No."

"You are no Solzhenitsyn. No Sakharov. You are Anton Epstein. The selfish bastard who is a greater threat to them than all the dissidents combined. And that, you stupid man, is why I told you."

Anton lowered his hand. For long moments the only sounds in the cabin were the wheels and rails and Anton's breathing.

He said, "I'll find a way to stop you."

The Russian lay on his berth. He rolled away to turn his heels and back to Timur.

Timur said, "You won't."

Timur had grown hungry. The dining car wouldn't open for another three hours. Outside in the midmorning, a breeze rippled the tasseled tops of the grasses. He spoke to Anton's back.

"Russia will feel one of us, Antosh. Perhaps both."

Past his shoulder, Anton said, "You're a monster."

"Some will say that of you."

Timur lay down, faceup on his own berth, knees bent, boots and head touching the walls.

"If you survive Moscow, beg them to exile you again. As quickly as they will send you. Go to Siberia. That should be far enough."

29

LARA

In the early afternoon, Moscow time, Gang brought Lara breakfast. He arrived with a plastic plate of scrambled eggs and black bread, plastic cutlery, and a teabag in a cup of blistering water from the samovar.

Lara considered inviting him in to talk while she ate. She'd been cooped up in her jostling cabin with nothing to see but the arid plain, half green, half blue. Gang did not leave her doorway after dropping off the food. He had his own cup of hot water; she thought they might share the teabag. They stood as they had last night, him in the corridor, Lara in her compartment.

She asked, "Would you like to come in?"

"I shouldn't."

"That's true." Lara held the plate and glass cup. Gang's cup steamed like hers. Lara said, "Just to be clear. Why not?"

"Because I want to."

Lara nodded. "That's good enough for me." She closed the door.

She ate quickly, annoyed and second-guessing herself. She stabbed at the eggs too hard and bits skittered off the plate. She scooped the spilled eggs off her lap to put them back on the plate.

———

KILOMETER 1303

The slowing of the train awoke Lara from a nap. The locomotive whistled greeting to a place Lara could not yet spot on the windswept steppe.

In the corridor, the conductress called: "Choir. Our stop is only fifteen minutes. You may stretch your legs. Do not leave the train platform. This is Choir."

Lara gathered her soil collection tools. Gang waited outside her door. Natalya fumbled with the vacuum, unreeling the power cord. In heels she stood taller than Lara, eye-to-eye with Gang.

The train lurched as it braked, Natalya stumbled. Gang flashed a hand to catch her. She nodded and looked him up and down.

Björn emerged from Sinjin's cabin with the Englishman. The two had become friendly while Lara was behind a locked door. Sinjin, garrulous, had a camera slung about his neck. Timur and Anton hadn't exited their compartment. Lara turned to knock; Gang stopped her.

"Let's not make friends."

The Agency man appeared from his room beside the samovar. He appeared relaxed and tucked-in; five-day train rides back and forth across Asia were his vocation. Everyone else in the corridor needed a shower, an iron, and a lint brush.

The train eased into a dusty Mongolian city. What ground wasn't blackened by industry was bald or paved. The place looked to be home to no more than ten thousand. After traveling across an endless meadowland, the train had entered a city in the center of the Gobi that seemed to have not one blade of grass. The place wasn't on Moscow time, so school had just let out; umber children in parkas and backpacks ran in the windswept streets.

The train came to a stop behind a station at the city limits; beyond it lay nothing but the rounding of the earth. The station was built of white stone under a green roof that made it resemble a vanilla cake with pistachio icing on a brown plate.

The instant the train came to a halt, Natalya lowered the metal steps. With her vacuum, she herded Lara and the rest out of the car. Sinjin and Björn hurried first down the metal stairs, then Gang followed Lara into the sunshine. A few hundred others climbed out from the lower-class carriages. Gang scanned them as if for threats, along with a dozen traders and their kiosks mounted on hand-pulled carts or mopeds. The vendors sold hot food cooked on mobile grills, and tulips and white flowers in pots. Gang's caution made Lara edge closer to him.

The Agency man trundled down out of second class. He approached Lara and Gang. She held up the trowel. "I need dirt."

Maxim led them around the stationhouse to the front façade. In a square of sandy soil beside a parking lot, she filled a sample bag at the foot of a steel statue of a silver man on a silver pedestal. The figure was naked save for a wrap flowing in a wind that probably blew a lot in Choir. He held aloft a toy rocket ship. Maxim said this was the first Mongolian cosmonaut. The statue looked as forgotten as the rest of the place.

Lara said, "I have to make a phone call."

Maxim did, too. He led them inside the station, a gold-plated, grandiose interior out of touch with the modesty of Choir. Maxim let Lara have the payphone first.

She dialed the Beijing embassy, reversing the charges.

After several minutes of ringing, Gang tapped his wristwatch to remind her that the *Rossiya* was going to pull out shortly. She was close to hanging up when Rudd came on the line.

She said, "I don't have long."

"Where are you?"

"In the middle of the Gobi. It's flat. What's the latest?"

"Radio Moscow finally issued a statement."

"Read it to me."

"Alright. Quote. An accident has taken place at the Chernobyl nuclear power plant. One of the atomic reactors has been damaged. Measures are being taken to eliminate the consequences of the accident. Aid is being given to those affected. A government commission has been set up. End quote."

"Son of a bitch. We were right. It's Chernobyl."

"It took the Soviets three days to send out this bullshit. They followed it with a list of nuclear incidents in the West."

"Any updates from the Swedes?"

"They're saying the plume's split into three traces, heading north, south, and west. The Poles are getting worried. We're getting reports of panic in Ukraine."

"Reagan said anything yet?"

"No. But you can bet he's got satellite photos on his desk. The Reds can't keep this quiet much longer. Everything alright on your end?"

"Fine."

Rudd asked, "What time is it there?"

"I don't know. I'll call you tonight."

"I'm sleeping in my office."

Lara hung up. Maxim stepped up for the payphone. He tossed in some coins; the phone tolled like wind chimes. The Agency man waited, one foot tapping. He got no answer until the *Rossiya* whistled a departure warning. Maxim hung up; they hustled out of the station onto the platform where passengers were climbing into the carriages and the vendors scattered. Gang bought two sausages wrapped in foil.

Nearing the second-class carriage, Maxim took off running at Sinjin who had his camera to his eye. The Englishman was trying to capture the disappearing perspective of the rails into the great blankness of the Gobi. Out over the desert, a pair of military helicopters beat the arid air.

The Agency man threw a hand over Sinjin's camera lens. An argument began; both waved at the Gobi and the sky. The train whistled again. Tall Natalya lost patience; she stalked over to put an end to the dispute. She marched both red-faced men to the Trans-Mongolian. Lara and Gang were the last passengers waiting to board. With a jerk of her head, Natalya got them up the steps.

The train shuffled forward just as Maxim slammed himself in his cabin. Sinjin did the same. Natalya eyeballed the corridor, then closed her door firmly.

Gang asked, "Should we check on Sinjin?"

Before Lara could agree, Björn burst out of his cabin. Like a hunter holding up three ducks, he showed off a trio of unlabeled bottles filled with clear liquid. Jammed-in corks stoppered all three.

He said, "Mongolian vodka. I got them on the platform."

Gang pulled the cork from one bottle with his teeth. He sniffed.

"Not the worst."

Björn said, "I think it's home brew." He said this as if it were a good thing.

The Swede slapped Gang's shoulder. "Bring Anton and Timur. I'll get Sinjin. We'll meet in the dining car."

He skipped up the passageway to Sinjin's door, rapped a knuckle on it, and was admitted.

Gang shrugged. He asked Lara, "What do you think?"

"There's nothing to see outside but more Gobi."

He said, "We've got 'til midnight."
"I could sit alone in my room."
"That's probably best."
She shrugged too. "Good enough. Let's go."

.

30

GANG

Kilometer 1313

G ang knocked. Timur answered through the door.
"What?"

"It's Gang."

"What do you want?"

"Björn bought a bunch of vodka from a vendor. He's waiting for everyone in the dining car."

"I don't drink."

The door opened so fast Gang fell back against Lara; Anton burst into the corridor and headed off down the passageway. The big Chechen ducked through the portal and followed with a huff.

Gang and Lara trailed Timur through the five lower-class cars to the restaurant. From the platforms between carriages, the Gobi rose like a sea before a storm. Dunes in flesh-tones and gold rumpled the wastelands all the way to the jagged line of a mountain range. The afternoon sky cured into rose and cobalt. The rushing air smelled scrubbed and fresh, the scent of the desert, of nothing.

In the restaurant car, the last breakfast dishes were cleared by small women in pink aprons and headscarves. A smattering of Chinese and Soviet passengers occupied some tables, all reading newspapers they'd picked up in Choir. At a corner booth sat Björn and Anton. Timur held his accustomed place at the neighboring table, blocking the aisle with his legs. Anton wore a burdened expression, slumped in his burgundy sweater. He gazed at the three bottles like a man longing.

Lara asked, "Where's Sinjin?"

Björn said, "He's coming."

Timur dwarfed everything. An aproned woman put glasses on the tables, Timur pushed his away. Björn didn't wait for Sinjin but pulled the cork on the first bottle. Anton gripped his glass while Björn poured. No one suggested a toast.

When all the glasses were filled, Sinjin entered the dining car with the Agency man. They came to stand between the booths.

Maxim said to them all, "I want to apologize. Mr. Alonso and I have come to an understanding. I wish to be welcome in your group."

Sinjin said, "There's a big Soviet military base outside Choir. I didn't know that."

The Agency man said, "I was simply doing my job, as I understand it."

Lara said, "Please join us."

Sinjin and Maxim took the open seats. Björn tipped out two more shots. All the drinkers held their glasses to each other.

Sinjin pronounced Choir's vodka as good an example of bad alcohol as he'd ever tasted.

———

Gang only sipped the homemade vodka. He'd need his head on straight tonight at Sukhbaatar to spirit Lara away.

They'd need to spend a few days on the border in

Sukhbaatar. Beijing-bound trains ran only twice a week on the Trans-Mongolian track. They'd get a hotel, separate rooms. Eat all their meals together. Maybe they'd take a camel tour of the Gobi, a sunset, a campfire.

Gang said little. At the table were three nuclear physicists, a rich dilettante, and a giant.

First, Sinjin gave a lesson on collecting mushrooms in the Urals: the delicious *obabok* which prefers the sun and damp of late spring; the season might be too early for the prized *boletus boletus*; and the poisonous *Amanita phalloides*, called the "death cap," which would not appear until June. None of the scientists nor Timur mentioned Chernobyl. Anton and Sinjin talked about tennis, Björn about skiing. Lara told another tale from her decade as a policewoman. She egged on reluctant Timur to describe coal mining. The enormous man's voice was a rumble, as if he could rip coal from the ground with his hands.

After an hour and a half of passing the bottles around, the conversation turned Maxim's way.

The Agency man had made the mistake of drinking to keep up with Björn and Sinjin, a Swede and a diplomat. The cheap vodka had him flummoxed.

Gang had never developed the taste for liquor. Alcohol made a person more of what they already were. Gang's father was a brute. Björn was kind. Anton was afraid. Maxim was hurt.

Anton, the other Russian at the table, asked after Maxim's home. The Agency man blew out his cheeks, as if suddenly he'd been asked a stupid question. But he raised a hand to the table, either to apologize or quell any response.

Maxim slurred a little. He was born in Volovo, a small farming *kolkhoz* four hundred kilometers south of Moscow. His father was a tractor mechanic, mother a greenhouse worker. The father had fought the Germans and lost a few toes to an Eastern Front winter.

By the time he was ten, Maxim was operating a tractor. By fifteen he drove crops in a big rig a hundred kilometers to the central *oblast* market. At eighteen he was drafted into the Red Army. He became a truck driver. At nineteen he shipped out to Afghanistan.

As his story waxed on, Maxim slipped lower in the booth, arms folded. His gaze fixed on a middle distance somewhere past his crossed feet.

"I liked driving. I like the world to move. I don't like to be still." Maxim spoke with deliberateness as if challenging some remark to the contrary.

Sinjin said, "So you ended up on the Trans-Mongolian. Excellent."

Björn, eager to placate, said, "I was lucky, too. I got to ski for a year in the Artic on the Russian border, keeping an eye on you lot."

Maxim made no eye contact, stared only away. Around him, the table quieted. Timur put his wide hands on his knees as if to push off.

He said to Anton, "Enough. Let's go."

Anton, somewhat drunk himself, didn't move, focused with the others on Maxim. Timur growled. He would not, for some reason, leave without Anton.

Björn asked, "How did you end up working on the Trans-Mongolian?"

Maxim said to his feet, "Medical discharge."

"May I ask what happened?"

Maxim replayed something in his head. He nodded and gave himself permission.

"I drove over a mine."

Maxim looked with hard eyes at the carpet as if he might project something there.

He said, "There was supposed to be a warning sign for the minefield." The Agency man shook his head, still arguing inside it. "There was no sign."

Björn, also a military man, leaned across the table. "Maxim." He rested a hand near the Agency man. "Maxim."

"What."

"Were there others in the truck?"

Maxim nodded. He blinked many times, either at welling tears or memory.

"I, um." Maxim cleared his throat. He was struggling whether to speak of the dead or not. One never knew which the dead preferred.

The faces at the table became sympathetic, except Timur; the Chechen stroked his beard. Maxim continued with a tinge of pugnacity.

"It took three days to find a plane to fly us to Vladivostok. I was to get surgery there. I waited in a tent at the airfield. Twenty bags lay out in the open. I unzipped every one and smeared bug juice on the faces so the ants wouldn't eat them."

Maxim stopped there. Anything else he meant to say got clogged in the telling. He pinched the bridge of his nose.

Björn uttered, "People die in wars, man. It wasn't your fault."

Maxim doubled over. Gang thought he might puke but Maxim tugged up his right pants leg. A ragged half of Maxim's calf had been ripped off by the mine.

Maxim dropped his trouser leg. "The Agency found me this job. Riding the train."

Maxim seemed done. The last of the bottles held more than enough for a final round. Lara poured for them all except Timur. Out in the passing desert, rock outcroppings broke the wastes, like rotting ships on a dried sea. The first strains of day's end ambered the light.

To change the mood, Lara joked they should drink up and go so the restaurant could set up for lunch. They all raised their glasses to each other.

Maxim tossed down his vodka in a way that told Gang he had more to say.

The Agency man did not set down his emptied glass. Holding it, he peeled away the index finger to point at Anton. "You."

Anton, unawares, asked, "Yes? Me?"

"Men died in Afghanistan."

Anton said, "I understand that."

"Men are dying now."

"That's regrettable. Of course."

Maxim said, "For Russia."

"Yes, Maxim. They died for Russia."

The Agency man sat straighter. Timur did the same, but Maxim did not see it.

Maxim put down his glass, hard for emphasis, but clumsily. "You want to disgrace Russia."

"I beg your pardon."

He swung his finger across the table.

"They all know. You told them. You told *me*. You're going to Moscow to say how terrible everything in Russia is. How bad we are. How backwards."

Anton said, "That's wrong. I want to help."

Sinjin interjected, "We're all a little drunk. Maybe let's continue later."

The Agency man stood. That same instant, Timur rose. Gang got to his feet beside Lara.

The big Chechen said, "Go back to your cabin."

Maxim said to him. "I almost died."

Timur tipped only a degree toward Maxim but enough for Gang to see what was intended. Maxim lacked the sobriety to know what he was looking at.

Timur said, "Almost."

Maxim, undaunted and foolish, sneered. "What unit, Timur Makhdi? In Afghanistan? Name your unit."

The big Chechen's teeth showed behind his beard. He said to Björn, "Take him away."

The Swede got up, leaving only Anton and Lara seated.

Björn's hold on the Agency man's arm offset any resistance. They left the dining car.

Timur looked down at Gang, "Why are you standing?"

"Because you're standing."

"What did you think I was going to do?"

"Something I might've had to stop you from doing."

The big Chechen gauged Gang up and down. To Anton, Timur said, "No more drinking."

The scientist rose. He and Timur filed out of the dining car.

Lara plucked the half-full bottle off the table. She stood with it. Moving down the aisle through the red booths and Mongolian carvings, Lara weaved. Gang hadn't noticed she'd drunk that much.

31

LARA

KILOMETER 1442

The train surged straight north into the desert. In the quivering of the train, the rhythm of the tracks, and the dying sunlight, she and Gang were left with nothing to do but look at each other if no one spoke. Gang crossed his legs under him, looking very composed.

Lara asked, "Are you wicked?"

"You're a little drunk."

"I wanted to ask you that way before I started drinking."

She'd kissed wicked men before, a few of them cops, one professor in grad school. She'd liked the kisses and regretted them later.

"No. I don't think I'm wicked."

"So." Lara felt a gesture was needed. She raised a finger, then dropped it.

Gang said, "So."

"Murder. Not wicked."

He uncrossed his legs to give a serious answer. Before he started, she said, "You murdered your father." Lara flicked a hand backwards. "Youthful indiscretion." *Pfff.*

Gang nodded. She could see he was weighing whether to answer.

"You going to remember this? Because I'm only going to say it once."

"I expect that'll be enough."

"Alright. You know how you hear about a wolf in a trap gnawing itself free? I grew up without a father. Then I found him. The man who'd abandoned me was disgusting. My father's my paw. I'll always be without him. But I had to get free."

"That was what you needed. Not sure getting run over suited your old man's needs. Or the others."

"The others I can explain."

Lara said, "Pfff," again.

"You're too sloshed to listen."

"Nope."

"Nope what?"

"Go ahead. Make it okay."

Gang sat back to consider, then stood. "Be right back."

"Where you going?"

She watched him exit her cabin. Gang in ebony pants and pullover moved like a black cat. Lara shook her head at herself. "What am I doing?"

He came back with a glass cup of steaming water, the tab of a teabag hanging out. Lara accepted it, then set the cup on the table, too scalding to hold. How had Gang held it? He sat across from her, again in lotus.

Gang said, "In our village, there were no sheriff and deputies. No cops. There wasn't a courthouse or a jail. There was just Li. The *Qiǎng Rèn*. The strongman."

Lara repeated, "Qiǎng Rèn" to show her cogency.

"Li and his guys lived off the village, everyone chipped in. If you refused, you got roughed up. Li kept the bad guys from other villages out. The other villages kept him out. When I was eleven, a man named Ho knifed Li and took over. Five years later, while I was in Baltimore, Ho got killed. I'm pretty sure there've been, like, three more since."

Lara blew over the surface of the teacup while Gang waited, until she found it less scorching. She almost forgot she was supposed to sip. Gang continued.

"Sometimes violence is the natural order. It doesn't work in a culture like yours, but in a simpler one, it can give balance."

He came to sit beside her. Gently, like stealing from her, Gang slipped the hot teacup out her hand.

He said, "Reactors work this way. Fission's made up of collisions. Violence makes energy. Sometimes humans are neutrons."

Lara liked the comparison, but it was too fleeting for her to hold onto through the vodka. Her comment was gone before she could make it.

Gang's dark eyes loomed close. Lara didn't retreat. Silently this time, she asked the deep place where alcohol couldn't reach, "What am I doing?" That bit of sobriety decided not to interfere.

She said, "Kiss me."

Out in the corridor, Maxim screamed.

32

ANTON

"Listen to me, both of you!"

The Agency man pounded on the door. Sitting on his berth, Timur grew veined and red-faced, fuming like a fuse.

In the passageway, Maxim bellowed: "Two hours from now this train will stop in Ulaanbaatar. I will make a phone call to the Agency. They will call the KGB. You, Anton Epstein, you Jew scientist, will be arrested for treason at the Russian border. For revealing state secrets. For goddam something! Your report is going to be thrown in a fucking waste bin. You will not be allowed to return and embarrass your own country. You'll be lucky if they don't throw you in the garbage, too."

Anton stood. "I'm going to talk to him."

Timur said, "No." Anton sat.

Maxim thumped another fist on the doorframe.

"And Timur Makhdi. Chechen. I don't believe you. I don't believe anything about you. Whoever you are and whatever you are doing, the KGB will be waiting for you, too."

Anton stood again, slowly so Timur would not feel dared.

"He's just drunk, Timur." Anton moved toward the door.

He had to make the Agency man be quiet. Maxim could stop Timur's horrifying plan. Maxim could make that call to the KGB and Timur would never reach Chernobyl. If Anton was arrested, too, such was the price. But Maxim had to be quiet.

Anton said again to Timur, patting the air before opening the door, "He's drunk."

Timur said, "Let him in."

33

GANG

G ang pinched Lara's chin.
"Hold that thought."

He hopped off the berth, leaving Lara to lean into the space he vacated.

Gang unlocked the door to peek into the passageway. The inebriated Agency man was out there inveighing against Anton and Timur, threatening them both with arrest. Maxim hammered on the door while yelling at the top of his lungs that he'd have the KGB waiting at the Russian border. He did this from the safety of the corridor. There was little chance he'd shout that way in Timur's face.

Then Timur's door opened. Anton asked Maxim to calm down, to come in and talk. When Maxim said, "Fuck you," an arm thick as a loaf of bread grabbed him by the collar and yanked him inside. The door slammed shut.

Gang glanced back at Lara. He sighed, "Goddamit."

He closed Lara in. All the other doors were shut except conductress Natalya's. The big blonde peeked out, her displeasure poorly veiled. Gang waved.

"I got it."

Natalya winced and ducked back into her cabin.

Gang pressed an ear to the door; he caught the muted noises of scraping and kicking, like the shuffling of rats in an attic. He clenched his jaw and tried the door. It was locked.

"Anton, open up. Let me in. Anton, come on, man."

With a fast metallic jangle, the lock was undone. Gang shouldered the door open and shoved Anton aside.

In the small cabin, Timur's back occupied more than half the space. The giant bore down on Maxim thrashing on a berth, his mitts clamped around the Agency man's throat. Maxim beat frantically at Timur's arms and chest.

Gang leaped onto the opposite cot, then skipped over the short tabletop between them. In a flash he landed on the berth where Timur was throttling Maxim. Gang straddled the Agency man and came eye-to-eye with Timur.

"Stop."

Timur was too enraged to hear him and too strong to grapple with. A man this powerful had only a few vulnerable spots.

Gang made a knife's edge of his right hand's fingertips. He punched, short and sharp, into Timur's Adam's apple.

Timur gagged as any man would have to. He backed off, bringing hands up to his own throat. On the berth, Anton curled into a ball, hiding behind raised knees.

Timur and Maxim both coughed for air. Maxim tried to sit up, but Gang squatted over him and pressed a heel into his neck to hold him down. Maxim's legs ran hard nowhere.

The Chechen finished rubbing his own throat. His eyes became slits. Timur surged again for Maxim. He seemed to not see Gang.

"Timur, no."

Gang fought off Timur's hands, windmilling faster than Timur could react. Gang flung a backhand knuckle into Timur's temple to snap him out of his fury.

Timur reared back. Under Gang's shoe, Maxim yelped; Gang smashed the flat of a hand into the Agency man's sternum to shut him up.

Timur rattled his head. He growled from his heaving chest, frustrated with Gang perched on top of Maxim.

"Get off him."

Stuffed in his corner, Anton said, "No. He'll kill him."

Under Gang's heel, Maxim squeaked.

Gang asked Timur, "Do you have to do this?"

"Yes."

"No matter what?"

The big Chechen's hands clutched and unclutched.

"Get off of him."

Gang said, "Timur, trust me. Just...just stay there. Anton."

The scientist started, surprised to have a role.

Gang said, "Lara's got half a bottle of vodka. Go get it. Go on."

Anton's focus flitted about as if he might find some alternative. On the berth, Gang's heel squashed Maxim's throat every time the man tried to move.

Anton got to his feet. Gang said, "Get the bottle. Don't say anything else."

The scientist bumbled from the cabin. Timur said, "Don't make me hurt you."

Gang shook his head to create some doubt that Timur could do that. But of course Timur could. Gang might have an advantage in open space, but in the tiny arena of the compartment, Gang would be done the second Timur laid hands on him.

"Listen to me, Timur. I need you to let me handle this."

The Chechen jabbed a massive hand at Maxim sprawled under Gang's shoe. "This *mudak* has to die."

"Alright. Just stand down."

Timur pointed between Gang's eyes to stamp the responsibility there.

Sheepish Anton returned with the vodka.

"She's asleep."

Gang stepped off Maxim's neck. The Agency man gasped like a landed fish. Anton and Timur sat side-by-side.

Gang helped Maxim come upright. The Agency man's face was flushed from straining to breathe.

Gang pressed on Maxim's shoulder to pin him against the cabin wall. He told Anton, "Uncork the bottle. Give it to him."

Anton handed the vodka to the Agency man.

Gang told Maxim, "Have a drink, man."

Maxim shook this off. Gang lowered his face and changed his tone. "Have a drink."

The Agency man took a pull off the bottle. Gang said, "One more." Maxim complied. Under Gang's hand, Maxim shuddered, not because he was a coward but because he wasn't stupid.

Gang took away the vodka. Without turning his head from the Agency man, he reached the bottle behind him. Anton grabbed it, and this freed up Gang's hand.

34

TIMUR

Kilometer 1466

G ang raised his right hand to his left ear as if to finger his lobe. Faster than Timur's eye could track, Gang struck the edge of his hand against the side of Maxim's neck.

The Agency man went slack, eyes closed, a puppet with the hand withdrawn.

Gang nestled two fingers under Maxim's jaw for a pulse. He nodded.

Anton sounded on the edge of retching. "Oh my God. What did you do?"

Timur spoke to Anton: "Be quiet. I am very serious about this. Be quiet."

Gang sat next to the slumped Maxim. He seemed bothered but not awfully so.

Timur asked, "Is he dead?"

"Unconscious."

"Move aside."

"No."

Timur seethed. "He is going to die. I ask you to move one more time. Or he will not die alone."

Gang cursed.

Lithe as a snake, he slipped behind the inert Agency man. Gang put Maxim's neck in a vise between his arms, then squeezed so hard his lips fleered back from his teeth. Maxim did not wake, did not squirm. Anton turned his face to the shivering wall.

For five minutes, Gang did not release or relax. He closed his own eyes and rested his chin on Maxim's shoulder while he crushed the sides of Maxim's neck, until it was done. Gang took another pulse, then clambered out to sit beside the dead Agency man.

Timur asked, "Why?"

Gang hitched his head and looked out the window. The sun tipped toward the pan of the desert in an unmarred sky. Night over the Gobi was going to be a spangled affair.

The Chinese ran a hand through his black hair. "You were going to kill him."

Anton whimpered but plugged up so Timur wouldn't turn on him.

Timur breathed in the new situation. He sat on the berth beside Anton. The Russian vibrated like a tuning fork.

Timur said to Gang, "I'm grateful. You were protecting me."

"I was protecting everybody."

"I think you've done this before."

Gang mumbled, "Ah, hell."

Timur asked, "Are you some sort of killer?"

"I have been."

"For money?"

"Sometimes."

Timur said, "I've known your kind."

"I thought you were a miner."

"I have been."

Timur offered Anton the remaining vodka. "Here."

"No." Anton pushed the bottle aside.

"Stop whining. This was your fault."

"Mine?"

"Your fucking bragging, about the rotten fucking reactor you built. How you are going to Moscow to fix everything."

Timur jammed the vodka bottle against Anton's chest. The scientist took it.

Timur continued to snarl. "I don't care how many this Chinese has killed. I don't care how many I have done." He pointed at the dead Maxim. "Or how many this prick killed when he drove over a mine. You, Antosh, and your reactor will kill more. So fucking drink, Russian."

Timur patted the scientist's hand on the bottle.

"Don't worry. You saw nothing. You were not here when this happened. As soon as you stop shaking, I want you to leave."

Timur turned on Gang, "So, little Chinese. Are you here for me?"

"No."

"Anton?"

"No."

"Then what are you doing on this train?"

"You've got enough problems, man."

Timur said, "True. You have a plan?"

"Sort of."

35

ANTON

KILOMETER 1472

"Throw him out the window?" Anton shot to his feet. "This is your plan?"

Gang let his palms fall into his lap. "You got a better idea?"

"I'm not a murderer like you two. How in the world would you expect that *I* have a better plan?"

The Chechen was placid, arms crossed. Gang spoke for them both.

"Look. We're in the middle of the Gobi Desert. It'll be pitch dark in an hour and a half. No one's going to find him until morning. He was already drunk, I made him take two more swallows. He was depressed, angry. Everyone heard that. We'll say he fell off the train, or he jumped. Who's going to say he didn't?"

Timur turned eyes like a dragon's to Anton.

"Only us."

"The way I did it, they won't be able to tell. No marks, no bruises. The fall off the train will be the cause of death."

The Chechen said, "Good."

Gang said, "We'll be in Ulaanbaatar in another hour and a half. Lara and I are getting off there."

Anton startled. "What? Why?"

"That's a need to know only. And you don't."

"Is she involved in all this?"

"No. And she stays that way."

Timur said, "I will leave at the first station inside Russia."

Gang checked his wristwatch. "That's Naushki. In nine hours. Three a.m."

Anton waved his hands as if trying to stop a car. "Wait. You're leaving me on the train?"

Timur said, "The Swede and that fool Englishman will be here."

Gang shook his head. "No, Sinjin's stopping in the Urals."

"Ah, yes. Mushrooms."

"And Björn will probably leave when he finds out Lara's gone."

Gang said, "So, you'll probably get to Moscow alone."

Timur added, "When you are there, if you must, tell them you believe this little Chinese did the killing." Timur opened a platter-like hand to Gang. "You won't mind. I assume you are not easy to find in China."

"I'm not."

Timur's evil glances made Anton shiver. Standing at the door, he wrapped his arms around his ribs. He needed to save himself. He could negotiate. Anton shot Timur a cold glance.

"What else shall I tell them in Moscow?"

"Whatever makes you feel safe, my friend. But some things you should know. First, I am very well financed, and very experienced at traveling unnoticed. A shave, a haircut, another passport, who's to say who I am? And do not forget. I work for the Afghans and the CIA. You think you should be afraid of the KGB?"

Timur wagged a finger between himself and Gang.

"We are ghosts, the two of us. But you, Antosh? *You* are very real."

Anton backed against the door. He could run. Through the carriages, to the locomotive, to the engineers. Tell them everything. Demand protection.

Behind his back, he touched the door handle. "Will you chase me?"

Timur said, "No." He gestured to the open space beside him. "But sit."

Gang said, "I would if I were you."

With caution, Anton sat beside Timur, across from Gang and the body. The giant blocked the window and the end of the desert day.

"The best thing for all of us is to stay in line. One story."

Anton said, "I didn't do anything."

"And you will have done nothing in the story. But consider if you make me and the Chinese your enemies. You are a smart man, Anton. But you are not clever, not in this. He and I will not break ranks. You will be in a Mongolian jail. We will ride on."

Anton plastered hands over his face to blind himself, to hear and feel only his own breathing. To take himself out of this moment, this fucking predicament.

He lowered his hands.

"Throw him out the window."

36

GANG

The corpse made the cabin feel smaller. When Timur stood, he didn't help.

Anton tugged at the Chechen. "No, no. Wait until after dark."

Timur brushed off the scientist's hand.

Gang said, "If we wait, we'll be throwing him out in the middle of the train station in Ulaanbaatar. It's got to be while we're still in the Gobi."

Timur pointed at the flatiron land. The *Rossiya* passed no camels or yurts, nothing but dunes and railroad tracks, simple and empty.

Timur said, "We do it now."

Anton urged, "What about other trains? What if they see the body?"

Reaching for the window to open it, Timur growled. "No one will stop."

Gang said, "They can't stop. They're all on schedules. Someone might radio it in. But Anton, we're in the real middle of nowhere. No one's coming out here anytime soon."

209

Timur grunted trying to slide the window down.

"Locked."

Gang popped off the berth, making dead Maxim fall over onto his side. Gang propped him back up; it was just easier to be in the room with the Agency man's body if he was sitting up.

Gang edged Timur aside. A pair of triangular-headed screws secured the two halves of the window frame together. They'd been too small to notice before.

"Try again. Maybe they'll break."

Timur brought all his weight to bear to budge the top pane. The screws held.

"Now what, little Chinese man?"

"We need a key."

"Who has a key?"

Anton said, "Natalya."

Gang asked the scientist, "How do you know?"

"Yesterday, in China. When we were all looking at the Great Wall. The fat porter opened the door to his cabin. You remember? A breeze came out. He had his window down, so he had a key. Natalya might have one, too."

Timur said, "No."

Anton flung up his hands. "Then what are you going to do? Drag a body down the corridor to throw it off the platform? Everyone will hear you."

Timur was not a giant to be scolded. He said, "The Russian woman will know if we go to her."

"There isn't any choice."

"I don't like it."

Gang said, "He's right, Timur."

"Don't agree just to placate him."

"I'm not. We can explain opening a window better than getting caught hauling a corpse down the hall."

Anton began to stand. "I'll go ask her."

Timur pushed him back down. "You are a terrible liar. The worst. No."

Gang said, "I'll go."

Timur frowned. He motioned to put himself on display, his shaggy head a centimeter from the ceiling. He pretended to be offended.

"Not me?"

Gang left the compartment for the corridor. He paused at Lara's door where inside she lay sleeping. He tiptoed to the last cabin.

Gang knocked. The portal cracked open. One mascara-lined blue eye filled the gap. The eye traveled down Gang's length, then climbed him. The door opened all the way.

Natalya wore a white T-shirt with no bra beneath and the bottoms of a crimson track suit with a stripe up the leg. Barefoot, she was considerably shorter. Her blonde locks were disarranged; she'd been sleeping, an afternoon nap on Moscow time.

"*Da?*"

"Sorry to bother you. I want to lower a window. I wonder if you have a key to undo the screws?"

Natalya seemed to have a hard time keeping her eyes on Gang's face.

"Why?"

"Maxim's had a lot to drink. He's also pretty upset. Some bad stuff he did in the war. We're trying to calm him down in Anton's cabin. I think he might throw up. We need to have the window down."

"Take him to the washroom."

"If he pukes in the corridor, or he misses the sink, you'll have to clean it up."

"Come in."

Gang stepped inside. With a lift of her nose, Natalya indicated for him to close the door.

The conductress's cabin was no different from the others

in second class: two berths, gooseneck lamps in the walls, a folding tabletop between the beds. On the stubby table stood a pot of white peonies she must have bought in Choir after stopping Maxim from accosting Sinjin and his camera. The barren Gobi rolled by as it did in every other window. Natalya made the compartment feel as small as Timur did. Her curves demanded space while her eyes invited closeness.

Natalya faced him. She peered down into the carpeted, trivial distance between them, then up to his face. The conductress let seconds fall between them like hourglass sand. She sighed, as if to say *It's only a stride, man.*

Natalya took it. Her bosom arrived at Gang first.

In a quieter place, not on a clacking train, she might've whispered something. Instead, chest pressed against him, she ran her hands over Gang.

The conductress trickled fingers down his ribs, then followed his belt around to his back, up his spine. Her touch feathered behind his neck, across his shoulders, down his arms to his wrists. She bent just slightly at the knees to lengthen her reach, to his rear, then his pockets. She roamed around front, then slipped both hands over his zipper.

In the short space between their faces, above her breasts, her mouth opened.

Natalya said, "Ah."

Gang moved only to smile.

"You are a stunning woman."

Willing or unwilling, Gang was responding under her hands working up and down, like sanding.

She said, "It is a very long way, this train."

He cleared his throat. "I have to get back to Maxim. Before he pukes."

Natalya's face evinced disappointment before her hands did. Gang backed away. She put one hand on a hip, the other cocked in the air, a teakettle pose. She was pointing.

A green ribbon hung from one gooseneck lamp. At its end dangled a brass wingnut resembling the key to wind a clock.

Gang slipped the ribbon off the lamp. "Thank you."

"Lock the window after."

"Alright."

"I don't want everyone knocking on my door."

Natalya put both fists on her hips, now a sugar bowl.

"You wouldn't do anything unauthorized, would you?"

"No."

"What about something authorized?"

He held up the key on the ribbon. "I'll bring this back."

"Do."

He left the conductress in her cabin. Passing Lara's room, still a little revved, Gang almost ducked in.

37

ANTON

P lay along. That was all he had to do, until three in the morning when Timur would leave the train.

With Gang out of the cabin, the Chechen stared off into the Gobi, surely hoping the wasteland would not run out before he could throw a body into it. Timur planted both palms against the wall as if he were pushing it.

Anton had never been this close to a corpse. Even at funerals, he shied from open caskets. He couldn't imagine what matters must be like at Chernobyl, in the medical wards, the morgue, the ruins of the reactor. Arranged to appear sitting, the Agency man's face was drained but his fingers pooled pink. Maxim sat unnaturally, terribly.

"Timur."

"What?" The Chechen spoke to the dirty windowpane, lit by the late day.

"We're at a turning point. Right here."

"Shut up, Anton."

"You didn't kill Maxim. Gang did. We can stop. We can say what happened. Then you can leave the train. Go home to your family in Chechnya, show them you're alive. They'll welcome you, Timur. Go reclaim what's been taken from you. It's not too late, you haven't gone too far. But in the next few minutes, you will. I beg you, stop everything. Right here."

Timur lifted his eyes to an opal sky.

He said, "Here's what will happen. The Chinese man will return. You tell him you've had a change of heart. He will murder you with one, maybe two chops of his hand. Then I will tell him the same. He will kill me, or I will kill him. And we're worse off than where we started."

Timur rapped a knuckle against the glass pane.

"I know the moment I am gone from the train you will blurt out everything. I have reasons for you to be dead. And reasons for you to live."

The giant turned from the window.

"So shut up, Antosh."

Gang returned. He held up a brass key hanging from a green ribbon. Timur snatched it.

38

GANG

T he lefthand screw put up a fight but loosened after a long grunt from Timur. The second screw wasn't having it.

Timur set both hands to the key; the small brass wings didn't give him much purchase. The Chechen strained and flushed as much as when he was choking Maxim. The screw didn't budge.

Gang said, "Stop, man. You'll strip it."

Huffing and thwarted, Timur backed off. Gang moved in to view the problem closer. The triangle-headed screw revealed glints of bare metal where Timur had shorn it. If the three-sided head rounded off, the screw would be impossible to turn.

Dead Maxim had slouched and turned his face, disinterested. He didn't care how he was ejected from the train. Timur was succumbing to frustration; the giant was on the verge of lugging the corpse down the corridor and flinging it off the platform to be done with it. Gang had no idea what to do next.

Anton said, "Step aside."

The Russian rose. Timur and Gang stood between him and the window. Anton said, "Move," and they shuffled aside. Anton rummaged in the pockets of his burgundy rollneck sweater for a pack of Chunghwa Filter Kings and a flick lighter.

Anton said nothing while examining the last screw. Timur asked Gang, "What is he doing?"

Anton lit a cigarette. "Shut up," he said. "Science."

He took a long pull on the cigarette to heat the tip to an ember. Anton touched the glowing end to the metal window frame around the screwhead. The smoke Anton blew on the pane curled back on him.

In two minutes he'd smoked the cigarette down to the butt. Between draws, Anton touched the glowing tip to the metal frame around the screw. He fired a second cigarette and did the same. Because the frame was unpainted metal, he left no scorch marks.

Anton snapped his fingers at Timur for the key.

The screw broke free; Anton augered it out it with little effort. He dropped the window enough for the tobacco haze to suck out into the desert; a cool and parched wind gushed in along with insect husks, cobwebs, leaves, and black chernozem dust.

Anton slid the window shut. He sat across from the corpse and did not look at it.

Gang said, "Brilliant."

The scientist said, "Heat expands."

Gang took back the key and ribbon. Timur nodded approval but the scientist wouldn't look up.

Gang checked his watch; dusk lay an hour away.

He said, "Anton, go into the corridor. Walk toward the platform between cars. Before you go outside, I want you to say 'We'll get some fresh air. It'll be alright.' Say it loud enough to be heard from the corridor. Wait on the platform two minutes. That's all. Then come straight back. Two minutes."

The scientist did not rise. Outside, the Gobi and the time to act streamed past.

Timur sat beside the scientist. He rested a hand on Anton's knee.

"Antosh, do what he says. Or I will throw you out the window too."

Anton left the cabin.

Gang sat beside the dead Maxim. Timur's assault had left no traces on his throat; neither had Gang's. Maxim wore a nice watch.

Gang asked Timur, "Are you going to try to throw me out the window?"

The Chechen shook his head. "I think it would be like trying to throw out a wildcat."

"What's gotten into you, man?"

"What do you mean?"

"Threatening Anton. Going after this guy."

"I had to make Anton move. He is a scientist; he does nothing quickly. That one? He threatened me with the KGB. I will not go back to prison."

"Who are you, Timur?"

Timur indicated the man Gang had killed. "You just killed a Russian. Maybe you will visit a Russian prison yourself. Then you'll see who I am."

They spoke no more until Anton returned.

The giant got to his feet. "Open it."

Anton yanked down the window frame. The burst of Gobi air riffled the curtains and flapped Timur's hair about his face. The mountains were not so distant, the desert was coming to a close. Timur scooped the corpse off the berth.

Gang lent a hand to raise the body face-up, headfirst to the open window. Before they heaved him out, Gang told Anton, "Throw out the vodka."

The scientist tossed the third-full bottle into the desert beside the tracks, then scurried out of the way.

Gang bore little of Maxim's weight. Mostly on Timur's strength, they raised the Agency man up to the gushing window, stuffed him through and sent him sailing into the open. The speed of the train swept the corpse away into the wind and shadowed dunes.

Gang poked out his head for a glimpse of the clump beside the rails. Another train might see Maxim before nightfall. Likely not. No one was going to reach the body before daybreak.

With the brass key, Gang secured the two screws. He wiped the window frame clean of Anton's cigarette ashes, then pocketed the ribbon.

Gang went to the samovar for hot water and a fresh teabag. He crept into Lara's cabin and locked the latch.

39

LARA

Kilometer 1491

Waking felt like rising through slush. The berth drew Lara down even as Gang's hand and voice tempted her upward.

"Hey, sit up. I brought tea."

Lara came upright. She batted her eyes to jumpstart them; warm mint drifted under her nose. Two-handed, she accepted a glass cup from Gang.

"Jesus, that's hot. How do you hold that?"

Gang took the tea back and set it on the table.

She asked, "Where are we?"

"An hour out of Ulaanbaatar."

"Wake me before we get there."

"No, no, sit up. Lara, come on. Some things have happened."

"Okay." She sniffed. "Alright."

Gang sat beside her. On the table the teacup steamed.

"What's going on?"

Gang made little halting gestures, a way to ask her to stay calm.

"Just tell me."

"Maxim, the Agency guy. He's dead."

Scalding or not, she grabbed the tea. The cup was very hot, but she held on.

"What happened?"

"You heard Maxim out in the hall yelling at Anton and Timur."

"Vaguely."

"He was threatening to call the KGB on them both. He was drunk but he meant it. Anton opened the door to talk. Then Timur hauled him in out of the corridor."

Lara said, "Wow," and sipped. The part of her that would always be a cop tamped down her reaction. This was a crime, a sad but common thing.

Gang said, "Yeah."

They'd all liked Timur. A massive man, intelligent. Brave, headed to Chernobyl to labor in the tunnel under the reactor. But the Chechen was no one to threaten.

Gang said, "Timur didn't do it."

"What? Who, Anton?"

"Not Anton."

The pieces fell together.

"Gang, no."

"I know."

"I'm not going to yell."

"That's a good idea."

"You said you were done. You looked me in the goddam face and said you were done."

"I know. I was."

"Why? Why on earth did you get involved?"

Softly Gang took the cup. He returned the steaming tea to the table, maybe so she wouldn't throw it on him, or to make it easier for her to hit him.

He said, "I need you to believe me."

"Then don't lie. About anything."

"Timur was going to choke Maxim to death. The look on Timur's face, Lara, there was nobody home. I swear, he was going to kill the guy. Then he was going to haul the body down the corridor and throw it off the train. And he'd have gotten caught. Natalya, Sinjin, Björn, one of them would've heard him or seen him. He was going to snap the guy's neck, break his windpipe, something obvious. Then when the body's found, probably tomorrow, Mongolian police and the KGB start looking for us. We'll all get detained as witnesses. Timur goes to jail. Probably Anton as an accessory."

"Tell me how this concerns you."

"You know who I am. I don't *get* detained. I don't witness. As far as the police are concerned, I don't exist."

Gang pointed at the wall behind him that separated Lara's cabin from Timur's.

"I went over there to calm things down. But I swear to you, Timur was five seconds from tearing off the guy's head."

"So you actually killed Maxim for him."

"Look, the guy went after Timur. He was drunk and stupid. I did the only thing I could think of to protect both of us."

"How were you protecting me?"

"Maxim was a Russian citizen. What happens if you're named a witness? You get taken back to Moscow to testify. There's a contract on you, Lara. Who's going to protect you? Some Russian cop will just take the mob's money and cut your throat. We've got to get you off this train and back to Beijing. That doesn't happen if Maxim's been murdered."

"But he was murdered."

"Not so anyone will be able to tell."

"Jesus, Gang. Alright. Tell me. How'd you do it?"

Gang touched a fingertip below her ear. "Knife-hand to collapse the carotid sinus. That knocked him out. Sleeper hold to cut off the carotid arteries. No bruise, no trace."

Gang shrugged to say he was sorry he knew how to do that.

"Where's the body?"

"Fifteen kilometers behind us."

"How'd you get it off the train?"

"We threw him out the window."

"Dear God." Lara rubbed her forehead. "I thought all the windows were locked."

"I had to go to the conductress's room for a key that could open the one in Timur's cabin."

"You had to?"

"Yeah."

"You were alone with Natalya?"

"I threw a body out a window. You're annoyed with me for going to see Natalya?"

"Why are you telling me all this?"

"About Natalya?"

"The part where you killed someone."

"Lara."

"What."

"Here's the truth."

"We are way too far into this for you to be telling me anything else."

"Alright. Of all the women I've known, you're the only one who knows me. The only one I haven't lied to. Much. I'm afraid."

"Of what?"

"That you'll be the last. I want to be straight with you. I've never done that, and I don't see it happening again. I want to try it now."

"You want to try it."

"Stop being a cop. You know what I mean."

Gang shuffled on her berth as though he might rise and exit.

"You say the word and I'll leave you out of it. When we

get off the train at Ulaanbaatar, you go your way, I'll go mine. You won't see me again."

Lara was on a train speeding across Mongolia, needing to decide right now if a man she found so compelling and repelling might ever get a chance to convince her that the way he'd lived his life hadn't made him a devil. Never get the shot to take her to dinner. Never get her drunk enough again for her to ask him for a kiss.

She said, "Let's go the same way for a while. See what happens."

"Alright."

"You can't kill anybody else." Lara shook her head. "And I can't believe I just said that."

Gang stood. His face was blank because now he had a course.

"Pack."

40

BAT

W alking a circle around the *ovoo*, Bat sprinkled vodka
on the stacked stones. He took a sip for himself. The
spirits did not like to drink alone.

After his third circuit around the altar, he placed three
rocks on the ancient wall, one each for his wife, son, and
daughter. He called his untethered horse to come to him, to
stow the vodka in the saddlebag. Bat had little taste for alcohol
anywhere but at prayer.

Bat crossed his legs and boots under him on the cool earth.
He arranged the hem of his duster over his knees and pulled
down his wide-brimmed bush hat. The prayer flags around
the ovoo snapped, the wind on the Choiriin mountaintop
never stilled. This was as it should be. The wind was the voice
of the *bogd*. So long as there was wind, the spirits and ancestors were here.

Someone had put a fresh set of ram's horns on the
rounded peak of the cairn. The rack was thick and gnarled, a
strong sheep had worn them. From where Bat sat in the dirt,
he imagined the horns were the twin arms of a slingshot. He

pulled back his wishes, aimed them at the spirits' home above the mountain, and let fly:

"Protect my son. Muunokhoi is not the fierce dog I named him to be. He is gentle and the city is not. His life there brings him too little joy.

"Protect my daughter. Enebish rides her prettiness away from her mother and me. I named her Not This One to keep her from the evil eye, but there are too many eyes on her.

"Protect Oyuun, my wife. She is the center of my life."

Bat sat comfortably. His old knees did not bother him today.

The sun wouldn't set for another hour. This was Bat's favorite time on the mountaintop, when the shadows of Choir five hundred meters below grew long, when the clean light sharpened the contours of the Gobi plain like a strop. For his last few minutes at the ovoo, Bat closed his eyes.

The banners whipped, the wind whistled, and all else stayed mum. The chill in the soil began to eke into his hips. Soon it would be time to ride down the mountain.

He opened his eyes before he was ready. The horse pawed the dirt and shook its mane. A deep thrum welled behind Bat, something descending over the desert.

He stayed cross-legged on the ground while the helicopter landed at his back.

———

The Mi-8 copter leaned north. Below, Bat's horse ambled down the mountain on the path of the dried ravine. The horse would trot straight to his barn and Oyuun would find the note Bat tucked in the saddlebag. Oyuun was well named; Patience.

The chopper leveled off at seven hundred meters. Through a porthole Bat saw his little house on the mountain slope approach, then sweep behind. Oyuun would hear the rotors and later know he was onboard. The city came and went next. From high above, Choir looked to be no more than a thumbprint on the Gobi.

The helicopter banked one more time to line up with the railroad. The pilots poured on the power.

The Mi-8 flew over desert that Bat knew well enough. He unclicked his seatbelt from the web seat attached to the fuselage and staggered toward the cockpit. The chopper bucked on the high desert winds, he needed handholds to move forward.

The pilot and copilot welcomed him to the jump seat between them. Both wore white helmets, they were young and wrapped in green Soviet Air Force flight suits festooned with pockets, zippers, and insignia. The copilot offered Bat a headset with a microphone. Bat tugged the earmuffs over his bush hat while the copilot plugged him into the intercom.

Bat said, "Thank you." His own electronic voice played in the headphones. Through the plexiglass windows at their feet, the railroad ran straight.

The pilot said, "Yes, Chief."

"May I ask a few questions? There wasn't time before we took off."

The pilot said, "You have the control." The copilot gave a thumbs up, then the pilot pivoted to Bat.

"Yes, Sir."

"Who found the body?"

"A crew doing a nav training flight. They were following the tracks north from the airbase. They radioed in as soon as they saw it."

"How long ago?'

"I don't know exactly. Inside the hour."

"Has anyone touched it?"

"They said they just hovered."

"How long until we get there?"

"We're doing two hundred kph. At current speed, twenty-five minutes."

"Can you go any faster, Captain? I'd like to beat the sun."

The Soviet pilot grinned. Turning to the windshield, he said, "I have the control."

The copilot raised his hands off the cyclic, the pilot put hands-on. He pushed the throttle to the stops. The Mi-8 leaned forward and the winds parted.

The pilot said, "Two-fifty, Chief."

Bat asked the pilot to set the Mi-8 down fifty meters from the body to blow no more sand over it.

The chopper touched wheels down lightly. The pilot sent the copilot out with Bat to be of assistance. He stayed in the cockpit to keep the rotors flipping and the turbines warm.

Bat had the copilot walk south along the track to look for nothing specific, just anything that caught his eye. Bat slid on leather gloves and approached the corpse.

A male, one meter three quarters tall, lying on his front. The right arm reached above the head as if greeting someone below him, the other arm was hidden under the torso. Both legs were akimbo. The corpse wore sand-colored slacks, leather shoes, a grit-covered brown sweater vest over a white long-sleeve shirt. Cropped brown hair. No visible wounds.

Ten meters south of the body, a divot in the sand marked the point of impact. A groove indicated that the man had not landed on his feet. He left dents where he'd rolled.

The trains through the Gobi traveled eighty kilometers per hour. At that speed, a tumble from one would be enough to kill. But the sand was also grainy enough to survive.

Bat withdrew a wallet from the back pocket. A state-issued ID read Maxim Maximovich Sprygin, a guide for the USSR's Intourist Agency. Another card listed membership in a Red Army veterans group. A driver's license showed a residence in Moscow. Maxim Maximovich Sprygin carried a hundred and ten rubles and fifteen Mongolian tugriks.

Nightfall would land in another thirty minutes. The copilot returned from walking along the rails. He took even strides and counted them. He'd found something.

Bat rolled the body over.

On the left wrist was a good watch. Cash in the wallet. This was no robbery.

No rips in the vest or shirt. No scuffs on the knuckles or scratches on the wrists, no bruising or friction burns on the throat. No broken fingernails, no scraped-off skin visible beneath the nails, no blood on the lips or in the ears. No outward signs of struggle.

Hair barbered. Physique lean, around thirty years old. Bat squeezed Maxim's cheeks to make him pucker. The flesh was rubbery, not yet stiff. Bat lifted one eyelid; the lid resisted enough to indicate the first stage of rigor. Maxim Maximovich Sprygin hadn't been lying here long. He was a blue-eyed Russian. The sclera was bloody.

Below the glassy eye, where the socket met the cheek, a tiny scarlet webwork marred the blanched skin. In the thinning light Bat bent close; he blew on the face to clear it, make certain that what he saw was not red quartz dust.

Almost beneath notice, the mark was the spidery lattice of petechiae, broken capillaries in the flesh of the cheek. They were formed post-mortem by the corpse lying face down. A sign of straining to breathe. Bat checked the other eyeball. It, too, was bloodshot.

Taken together, these were indicators of choking.

Bat removed his gloves to palpate the throat. The windpipe was intact. He probed the back of the neck; the vertebrae of the cervical spine were misaligned. Bat took Maxim's head in his hands. He turned the chin left then right, felt the crunch of displaced bones. Bat pulled the head to him. The neck stretched ten centimeters.

Maxim Maximovich Sprygin's neck was snapped.

The copilot returned. Wearing gloves too, he held out a glass bottle, corked, one-third full of clear liquid. Bat lowered Maxim's jaw. He pushed on the chest to bellows some air, then bent for a sniff. Vodka. He checked the airway, found no blockage.

The copilot pointed south down the tracks where he'd found the bottle. "Two hundred meters."

Maxim Maximovich Sprygin was an Intourist Agency man riding a passenger train north. An Army veteran. A drinker. He'd likely been strangled, but choking didn't seem to be what killed him. He'd not been robbed. He'd fallen from a moving train. The fall did or did not break his neck. He'd been either dead or alive when he hit the desert.

The copilot asked, "How long has he been here?"

"About an hour."

"Do you want to take him back to Choir?"

Bat stood over the body.

"No."

Bat hurried to the helicopter ahead of the copilot. They ducked under the desultory spinning blades; Bat climbed in. The Air Force Mi-8 wasn't making so much racket now, the pilot greeted him with a shout over the idling turbines.

"What have you got?"

Bat said, "A dead veteran."

"Damn."

"I need you to radio your base. Have them fly my deputy out here."

"When?"

"Tonight. Now."

"Chief, that's going to be tough."

"I want the body out of the desert before the vultures get to it. Or a bear or a polecat. Can you do that? For a veteran?"

"I'll try."

"Thank you."

Bat bounced to the jump seat so the copilot could clamber into the cockpit.

He said to the pilot, "The train is about eighty kilometers north of us. Can you catch it before it gets to Ulaanbaatar?"

The pilot handed him the headphones. Bat spread them over his ears as the turbines began to howl.

On the intercom, the pilot told his copilot to chart their present coordinates; the copilot strapped a plastic map to his thigh and got busy.

With luck, the body wouldn't lie in the open much longer, another hour, just after dark. It was too late to ask the desert sprits to protect Maxim Maximovich Sprygin. Bat's deputies would find him with spotlights, following the railroad and the wind.

———

The two young Soviet fliers delighted in flying nap-of-the-earth. They rolled with the twists in the rails and the humps of the Gobi, chasing down the Trans-Mongolian a few meters above the tracks. With twilight descending they turned on powerful floodlights. Closing in on Ulaanbaatar, home to a million, a few villages cropped up along the tracks. The pilot flew barely above them, zooming past at top speed.

For ten minutes Bat said nothing while the pilot convinced his air wing to send another helicopter to retrieve Maxim Maximovich Sprygin. Bat's deputy was rousted from his dinner to go along. Once the radio confirmed all this, Bat radioed ahead some instructions to his police counterpart in Ulaanbaatar, then settled in for the rollercoaster flight.

Dusk made little difference in the tones of the fading desert, brown shifted into gray. The sky turned indigo, then starlit. The pilot added altitude for safety while the copilot kept an eye on the tracks. In the middle distance, lights gleamed in some of Ulaanbaatar's taller towers. Bat's son Muunokhoi was in the city somewhere, but Bat had no time for him right now.

The train was easy enough to spot, like a glowing centipede on a dark floor. It seemed to move in slow motion below the racing Mi-8. The pilot flew directly up the spine of the train.

On the intercom, Bat said, "Stop the train."

The Mi-8 bled airspeed to match the pace of the locomotive, then banked to run alongside. The pilot eased the cyclic to drop altitude until the chopper coursed only meters above the desert, eye-level with the locomotive. The Gobi rushed very close below Bat's feet.

Through the headphones and whirling blades, Bat heard the train whistle. The Trans-Mongolian wasn't slowing.

The pilot looked inquisitively at Bat, to ask: How bad do you want to do this?

Bat said, "Go."

The pilot pushed the throttle; the helicopter shot ahead.

In thirty seconds, they'd gained a kilometer on the train. The pilot decelerated sharply, making Bat take hold of his seatbelt. The chopper rounded into a tight U-turn as the pilot shed all velocity.

He came to a low hover directly above the rails. On the dark flatland before Ulaanbaatar, the Mi-8 aimed both floodlights right at the onrushing train. The Trans-Mongolian's one strong headlight shined back.

41

TIMUR

O ut in the corridor, the conductress called, "Ulaanbaatar in fifteen minutes. The *Rossiya* will stop for one half hour. Ulaanbaatar in fifteen minutes. Ulaanbaatar."

Finished with her announcement, she cranked up the vacuum.

From his berth, Timur told Anton, "We'll stay right here."

The Russian sat up from lying on his back.

"I should like to get out for a bit. Buy some food and cigarettes from the vendors. I wish to stretch my legs."

"What you wish," Timur said, "is to find a policeman or two."

"I don't assume for a moment I will be allowed outside of choking range from you."

It was a venomous thing to say, but not angry. Anton hadn't recovered from the Agency man's killing. Nor had Anton put down his guilt over the accident at Chernobyl. Probably, too, he was trying to figure out a way to stop Timur from destroying Russia. So Anton was unpleasant.

Timur said again, "We'll stay right here, until I leave the train. Go back to sleep."

With a jolt the train braked, rocking Timur forward. The locomotive squealed to slow its great momentum; the second-class carriage jostled with the linked cars front and back. This was not the Trans-Mongolian's arrival into Ulaanbaatar.

Timur looked out the window. The train was decelerating in a gloomy nowhere.

"Don't leave the cabin."

He opened the door to duck into the corridor. The blonde conductress dragged her vacuum aside to let Timur pass.

He hurried out onto the short platform between cars. Timur leaned out to see beyond the locomotive.

A large military helicopter had landed beside the railroad mound, rotors beating fast. A figure in silhouette trod in the beams of searchlights from under the copter's nose. In the near distance, Ulaanbaatar cast a dome of light against the night. The air bore a chill.

The silhouette approached the locomotive, then climbed a ladder up into it. The helicopter stood vigil. Then the train lurched and the helicopter watched it go. Before the train regained too much velocity, Timur considered jumping off and running.

No. He had to clear the border. He was expected in Russia.

Timur returned to his cabin.

Anton's expression had changed, not so lost. He gazed at Timur as he had yesterday when they'd first met—complicated, and a little smug.

Timur sat with a thump. "It appears, Antosh, you have gotten your wish."

"Yes?"

"The police have come to you."

42

GANG

"Now," Gang said, "slow."

Face-to-face in the gap between berths, Björn tried to stab Gang with an ink pen.

Gang pivoted his hips away from the pen, a move he called "the swinging gate." The pen jabbed only air. The flat of Gang's left hand fired out, pushing Björn's arm and the pen away. In the same motion, Gang gripped the Swede's wrist; Gang's right palm snapped into Björn's knuckles, forcing the hand inward and open. The pen landed on the carpet.

Gang grabbed it off the rug.

"When a hand is bent in like that, it can't stay closed. That's how you take away a knife."

Gang handed the pen to Björn.

"Now fast."

The Swede stabbed. The pen ended up in Gang's hand. The third time it flashed at Björn's throat.

A knock came at the door. Lara entered. She sighed to see the two of them on their feet, slapping at each other again.

"I don't want to know." She took a berth. Gang plopped beside her, Björn across from them.

Lara asked, "Why'd the train stop?"

Gang and Björn shrugged together. They'd barely noticed.

She said to Björn, "There's something I need to tell you."

Björn grinned, a little sheepish. "I think I know what it is."

"What?"

"It's kind of obvious."

"What is?"

"You two."

Lara pulled her head back like a turtle. "What? No."

"It's okay."

Gang jumped in. "Thanks. I didn't know how to tell you."

Björn said, "It's fine. Lara and I are just friends."

She threw out a hand between the two of them.

"Hey."

Gang eased her arm down.

"Look. The thing is, Lara and I are getting off the train at this stop. We're going to take some time together, hang out in Mongolia a few days. Ride some camels, rent a yurt."

Björn asked Lara, "What about the job?"

Gang squeezed Lara's hand hard enough to make her fidget. He lied for her.

"There's another train to Moscow on Saturday. We'll take that. Be right behind you."

Björn stayed focused on Lara. "The soil collection? Your equipment?"

She said, "You can handle it. Just take a sample at every stop and label it. Take all the equipment to the US embassy in Moscow. I'll get it next week."

Now that she was playing along, Gang eased his grip.

Björn was typically agreeable. If he was disappointed personally or professionally, he kept it in check behind his manners. Gang grabbed his shoulder bag from under his berth.

The train slowed through the outskirts of Ulaanbaatar. After a day and five hundred kilometers across the vast Gobi Desert, the sudden presence of electricity, pavement, and pollution made even a city of a million feel like an outpost.

In the passageway, Natalya pronounced: "All passengers in second class, report immediately to the dining car. Everyone go to the dining car."

To enforce her decree, Natalya banged on doors. She knocked on Lara's but received no answer. Anton and Timur were next. Gang didn't hear what Anton told her but Natalya barked, "Now."

She rapped on Gang's door, didn't wait for a reply, and opened up. She raised an eyebrow to see Gang seated next to Lara.

Natalya said, "All passengers."

They filed out of the cabin, Gang last. Passing Natalya, he handed her the window key on a green ribbon. She patted his behind.

43

BAT

The first of the second-class passengers to arrive and take a booth was a thin, fair-haired young man, a fop in a belted travel coat and fleece slippers.

The next two arrived in a pair. A European-looking chap in a seaman's sweater and khakis who made no eye contact with Bat, nor did he look at the giant who struggled to fit into the booth across from him. The titan was broad and thick-limbed, part Asian in physiognomy. His long hair and see-through beard were the kind a man grew for the purposes of cutting them should he need to.

The last entered the dining car in a trio. They were all attractive sorts. The first was a muscular Nordic who waved to the fop then joined him in his booth. Next, a tall brunette in black slacks and top; she had a keen eye. Close at her back moved a Chinese man, also in black slacks and tunic. He sat across from the woman in their own booth. His black polyester jacket implied he was ready to go someplace. While the woman surveyed the car, the Chinese examined only Bat. If

238

the lights went out, this fellow might be the one missing when they came back on.

The last to enter the restaurant was the tall yellow-haired conductress of the second-class carriage. Thousands of years of Mongolian history had never produced a woman like that. She stood in the aisle to lean a hip against a booth, arms and ankles crossed.

Bat stood in the aisle while they assembled. He hadn't removed his bush hat. He had sand in his boots. In one deep pocket of his long duster he kept a pistol, and in the other, a small drum.

All their tickets were stamped for Russia. Bat greeted them with, "*Privet.*"

They nodded.

In Russian, he continued: "My name is Bat, Police Chief of the Choir *aimag*. Thank you for coming on such short notice."

Bat walked the aisle.

"The train is approaching the Ulaanbaatar station. I will not take much of your time, though I understand none of you are scheduled to depart there. Am I correct?"

No voice or gesture told Bat he was wrong. The fop and the Nord did not look at each other. The others in their pairs did.

"I've come to tell you that the body of Maxim Maximovich Sprygin has been found beside the railroad tracks one hundred kilometers to the south, in the desert. In my aimag."

Like opening the cages to six birds, the gazes of the passengers darted in every direction. Some birds were slower than others, some settled before taking flight again.

"Maxim Maximovich Sprygin was spotted by a military helicopter from a Soviet military base outside Choir. He was an employee of the Soviet Intourist Agency, assigned to this train, to your carriage. Another helicopter brought me here."

Bat pulled his gaze off the passengers to fix his eye out a

window, to the train's slow arrival into the hardness of Ulaan-baatar. If there were factions among the passengers, secrets to be communicated with their faces, he let them have a few private moments to do it. He'd catch them at it later.

He stayed silent striding toward the conductress. The closer he got, the more he felt the urge to turn away.

"I know nothing about any of you. I know about Maxim Maximovich Sprygin only what his corpse could tell me."

The voice that spoke first was not the one Bat would have guessed.

The woman asked, "What did his corpse tell you, Chief?"

"Only half the story, I think."

No one exchanged glances. Good. They'd done that behind his back.

Bat said, "You passengers of the second-class carriage. You will tell me the other half."

The train made more noise creeping into the city than it did racing over the open plains. Every rail and wheel, each squeak of the old springs, all things metal clattered, and the glassware on the tables rang. The second-class passengers quieted under the sounds, the way a house hushes with rain on the roof.

The train eased to a halt. Bat nodded to the conductress; she left to return to her station outside the second-class car.

Bat said to the passengers, "Seven hours from now this train will arrive at Sukhbaatar on the Russian border. Before that time, I will speak to each of you. I will make a determina-tion as to the cause of Maxim Maximovich Sprygin's death."

At the Ulaanbaatar station, several of the hundreds trav-eling on the Trans-Mongolian debarked onto the arrival plat-form. Vendors swarmed them, maneuvering bicycles, motor-scooters and hand-pulled carts with charcoal braziers, boxes of treats, colas in ice chests, selling to the arrivals and wandering among them to pickpocket. In the dining car, everyone rose from their booths.

Bat raised his hands.

"None of you are allowed to leave the train."

The Chinese had a hand already at the base of the woman's back. He asked, "What do you mean 'not allowed'?"

"Please everyone. Be seated one more minute."

The passengers took their booths. The giant was the last to fold into a booth.

Bat said, "Until the cause of Maxim Maximovich Sprygin's death has been determined, none of you may leave the train. At every station, until I say otherwise, you will remain in your compartments."

The fop asked, "What happens when we get to the Russian border?"

"I have notified my department and my wife that I will stay with this train as far as necessary. To Moscow, if that is called for."

"But I'm not going to Moscow."

"We will see where you are going, my friend."

The giant challenged next.

"By what authority?"

"I have the authority to remove all of you from this train right now and transport you back to Choir. I am being considerate by allowing the questioning to take place on your journey. I assume you do not wish that to change?"

The big man inclined his head, a pragmatist. "I do not."

"That is appreciated."

The second-class passengers took this to mean they had been excused. They rose again from the booths with a variety of expressions and whispers.

Bat said over them, "I beg your pardon. We're not quite done. Please sit."

Once more they took to the booths. The giant sat so hard the carriage shivered.

"I will say this once and hope not to repeat it. If for any reason any one of you leave this train without my permission, at any time or any place, I will immediately have all of you returned to Choir for interrogation."

Bat trod the aisle again to look in every eye.

"Understand, my friends. Though Mongolia is an independent nation, we are still very much under the influence of the Soviets. One of their legacies is a highly efficient police and intelligence network. Mongolia is a nation of two million people. Half our population lives here in Ulaanbaatar. The rest are scattered across open spaces. None of you looks nor speaks Mongolian. We are a close-knit people. Strangers among us are noted quickly. I will not have a difficult time finding you."

As before, Bat looked out the windows, allowing the passengers to be clandestine, to firm their alliances.

"If my investigation has not concluded before we reach Russia, I will collect your passports in Naushki."

The fop said, "Mine is a diplomatic passport. I don't surrender it to anybody."

"I understand. But would you prefer I request the Soviet police in Naushki to discuss this with you?"

The young man searched for a response. Bat gave him no time.

"You should all be aware that I have arranged for Soviet police and KGB to be at every platform, all the way to Moscow. They have taken the death of one of their Intourist guides quite to heart. Should you leave the train without my permission, I will report you immediately and you will be arrested not long after. And trust me, my friends. If you are going to try your luck, I suggest you do it against me in Mongolia, rather than the KGB in Russia."

Bat stopped walking. He turned, ready to release them back to their cabins. Before he could excuse them, the woman stood.

"Chief."

"Yes?"

"You mentioned 'arrest.'"

"I did."

"I'm an American diplomat with the US embassy in Beijing." She indicated the fop and the Nord. "They're diplomats, too, with the English and Swedish missions."

"Are you asking me if you have diplomatic immunity?"

"I'm telling you we have diplomatic immunity. We can't be arrested or forced to testify."

"Your name, please?"

"Dr. Lara Dill."

"Dr. Dill, thank you. Are you the American ambassador to China?"

"No, of course not."

"Ah, of course not. In that case, two items come to mind. First, Mongolia does not have diplomatic relations with the United States. Second, as I'm sure you're aware, diplomatic immunity in the instance of a serious crime relies greatly on rank. You are not an ambassador. Are they?"

"No."

"Forgive me, Doctor, but if any of you leave the train during my investigation, at any time or place between here and Moscow, you will be placed under immediate suspicion, and considered a suspect. Neither in Mongolia or Russia will you be immune. You are all on this train until I say otherwise."

The woman sat, tight-lipped and laser-focused on the Chinese man in her booth.

The Swede stood. "What serious crime?"

Bat approached. He rested a hand on the man's thick shoulder.

"Was he a friend?"

"Who? Maxim? I barely knew him."

"What is your name, please?"

"Dr. Björn Landsee."

"If you don't mind, Dr. Landsee, I'd like to speak with you first."

The big Swede rolled his shoulder from under Bat's hand. "About what?"

Bat turned to all the passengers in the booths.

"I'm sorry. Have I been unclear?"

The fop said, "Very."

Bat finally removed his bush hat.

"I believe Maxim Maximovich Sprygin was murdered."

Bat put his hat back on.

44

LARA

With a yellow wooden baton, Natalya blockaded the steps down from the second-class car. Hundreds of passengers flowed out of the lower-class cars. More from Ulaanbaatar replaced them for the journey into Russia.

Gang fidgeted. He watched out the window, crossing and uncrossing his legs. He tried to pace but the cabin gave him only space for two strides in each direction.

Lara said, "I know."

Gang sat across from her. He rubbed his hands as if to warm his palms.

Gang asked, "What do you know?"

"You can get off the train. You can get past Natalya and disappear. Be back in your expensive house in a few days. But you won't leave me."

"If I go and you're still on the train when it crosses the border, someone will kill you."

"And if you stay, someone will try to kill you."

The Mongolian evening seemed clement. No one coming

or going on the Ulaanbaatar platform was bundled up, none of the flags stood at attention.

Lara asked, "Who do you think it is?"

"There's a couple hundred other passengers on this train. We walk by every one of them going to the dining car. There's the restaurant staff. There's ten more stops between here and Moscow. Maybe they're not even on the train yet. It's impossible to guess."

Parents and grandparents bought treats from kiosks for their little ones, meats and cooked walnuts for themselves. Some vendors sold tchotchkes, small carved camels and dinosaurs, souvenirs of Mongolia.

Gang said, "You could try."

"No."

"Even if you get arrested, you'll be alive. Your government will get you out of it."

"Gang, I've got no immunity here. No American embassy to help me. I don't want to think what a Mongolian prison looks like. You heard him, this is a murder investigation. I'm trapped on this train."

She leaned forward to bounce a fist off his knee.

"And here's the kicker. I actually *am* guilty. I'm an accessory to murder. I know who did it."

Gang said, "You're not trapped."

"No?"

"You could turn me in."

"And what if I said yes? Would you let me out of this cabin alive?"

"I would."

"What would you do?"

"Probably have to kill Bat. Maybe Natalya. Maybe whoever Bat has waiting for us. Whatever I have to do."

Lara paused, a little stunned.

He added, "Not you."

She couldn't imagine how dangerous Gang must be. She

felt no fear of him.

"I'm not going to turn you in."

"Good. Then what are you going to do?"

"Trust you to keep us both safe until we can figure this out. If I have to bolt the train, I'll do it somewhere in Russia. The US has diplomatic relations there. I'll stand a better chance. Sound like a plan?"

Gang stood. "I have to move in here."

He left the cabin. In a minute, he returned with a soft travel bag that he tossed under the free berth. Gang gathered up the ionization chamber, Geiger counter, Lara's backpack and collection equipment, the trowel, and stashed them all under the bed, too.

He sat beside her. His left leg bounced like it was ticking.

She asked, "What are you so nervous about?"

"Aren't you?"

"Yeah, but not like that. You're supposed to be the professional here."

"Look, this is as close to the police as I've ever been. Bat's in the dining car looking for me." Gang jumped up to sit across from Lara again, giving himself more room to move.

A knock came at the door. Gang went on alert.

Lara said, "Yes?"

Björn identified himself. Lara told him to enter. The Swede came in and took the open space beside Lara.

"*Vad fan hände?*"

She interpreted for Gang, "What the fuck happened?"

"You speak Swedish now?"

"No, but how hard is it?"

Björn stamped a foot. "*What* the fuck happened?"

The lie came to her quickly, like drawing a sidearm, one of the things she'd done to survive.

"We don't know. Maxim's dead. He fell off the train. Or he jumped."

247

"Or someone murdered him. That's what the Mongolian said."

"We don't know anything."

Björn pointed under the berth where Gang sat. "That's your bag."

"It is."

"You're moving in here now?"

"Just 'til we know what's going on. You can take care of yourself."

Björn nodded, his good nature trying to bubble up.

Lara asked, "What did Bat want to know?"

"Little things. Timelines. Conversations. My background."

"That didn't take long."

"I didn't know much about anyone else. I've been drinking a lot."

"You know about me."

"That's why he sent me to tell you."

Lara asked, "Tell me what?"

"He wants to see you next."

45
BAT

S he arrived carrying a garden tool and a plastic bag.
Bat stood from the booth. "Dr. Dill." He extended a hand. She did not take it and did not sit. Bat reeled in his hand.

She said, "I need to get off the train for a few minutes."

"You already know my answer."

"I work for the US embassy in Beijing. I'm an ionizing radiation expert. You've heard about Chernobyl?"

"What is that?"

In a few terse sentences, the American explained the emerging calamity in Ukraine and her duties collecting dirt, which sounded to Bat like a flimsy cover for espionage. But he saw no harm.

"I will go with you. There are only a few minutes left."

Leaving the dining car, he stepped down in front of her. The platform had begun to clear, the Trans-Mongolian blew its whistle. The American couldn't find soil without going to the far ends of the pavement; Bat wouldn't allow it. She threw a few bits of blue granite in her plastic bag, then the locomo-

249

DAVID L. ROBBINS

tive chugged and blasted steam. Bat and the American woman jumped onboard the diner car moments before it crept forward.

They returned to the booth where he'd set up shop.

"Please sit."

She took the cushioned bench on the other side of the table. The train trundled ahead, shaking itself to gain pace. Ulaanbaatar slid past. For the past six years, Bat only came to the city when he could visit his son, once or twice a year, always by a *marshrutka* shared taxi. He'd had no occasion to see this sooty railyard.

The American grew impatient.

"Are you going to ask me questions?"

He was older than the American woman by ten, fifteen years.

"I apologize. I'm not often away from home. Never without my wife."

"Let's see if we can't get you back to her quick enough."

"That would be excellent. We Mongolians are very close to our families. Did you know that during the time of the Mongol conquests, the wives and children of the warriors traveled with the horde?"

She shook her head and would not engage.

"You are not married, Doctor."

"And how would you know that?"

"It is a guess, like so much of what I am asked to do. On the passenger manifest, you are listed by the name in your passport. Luba Mikhailovna Dilkova. The married version would be Dilkovna."

"I'm from a country that isn't comfortable with Russia."

"As am I."

"So I go by Dill."

"You are Russian-born?"

"Yes."

"I understand this. The Russians have been in my country

250

for seventy years. They have tried to change a great many things in our culture. One was to ban the use of our clan names, as a way to force us to identify as Soviets rather than Mongolians. My name, for example, is Ovog Sükhii Bat. Sukh was my father. Bat is my given name. I chose a clan name the Soviets would not object to. Ovog simply means 'clan name.' But my true clan is Borjigon. It means Golden family of Genghis Khan. Once the Soviets are gone, I will reclaim it."

"Are you related to Genghis Khan?"

This made Bat laugh.

"Of course, Doctor. *You* are probably related to Genghis Khan."

"What can I help you with, Chief?"

"You can help me understand what happened on this train."

"What did Björn tell you?"

"Not very much. Your Swedish friend drinks too much."

"I don't tell him how to live. What did he say about me?"

"Nothing pertinent. Did you know? Genghis Khan said if a man gets drunk three times a month, it is a punishable offense. If he is drunk only twice a month, that is better. Once a month is praiseworthy. What could be better than not to drink at all? But where shall we find a man who never drinks?"

The American said, "I know what you're doing."

Bat could see that she did. So he continued.

"The Russians tore down all of the Great Khan's statues. They erased his image from our money, his name from our villages. Did you know Genghis Khan's real name was Temüüjin? It means blacksmith. The Soviets took away our national hero. In his place they brought vodka."

Dr. Dill flattened a hand on the tabletop. It lay there as a notice that she might smack the table.

She said, "You can stop now."

How badly was she trying to hide something?

Bat said, "We are slowly shedding the Soviets. All the

Lenin and Stalin statues have been taken down. We have our independence, and soon we will regain our culture. The whispers are that the new man in the Kremlin, Gorbachev, is going to pull out all Soviet troops."

The American woman tapped an index finger on the table. This was Bat's last warning.

"Mongolians understand why the Russians despise us. After all, we did conquer them."

Bat raised his own hand just as she raised hers.

"Dr. Dill."

"What?"

"Tell me what I am doing."

She lowered her palm. Her fingers squirmed on the wooden surface, massaging it until she could speak without rancor. The train picked up speed. The last industrial ugliness of the million-person city slid past in ill lighting. Bat said farewell to his son somewhere behind him.

The American said, "You're bullshitting. Just rambling. You want me to think you don't know anything, so you're playing confused cop. Good cop. You'll play somebody different for every one of us."

"Excellent."

"You haven't asked me any questions."

"To each according to his need. From each according to his ability. The Soviets taught us that, too. But, here, Doctor, I have a question for you."

Bat lay his hands on the table and leaned over them, a way to make her feel he was peering deep.

"Have you played good cop before?"

"And bad cop."

"You were an American policewoman."

"Ten years."

"Marvelous. I will enjoy our next conversation even more."

"Are we done?'

"This is just the introductory round."

"Why did you say you think Maxim was murdered?"

Bat consulted his watch. The time was nine p.m.

"It is almost five o'clock Moscow time. The restaurant will start dinner in a few minutes. We will talk again."

Bat rose to excuse her. Dr. Dill got to her feet. She wore her concern too plainly; for someone ticketed to ride all the way to Moscow, she appeared quite invested in being able to get off the train before then.

Dr. Dill slid out from the booth. Bat wouldn't call anyone else to question for another hour or so. Let the clock tick. If the passengers in second class were desperate, let them get a little more desperate.

46

GANG

On the platform before the dining car, Gang huddled in his polyester jacket. Chilly gusts razored up his sleeves and under his shirt; he'd not brought the right clothes for standing in the open on a train speeding toward Siberia.

He didn't peek inside the carriage door at Lara sitting with the Mongolian cop. Gang didn't want to be caught watching over her.

Twenty kilometers outside Ulaanbaatar, the rails rounded north. The open mesas and endless steppe grasses were done. The land rose on low hills and lapsed into valleys. The gray slumber of winter hadn't been shirked here. At home in Baoding, the greening of spring had taken hold in crocuses and cherry blossoms, but in these last stretches of Mongolia, under a starlit and gaudy sky, tendrils of snow lay in crevices like the fingers of a white witch.

When Lara emerged, Gang was half frozen, patting at his arms. He led the way back to the second-class carriage, warming slowly. Although the dining car was on Moscow time, the hundreds of passengers in the hard-class cars had kept to the schedules of their stomachs. They'd finished supper, tucked away their children, and gathered around cigarettes, pipes, vodka, and a violin and balalaika.

Gang put Lara in her cabin, then retrieved two cups of hot tea. Entering, he set hers on the table to cool.

He asked, "How'd it go?"

"He got under my skin a little." Lara ogled the steam rising from her cup while Gang sipped his. "He didn't ask me anything about Maxim, or anyone else. He just sat there going on about the Soviets, his family, and Genghis Khan."

"Anything else?"

"He was almost nice."

"That pissed you off?"

"Hand me the tea." When Gang hesitated, she pointed. "Give me the goddam tea."

Lara accepted the glass cup, held it to her lips and blew. She swapped the tea between hands as her fingertips scalded. The discomfort settled her even as it hurt.

"Sorry."

"It's okay."

"Russia's five hours away. He's in the dining car ordering fucking borscht."

"You hungry?"

"No. This…" Lara composed herself anew. "This is a sixty-year-old cop from a Podunk town in the middle of Mongolia."

"You said your father was a sixty-year-old cop."

"That's why Bat scares me."

"Yeah?"

"He's like my dad."

"How?"

Lara tried a sip of tea. She found it doable.

"He's good."

47

ANTON

KILOMETER 1671

Anton lay on his back, hands crossed at the belt, shoes on. Timur rested on his berth, dressed too, and in his boots.

Every several minutes the blackness in the cabin jittered when the *Rossiya* raced through a village. Lights beside the tracks made the compartment blink unsettlingly, as if sand were thrown in the eyes. The train ran through crossroads and lowered warning gates that rang loud, then dim, then gone. Sometimes the racket of the rails dissipated into the swales and open spaces; in others where the hills rose close to the tracks, or in towns where the sound echoed off the station-house or warehouses, the clatter swelled. Anton could not rest.

In the flashes of one passing village, he checked his watch. It told him what he knew, that dinner was served in the dining car.

Timur must have seen him move.

"I'm sorry, Antosh."

Anton sat up on his berth. In the feeble light the Chechen lay squashed between walls, knees up.

256

"No you're not."

Timur did not rise to speak. "I intended to leave the train, just as I said I would. Now I cannot."

"The Mongolian will figure it out. He'll catch you."

"He won't."

Anton got to his feet. "I'm going to go tell him."

"Alright."

Timur rolled his boots off the berth, down to the carpet. Sitting up, he seemed to follow his legs, they made up so much of him.

He said, "Think first."

"About what? The truth?"

The train coursed over moonless, starless ground under a tufted cloud cover. In the bleak light, Timur pointed at Anton's berth.

"Sit for a moment, Antosh."

Anton lowered to the edge of the berth. He buttressed his arms on his knees to show that he might stand at any moment of his own choosing.

He said, "I'm not afraid of you anymore."

"I can see that."

Timur folded arms across his great chest and said no more while the lights and noise of another village flared. He regarded Anton with a thin smirk that appeared and disappeared with the village.

Timur said, "So you will tell the Mongolian the truth."

"Yes."

"Which truth?"

"The one where you tried to strangle Maxim to death. Then Gang did it for you and you threw the body out this window. Where you are a beast who will try to destroy Russia."

Timur chortled in the resurgent dark.

"Do you hear yourself?"

Anton prepared to launch himself to the door. Out to the passageway. Run to the dining car.

"What do you mean?"

"I mean there are other, far more plausible truths at hand, Antosh."

Anton squeezed his own knees as if urging them to straighten, escape. He shouldn't listen to another word from Timur, a creature formed in jails, caves, tunnels, cold, anger.

Timur said, "Perhaps I will tell Bat the Mongolian that you threw Maxim off the train."

Anton drew back as if pushed. "That's ridiculous."

"Is it? Who was it everyone heard Maxim threatening? I was mentioned once, but he was very specific about the Jew scientist. Very heated, I recall."

"Bat wouldn't believe you."

"Wouldn't? I've told you, you're stupid. Why do you think Gang told you to go to the platform? Why did he have you talk loudly, as if you were ushering Maxim out there for some fresh air? Others heard you in the hallway, Antosh."

Anton's arms began to tremble. His hands lost their grip on his knees.

Timur said, "You were drinking all evening, we all saw it. Everyone knows you are frantic to get to Moscow to redeem yourself on a soapbox with your report about your runaway reactor. You argued with Maxim on the platform. He was depressed, insulting you that you do not love Mother Russia, you do not respect the dead of Afghanistan. But Maxim went too far. You are a proud man, an intellectual. Two drunks fighting. You pushed him off the platform. He fell. He died."

Timur wagged a finger. "And if you are considering telling the Mongolian that Gang did the killing? Oh my, Antosh. I would have my affairs in order."

The Chechen stood from his berth. He took up so much room that Anton recoiled. He had to look almost straight up into Timur's shadowed face.

"As for me traveling to Ukraine to blow up the Soviet Union? That is a bit grandiose, and without evidence. Just another lie from the murderer."

Timur opened the cabin door and ducked into the corridor. He left the door open for Anton to follow him to dinner.

48

BAT

E very booth in the restaurant car was filled by Mongols, Asians, and Russians who'd boarded in Ulaanbaatar. The servers were kept busy in a half-dozen languages.

Bat finished the last spoonful of an excellent beet soup. He brushed a last bit of black bread around the bowl. He emptied a second pot of tea. He should vacate the booth; others may be waiting to dine. The conductress had put him in Maxim Maximovich Sprygin's cabin. Bat hadn't entered it yet. He wanted context for the Agency man before he rifled through Maxim's privacy. That context would come from the second-class passengers, so Bat kept the booth.

The Trans-Mongolian knifed in and out of nighttime villages, terrifically isolated places except for the railroad track running through them. No celestial lights lit the black earth tonight; the barreling train felt lonely and remote, too.

Bat had traveled all over Mongolia, hunted it with rifle and bow, hound and hawk, ridden and walked it with Oyuun and his little ones, but he'd never left his country. He needed no visa to cross into Russia, but there had never been a border between himself and his family. Bat wanted to get off the train, too.

At the opposite end of the restaurant, the big Swede Björn ate with the English dandy. The Englishman had been eyeing Bat throughout the meal. When Bat dipped his last bread and poured his final drop of tea, the fop stood. The Swede left the dining car while the Englishman approached.

Standing before Bat's booth, he asked, "*Sain baina un?*"

"*Sain, ta sain baina un?*"

"*Sain.*"

The young Englishman switched to Russian: "May I join you?"

Bat motioned him to sit. "That was very good Mongolian. Do you speak it?"

"I have an ear for languages. I picked up a bit."

"Excellent." Bat snapped his fingers for a rotund Mongolian girl to clear the table, bring more tea, and an extra cup.

Bat kept his hands in his lap and did not reach for a handshake. He didn't yet know what part to play with this one.

"My name is Sinjin Alonso. I'm a diplomat with the British embassy in Beijing."

Sinjin Alonso had dressed for dinner in a pale-yellow silk jacket, threaded with greens and blues, a coat for a spring day. At his throat above a white Oxford shirt, a cravat copied the hues of the jacket. Sinjin Alonso's cuticles were trimmed, his nails buffed. His manner was like a white rabbit, innocent, quick, wary in the garden.

"How may I help you, Mr. Alonso?"

The Englishman immediately brightened. He leaned closer, covert, though no one in the busy dining carriage could hear their conversation.

"I'm the only one in second class who isn't going to Moscow."

"I've been shown the manifest. Your destination is Novosibirsk. What is your business there?"

"I'm on vacation. Collecting mushrooms in the Urals."

"A fascinating hobby. Beware of the *Amanita*."

"Yes!"

Bat asked, "Is this a tradition in your family?"

"I learned it from my father. I did quite a lot of it a few years back in the Irish forests. Beijing is too big, there's not enough open land."

"Work on your Mongolian, Mr. Alonso. We have room for you to wander."

"A beautiful country. I shall return."

Bat sat back to gain a moment of study across from Sinjin Alonso. This fop was not the sort to answer a direct question. He had to be come at it from the side.

Bat said, "Like you English, Mongolians put great stock in tradition, though the Soviets have tried to repress our ways. Many of us are Lamaistic Buddhists. Followers of the Dalai Lama. The Soviets made his teachings illegal and demolished temples. For the Soviets, faith means only brotherhood with Russia, acceptance of their leaders as our gods. But Mongolians have persevered in our worship. The Soviets are here today, they will be gone tomorrow. That is time measured by man. The spirits are here always. That is time measured by the infinite."

Sinjin Alonso asked, "If you don't mind, what faith are you?"

"I do not mind, Mr. Alonso. I can see you are an inquisitive and gifted young man."

The Englishman touched his hand to his breast.

Bat said, "Shamanism is also strong in our land. I wish to carry on the old ways, the ancestral voices and forces that flowed in Mongolia in millennia past. I am a shaman. Only a small one."

"Do you have children?"

"A boy and a girl."

"Will they be shamans?"

"A father wishes that his children may be anything, Mr. Alonso. My children will be anything but shamans. Here, since you seem interested."

Bat dug into one pocket for his small goatskin drum and the stick carved from a dwarf elm. He handed them across the table. The Englishman accepted them admiringly.

"What are these for?"

"The shaman's drum is how we call and answer the spirits. With the proper rhythm, a shaman can travel the unseen world."

Bat tapped a finger against the goat hide stretched over a wooden frame. The drum throbbed a tone deeper than its diminutive size.

"This is my travel drum."

Alonso held up the stick. "May I?"

"I would use caution, Mr. Alonso. There are white spirits and there are dark. You may call either without knowing it."

The young Englishman dipped his brow, then returned the drum and stick. Bat stowed them in his coat for later, when he would be alone in a dead man's cabin on a night train to Russia.

The Englishman rested his silk sleeves on the table, palms turned down, about to barter.

Bat asked, "How can I help you, Mr. Alonso?"

The fop rapped a knuckle on the table, pretending he'd just that instant thought of something.

"I suppose I'd like to be able to keep my appointments. In case you're still on the train all the way to Moscow."

"When do you arrive in Novosibirsk?"

"Day after tomorrow."

"I wish to be home with my family by then, Mr. Alonso. Perhaps we can assist each other?"

"My thought exactly."

"Please. Continue."

"I hope if I tell you what I know, you'll have no further need for me. And I may go my way."

"That would be ideal, of course. Would you like to begin now?"

Sinjin Alonso started with his description of Dr. Lara Dill, then the mysterious Chinese man Gang for whom she'd developed an affinity. He told what he knew of the Chechen mountain Timur and his unlikely friendship with the haughty Russian scientist Anton Epstein. Alonso was generous in his assessment of the good-natured Swede Björn Landsee.

Alonso said to Bat little of note, nothing the Swede or the American woman hadn't revealed, or Bat hadn't gleaned. He let the young Englishman prattle about Lara Dill's beauty; he called her a tough cookie, an arcane term that suited Alonso's own popinjay style. Anton Epstein was haughty, yet remorseful over Chernobyl; he felt responsible. The Chechen giant was reticent and unexpectedly intelligent, mystery wafted about him. Gang was a remarkable martial artist, hands fast as starlings, and had struck up an affinity with Lara Dill. Björn was kind, powerful, vulnerable, and private. Sinjin Alonso reserved none of his descriptive depth for himself. He observed only that he was rich and underutilized.

He supposed the people of the second-class car were good enough sorts. Bat taught him two more Mongolian words: the others in the carriage were *tanil*, his acquaintances, not *naiz*, friends.

The dining car cleared out. The Mongolian staff bussed the last booths. Bat held up a hand to stop the Englishman. He'd poured four pots of tea during their talk and soon would have to attend to his own kidneys.

Finally, Bat asked, "What of Maxim Maximovich Sprygin?"

"Him? A complicated man, I think."

"How so?"

"He started off stiff, you know? A bit Soviet. Pleasant

enough, in a professional sort of way. Then he literally assaulted me when I tried to take pictures of the desert in Choir. Threw his hand over my camera lens, almost knocked me down."

"This came as a surprise?"

"Quite."

"Though he was doing his job. There is a missile base in Choir."

"Didn't have to do it that way, mate."

"Do you feel Maxim had a temper?"

"Can't say I knew him well enough for that. He did apologize. We let him sit with us."

"We?"

"Everyone in second class. Björn picked up three bottles of vodka in Choir. We had drinks here in the diner. All but Timur, he doesn't touch the stuff."

"I know that vendor. His vodka makes a better disinfectant."

"I'll grant, the second bottle was better than the first."

"What sort of bottles were they? How many?"

"Three. All clear glass."

"What kind of stopper? Rag?"

"Corks."

"Did Maxim drink with the passengers?"

"Yeah. He got a bit in his cups."

"How did he behave after he apologized? With the group?"

"He buttoned up while the rest of us nattered. After a while, Anton asked him about himself. Maxim told us about his parents. He got a bit maudlin when he talked about Afghanistan."

"I know he was in the Red Army."

"Some mine he drove over, killed a bunch of his Russian boys. Maxim was pretty down in the mouth over that."

"Would you go so far as to say he appeared depressed?"

"Yeah. And drunk."

With that, Sinjin Alonso ground to a halt. He rested elbows on the table then knit his manicured fingers. The colorful Englishman looked at his joined hands as though to consider their worth. After thoughtful moments and a sigh, two affectations of a diplomat, he opened them, signaling that he had arrived at the core of the matter. That he'd wrestled with a difficult decision and had chosen to speak, to further justice.

Sinjin Alonso said, "I'm afraid Maxim got into a row at the table."

"Really? With whom?"

"Anton."

"Had he been drinking?"

"Oh, yeah. Him and Maxim both. You know, Russians. Maxim in particular got pretty sloshed, and quite wretched about Afghanistan. I suppose he wasn't the first fellow to see too much in a war."

Bat checked his watch. Four more hours to Sukhbaatar. He needed to visit the water closet and it could not be put off any longer. The earlier events at the table with three bottles of homebrew vodka, six second-class passengers, one killer, one victim, could wait.

"Thank you, Mr. Alonso. I'll take it from there with Dr. Epstein."

"We're finished?"

"You've been very helpful. We will speak again in a few hours. Would you please send Dr. Epstein to the diner?"

Sinjin Alonso was slow to be dismissed.

"Alright then. One last thing?"

"Yes?"

"Later, after we all went to our cabins, I heard Anton walk Maxim out to the landing. Anton said they should get some fresh air."

"Thank you for your observations, Mr. Alonso."

Standing, the Englishman swung his head, somber. This plain show of grief was a reminder that he found the whole affair distressing, that he was innocent, and that he and Bat had an understanding. The fop reached for a handshake to seal it.

If Bat was still on the train in Novosibirsk, or farther, he would not let Sinjin Alonso go. Or anyone else in second class. But right now, he saw no reason to take the carrot from this nibbling rabbit.

Bat shook hands. Sinjin Alonso turned away. When the diner's door closed behind him, Bat hurried from the booth.

49

ANTON

APRIL 29
KILOMETER 1727

S talin's favorite movies were American westerns, this was common knowledge. For decades, even after his death, millions of Soviet children, boys especially, were raised on the quick-draw sheriff, the dark-hatted villain, the brave and brutal red man, the plains pioneer, working violence on one another.

The fellow sitting in the diner booth, who did not stand when Anton entered, looked like a myth from those American movies. He wore a broad-shouldered saddle coat and boots. He was thick-bellied, unshaven, and dusty enough. He did not remove his wide-brim hat.

The Mongolian opened a hand to indicate the cushioned bench across from him.

"Dr. Epstein. Please."

Anton slid into the booth. "It's midnight."

"Or it is eight p.m.? Does this not drive you crazy?"

"I consider it inconvenient. Logic often is. What can I do for you, Mr. Bat?"

"Chief Bat."

The Mongolian did not shake hands. He insisted on his title.

"Chief. How may I help?"

"You boarded the train yesterday morning."

"In Beijing. At dawn."

"My goodness, Dr. Epstein. What does one do on a train for so long? With so far to go?"

"Sleep. Eat. Look out the window at various versions of nothing."

"Drink?"

The question felt sudden and rude.

"Occasionally."

"I understand you are a scientist."

"A nuclear physicist. We are called atomschiki."

If Bat could insist on his title, so could Anton.

"A moment ago, you mentioned logic. I imagine every atomschiki, every scientist, must be to varying degrees a logician. To arrange the known in its proper order. Sometimes even to skip over the unknown, to find the next step."

"You could put it like that."

Chief Bat lay his wrists on the table and leaned onto them. His oilcloth greatcoat creaked. Wind would not pierce it, a mantle across his shoulders would shrug off rain and snow. What type of man was inside such a coat? Bat had the badge of a sheriff, the ruddy face of the natives in the old Westerns, a hat filthy and brown; he smelled of soil and horse.

Bat said, "When my son was very young, our favorite place in Ulaanbaatar was the International Intellectual Museum. It's full of puzzles, conundrums, and logic games. To be honest, I enjoyed it more than my son. These days when I visit him in the city, I go there alone."

Anton said, "You might have made a fine scientist."

Bat smiled this away. "The spirits made no such mistake with me. I am what I always was."

DAVID L. ROBBINS

"Chief. Despite the Moscow clock, we'll be at the border in three hours. I'd like to sleep some if I can. If I can assist you with your investigation, I'd like to get to it."

"Certainly, Doctor. My apologies. I tend to maunder. My wife tells me the only time I follow a straight line is when I'm in a saddle."

Anton was not tempted to smile. The hour was late. And he was wary of the Mongolian.

Bat said, "Tell me why you feel responsible for Chernobyl?"

Anton did not mean to react, did not realize he had. Something in the way he held himself made Bat lift a finger off the table.

He said, "These are someone else's words, not mine."

There was the opening gambit. The magician's left hand, distracting from the right. Anton, Björn, Sinjin, Lara, the ones Bat had spoken to so far. He was pitting them against each other. A tournament of words. What was it Timur said? One story.

Anton asked, "What does this have to do with Maxim's death?"

"Logic, Doctor. Puzzles. Leaps across the chasms of the unknown."

Anton had left Beijing expecting to be interrogated, by the press, the Soviet scientific community, the government, he'd imagined perhaps even Gorbachev sitting him down for a debate. But not like this, in the small hours in a railroad dining car, questioned by a Mongolian sheriff who dressed like a cowboy. Anton was versed in the greatest power on earth, nuclear power that could electrify or destroy the planet. Not museum riddles and small-town petty thefts. The RBMK reactor which he helped create had riveted the attention of the world, a spectacle even as it died. He, an atomschiki, was enduring a slow, miserable train ride with an assemblage of sots, peacocks, and murderers, in order to

270

ride into Moscow where he was going to testify before the world.

"I was a senior engineer at the Chernobyl nuclear power station in Ukraine. Four years ago, I conducted a study that uncovered several risks we had designed into the Chernobyl reactors. These risks were theoretical, taken for the purposes of efficiency and cost. Apparently, they have become reality."

"Why were you in Beijing and not Ukraine?"

If Bat were asking this, he did not know. Or he did.

One story.

"My report was rejected. As a result, I was exiled to China."

"I'm sorry. And now you are defying your exile?"

"I am."

"Dr. Epstein. That must fill you with pride. And some trepidation."

"A bit of each."

"You are going home." Bat said this wistfully, the notion of home. He shook a thick finger at Anton. "I know what you are."

"What is that?"

"A truthteller."

"Perhaps."

"You know, there are truth-telling spirits."

"Chief Bat, I don't mean to be impolite, but I have no interest in spirits. My work is in the realm of mankind."

"Just as well. Like you, those spirits rarely tell us what we want to hear. Perhaps you are like...what is his name? The gulag fellow."

"Solzhenitsyn."

"Him."

"No."

Bat leaned back to behold Anton. He tugged the brim of his hat, working on his puzzle.

Anton prodded. "Chief."

Bat animated out of his short reverie. "Dr. Dill has described the consequences of the accident in Chernobyl. They sound horrific. You say they were predicted by you. You are returning to Moscow to reveal state secrets. Name names, as they say. I wish you luck."

"Why is that?"

"I am Mongolian. We are no longer enamored of Russia. Tell me about the argument with Maxim in the dining car."

Anton couldn't get a fix on Bat's quicksilver moods, whirligig ploys, and logic games.

"I did not kill him."

The Chief cocked his head. "Why would you make that your answer?"

"Because that is what lies behind your question."

The Chief leaned in again, hands in his lap.

"Please answer my question."

"Maxim told us about a terrible incident in Afghanistan. Soldiers died, his friends. He believed he bore the fault. I'd shared with him my purpose for returning to Russia. I suppose he took it that I was being insufficiently patriotic. He felt mocked. By criticizing the Soviet government, I was making light of the sacrifice of his comrades in Afghanistan."

"But you weren't."

"Of course not."

"It does seem, however, Doctor, that you do intend to do exactly what Maxim feared. You will publicly accuse the USSR of malfeasance for the reactor accident in Chernobyl. You plan to reveal that it was preventable. That _you_ could have prevented it, if they had allowed it. They did not, they sent you away, and that is to the Soviet Union's shame."

"I don't view it like that. I want to make nuclear power safer. To make my country better. More transparent. This is in line with the thinking of our new First Secretary Gorbachev."

"Maxim didn't see how similar you two were."

"I beg your pardon?"

"You both carried burdens of regret. You feel the weight of deaths on your hands. His remorse drove him to suffer. Yours drives you to Moscow. He did not deserve to die, Doctor."

"No, he did not."

"Nor do you. You should be aware that we have the death penalty in Mongolia for murder. For a nation of very few, we use it surprisingly often."

"What are you saying?"

"Something happened in the second-class carriage. There are six passengers. You are too clever not to know something about the death of Maxim Maximovich Sprygin. Tell me about the events after the argument."

Anton felt punched. He worked his jaw as if it had really happened. Death penalty? He'd done nothing wrong. In fact, he'd done much right, much to be proud of, with more to do. Maxim had mourned twenty soldiers lost in a foreign war. Maxim was dead, lamentably, but the argument could be made that there was something wrong with him, whether it was anger, depression, alcohol, all of it, some of it. Maxim's fate may have been inevitable. It may have caught up with him.

Anton's tasks were to prevent the murder of millions, stop the lies of the USSR, and set the record straight of his own exile. A lie or two to this Mongolian was nothing.

"Are you trying to threaten me, Chief Bat?"

"I am trying to get off this train, Doctor."

"Björn led Maxim back to the second-class carriage. The mood around the table was spoiled, of course, so the rest of us returned to our rooms, as well."

"All of you at the same time?"

"Yes. We've become somewhat friendly crawling across Asia."

"Then what, Doctor?"

"Timur and I settled into our cabin to rest before arriving at the border."

"Timur, the big Chechen. Did he respond to Maxim at the table? Before everyone went their separate ways?"

"He rose to his feet to defend me."

Now the moment had arrived, for Anton to put Bat on a new scent.

Anton said, "Or."

Bat repeated this as a question. "Or?"

"Perhaps he was upset."

"What would he be upset about?"

"Some things Maxim said about him."

The Mongolian blinked, a small motion, the click of an abacus.

"Such as?"

"Maxim questioned Timur's service in Afghanistan."

"Alright, Doctor. Following that, you and Timur returned to your cabin. Did Timur seem upset?"

"A bit. He calmed down once we were away from the others."

"Were you bothered by Maxim?"

"There was no cause. Maxim was a stranger to me. And frankly, a little pitiable."

"Then what?"

"A few minutes later, Maxim arrived outside our door. He pounded on it and shouted threats."

"Threats?"

"He claimed he would have the KGB waiting for me in Naushki, to be arrested as a traitor. And he would demand they investigate Timur."

"Why Timur?"

"I have no idea. I assume you will ask him."

Bat grinned. Anton feared he'd overplayed his hand. Best to leave Timur to Timur. One story.

"Continue, Doctor."

"Maxim was making quite the infuriated scene in the corridor. We opened the door to invite him in. To talk. Assure him I meant no injury or insult to him or the Soviet Union. Maxim and I began to get on well enough."

"And Timur?"

Anton had to lie coolly.

"Timur did little talking. Then Gang came into the cabin."

"What was his purpose?"

"He'd heard the threats and banging. I suppose he thought he could help us quiet Maxim down. If I recall correctly, it was Gang who suggested I walk Maxim out to the landing for some fresh air."

"Did you?"

Here was the first snare. Anton was about to place himself on the open platform with Maxim moments before the Agency man's supposed leap or fall. Gang had fixed Anton in the corridor talking with an imaginary Maxim. Someone had heard him speak. Sinjin, Lara, Björn.

No way to lie here.

"Yes."

"Did you take a vodka bottle with you?"

With the speed of thought, keeping a blank face, Anton replayed the actual events. Gang sent him to retrieve the vodka from Lara's room. Gang made Maxim drink. Then Maxim died. The bottle went out the window. Then Maxim.

"Lara Dill had taken the last vodka bottle from the table. Gang sent me to her room for it. I knocked but she was asleep. I entered, found the bottle, and brought it back to my cabin."

"Maxim drank more?"

"He did."

"Did you?"

"No."

"Did the bottle go with you two out to the landing?"

"Maxim carried it."

"What happened on the platform?"

"Maxim and I talked for two or three minutes. He seemed resolved that he'd behaved badly. He said he was very sorry. He brought up Afghanistan again and appeared terribly sad. I felt it best to leave him to his thoughts. I returned to my cabin."

"You left him out on the platform with the vodka bottle, drinking."

"Yes."

Bat said, "And that's the end of it."

"Until you arrived in dramatic fashion."

Bat dipped his brow. He seemed satisfied and inscrutable, all at once.

Had Anton been convincing? Told his story and masked his intent well enough? Had he left anything out?

Damn it. The window. The opened window.

Bat had spoken to Natalya. Had she mentioned Gang's visit, the triangle key?

Anton should snap his fingers, bring up the window. No, that would put too much emphasis on it, make the window and the key objects of interest. Better to claim later that he'd forgotten them as irrelevant details.

What if Timur or Gang report the window in their upcoming conversations with the Mongolian? Anton's omission will be suspicious.

Did the Mongolian already know? Did he not? In that moment, Anton hated Bat.

Under the table, his hands balled. Anton was unaccustomed to the murkiness of lying. Science had none of it. Science was cold and clear, neither good nor bad. He had to leave the diner car before he betrayed himself.

Anton stood without asking if they were done. The Mongolian raised a hand.

"One more question."

Anton eyed the door out of the dining car.

"Yes?"

"Doctor, what do you think happened?"

"Maxim was intoxicated. He was wobbling when I left him on the platform. He may have fallen."

Bat rose from the booth to face Anton. His greatcoat fell past his calves, the hat shaded his eyes.

"Come with me."

The Mongolian headed for the portal out of the restaurant car. He didn't look back, expecting Anton to follow.

The platform between carriages was lit only vaguely through the dining car window. In the moonless night the rushing train lit a nondescript ground of weed and gorse. The squeals of wheels and springs made Bat raise his voice.

"The body was found in the desert beside a long straightaway in the tracks."

Anton said, "A drunkard will stumble."

"True. You say Maxim was drinking heavily from the bottle."

"Yes."

"The bottle was found corked."

"He may have had his fill."

Again, Bat said, "True," and nodded to himself. Loudly, he added, "But."

The Mongolian leaned far out to point the direction the train left behind. His long coat flapped around his legs.

"The bottle was found two hundred meters up the track. Through the Gobi, the Trans-Mongolian averages eighty kilometers per hour. That means ten seconds before Maxim lost his balance, so badly he plummeted off the train, he let go of the bottle. One would think these two incidents might be more simultaneous."

Bat reeled himself in from the wind.

"Your thoughts?"

"Perhaps he jumped."

Bat rubbed the stubble on his round brown chin. He feigned as if he were considering this for the first time.

"Maxim Maximovich Sprygin was depressed. Very drunk. Traumatized from the war. That was the condition in which you brought him out onto the landing, yes?"

"It was."

"And that was how you left him. Troubled. Drinking. Alone. Perhaps on the verge of suicide."

"Yes."

"A jump from the train is possible."

"I agree."

Bat wrapped both hands around the platform railing to gaze down. He shouted over the swirling night.

"Leaving him out here in that condition seems unkind, Doctor."

Anton said, "Goodnight, Chief." He turned for the door handle, knowing how much he should walk away.

Bat asked, "Did you argue with Maxim on the platform? Was there an altercation?"

Anton dropped his chin and turned from the door.

"What are you implying?"

"I imply nothing. I am asking transparent questions. I want you to see what I see."

"And that is?"

"According to the story you relate and the observations of others, you were the last passenger with Maxim Maximovich Sprygin. You had argued. You were both intoxicated. You were alone with him on a platform between carriages. It is difficult to envision that he fell by accident on a straight stretch of track. And I remain unconvinced that he leaped."

Bat rested a hand on Anton's shoulder.

"When Maxim Maximovich Sprygin left the train, he did not land on his feet. He struck first on his head. This snapped his neck."

"Then that is what killed him."

Bat lay his other hand on Anton's open shoulder. Anton couldn't tell whether Bat was being sympathetic or recreating a tussle with him out here on the platform.

"I try to believe the spirits when they talk, Doctor. I wish to believe my fellow man. But when logic speaks, I trust it most of all."

Face-to-face, closer than they'd been across the booth, Bat in his cowboy getup would make most men take a back step. Anton would have, but Bat held him by the shoulder.

Bat said, "In Mongolia, there is a saying. Many will put their finger in the mouth of a dead bear."

"What does that mean?"

"That the danger for you has passed. I am here. I will protect you. If you will tell me what happened."

Bat shook Anton by the shoulders, just a little more than the train shook them both.

What would Anton say? Gang was the killer? Invite Bat to come see the window in the cabin where the body went out?

Or he could lay the murder on Timur? Have him arrested in Mongolia, far from Chernobyl?

But Timur didn't do it, and there was not a speck of proof that he did.

Nor did anything implicate Gang.

What of the lies Anton had already told? What of the fact that he'd helped Gang and Timur dispose of Maxim? He had thrown out the damn bottle.

Timur had warned that he and Gang would join to say it was Anton. Two drunks fought on the platform. Maybe the bottle was used as a club between them and flew out of a hand ten seconds before Maxim was shoved over the railing, landing on his head.

This version actually fit Bat's spatter of facts.

Gang and Timur were the phantoms of powerful, sinister forces. Timur was a mujahideen. Gang, an assassin. There would be a blood price for pointing the finger at either of them.

The air whipping Bat's long coat and hair gave him the appearance of floating.

But the Mongolian didn't yet know what happened to Maxim on this train. Bat had only guesses that he called logic. Circumstances he pretended were evidence. He was resorting to threats, and empathy.

Bat hadn't solved it. He would not solve it.

One story. The story where Anton was innocent. Where he found a way to stop Timur. Where Anton returned to Moscow and was hailed.

Anton said, "Maxim fell. Or he jumped. Or he argued and struggled with one of the other five hundred people on this train. That is all."

He stepped back, breaking contact with Bat's hands. The Mongolian dropped both arms, his face soft with fatigue. Anton left him in the wind.

50

TIMUR

Anton entered the cabin agitated. He plopped on the edge of the berth, then gripped the cushion. He looked like a man on the lid of a casket that was trying to open under him.

He spoke without looking up at Timur. "I hate that I have nowhere else to go but in here."

Timur hadn't moved from the moment Anton returned. He didn't uncross his arms or sit away from the always shuddering wall.

"We have three more days of this, Antosh."

Anton chewed his lower lip. Timur wondered if the scientist had another sweater to wear. Three more days of looking at him.

"What happened with the Mongolian?"

"I don't know. Nothing. Something."

"Did you say anything regrettable, Antosh?"

"No. But he tried. He interrogated me."

"Have you never been interrogated?"

Anton released his clutch on the mattress to emphasize his frustration with the question.

"Why on earth would I have been?" He gripped the cushion again. The casket under him may have moved.

Timur sat forward. He knocked the back of his hand against Anton's knee.

"Antosh?"

The scientist worked to ignore him, dropping his chin to his chest like a child. Timur rapped his knee harder. "Lift your face. This is no time to cry."

"Fuck you."

"There we are."

When Anton glanced up, he was startled that Timur had come so close to him, filling the space between them. Anton sat back.

Timur said, "Interrogators don't look first for answers. They look for who *has* the answers. It is always the ones who try to outthink them. Did you do this?"

"I don't know."

"Then you did. How did you leave it?"

"Bat doesn't believe Maxim fell off the train. Or that he jumped."

"Good for him. He's correct."

Anton explained the Mongolian's theories, the discovery of the corked vodka bottle ten seconds up the track, the straightaway stretch of rail through the Gobi. How Maxim landed on his head and broke his neck.

Timur asked, "Did you stick to the story?"

"You mean the one where I'm the last person to see Maxim?"

"Yes, Antosh. That one."

"I did. You and Gang are bastards."

Timur shut off the gooseneck lamp in the wall. He stretched out as best he could. For the first time, he kicked off his boots. This was a swipe at Anton, that he intended to, and could, rest.

Anton worked his hands again, at Timur's silence.

The scientist remained on the edge of his berth, shoes planted on the carpet, ready for something. He wanted Timur to explain things, say all was well and they were safe. He wanted so much for Timur to be the only villain in the cabin.

The Mongolian had shared the direction of his investigation with Anton. Why? Why tell Anton?

To drop the first stone into the pond, then watch where the ripples go.

Bat suspected one of two things: Anton had killed Maxim, or Anton knew who did. If Anton was indeed the murderer, he would tell no one of their conversation. If Anton was not the killer but knew who was, he would warn them. Bat was playing a game far beyond Anton's understanding.

Timur checked his watch. Sukhbaatar in a hundred minutes. Then the Russian border.

The Mongolian would knock on their cabin door soon. Timur shut his eyes.

51

BAT

The conductress unlocked Maxim's cabin for Bat. She
stepped back but not very far.

"Here you go, Chief."

In the narrow corridor, he brushed past. The woman was
compelling. She was a lure and a warning together, like the
mouth of a cave.

Natalya waited until Bat had turned on the table lamp
before closing him in. He spread the vents of his greatcoat to
sit on the dead man's berth. The cabin was neat, the berth
unslept in. Maxim Maximovich Sprygin had not lived a day
and a night on this train.

The last open spaces of Mongolia rolled past in a blind
night. Bat clicked off the lamp to let the dark flow in and
release himself into it. He tried to lower the window to invite
the wind but found the frame screwed shut. Every tock of the
wheels beneath him swept him farther from his home. He
wondered what he would be barred from beyond the border,
what would be denied him in Russia.

Bat had no hope to find clues in Maxim's cabin. The

Agency man's wounds had been deeper than his body, cut into his soul. Maxim had gotten drunk and opened himself to wrath. The spirits of his soldier friends had flocked to his anger, fed themselves on it, all of them killed too young, died in flame on foreign earth. They had no voice for their pain but Maxim.

From his pocket, Bat pulled his drum and stick. He struck the skin once but the sound had no resonance in the quaking, squeaking compartment. The *ongods*, the ancients, ancestors and shamans before him, were not with him leaving Mongolia.

Bat set aside the drum and stick. He could summon no spirit with them, and Maxim did not linger in this room. Bat peered into the tarry night.

For thirty minutes he sat as emptily as he could. He did not tote up facts or speculate, prove and disprove, label lies or truths. There was no then, there was no now, all was always, and the barriers were only what he believed. Bat did not listen to the steel train or sense its shakes, he heard and felt nothing, and in the nothing lay everything.

On the dark flatlands, entering no village, for no reason Bat could figure, the locomotive whistled. Perhaps the engineer had gone too long with silence and wanted in his ear a voice he understood and loved. So he summoned his train to hoot at the blackness.

Bat turned on the cabin light.

52

TIMUR

When the tap came at the door, Timur let Anton answer it. He stayed supine on his berth in his stocking feet.

The Mongolian entered, apologetic for the hour. Timur remained still while the policeman sat next to Anton. Timur came upright but did not click on the gooseneck lamp behind him. Bat and Anton sat in light, Timur in half-dark.

He checked his watch. 2:30 a.m. Beijing time. Who gave a fuck what time it was in Moscow?

Timur asked, "Sukhbaatar in thirty minutes. Are you coming with us to Russia?"

The Mongolian nodded. "It appears so."

Bat had not removed his hat or oilcloth coat; the man looked capable of being dropped anywhere on earth and surviving. The Afghan fighters were like this, hardy as mountain goats, living outdoors as much as under a roof. Timur had become this, too, sleeping in caves and mines, feral by firelight, in the company of hunger, fear, and cold as often as with

286

men. Anton, the civilized Russian, was nothing like the two of them.

The Mongolian looked worn out.

Timur said, "You have had a long day. Would you like to continue in the morning?"

The policeman exhaled a deep breath and surveyed the cabin. He inclined his head to see from under his brim. Bat might have been in the sun the way he winced; he seemed to see a great distance, though everything but the ceiling was close enough for Timur to touch without standing, and he would scrape the ceiling with his head if he did stand.

Bat sighed. "In fact, yes. Thank you."

Anton and Bat sat side by side. Bat paid him no attention.

The Mongolians said, "One question."

"Of course."

"Maxim banged on your door, shouting."

"He was threatening Anton."

"I understand he was also threatening you."

"After a fashion."

"Over what?"

"I don't believe he knew. He was hurt, and very drunk."

"You must be able to guess."

"Of course I can." Timur opened his palms. "I was a mujahideen in Afghanistan."

Bat leaned away a few centimeters to cross his arms over his chest. His tired face scrunched. Anton lofted both eyebrows; in the circumstance, that was all he could do.

It was clear Anton hadn't told Bat this.

The Mongolian said, "You are Moslem."

"Yes. I think the Agency man sensed it. His time in the war had taught him to love all things Russian. And to hate his enemies."

"Were you his enemy?"

"I was once. But no more, Chief, no, no. I spent four years

287

at forced labor in Soviet mines. My wife died in a Russian torture cell. That cured me of caring enough about the Soviets to oppose them. I have no desire to repeat the experience."

Bat looked into his own lap, then cocked his head Anton's way. He wanted to ask Anton why he'd said nothing of this. When he did not, Timur asked for him.

"Antosh, you did not tell him?"

The scientist flubbered. "These are not the sort of things one shares about another."

"Of course, of course. Thank you for protecting my privacy."

Timur addressed Bat. "Anton and I have become friendly. As much as I will be friends with a Russian."

The Mongolian's nod showed his sympathy on this point.

Bat stood from the berth. He and Anton had not exchanged a single look. Bat had not come to talk to Timur, but to talk to Timur *in front* of Anton.

The Mongolian asked, "Why were you in Beijing?"

"I have a wealthy friend there, a Uyghur. Shah Barat. He runs his family's construction business. I went to ask for work. Shah Barat will confirm this."

"I am certain. Where do you live?"

"I keep a flat in Peshawar. I can give you the address."

"What is your business in Moscow?"

"I am a miner by trade. There is good paying work in Ukraine."

"Where?"

"At Chernobyl."

"Truly? The ruined plant?"

"They're digging a tunnel under it to stop the nuclear material from burning into the ground."

"It sounds dangerous."

"Have you ever been in a mine?"

Bat waved it all away. "We'll continue in the morning." He nodded to Timur, and curtly to Anton. "Please stay in your cabin. The stop in Sukhbaatar will be hours-long for customs."

Once the Mongolian had left, Timur lay back, arms behind his head.

Anton hissed, "Why did you do that?"

"Do what?"

"Tell him about Afghanistan, prison, the mines."

"I had no idea if you had told him or not. I thought it best not to hide it."

"But I *didn't* tell him."

"You should have. It is a game. You have three days to learn it."

Timur had asked Bat nothing about the vodka bottle, the Agency man's broken neck, none of the ripples the policeman had dropped in Anton.

Anton said, "Now he thinks I'm being secretive."

Timur shut his eyes. Twenty minutes to Sukhbaatar.

"You are, Antosh. But you did not kill anyone, and the Mongolian cannot prove you did. So close your mouth and give me twenty minutes of peace."

53

LARA

G ang lay on his berth like he was dead, as though a coroner had arranged him. Face up, toes up, arms at his sides, hands beside his pockets, thumbs up. He wore all black and in the dark cabin Lara could not see him breathe.

She didn't remember lying down on her own berth, just sitting with her head on his shoulder. Gang must have arranged her once she fell asleep. The door was locked. Lara rolled onto a shoulder to look across the carpet at him.

She had no notion where the train was, how close to the Russian border. The world was lightless, the clack of the rails softened through the berth's cushion and the pillow. Eyes on Gang, Lara contemplated how every one of her options came back to him.

In minutes, the train stuttered, the first tap on the brakes. In the corridor, the conductress rang out, always like a circus master: "This is Sukhbaatar. Sukhbaatar. The train will stop for three hours. Please stay in your cabins. Customs agents will come aboard. Have all luggage ready to be inspected. This is Sukhbaatar."

Natalya began to vacuum.

Gang didn't stir. She sensed he was awake, heedful. The Trans-Mongolian slowed in the first outskirts of the last Mongolian city. Stripes of yellow light played over Gang. Lara sat up. His hands left his sides.

She shushed him.

"Stay."

The train lurched as Lara moved to him across the small divide. She lay down with him, her back to his chest. When Gang did not put a hand on her, she groped behind to pull his arm across her waist like a blanket. She fit her fingers into the grooves between his knuckles.

He breathed against her ribs, his nose peeking through the drape of her hair against her nape. The locomotive sighed to stop itself; in the corridor the vacuum howled. More electric lights spilled through the window as the city thickened around the tracks, but Lara shut her eyes against it all so the night and Gang's closeness would not dispel.

54

GANG

April 30
Kilometer 1928

Sukhbaatar's customs man came into the second-class carriage with the first slips of dawn. He was pudgy in a city-dweller's way, with a drinker's knobby nose and the jet hair of a Mongolian. Lacy light lit him while he unzipped Gang's soft bag and opened Lara's small luggage, backpack, and soil collection case. He tipped a toe against the yellow Geiger counter and the ionization chamber beneath the berth where Gang had slept and she had joined him. The portly man scribbled something on a thin page, tossed it on the empty berth, dipped his head Good morning, and left.

Sitting up beside each other, Gang and Lara shared the same little head shakes. After hours of lying entwined, breathing in pace, dozing, it seemed wrong to have been interrupted by such an officious and unhandsome man in gray light.

Lara kissed his cheek. It was the first time she'd kissed him, but lovely. It felt like it had come after many such things.

She said, "I have to go out. Soil sample."

"Leave it, Lara."

"No." She fell away from him to sit up. She said, "Go get tea."

Gang slipped past her on the berth, unlocked the cabin door and stepped out. The row of windows in the corridor showed the cordovan hills that cupped the small city, and the grime of Sukhbaatar's train station. Freight cars waited on side rails; oil spills, litter, and smutty gravel blotched the earth; and squat Mongolians moved about in sooty jackets. Everything about Sukhbaatar looked chilly. A few dozen bundled-up passengers arrived hefting luggage toward the hard-class cars for the journey into Russia.

At the samovar, Gang filled a steaming cup. He dropped in a teabag. The Mongolian policeman in his brimmed hat and greatcoat climbed the steps.

They greeted each other in Russian.

"*Privet.*"

Gang asked, "Where were you?"

Bat removed his hat. Black strands of hair were swept back off his broad forehead, matted by too many hours under the hat. One lock fell loose; Bat tucked it behind a thick ear.

"I had to step out for a few minutes. Some brisk air to wake me up."

"You've been standing here the whole time we've been in the station?"

"I'll sleep after Naushki. Anyone who wants to leave the train while we're moving can just jump." Bat caught himself. He said, "I'm sorry, that was poor humor. I'm tired."

"Do you really have police in the train station?"

"No. There wasn't time."

"So I can just walk off?"

"Mr. Gang, is it?"

"Just Gang."

"I did not lie, Gang, when I said I could have any of you

found in an hour in Mongolia. Another troubling legacy of Soviet occupation is a robust network of informants."

"How about in Russia?"

"I've been told there will be officers at every station. One of you may try. We will find out."

The Mongolian returned his hat to his head, his short break over.

"You and I have not spoken yet, Gang. I will need some rest first."

"I'll see you in Russia."

"In Russia, then."

Gang handed the Mongolian the hot cup. Bat took it in a hand that looked like it could hold embers.

In the middle of the carriage, Lara shambled out from her cabin. She approached carrying her trowel and a plastic bag. She'd wrapped herself in a green shawl.

"You gave him my tea."

She'd said this in English. The Mongolian did not understand; he raised the cup in greeting.

Lara took the gesture wrong. "That's my fucking tea."

Gang said, "I'll make another one. Go."

Lara led the Mongolian down the short steps, grumpily on a search for a patch of soil. Gang drained more scalding water from the samovar into a cup. He tossed in a teabag, then set the cup on a stair leading down from second class. The hot water misted into the morning, cooling, because that was how Lara liked her tea.

RUSSIA

55

BAT

KILOMETER 1951

B at sat at the window waiting for the sliding land to change names, histories, ghosts.

Soon the train clattered over a bridge and a river wide enough for fishing boats and a barge. A sign named the ribbon of water the Selenge River. Nothing else said welcome to Russia.

Bat felt no different outside Mongolia. This disappointed him a mite. Perhaps some ancestor might have sent him a shiver or an ache, something to bid farewell or a warning. In dead Maxim's cabin, Bat sat alone. His other self, far behind in the Gobi, had never been this alone.

On the north bank of the river, the train whistled to tell the border town ahead that it was coming. The Selenge wandered away west but not out of sight. Bat imagined himself on the water, on a raft with fish jumping at bugs now that the sun was up, drifting south to home.

He left Maxim's cabin as the train decelerated into Naushki. No one else was in the corridor yet, not even Natalya. Bat visited the water closet. He could barely piss,

297

he'd had so little water through the night. The mirror reflected him rumpled and sleep-deprived. Bat tugged down his brim as if he might hide from his image.

In the corridor, Natalya announced the train's arrival. Even at dawn the woman looked honed, impervious to the hours.

"This is Naushki. All passengers must bring out their paperwork for passport control. The train will stay here one hour. This is Naushki."

She did not vacuum but stationed herself at the samovar, blocking the way to the steps down from second class. Bat knocked on every door to gather passports and diplomatic visas. Gang opened Dr. Dill's cabin to hand over their papers. Gang kept the door partly closed; the air around him suggested he could use a change of clothes. Gang had not expected to be on this train long.

Bat said, "It's Russia now."

"I'll come talk to you."

"After I get some rest. Will Dr. Dill want to collect her dirt?"

"She'll skip this one."

Bat carried the passengers' travel documents into the station, a stout yellow and gray structure of rectangles and arched windows. Viewed from the tracks, the town appeared valued by the Soviets only for the trains. A few thousand Soviets lived here on the edge of the empire. Naushki had her purpose and was left to it.

Bat used his badge to cut to the front of the long customs line. He got stamps on all the papers and a visa for his police business in the USSR. Headed back to the train across terracotta tiles, Bat took in the view of Naushki, a town of boxy buildings and square homes packed like groceries on a shelf. No arid Gobi wind crossed his cheek, just the damp of a river. The Russians were white as a deer's tail, Bat was the color of a fox. He'd travelled just ten kilometers into Russia and already couldn't shake how foreign he felt.

Overhead, the morning mist off the river melted away. Bat pushed his hand onto a patch of grass to rub the cool dew over his face and stay wakeful. He breathed in the Trans-Mongolian's diesel tang, a curling finger to bring him back onboard and farther into Russia.

Bat needed to sleep.

Then, he'd have to unravel why one screw in the window of Anton's and Timur's cabin was newly stripped.

56

LARA

KILOMETER 2167

For hours north out of Naushki, the tracks played hide and seek with a black river. A long sere ridge hid the view to the west while the east remained a green tableland riven with creeks. Villages flashed by, all of them wooden homes behind pastel shutters, wood smoke overhead and milk cows in the yards.

Lara and Gang did not leave their cabin, separated by the arms-length between berths; sometimes Lara stretched a socked foot to kick him for saying something funny or off-color. Gang told stories of growing up in rural China and said nothing more of his short time in America.

His mother's name had been Jing, which meant Quiet. She'd been this, if only because she suffered, and Gang never knew it. He told Lara about the nuns who'd raised him after his mother's passing. The Catholic women were harsh and loving, so that was what Gang knew of love. He'd managed to avoid the nuns' religion but did admire them, and to this day dressed only in black and white like them.

Lara didn't speak about her time in the Boston police.

This seemed an instinctive topic to omit when talking to an assassin, like talking to a cat about dogs. Like Gang, she focused on her childhood; those were the years when she and he were so different than who they were now, and they had no chance to know each other wholly without knowing each other as children.

Also like Gang, she'd avoided picking up the Catholicism of the cops in South Boston. They were named Tony, Pauly, Nicky, and Ricky, all of them. Her father was Vlad and they called him Eddie. He was a redhead, and they could not figure how he could be Russian. He was an engineer and an Eastern Front warrior, so he became the precinct's armorer. He knew everything about weapons, how to fix them, unjam them, alter them, but he could not outshoot the other cops because firing a gun made him shake. They understood, so long as Eddie did what he had to when he had to.

At midmorning, just as the tracks pierced a hamlet on the western shore of a large indigo lake, the sky cleared. A colony of gray-necked geese an acre wide watched the *Rossiya* power past; they did not take flight, they'd seen many trains. Gang checked the time; he guessed that breakfast had begun in the dining car. After he left, Lara locked the door. While he was away, she weighed the difference in the cabin between Gang being there and him gone. This made her eager for his return and a little afraid to be without him.

Gang knocked sooner than she'd expected. It turned out that entering the USSR meant another hour had been added to the nonsense of living on Moscow time. He tapped his watch and groused that breakfast wouldn't start until one o'clock.

———

The tracks followed the loops of the Selenge River for a long time. The sun climbed and sometimes the Trans-Mongolian's shadow touched the river's muddy edge. Just past noon, the train crossed to the right bank of the Selenge over a five-span bridge that Maxim would not have allowed Sinjin to photograph. From their two berths, Lara and Gang leaned toward the window to gaze down. They touched shoulders.

In the corridor, the conductress intoned, "Ulan Ude in fifteen minutes. The train will stop for forty-five minutes. Ulan Ude."

A knock was followed by Bat's bass voice. Gang unlocked the door, Lara called, "Come in."

The Mongolian entered. Gang vacated his berth to sit beside Lara. Bat looked rested, less dusty and ridden. His hat stayed on, his coat hung to his calves. He smelled of soap.

Gang said, "You've slept. You needed it."

The Mongolian laughed, freshened and jolly. "It seems when I'm away from my wife I'm not able to care for myself."

Gang asked, "Are you going to give us back our passports?"

"They will be returned when I conclude my investigation. Or in Moscow if I have not."

"So you still think the Agency man was murdered."

"I have reason to suspect that, yes."

"Are you worried, you know, for your own safety?"

Bat didn't drop his affable face. "Is that a warning, Gang?"

"No. But you're stuck on the train with us."

"I do not worry. If there is a killer among you, it was not a planned thing. The one who did it is merely hoping to stay undiscovered a few more days. The killer knows it will be very hard to conceal two murders. I fear only my wife."

Gang jutted a finger at Bat. "You look like you can handle yourself."

"There are so few Mongolians, we have learned to excel in individual sports. There was a time when I was a champion wrestler."

"I believe it."

"So was Oyuun. That is how we met." Bat pointed back at Gang. "I understand you are quite the martial artist."

Gang nodded for his answer, spotting the trap door Bat had laid out for him.

"I'd like to ask about the timeline."

Gang said, "Alright."

Bat ticked items off on his fingers: "Yesterday, after the train left Choir, all six passengers and the Agency man gathered in the diner. All but the Chechen shared three bottles of vodka that your Swedish friend purchased on the platform. Maxim Maximovich Sprygin told a story from his time in the Red Army. He grew upset with the scientist Epstein, and to a lesser degree with the Chechen. The Swede escorted Maxim back to his cabin. The gathering broke up."

"So far, so good."

"Dr. Dill carried the last of the three vodka bottles back here to her cabin."

Lara only nodded. The Mongolian hadn't phrased it as a question.

Bat said to Gang, "A short time later, Maxim began to shout through the door at Epstein and the Chechen."

"Yes."

"Where were you when you heard Maxim yelling?"

"In here."

"With Dr. Dill."

"This is her cabin."

"Along with the vodka bottle."

"Right there, Chief, is where you stop asking."

Bat leaned back and tucked his boots under the berth.

"Please understand. I have no curiosity beyond the order of events."

"I'll hold you to that. Go on."

"You left Dr. Dill to go out into the corridor. Why?"

"To see if I could help quiet Maxim down."

"Anton Epstein has said he opened his door to let Maxim in, to talk with him and the Chechen. I assume matters quieted down after that."

"They did."

"Then why did you feel your help was still needed?"

Bat twined his fingers in his lap. He kicked his feet under the berth.

Gang said, "To be honest, Anton can be a dick. And you may have noticed that Timur isn't so great with people. I figured I might be able to smooth things down better than them. Maxim didn't seem like a bad guy. Just troubled."

"That was generous of you. Considering." Bat cut his eyes at Lara, meaning "considering you left this woman and a bottle of vodka." She wanted to punch him. She checked on Gang fast to see if he was smirking to indulge the Mongolian. Gang didn't.

The brakes of the Trans-Mongolian seized and released on the approach to Ulan Ude. The tracks followed another tight bend in the river, making Lara, Bat, and Gang sway together. The emerald plain beyond the river gave way to humble farms, greasy warehouses, bare ground, more tethered animals.

Bat said, "Tell me what happened in the cabin with Maxim."

"He started crying. He told Anton he was sorry for how he acted at the table. He blamed himself for getting a bunch of his friends killed in Afghanistan."

"He was weeping."

"That's a word for it."

"And drunk."

"Pretty much.

"Whose idea was it to give him more to drink?"

"Mine."

"Why on earth?"

"I figured if he drank enough, he'd pass out."

"You sent Dr. Epstein over here for the bottle."

"I did."

"Then Maxim drank more in Timur's cabin."

"Correct."

"Then Anton Epstein escorted Maxim outside to the platform."

"My mistake. Maxim was a Russian. Russians don't pass out."

"Why did you not come to Dr. Dill's room yourself? I mean no disrespect, but was that not an invasion of her privacy?"

Lara was tired of shadowboxing and being snubbed in her own cabin. She spread an arm across Gang's chest the way a mother would to hold back a child.

"That's it, no. You don't get to ask him about *my* privacy."

"Doctor?"

"Anton and I are colleagues. It was goddam fine for him to come in here and Gang would know that."

"Were you asleep when Dr. Epstein entered your room?"

"What does that matter?"

"I won't know until I hear your answer."

"Yes, I was asleep. Does that fit with what someone else told you?"

"It does."

"You finished?"

"For the moment."

Lara said, "Now I've got a question for you."

Bat shrugged with his hands, for her to proceed.

"Do you fucking aggravate me on purpose?"

The Mongolian blinked enough times for Lara to wonder if he'd forgotten the question. Then Bat grinned. He removed his hat and held it over his heart; it seemed a gesture of respect. Bat's hair was ebon and lusterless, nothing about it shined. This made the gleam in his oblong eyes brighter.

He said, "I do."

"You want to tell me why?"

"Doctor, you said it yourself. I play the good cop, the bad cop, all the cops."

Bat held out his hat at the cabin door to imply the other compartments in second class.

"The Englishman Alonso is a narcissist. I flatter him and he talks. The big Chechen is like a forest animal. If you approach him the wrong way he will roar and disappear. I speak to him with diffidence. The Swede is a pleasant alcoholic who has managed to sleep through the entire affair, so I ask only generalities. The Russian scientist is a know-it-all. I treat him like he knows nothing to make him prove me wrong. Gang is a riddle. Riddles cannot be solved head-on, so I engage from many angles. You, Dr. Dill, are a modern American woman. A former police officer, a prominent scientist. You will not be ignored. So I ignore you."

Bat returned his hat to his black crown.

"And you talk."

The train squealed its arrival to Ulan Ude. Bat stood, framed in his long duster coat. He looked like a gunfighter.

"Something terrible happened to Maxim Maximovich Sprygin on this train. Each of you knows some part of it, or all of it. I must find out. So I am setting you against each other. You cannot be surprised, Doctor."

Bat turned for the door. The train joggled, an ungainly halt that did not unbalance Bat, the Mongolian was sure on his boots.

"Dr. Dill. Would you like to walk with me into town?"

57

BAT

KILOMETER 2207

L ara Dill found dirt under a poplar tree in the train
station plaza. She sealed a scoop in a plastic bag then
scribbled on it. She asked permission to make a phone call.

Bat stood aside while she worked a payphone. Dr. Dill
looked skittishly about the Ulan Ude station platform; an
armed trio of Soviet police in olive drab strolled among the
hundred boarding and the hundred leaving the train. Bat had
no guarantee that the officers were here for his purpose.

The station had three sets of rails; the Trans-Mongolian
filled one track while a pair of kilometer-long cargo trains
idled on the other two. The big station house was a bland
design, pastel blue and beige in straight lines, nothing
contrasting, rounded, or diagonal. The station seemed
designed without architectural goals except size and sturdi-
ness, which made it Soviet.

Lara Dill spent five minutes on the phone. When she hung
up, her strides to Bat were elongated, walking off some agita-
tion. She stopped in front of him, hands in pockets.

He asked, "Would you like to see a bit of Ulan Ude? We have some time."

"Are you done ignoring me?"

"Don't be petulant, Doctor. Shall we?"

She fell in beside him.

He asked, "Was it a bad phone call?"

"Standard."

"The reactor in Ukraine?"

She nodded at her tramping feet, hands still stuffed away.

Dr. Dill described the call to her American embassy in Beijing. The latest reports had the radioactive plume from the ruined reactor slowing its advance north, turning south. Rain was sewing a band of dangerous isotopes across Germany, Poland, and Czechoslovakia, drifting toward France. Europe was furious with Moscow for hiding news of the explosion so long. The Soviets had reached out to West German scientists for advice on how to fight a fire of burning graphite.

"The death toll at Chernobyl is being reported in the press at two thousand."

Bat said, "That sounds terrible."

"Four thousand work at the whole power plant. So it's probably an exaggeration."

"But there have been deaths?"

"Count on it."

In freighted silence, they climbed a walking bridge that crossed over the rails. From this height Bat could look into some side streets of Ulan Ude. Women filled buckets from metal standpipes at corners, then bore them away on yokes across their shoulders. Children home from school played chalk hopscotch. On the bridge, arrows pointed Bat and Lara to the city center. They walked above the backs of the Trans-Mongolian, over passenger carriages, freight cars, open coal cars, and steel tube liquid cars. A verdant breeze glided to them off the Selenge two hundred meters away. A delta of ducks winged west deeper into Siberia.

Off the bridge, a manicured pedestrian lane led to a shopping street named Ulitsa Lenina. Ulan Ude looked to be a pleasant enough place to spend a life for a few hundred thousand hardy Russians. In a bend of the river, the little city greened at the backend of May. The sylvan caps of a small mountain range limited the view north. Another sign pointed farther down Ulitsa Lenina, reading: *Lenin's Head*.

Bat said, "We must see Lenin's head."

All the shops and houses on Ulitsa Lenina were wooden, some grand, decorated with eye-catching hues, ornate gingerbread, festooned with onion domes. The century-old lane mixed vintage monarchy and the frontier; it had been laid out before the Revolution by defrocked Imperials exiled to Siberia from the Romanov's court, reminders of old St. Petersburg. Poplars and cheromka trees bursting with green berries lined the leafy avenue. Button-nosed Buryats, slant-eyed Mongols, and European Russians, men and women carrying empty mesh baskets, chattered in queues stretching out of the stores onto the sidewalks. Bat paused at one shop window to gander at a display of heavy cast-iron skillets with enameled interiors, selling for one ruble fifty kopeks. He would have bought one—Dr. Dill offered to lend him the Russian currency—but the pan looked to weigh at least ten kilograms. Bat would have to haul it across the face of Asia and back again to put it in the hands of Oyuun.

The second block of Ulitsa Lenina opened onto a grassy common presided over by a colossal bronze bust of Vladimir Lenin. Resting on a marble pedestal, the head rose eight meters above the lawn. The colossal, bald Lenin wore his signature Vandyke and high-cheeked narrow gaze. A passerby told Bat and Lara the locals called the statue *Jewish Lenin* because in winter the bust wore a cap of snow like a white *kippah*.

Walking away from the statue, Dr. Dill asked, "Am I a suspect?"

"No, Dr. Dill. Others said you were asleep. You said the same. I believe you."

"You can make it Lara."

"Thank you. Lara."

"Then why do I need an escort off the train?"

"Because you have not told me everything you know. You are a material witness."

"When do I get my passport back?"

"When I believe otherwise."

They headed back to the train past the lines of shoppers. Lara Dill asked, "How many murders have you investigated in the middle of the Gobi Desert?'

"How many murder cases did you deal with in Boston?"

"One or two a year, for ten years."

"That's quite a lot."

"It felt like it."

"In Choir, there are fifty thousand Mongols. Ten thousand Russians live outside the city on a military base. Of the sixty thousand people around me in the middle of the Gobi Desert, fifty thousand drink. I investigate ten murders every year. For thirty years."

Lara Dill's gait slowed as if Bat had handed her ten iron skillets. He let her catch up.

"Lara."

"What."

"Why does Gang have a ticket for a five-day journey, but no change of clothes?"

"Why do you say that?"

"In your cabin. I kicked his bag under the berth. It is essentially empty."

"You'll have to ask him."

"He will lie."

"I have no idea what he'll do."

"Gang began the trip sharing a cabin with the Swede. He moved in with you after Maxim's death. Why?"

Ascending the bridge, Lara Dill's brown hair obscured her face.

"I don't have to answer."

"What are you afraid of?"

"I said I don't have to answer."

"No, you do not."

Above the tracks, with the river behind them and the Trans-Mongolian below, with geese in the sky, Bat laid a hand on Lara Dill's wrist. He stopped her.

"And if you do not answer, I will note that you have been evasive in a murder investigation. Lara, you know how this works."

Bat sliced a hand through the air at the empty bridge. No one else would hear what she had to say. This was the place to say it.

"I won't ask you again. I will ask others."

Ahead on the tracks facing west, the Trans-Mongolian's locomotive keened once to announce its imminent departure. Bat shrugged and turned away from Lara Dill.

She grabbed his arm to turn him back.

"Four years ago, at the Moscow embassy, I dug up some suspicious stuff about the CIA and the Russian mob selling nuclear material to the Afghans for dirty bombs. I wrote an embassy report. The mob got their hands on it somehow. They kidnapped me and told me never to come back to Russia."

"You were exiled to Beijing, too."

"I was."

"Let's walk, Lara. Ulan Ude is not a place for either of us."

They continued across the bridge. Beneath their feet, the train cars jostled, tightening their ranks.

"Go on."

She said, "Chernobyl happened three days ago. I'm the only American diplomat in the region with expertise in ionizing radiation. The US embassy in Moscow got in touch with the local mafia. Apparently, they gave me permission to come back to do this one job, get information on Chernobyl, lend a hand if I can, then go back to China."

"Why do you say apparently?"

"Halfway across China, the deal changed. The guy who guaranteed my safety was… replaced."

"I understand."

"Now, it turns out that if I come back to Russia, they'll have me killed."

Lara threw out a hand at Ulan Ude. At Russia.

Bat asked, "Who is Gang?"

"He was sent to warn me."

"By the mob?"

"That's what he told me."

Bat said, "This is truly incredible."

"No one else knows."

"You do."

"He's just a messenger."

"Will Gang corroborate this?"

"Will you arrest him for it?"

"If he's done nothing wrong in Mongolia, I have no authority."

They descended the steps of the bridge, the last two passengers on the wide concrete platform. All the vendor carts, send-off well-wishers, and police were gone; only blonde Natalya stood outside the train, the canary yellow baton in hand. Bat and Lara hurried alongside the Trans-Mongolian. The long vents of his duster coat bounded at his sides like hunting dogs.

Lara Dill spoke quickly, wanting to finish before they reached the second-class carriage.

"Gang and I were going to get off at Sukhbaatar. That's why he brought no clothes. Then Maxim died. You flew in and told us no one leaves the train. So I'm stuck. Gang moved into my cabin to protect me. That's all."

They reached the second-class car. Natalya jerked the baton for them to get onboard. Lara stopped walking, Bat too.

She said, "Now that you know my fucking life is in danger, will you please go onboard and send Gang out so we can get the hell out of Russia? Chief?"

The green second-class carriage loomed broadside behind her. At the steps, Natalya scowled. In the windows, hung behind Lara Dill's head like a gallery, a witness or a killer peered down at the two of them talking alone on the platform. The Swede looked quizzical. Massive Timur studied them and said nothing to the Russian scientist beside him. Gang watched coolly. English Sinjin took their photograph. The rectangle of Maxim Maximovich Sprygin's window was empty.

The brow above each second-class window was clotted with grime, tangled cobwebs, trapped leaves, soot and dust, dead insects, all the detritus whipped up when a train this large roared through the most remote passages of Asia. Only the tops of two window frames appeared swept clean: the conductress's window at the end of the carriage; and in the center, the mantle above Anton's and Timur's faces.

Lara repeated, "Will you let Gang and me leave?"

Bat said, "No."

58

ANTON

KILOMETER 2230

T wenty minutes north of Ulan Ude, the *Rossiya* crossed a wide steel span to the river's left bank. Ten kilometers later, the train followed a crook in the Selenge due west. A series of islands cropped up in the river, then the river faded, replaced by villages and meadows, dots and dashes along the rails like code. The villages were built of wood, farms, homes, and shops dabbed in bright colors to counter the long months of white winter. Every hamlet hosted a lumberyard to mill the Siberian birch, pine, and cedar out of forests with shadows so deep the snow loitered on the loam late into April.

Ahead in the distance, the western horizon flattened and glistened. The train was approaching the immense Siberian lake, Baikal.

Natalya knocked. Timur spoke his first words since Ulan Ude.

"Go away."

Unmoved, the conductress called through the door, "I have cakes."

Timur sat up from lying curled on his berth.

"Come."

The tall conductress entered balancing a tray of sweets on little paper platters. She called the treats *romavaya baba*, Roman woman. Raisins and powdered sugar coated each; they cost ten kopeks apiece. Timur bought two; Natalya left.

Anton did not assume Timur would share, but he was mistaken. Timur offered one. Anton ignored it and rose.

Timur asked, "Where are you going?"

"It's two o'clock. Breakfast is being served in the dining car."

"We're staying here."

"No, Timur. I'm going to have a proper meal. You can stuff me out the window, or you can stay here and stuff yourself on cake."

Anton leaned in toward the Chechen.

"You say I'm stupid, but I don't say that about you. I believe you understand the Mongolian might take a different view of matters if you lay hands on me. I'm going to breakfast."

Before twisting the door handle, Anton glanced back to gauge Timur's reaction. The big Chechen wiped powdered sugar out of his paltry moustache. He crammed the second cake across his lips and chewed cogitatively. Timur nodded Anton out the door.

———

KILOMETER 2268

Anton paused on the platform outside the dining car, clinging to a handhold while a cargo train pulled by a quartet of locomotives rumbled by. Everything on the *Rossiya* trembled, the wind flipped up the collar of his sweater. Such a maelstrom made it plausible, even past Bat's skepticism, that a drunken Maxim might have tottered off the platform.

Anton managed to light one cigarette, smoked it, then entered the restaurant. A new diner had been inserted at Naushki; the Mongol motif of plains horsemen, camels and carved wood had been swapped for the ornamentation of a Russian tearoom. The carpet and draperies were bloodred, the booths had been exchanged for a dozen four-top tables set with doilies and delicate glassware. Tassels hung from every lampshade, gold embossed hammers and sickles were impressed into the cushions of every chair. The walls were murals of infinite sky and lush fields worked by thick-wristed comrades fashioning sheaves under factory smoke. Dead Lenin gazed at the future from black frames above both doors.

At a table, the Swede sat alone. His silverware lay crossed on an empty plate beside a half-full teacup and an aluminum teakettle. Anton invited himself to sit across from Björn. He waved for a waif-looking waitress in an apron and headscarf to come. Anton ordered whatever Björn had eaten and a fresh kettle.

Björn gave a distracted smile. His hands rested in his lap below the table, broad shoulders slouched. He gazed out at the afternoon countryside. "It feels stupid to say good morning."

Anton said, "It's a peculiarity of the Russian. We create processes to benefit the people. Then we admire our processes more than people."

The landscape scurried by on the constant clack of wheels on rails. The wide fields were brown by the plow. To the horizon, it seemed, tractors turned the earth, dusty farm trucks crisscrossed on dirt lanes, robust men and women swung scythes to fell the winter groundcover. The sky capped it all in azure like the murals of the dining car.

Anton asked, "What do you make of things?"

"Terrible."

A fresh teakettle and cup arrived. Anton poured first for Björn, then himself. He took a sip and for a while said nothing, to show his concurrence and concern. Timur had told Anton to play the game. Anton would play.

Björn filled in the silence, as Anton intended.

"Maxim's dead. We're trapped on a train. I can't get any news from home about that *jävla* radioactive plume. I can't do my job. There's three more days of this."

"What do you make of the Mongolian?"

"He looks like a fool. He's not."

"What do you think happened to Maxim?"

"I don't know. I'm done drinking."

"Why?"

"I might have been able to do something."

"Perhaps we all could have been kinder. Braver. It's natural to think that after a tragedy."

Anton lifted his teacup. He paused the porcelain at his lips to speak through the steam. The samovar made ridiculously scalding water.

"That's why I'm going back to Moscow. To try to be brave."

Björn raised his own steaming teacup. Together they blew across their surfaces, then slurped.

Anton let another minute roll by under the cadence of the train. The Swede sank disconsolately into himself as if he had a vodka bottle on the table.

Anton's breakfast arrived, two soft eggs, a scoop of fatty red hash, and black bread. Anton took up his utensils but held them beside the plate as if he had something more important on his mind than food.

"Björn?"

"*Ja?*"

"What if I told you there might be a way for you to help?"

"What are you talking about?"

"What if it was for Sweden?"

"Anton. Make sense."

"I can't tell you just now. But if you're willing to trust me, I may need you, sometime before Moscow."

"To do what?"

"A hard thing, Björn. But no one better than you to do it."

Björn surrounded the teacup with both palms as if to draw the heat into himself.

Anton repeated, silkily, "It will be for Sweden, my friend."

He did not lift the knife and fork but held them clutched in fists.

He said, "And the world."

59

TIMUR

A nton stayed away from the cabin for hours. Just as well. Timur did not have to lie back on his berth and feign indifference.

He sat with legs crossed, arms over knee, sometimes chin in hand, watching the beauty of Lake Baikal unfold.

Baikal was too wide for the train to cross the water. The lake held one-sixteenth of all the fresh water on earth. It was the oldest lake, the deepest, the bluest, in the world. The rails traced the lake's great rim, clinging to cliffs, trestles strung across precipices, bridges over chasms, views straight down into the lake. The setting sun turned the rock faces blush, the water purple.

At Baikal's western corner, the rails pierced a pair of villages; signs read Slyudlanka and Kultuk. Maybe ten thousand Russians lived in them. Both looked haggard, treeless, built low and colorless, cowering as if frightened of the lake. Only Slyudlanka's train station had color, built of white and pink marble. Factory buildings whooshed by, their grounds looked defiled. Though both settlements were on the lakefront, not a single vessel rode at their little harbors, only one rusted barge. Timur imagined blizzards and icy, knife-edge winds. Baikal, serene today, must have been a moody Siberian mistress.

The rails rounded to the lake's long northern rim, across more precarious bridges, then into a tunnel. The train popped out into the reddening day before diving instantly into another tunnel, like a blink. Timur had never worked on anything like these kilometer-long tunnels. He'd never punched into a mountain so hard he came out the other side.

At twilight, he stopped counting bridges at a hundred, tunnels at thirty. The train spent as much time rushing through the dark as it did in the waning sun. Wind whipped up the waters of Baikal, a night witch coming.

Chernobyl smoldered three thousand kilometers away. Timur didn't know if what he planned to do there would affect the lives of the people who lived here beside Baikal's tempers. He thought it might not. If it did, if it made them move away, that might be a mercy.

60

BAT

P ast dark, past breakfast and lunch, Bat stayed in Maxim's room. The Siberian lake transfixed him. He'd never seen a body of water so huge. As a boy he and his father had hunted the far corners of Mongolia, fished in lakes Khovsgol and Uvs, but both would struggle to fill one corner of Baikal.

The railway teetered above the water, tiptoed across gorges, drilled through mountains, clutched at the faces of cliffs. Bat had grown up under Russian conquerors and felt no love for them, but even with that coldness he had room for awe.

He dozed a bit, then in the afternoon, seated alone before the window, he began to comb through Maxim's few belongings. The young Agency man was no intellectual; he travelled with neither books nor anything with which to write. He had some candies Bat helped himself to. Maxim had tried to dress well.

Bat prayed for a while. He tapped one finger on the travel drum to stay quiet in the cabin. He expected no response from the dead, but maybe some ancestor might be drawn to the

321

drum, a spirit who might have tagged along so far from home with Bat, just to see Baikal, too.

When the sun doused, the lake began to froth under a rising wind. A loop to the north swept the tracks away from Baikal; the train raced along the left bank of another river, the Angara. Another full night fell. The only pearls of light glowed on the river or in cabins up in the hills.

The next city, Irkutsk, Siberia's capital, was an hour away. Beyond Irkutsk, Bat knew little of Russia's geography. He'd waited long enough in private, let the passengers and the killer speculate—where was the Mongolian?

Bat put on his hat. He opened Maxim's door and stepped into the passageway. The corridor windows faced a pitch, passing night.

He walked the length of the carriage, past all the cabin doors. Bat slowed at each, like a father strolling the hall of his children's rooms.

He knocked on the conductress's door.

Natalya opened part way. She stood barefoot, the top two buttons of her white blouse undone, and her hair disordered. The conductress had the look of a woman who was not alone. Seeing it was only Bat at her door, she opened the rest of the way. He entered to find that Natalya was by herself. Even with no one around she was seductive.

She asked, "What can I do for you, Chief?"

"May I?"

Natalya shrugged, a sloppy gesture. Bat sniffed a whiff of vodka in the cabin.

Entering, he went to her window. He pressed down; the frame slid open easily.

"The window in my room is locked."

"They're locked in all the cabins."

"Why?"

"Railroad policy."

Bat sat on the berth which had not been unmade. She took the one that served as her bed.

"Tell me the purpose of that policy."

"The government doesn't want passengers to pass items through the windows at stations. Also, it stops vendors from approaching the train."

"I see. Your window opens."

"I work for the state."

"If a window were to be opened, how would that happen?"

"I have the only window key for this car."

"You."

She said, "Yes."

"No one else?"

The Russian woman crossed her long legs. Her ankle was very loose, her bare toes pointed straight at the carpet, like a dancer.

Natalya bit her lip. "Am I in trouble?"

"I don't know. Should you be?"

She lowered her head to pinch her nose, then covered her mouth and breathed behind a palm. A sheen rimmed her eyes.

"He asked."

Bat let a few seconds stretch for the conductress to simmer in her tears.

"Who asked?"

The conductress's head jerked out of her hand. She'd believed that he already knew. Natalya pulled in her lips so tight her teeth showed. Animals did this when caught in a snare.

"Gang."

"May I see the key?"

She stabbed a finger at the gooseneck lamp behind Bat. A small tool resembling a brass butterfly hung at the end of a ribbon. He fingered it, then left it dangling.

"Why did you give this to Gang?"

"He said he was trying to calm Maxim down in Anton's cabin. Maxim was drunk and might puke, so Gang wanted the window open."

"Why didn't you tell him no? Railroad policy."

Natalya's reply was not in words but a glance down at herself, into the open buttons and the separation of her breasts. She drew in her hands from her knees to run them up the insides of her thighs before crossing her arms over her chest. Natalya was the conductress on a seven-thousand-kilometer train ride. She was too beautiful to cross Asia always alone.

Bat said, "I understand. No harm in that."

With shining eyes the blue of Baikal, Natalya glowered at Bat for tricking her.

She said, "None."

"But there is harm in hiding information."

"You didn't ask."

"That is true, and it is evasive."

Bat stood.

"I understand you are Russian, and you feel safe in Russia. Do not withhold information from me again, or we will test that theory. Is there anything else I should know?"

Natalya kept her seat on the berth. "No."

"Can I still rely on you?"

"Yes."

Bat scanned the cabin, slowly for the conductress to see that he would search everywhere for evidence that she or anyone might be a liar. He tipped the brim of his hat and let himself out.

61

GANG

Kilometer 2663

As the train settled into Irkutsk, Bat came for Lara. She took her trowel and disappeared with him across the platform under electric lamps. A hundred passengers got on the night train, a hundred stepped off.

Gang had nothing else to look at but the backside of Irkutsk's turn-of-the-century train station. The long building was another in the ornate imperial style that had disappeared under the boxy communists. The spired cupolas and quarried stone held Gang's interest until Natalya's vacuum hummed in the corridor.

He left Lara's cabin and walked the electric cord to the vacuum. Only he and the conductress occupied the passageway. She did not turn off the vacuum but held up a hand to stop him. Natalya curled fingers around his lapel to pull Gang near.

"The Mongolian knows."

"About what?"

"The key. He knows you came for it to put down the window in Anton's room."

325

Gang peeled her hand off his jacket. "Why should I care if he knows?"

She put her mouth against his ear. The woman's breath felt as warm as the tea.

"Because when he asked me, he did not already know."

"You hadn't told him?"

"No."

"Why not?"

Natalya answered, stroking his arm. "I was protecting you."

"From what?"

"I don't know or care. But now the Mongolian thinks the window is important."

In heels, she stood at Gang's height; they almost touched noses. She whispered and breathed so lightly he had to read her lips to understand.

"That was a mistake, Gang."

She touched him on the shoulder to push him along, then guided the vacuum away, her back to him.

———

Gang passed through the six cars to reach the diner. The new passengers in the hard-class carriages claimed bunks by slapping luggage onto the thin mattresses. Porters clipped holes in tickets, children got a jump on their running about, matrons inspected their new lodgings for cleanliness, old men lit pipes before bed. Soldiers pulled out bottles smuggled onto the *Rossiya* in their greatcoat pockets. Gang assessed everyone who came within arm's reach or brushed him in the corridors.

In the dining car, he found Timur and Sinjin seated across from each other at a table. The Russians had inserted their own brand of rolling restaurant into the train, all crimson and gold, every wall a mural of the power of people pulling together, Lenin looking over their heads as if the people were beneath him.

Gang approached Timur and the Englishman. They'd been dining in silence, arms crooked around their plates like convicts. Sinjin's camera lay on the table. Gang took the chair beside Timur; this annoyed the big man and made him scoot closer to the window.

A toothy waitress took Gang's order. Gang pointed to the remains of Sinjin's plate and told her without knowing what it was to bring him that, and tea.

Sinjin seemed glad of Gang's company. Likely Timur had not been chatty enough.

"I've always wanted to see Irkutsk." Sinjin indicated the window, out to the lightless river beside the tracks.

Timur lifted his heavy brow from his food. "Why?"

"Irkutsk has one of the great collections of nineteenth-century Russian architecture."

Timur asked again, "Why do you care?"

"Because it's interesting. I read a book. Have you never read a book?"

"There wasn't much light in the mines."

Sinjin, who never seemed daunted, or perhaps he simply could not read people, spoke to the top of Timur's great head.

"How can you care so little about the world?"

Timur's head came up. Gang rested a hand on his shoulder. Timur lowered his face to the last bites of his meal, but his eyes were slow to follow.

Gang said, "Sinjin."

The young Englishman was quick to smile, mercurial. He seemed to have little stomach for conflict, even when he was the cause.

"Yes?"

"How'd you like to go take some photos of Irkutsk?"

"Of course I would. But we can't leave the train."

Gang shrugged.

Sinjin's jaw dropped. "You mean, *leave* the train?"

"We're here for an hour. There's time. It's a nice night, you'll get some good shots."

"What about the police? The KGB? The Mongolian said they'd be waiting at every station."

"I think he's bluffing."

"What if he's not?"

"Then we'll turn around."

"I don't know."

"We'll be in Novosibirsk in a day and a half. When we get there, wouldn't it be nice to tell Bat you know he has no cops at the stations and to fuck himself? Then you go get your mushrooms."

Sinjin raised his eyebrows; the notion was a gamble, but appealing.

Gang said, "Timur?"

The giant wiped his mouth with a napkin. He threw it into the middle of his plate.

Timur rose. "I've seen enough of Siberia." He edged behind Gang's chair, into the aisle, then lumbered away.

With Timur gone, Sinjin asked, "Why do *you* want to test Bat?"

Gang showed his palms, to appear innocent.

"I might not want to go all the way to Moscow, either."

———

Ten strides from the dining car, against the flow of travelers headed to the train, Sinjin was struck by a truncheon between the shoulder blades.

Gang spun to the threat.

Two bullyboys in plain clothes holding riot batons, plus one chubby stump with his hands in his pockets, faced them. All wore felt hats and leather coats, unpressed pants, unpolished brogans. Gang judged them to be undercover police, maybe KGB. Sinjin dropped to a knee.

The second one aimed the nub of his baton at Gang's nose. The lunk who'd hit Sinjin patted the barrel of his bludgeon into his palm.

The young Englishman shook his head as if it were wet. He wobbled to his feet. Steadying, he pressed his shoulder against Gang's.

Sinjin slid the camera around his chest to put it behind his back. He said to the fellow who'd hit him, "Try that again, boyo."

Though the Russians didn't speak English, Sinjin's meaning was clear. The man stopped patting the club into his hand.

The crowd peeled away. Gang did not take his eyes off the baton pointed between them. On instinct, the people on the platform formed a circle around them.

The short one, the leader, said, "You're both under arrest."

Gang said, "We'll go back to the train."

"Too late for that." The leader said to his men, "Do it."

Sinjin's cop stepped up, baton raised for another blow.

Sinjin landed a roundhouse into the man's jowl. The man staggered backwards, hat knocked off, then collapsed on his rump. Bouncing on his toes, Sinjin pistoned both fists over him in little circles like an old-fashioned pugilist.

Gang flung his left arm in the air, then windmilled it down to trap the threatening baton under his armpit. He dropped low to broaden his base and with his free hand shot a palm-strike into the Russian's thorax. The man stumbled backwards, the wind knocked out of him. On his way down, Gang twisted the club out of his grasp. The disarmed agent sprawled on his backside. The crowd caught its breath. Gang tossed the truncheon onto the man's gasping chest.

Gang had taken his focus off the short one for only a

moment, long enough for the last agent standing to shove a pistol against his forehead.

For so long, life had been a commodity. Lives traded for money. In this moment, perhaps among his last, Gang was heart-struck that right now he might die, really, for nothing.

He raised both hands, not in surrender.

62

BAT

The Chinese moved at a speed Bat had not seen before in a man. He'd known wrestlers who were cat-quick, but not like this. This was no cat, but a kestrel.

The KGB agent made a mistake pressing the pistol against Gang's head. He should never have come within arm's reach. Gang lifted his own hands to make the agent think he was done. Then he disappeared from the barrel, peeled away so swiftly Bat's eye could only register where Gang started and where he finished.

With hands already up, Gang gripped the agent's wrist, flashed his free hand across the knuckles, and in one movement held the revolver. He turned the snub barrel to the night sky, flicked open the cylinder and poured out six bullets. They clattered on the platform. Gang returned the KGB man his gun.

Lara Dill arrived at his side, late from pushing through the crowd, shouting, "No, no, no!"

The two agents on their backsides climbed to their feet. One rubbed his ribs, the other his jaw. Gang, standing amid the spilled bullets, smiled at Lara, then put her behind him, facing the three. The Englishman kept his fists at the ready.

Bat stepped into the arena of the crowd under the electric lights. He presented his police credentials to the short, heavyset man. A few minutes' conversation ensued; Bat insisted that Gang and Sinjin were material witnesses to a murder and were required to continue on the train. The man demanded they answer for striking him and his men. Bat parlayed that he might have to report how his KGB boys attacked foreigners first without identifying themselves, the one they managed to hit from behind was a British diplomat, both felt the need to defend themselves, the two agents had been knocked off their feet, and he, their leader, had his weapon taken from him.

Walking back to the second-class carriage, Bat stopped Gang, Sinjin, and Lara from speaking. He loaded them into their car past a glowering Natalya who bounced her wooden baton off her hand.

In the corridor, Bat excused Sinjin to return to his compartment. The Englishman tried to lay a hand on his shoulder in gratitude, but Bat raised a finger to halt him. To Lara and Gang, he said, "Go to your cabin."

He followed through Lara Dill's door and shut it behind him. The Mongolian sat on the berth across from them, his greatcoat spread wide under him and touching the floor.

He said, "I have a son who believes in nothing. He has taken from me only some traits of the face. None of our ancestors will speak to him because he will not hear. No animal will eat at his hands or die at his hands in the city where he lives. His life is a bank and a clock and a weekend."

Lara and Gang glanced to each other, unsure.

"My daughter has strength but lacks patience. She is selfish and clever. Next year when her schooling is done, she will go out into the world. It may break her because we have loved her too much to teach her to bend."

Bat removed his hat to speak of his wife as if he were in her presence.

"I have left Oyuun alone with our children. With my horse. To go to Moscow."

Bat returned his hat to his head.

"The next time either of you, *any* of you, leave this train against my orders, I will let the KGB, or the police, or whoever is waiting, have you. I will say that person is the murderer, even if I do not believe it. I will close this case. Then I will go home."

Bat stood. The heavy oilcloth of his coat fell into shape around him.

"Do not think you have the luxury of doing that again."

Bat opened the cabin door. He spoke to Lara Dill and Gang without glancing back.

"Tell the others."

63

LARA

KILOMETER 2663

The instant Bat left the cabin, the Trans-Mongolian surged forward, as if his slamming the door shook the train.

Lara turned on Gang beside her. "Goddammit." She gestured at the empty berth across from her. "Go sit over there."

Gang locked the door, then complied, hands in his lap. Lara had been with him for most of the last three days. She had no idea what sorrow might look like on Gang. If he was sorry now, he showed nothing of it.

She said again, "Goddammit."

"May I?"

"May you *what?* Explain to me why you risked getting arrested and leaving me on this train alone to get fucking killed?"

Gang lifted a finger, trying to object.

"*And.*" Lara leaned across the gap to push down his hand, a way to say shut up. "And what about the risk to you? If you get arrested, you're dead. You said that."

334

He nodded. He had no choice.

"And Sinjin? You involved *Sinjin*? What the hell were you thinking?"

If Gang lifted a finger again, Lara quietly swore to God, she would try to rip it off.

He said, "To be fair. I had no idea he was going to slug a cop."

"Here's a thought. If he's not leaving the train, then he doesn't hit a cop. Why did you take him?"

"For cover. Sinjin lugs his camera everywhere. I figured if we got caught, we could say he was just going to snap a few photos around the train station. No harm."

"Alright." Lara lifted her own finger between them. "Alright, that actually makes sense."

The train trundled past an ever-speeding string of light poles, flickering the cabin. Irkutsk devolved into warehouses and hovels, roughnecks, men in hardhats, container cars on side rails, a feral dog limping. The city rolled away while the lava of Lara's anger cooled. A minute out of the station, the tracks looped west, then crossed a river bridge.

On the bridge, over black water, Lara asked, "Why'd you leave the train?"

"I needed to find out if Bat was bullshitting about having cops at every station."

"He's not."

"Okay, that's clear now. *Because* I got off the train."

"Another fair point. Stop that."

Gang said, "And I think he's closing in."

"Why?"

"He knows about the window in Timur's cabin."

"So?"

"He knows I went to Natalya for the key. He asked her about it tonight."

"Why did she wait to tell him?"

"No idea. Timur didn't mention it, either. Or Anton."

Lara said, "Or you."

"We've all been figuring someone else would tell him. No one did. Now Bat thinks it's something we kept from him."

"Because you did."

Lara had never been in this place before, on both sides of a crime, knowing the facts and watching a cop assemble them. Evidence was always a jumble of disconnected events, clues, hints, and testimony, pieces without meaning or place until an investigator gave it to them. A puzzle. Bat loved puzzles. All cops did.

Lara said, "The window doesn't matter. The story about needing it open in case Maxim threw up, that'll hold. No one mentioned it to Bat because no one thought it was important. He knows that. It's not why he's closing in."

"Then why?"

"He knows something you don't."

The gooseneck lamp behind her shined in Gang's face. Lara clicked it off. She patted the mattress beside her hip, then lay down. Obedient to get out of the doghouse, Gang moved in the dark to fold behind her, chest to her spine, chin on her nape.

She tucked his arm around her. Lara wriggled backwards until she felt Gang pressed against the bulkhead.

"Do you know how frightened you made me?"

"I'm sorry."

She asked, "Where's the next station?"

"Krasnoyarsk." His breath warmed the back of her ear. "Eleven hundred kilometers. Seventeen hours."

He kicked off his shoes. His lashes batted on her neck as he blinked.

He asked, "How's Chernobyl?"

"Rudd said the winds have shifted south. The plume's blowing back toward Kiev and the Black Sea."

"Is that as bad as it sounds?"

"Worse. Tomorrow's May Day, the biggest holiday in the

Soviet Union. Forty million people in Ukraine will be outside watching parades. The cloud's going to carry alpha and beta particles right over their heads. Iodine 131 gamma radiation concentrates worst in the thyroids of children."

Gang kneaded her shoulder. He held her and protected her, comforted her. He'd tested Bat, risked his own life, for her. But there was nothing she could do to protect him. Not from Bat. Not from whoever was coming for them both.

Lara stayed in her shoes, awake. The *Rossiya* plunged into the night, westward through more villages that strobed the cabin, past trains that shuddered the berth under her in Gang's sleeping arms.

64

BAT

May 1
Kilometer 3087

B at woke an hour before dawn. This was the time for chores, digging away snow and manure, for carrying wood, when the light below the horizon was not yet a rising sun but a lantern entering the barn. He'd gotten out of bed at this time every day of his childhood and adult life.

Bat left Maxim's cabin for the washroom. His hat and greatcoat stayed behind, along with his boots. He hurried in his ablutions, not wanting to be seen by the passengers in his sleeves and stocking feet. He looked too much like a traveler, one of them. They mustn't be allowed to forget he was not.

Returning to his cabin, Bat stopped outside his door. In the relative silence, the wheels on the endless rails crackled like a woodfire. Bat did not say a prayer; he was on his own in Russia. He closed his eyes and exhaled long, to go elsewhere, into the puzzle, to become Maxim Maximovich Sprygin.

Bat made a fist to bang on the door, stopping shy of striking it. He raised his voice without sound and cursed without profaning. He threatened Anton for betraying the

338

Soviet Union, for demeaning the deaths of his war comrades. He shouted he would have the KGB waiting in Moscow for you.

Bat jiggled his head hard to make himself muzzy, drunk.

And you, Chechen. I distrust something about you. I cannot know you were a mujahideen in Afghanistan, but if I had lived, I would have learned it. You are my enemy and I sense it.

The cabin door opens. Maxim steps inside.

He sits on a berth. Across from him are Timur and Anton. They are not angry but conciliatory.

On the other side of the bulkhead, Gang, a Chinese with underworld connections, lies with the American woman. He hears the commotion in the hall and rises because he believes he can help calm matters in Anton's room. But matters have already calmed. Maxim's shouting has stopped.

Still, Gang leaves the bed of Lara Dill.

Gang enters to find a weeping Maxim apologizing to Anton and the giant Timur. Maxim accepts that his behavior tonight has been poor, that the blame for the deaths of his Red Army friends in Afghanistan is his own. His threats of exposing Anton and Timur are rescinded.

Gang sends Anton to fetch the vodka bottle from the cabin of a sleeping Lara Dill.

Anton does not wake Lara Dill. Returning, he hands the bottle to the miserable Maxim. Maxim swallows more vodka, enough that soon it will be fresh on his dead breath.

Maxim grows nauseated. He may vomit.

They attempt to open the window so Maxim may hang out his head into some cool air, maybe empty his gut.

The window is locked by a pair of three-sided screws. Timur the giant cannot budge it.

Gang, who for some reason could not leave the cabin for the few moments needed to grab the vodka from his inamorata's room, now embarks down the corridor to convince

Natalya to trust him with the triangular key. The conductress flirts. Gang responds in some way, big or small, but enough for her to become protective of him for her own purposes. Later, she volunteers no mention of this interlude with Gang for the key.

Opening the window is a struggle. With the key, Timur almost strips one of the screws, but the window succumbs and slides down. Maxim does not vomit. Anton accompanies him out of the cabin, onto the platform. In the corridor where Sinjin hears him, Anton remarks that Maxim could use some fresh air which, unexplained, was not available from a downed window.

Maxim carries the vodka bottle. After all these sorry events, he has not had enough to drink.

Sitting on Maxim's berth in plummy dawn light, Bat donned his boots, coat, and hat. He stepped into the corridor where the samovar sat on its blue ring of fire always boiling water.

He moved out onto the jangling platform and wind between carriages. Minutes before he died, Maxim stood here at the opposite end of a day, at a setting sun.

Anton and Maxim talk more on the platform. Maxim drinks again. Anton leaves him in a badly depressed state, in a gathering Gobi dusk.

Maxim corks the bottle. He has had enough.

Maxim moves to the railing to peer down at the sundown desert racing by at a hundred kilometers per hour. He is drunk, morose. He throws away the bottle.

Ten second later, Maxim Maximovich Sprygin jumps off the train.

Except.

He doesn't jump. He dives. He lands on his head and snaps his neck.

Or.

Another train barrels past. A big train like the Trans-

Mongolian, it makes the platform shudder. The vacuumed air sucks Maxim closer to the railing. Enough vodka in his blood, enough anguish in his heart, Maxim tumbles over the rail. He lands on his head. His neck is snapped.

But.

There is no train rushing in the other direction across the Gobi. In China and Russia, the tracks are doubled, but in all of Mongolia, the trains run on only one track.

Standing at the railing, wind whipped the hem of Bat's greatcoat about his boots. The wind tugged him backwards, like a spirit telling him No, the truth is not here.

Bat retreated from the rail, and the wind eased.

Anton does not escort Maxim onto this platform or speak to him in the corridor. Maxim does not stumble or dive off the train. He does not breathe his last standing at the railing.

He dies in Anton's and Timur's cabin. Gang is present. Maxim's corpse goes out the window. He sails headfirst, lands that way, and the bones of his neck snap. He rolls, then comes to rest facedown.

This was the purpose of puzzles. Only the truth solved them.

The last two pieces: Whose hands choke Maxim Maximovich Sprygin without a fight, without leaving a mark? And how does Maxim Maximovich Sprygin die?

The rim of the rising sun yellowed the steppe. Bat stretched and spit, the way he always did when his chores were done.

65

TIMUR

T imur did not sleep.

There was nothing new in that. In the last six years, he'd rarely slept a full night. In Afghanistan, he'd hunkered with Marisa trading hours on watch, or lying with her, not sleeping. In the Soviets' coal mines, he saw so little sun that when night came it didn't trigger rest. In those prison barracks Timur lay by his hatred in the dark like a campfire. Returning to Afghanistan, digging burrows for the mujahideen, he worked to exhaustion before falling onto a pallet any time of day or night, and if he'd slept well, it was there.

Through the window, Timur watched Russia slip past in gouts of distance, hundreds of kilometers at a leap. After midnight, a few hours out of Irkutsk, the train entered the Cheremkhovo coalfields. Factories and refineries dotted the darkness in spurts of flame and chimneys so tall they flashed lights to keep planes from running into them. The coal-burning stink of the mills drifted up from the black valleys.

With dawn hinting, Timur did not move from his berth. He closed his eyes for short stretches, but they were waking, gathering minutes. He spooled to himself, as if reeling a bucket up from a well, the things he would destroy, the cities and towns to depopulate, the factories he would silence, chimneys he would snuff. Timur reveled in the vastness, quietly amazed at what he might do to all of this Russia.

He spent some time, too, thinking he might kill Anton in his sleep. Anton must have been aware of this. Timur marveled the man could ever close his eyes around him.

In his mind's theater, Timur throttled the life out of the Russian. Anton died pitifully. Then Timur strode the length of the second-class carriage. First, he would kill Natalya for her keys to enter the other cabins. A shame, a beautiful woman. Then Björn. The muscular Swede would need to be surprised or else he would put up an admirable fight. Next was Lara Dill's cabin. The American woman posed no threat; but she lay with the Chinese who had a cobra-like quality, a speed and danger Timur wasn't certain he could counter. He skipped the door of Lara Dill for now. Next came Sinjin. The mouthy Englishman would have to die only because if he awoke to a car full of dead people, he would be insufferable.

Last came Bat. Timur imagined him also not sleeping tonight. The burly Mongolian had a penchant for disappearing into dead Maxim's cabin for long hours. This unnerved everyone; why was he hiding out when he was supposed to be solving a murder? This, of course, was his purpose. Whenever Bat emerged, he wore his wide hat, duster coat, and boots, looking the part of the lawman. He was broader even than Timur, he filled the corridor from wall to windows. When the Mongolian asked questions, they were as pointed as knives, then he vanished again for lengths measured by the sun and moon. Timur, on his way to the dining car, the samovar, or the water closet, might hear Bat behind Maxim's door tapping on a little drum.

Timur envisioned himself unlocking Bat's door with a dead Natalya's key. He eased inside to sit on an empty berth.

He and Bat talked, Chechen to Mongolian, about their loathing of Russia. They'd tell each other of Bat's desert and Timur's mountains, their homes, families, and griefs. Perhaps Bat would tell him about the little drum and magic. Then they would decide together if Bat had to die.

The black Russian steppe lit to gray, then to gold. Timur pulled on his shoes and his jacket. Before ducking into the passageway, he gazed down on Anton.

He spoke not in a whisper but loud enough so Anton might hear and know he could sleep on, safe from Timur.

"Hero."

He left the cabin. Timur was not surprised to find Bat on the cold platform between cars. Gusts whisked the Mongolian's greatcoat around his squat form as if he stood in the heart of a whirlwind.

Timur stepped to the railing. The carriages clacked on the rails with the rhythm of panting horses. A village swept up; a streetlight burned on one corner, then another, and the village was gone.

The Mongolian stepped beside Timur. Side-by-side, they were as wide as the railing and had to share it. Their shoulders touched and their hands.

Bat looked up at him. Both had hair long enough to whip their faces.

While they stood at the rail, the train could not find a straight stretch through the Siberian highland. The tracks scrawled to accommodate a hill and a stream, a wood and another hamlet. For minutes, Timur and Bat had to hang on or else be shook free from the railing. They swayed in unison, and this reminded Timur of the sunrise prayer he had not yet done.

The Mongolian said, "I don't think you killed him."

"Why do you think that?"

"He was choked, but there were no signs of struggle on Maxim Maximovich Sprygin. His windpipe was not collapsed, his throat showed no bruising. No cut lip, no blood in the nose or ears. No loose teeth or jaw. You, Timur Makhdi, would have left evidence of yourself on a man you killed with your hands."

Timur nodded out to the passing land, a little flattered.

The Mongolian said, "The Russian Anton did not do it."

"How so?"

"He left the compartment to bring back the vodka bottle. Maxim was alive at the time. Maxim drank. The vodka was on his body's breath. A man in the middle of a murder doesn't leave it to fetch a bottle."

The train rumbled onto a steel span across a waterway, entering a gridwork of girders that echoed the train. A sign named the river, the Reka Uda. On the west bank a second sign marked the crossing of another time zone, into the Kras-noyarsk region. Moscow's clock was now only four hours behind. That brought breakfast a little closer.

Timur said, "Perhaps they argued on the platform."

"Anton is soft. Even drunk, Maxim was a soldier. No."

The next instant, the Reka Uda and the tracks split another dull village. Quickly, as if to seek more interesting company elsewhere, the river wended away north. The speeding train put the river and the town behind it.

The Mongolian said, "Maxim Maximovich Sprygin gets drunk and insults you and Anton, threatens you both with police. Even if the two of you have reasons to want him harmed, neither of you did it."

Bat raised a finger above the swift flowing railroad ties. He curled the finger downward to describe an arc.

"Maxim did not leap or stumble from this platform. Nothing indicates that."

Timur said, "As you say."

Another loop in the train's path pressed Bat against Timur. They stood on the spot of the lie of Maxim's death. With no space between them, Bat was letting Timur know that he had no fear of him.

Bat said, "That leaves Gang."

"Does it?"

"He was the only one in the cabin with no reason to kill Maxim. No threat nor malice. This means he had no reason to do it. And no reason not to."

"That is an odd logic."

"That is the puzzle."

Bat's hand, next to Timur's on the rail, covered Timur's knuckles. Bat's mitt had heft. His touch was not strange but somehow called for, Mongolian to Chechen.

Bat said, "Gang sent the Russian into Lara Dill's room for a vodka bottle. He sent a man, a relative stranger, into the room where he had just lain with the woman inside. I have been married a long time, but I know this is something one does at one's peril. Lara Dill defends this action, but it goes against logic and experience."

If Marisa were in that cabin, the man who entered without her permission would stagger out with a knife hilt protruding from him like a windup toy.

Bat said, "Gang stayed behind in your cabin. With you and Maxim Maximovich Sprygin. Why?"

Timur said, "Yes. Why?"

"That is the piece I do not have. I feel it is the last."

Bat tapped Timur's wrist with his next words. "Will you tell me the truth?"

The Mongolian looked out at the dawn-blushed steppe. The tracks sang loudly enough. Timur allowed himself a laugh Bat would neither see nor hear.

He said, "I think there are not many Moslems in Mongolia."

"Very few."

"Do you know any?"

"No."

"If you did, they would tell you the great importance Islam puts on truth. To lie is *haram*. Forbidden."

"As it should be."

"There are three instances in which a lie is permitted. Where it is *halal*. Would you like to know?"

"I see you want to tell me."

"A Moslem may lie to reconcile between people. He may lie to please his wife. And he may lie to an enemy."

Bat did not break his gaze from the sparkle of dew on the rolling plain. Timur peered down on the top of the Mongolian's hat. The hat bobbed once, a short, decisive nod. Bat patted the back of Timur's hand, also once. The Mongolian walked out of the wind, inside the carriage.

66

ANTON

The *Rossiya* spent the drizzly afternoon coursing through birch *taiga* and dodging mountain spurs. In the passageway, Anton smoked the last of his cigarettes to avoid being alone in the cabin with Timur. Anton had grown up a scientific boy, so he did not imagine faeries and fabulous beasts in the green shadows of the woods.

One by one, the others, even Timur, walked by and invited him to lunch now that it was being served. Anton held his place in the windows of the second-class carriage.

At 4 p.m., the train crossed another river, the Yenesei, over a thousand-meter six-span bridge. The steelwork and stone abutments of the overpass looked to be from another century. Sinjin emerged with his camera. Natalya, by some sixth sense, came out to shoo him away from the windows. She held up a big palm to remind him she would use it.

The conductress called out: "This is Krasnoyarsk. The train will stop for fifteen minutes while we take on a new locomotive. Krasnoyarsk."

The train creaked into the station as if the dreary day had

made it stiff. Huts and parked boxcars failed to block the view of the river where gulls dove on a garbage scow. On the other side of the tracks, a steep slope hid the city built on the heights above the river and the railyard.

Lara Dill left the train unescorted; Gang watched her from the top of the steps. He seemed ready to take flight. The Mongolian stayed quiet in Maxim's cabin. He must have decided the KGB run-in with Sinjin and Gang in Irkutsk was a sufficient deterrent to anyone making a serious run for it. Even so, on the platform outside the second-class carriage, two policemen took up station. A stout fellow in a mackintosh and trilby hat held the leash of a muzzled brindle dog that resembled a wolf. Watched by the animal and its handler, Lara Dill kicked aside blackened gravel to scoop up her soil sample, then made a call from a payphone. When she returned onboard, Gang joined her inside her cabin.

Natalya's vacuum made Anton skip out of the way. The woman cleaned the carpet like she was annoyed with it. The train lurched backwards with a *thunk* when the new locomotive backed up to it, then eased forward and gained pace out of Krasnoyarsk. The conductress stowed her vacuum behind the samovar and herself in her cabin.

Beyond the city, the *Rossiya* entered a country of dark earth plowed by horses. Much of the land had been recently cleared; mounds of overturned stumps were being torched by farmers. The train rolled through flames and smoke like a warzone. Beyond the fields stood klatches of brightly painted *dachas*—blue, green, and yellow—never a red one. Again the scenery closed in around the tracks, dense forests under a gloomy sky. Anton knocked on Björn's cabin door.

The Swede invited him in. The cabin was neat, a book and reading spectacles on the table.

Anton settled across from him. The big Scandinavian wore a white Oxford shirt and khaki slacks, yellow hair touching his collar.

Facing each other, Björn said only, "Yes?"

In private, Anton saw that Björn did not like him. They were both physicists and men who loved their countries. But Björn was a soldier, he had not been exiled, and Anton's country was poisoning his.

"I have to speak with you about Timur."

"Did he kill Maxim?"

"He did not."

Anton expected Björn to ask next, "Did you kill Maxim?" but the Swede crossed his arms. Anton waited in case he might; when Björn did not, Anton felt a barb, that the Swede didn't feel him capable enough to even inquire.

He said, "Maxim fell. That is what I believe."

"I don't know what, or who, to believe on this train."

Anton said, "Forget Maxim for the moment."

"Easier said than done."

"Listen to me. Timur claims he is going to Ukraine. In Chernobyl, he'll take part in excavating the tunnel under the ruined reactor."

"What's wrong with that? If the Chechen wants to dig, let him dig."

"He's not going to dig. He's planning to sabotage the tunnel."

The Swede's handsome face soured. "This I don't believe."

"Timur Makhdi is more ruthless than you can imagine."

"How do you know this? About Chernobyl?"

"He told me."

Björn's arms unfolded.

"Anton, do you think fabricating stories about the other passengers is a good idea right now? There's a policeman onboard. There's been a murder."

"You think I'm lying?"

"I'm not sure what to think. But this? This is too incredible to be true. Why? Why would Timur tell you such a thing?"

"He thinks we're comrades. Both of us trying to hurt Russia."

"This is what Maxim said."

"But it's not true." Anton covered his heart. "Not about me."

"Ruin the tunnel, how? How can he do it?"

"He'll be one of six hundred miners. Timur knows how to handle dynamite. He'll find a way to wreck the tunnel, cause a cave-in."

Björn's gaze dropped, visualizing. The Swede seemed to find it at least plausible.

"Why? Why would he do it?"

"Timur is a mujahideen."

"What? No."

"He's a Moslem. He was in Afghanistan fighting for the Afghans. The Russians captured him and sent him to Siberia to mine coal. His Afghan wife was murdered in a Soviet prison in Kabul. Ask Timur, he'll tell you this. He's already told the Mongolian."

"Alright. But Chernobyl? Wrecking the tunnel?"

"It's almost inconceivable. I accept that. But Timur hates Russia with a fury that defies description. It's driven him mad. Björn, listen to me. I'm telling the truth."

"You can't be."

"I ask you to consider the cost if I am."

Björn played another scene in his head, slowly, terribly.

The Swede said, "If the reactor core reaches the underground water…"

Anton finished his sentence, "…it will unleash a catastrophe unrivalled in human history."

Anton leaned over to put a finger into Björn's chest.

"Consider the cost to Sweden."

The Swede shook his mane, fighting off the notion, but Anton could see it gaining traction. He pressed.

"Tomorrow at sunup, the train pulls into Novosibirsk. The

morning after that, Yekaterinburg. The next dawn, Moscow. Björn."

"*Ja?*"

"If Timur reaches Chernobyl, there'll be no one to stop him."

Björn sat back against the wall, arms folded again. The Swede muttered, "*Åh, fan mig.*"

67

GANG

Kɪʟᴏᴍᴇᴛᴇʀ 3810

L ara returned to the cabin troubled. She tucked the
Krasnoyarsk soil sample into her collection case and
tossed aside the trowel. She did not sit, only stared at Gang's
feet displeased, as if he'd stepped in something. She moved for
the door.

"Where are you going?"

She said, "Tea."

"I'll get it. Stay in here. Lock the door."

"You make it too hot."

"Don't care. Sit."

"There's someone out there to kill you, too, you know."

Gang said, "That's sweet." In the passageway, he paused
outside the door until he heard the latch. For the first time in
hours, Anton wasn't in the corridor focused on the rainy day,
smoking, surly and alone. Gang made two teas in glass cups
etched with likenesses of cosmonaut dogs.

Lara let him in at his knock. Gang set the teas on the table,
relocked the cabin, and sat across from her. She looked no
happier than when he left.

He asked, "You want to tell me?"

"Chernobyl."

"Your phone call?"

"Yeah."

"Not going well?"

Lara attempted to pick up her tea, then set it down, freshly bothered by how he could hold the burning glass.

She cleared her throat. Lara worked her hands in the air as if she were rummaging. She was trying to make sense of something.

"For the last four days, helicopters have been dropping sand, lead, and dolomite on the reactor fire. The Beijing embassy's getting reports that the Soviets have thrown five thousand tons on the core. The level of radionuclides rising out of the fire dropped from six million curies to three million."

"That's good, right?"

"It was."

"Was?"

Lara waved her open palm above her teacup on the table. Steam rose through her fingers.

"The radiation levels went back up again overnight. Six million curies. The Soviets are so bad with their technology, there's a 50 percent chance even these measurements are off."

"So it could even be worse."

"And the temperature from the reactor's going up. Seventeen hundred degrees Centigrade. The Russians aren't sure why."

Gang touched her knee. "But you are."

"I think so."

"Try your tea."

Lara wrapped both hands around the glass. She took a swallow like a little girl, with an audible sip and a gasp. She returned the tea to the table.

Gang asked, "What do you think's happening?"

She made a dome of her hands, pushing them downward, packing.

"The uranium dioxide fuel and the zirconium casings still inside the reactor core probably got so hot they fused into a sort of radioactive lava. If the core temperature keeps growing, say to 2,800 Centigrade, it can melt through the concrete floor of the reactor vault. Gang, that's half the temperature of the sun."

"Then?"

"Then you add in the five thousand tons of material they've already dropped on top of the core. That's a lot of pressure eating down into the earth."

"That's the China Syndrome."

Lara lofted her eyebrows, straining to stay patient.

"Which is bullshit and the name of a bad movie. For the last seven years since Three Mile Island, we've been doing computer modeling for worst-case scenarios like this. The core will *not* eat through the center of the earth. That defies geology and physics. But now that it's happening in real time, and behind the Iron Curtain, we can only make guesses how far a melted reactor core will drill into the ground. Understand, in this case, it doesn't have to go very far. If that lava bores down just twenty feet below Reactor Four, it'll hit the water table. Then."

Lara tossed up her hands. She had no more scientific terms or analysis.

"Then the world is fucked."

She lay faceup on her berth. She kicked off both shoes. Lara did not close her eyes but stared at the cabin ceiling.

The steppe rolled by, another endless emerald panorama at late day. Mist blanketed the land and scudding clouds snagged on the hilltops like banners. If he were home in Baoding, Gang would light a fire to chase the damp. He might read, or cook, or listen to a phonograph.

He kicked off his own shoes. In his socks, he moved the

short distance to her. He lay behind Lara in the little space she left against the wall. Gang expected her to roll away and give him her back, but Lara turned to face him.

She kissed him without preamble. They both kept their hands out of it. She broke the kiss, pulling back to focus. He smiled but she did not.

Lara said, "I'm sad and this is a bad idea."

Gang nodded. When he pushed himself up to rise, she pressed a palm to his chest.

"All I said was it was a bad idea."

68

TIMUR

Timur awoke to Anton's absence. He'd not heard the Russian slip out.

Dawn was a suggestion in the east; the train barreled west. Perhaps Anton was standing in the corridor again, brooding to start his day, watching the tracks swerve around marshes and hills and cut through villages.

Timur rolled off the berth onto his knees. He lowered his forehead to the cool carpet to begin the *fajr* prayer. He recited the first words, found calm, and offered his spirit to God. He asked in return that, like a blacksmith, God make every beat of his heart a hammer to harden him.

When the *fajr* was finished, Timur needed the berth to help him push off his knees. He thought, Not much longer, God.

Timur sat. Rubbing his legs, he glanced out the window. The early light had swelled enough on the forests for him to curse.

"Fuck."

This was haram so he apologized, feeling God near after his prayer. Timur said to the window, "I know these hills."

He slipped into his boots and jacket and tied back his hair with a leather lace. In the passageway, as he'd suspected, Anton stood gazing out a window.

Timur sidled beside him. The Russian did not recoil or turn away from the cold glass.

Timur said, "I prayed this morning."

"Good for you."

"Did you pray, Antosh?"

"I did not."

Timur rested a hand on Anton's shoulder. The Russian did not flinch.

Timur said, "Moscow lies ahead for us both." He dropped his hand and walked away.

Anton said, "God knows what you're doing."

Timur turned in the corridor. He covered his own heart to speak of God.

"I know. I told Him."

Timur moved through the carriage quietly to disturb no one. The samovar greeted him with warmth. He slid the door aside to step out onto the platform.

Timur zipped up his jacket. He stepped to the railing, into the gushing wind, to see daybreak over the Kuzbass. His grip tightened on the chilly steel.

For four years he'd been carted among these hills, ridden the rails and backroads through these woods. He'd shivered when he'd been given no blanket, sweltered when there was no shade nor water. For his first year in Russian hands, he traveled shackled. Once he'd been broken of the belief that he might flee, he was left free to move about the cattle carriages and truck beds that carried the prisoners between coal mines and camps. Chuvashka, Bachatsky, Kemerovo on the Tom

River, Kiselyovsk; it seemed that Siberia was nothing more than one great forest and one giant pit.

Timur spit off the train, into the Kuzbass.

Behind him, the portal opened. Out of the second-class carriage stepped the big Swede. He wore no jacket, only a riffling white shirt, slacks, and boots. His blond hair waved about his head. He looked untouched by the blowing cold.

Breakfast wouldn't be served for another six hours. Timur had not seen Björn up and about before sunup. He turned from the railing to greet the Swede face-to-face.

"Yes?"

Björn shouted over the swirling air and the friction of steel.

"I'm sorry, Timur."

Timur had to shout, too.

"Don't be."

"What are you going to do in Chernobyl?"

"Dig a tunnel."

"Are you going to destroy it?"

"Who is asking? You or Anton?"

"Me."

"What do you want, Swede?"

"To protect my country."

"From me?"

"Yes."

So here it was. Anton had made his move.

Björn called, "Is it true, Timur?"

Timur could lie; he had a falsehood already planned out, about Anton and Maxim, secrets, murder, the melting reactor in Ukraine. Anton was the murderer, Maxim a drunkard, the Swede a pawn.

Björn strode to the center of the platform, feet spread. The wind billowed his shirt, a powerful man.

The Swede was only doing the same as Timur, trying to keep his homeland, kin, and loved ones safe. By stepping onto this platform at dawn, Björn was willing to put himself in harm's way. Did he deserve to be lied to?

Timur asked, "What do you think?"

"I can't risk it."

If Timur would lie, he must do it now.

Or he could honor the Swede and be that harm.

Timur felt no more urge to lie. Anton and the Swede were both scientists, they spoke a language Timur was not fluent in. The Swede had been convinced enough to stand here.

And Timur felt no fear. Björn would not try to take his life, but subdue him, tie him up, keep him in his cabin, turn him over to Bat or the KGB.

Timur, for his part, was going to kill the Swede.

"Come on, then."

Björn rushed at him. Good. Fighting a brave man was better than a coward.

The Swede extended his left arm as if to shove through a door. Timur tried to deflect the blow, but the man had girth and strength. Björn's grasp took hold of Timur's jacket to drive him against the railing. Timur curved backwards, over the speeding ground and clacking wheels. The Swede was trying to push him off the train.

Timur grabbed the back of Björn's neck. He hauled himself upright, even against Björn's strongest heave. Timur cocked an arm to smash Björn, stun him. But why was the Swede using only one arm?

The answer came with the knife into Timur's gut.

Björn didn't look down to gauge the damage but pressed in close, chest to chest, as he thrust the blade in again.

Timur drew back his head enough to howl at the last stars of the morning over the Kuzbass, then bashed his forehead into Björn's. The Swede stumbled but kept his grip on Timur's jacket. The headbutt wracked Timur's own balance, he saw glimmers on the Swede's face. Blindly, he struck his fist into the pins of light.

Björn let go of Timur's jacket. He reeled to the center of the platform, a hand pressed to his forehead. In his other hand the Swede gripped a Swiss Army knife with a silver blade folded out.

Timur yanked up his jacket and shirt. Both wounds in his abdomen bled onto his belt. He pushed fingers into the twin slashes to test if he could stand the pain of them. Timur gritted his teeth, his nostrils sucked in a sharp, frigid breath. He spit to taste for blood and found none. Timur stomped toward the Swede.

Björn, still unsteady, led with the knife. He swept it between them to keep Timur at bay until his head cleared. Timur dodged the first arc; before Björn could swing the blade back in play, Timur bull-rushed him. He rammed a shoulder into the Swede's exposed side, backpedaling him into the railing on the other side of the platform.

Timur surged in tight, trapping Björn's knife-arm between them. The Swede smashed the knuckles of his free hand into Timur's eye socket but too late, Timur had him by the throat.

Timur squeezed with all he had. The Swede, even stymied and staggered, was a beast against the railing. He battered Timur's face with his loose fist, picked at Timur's side with the Swiss Army knife. Timur bared his teeth and choked Björn hard. He felt with his thumbs for the man's windpipe.

The Swede's flogging grew manic, he hammered Timur's nose with an elbow. Timur bore down to crush Björn's throat. The Swede punched a knee into Timur's groin, but his power was fading, Timur endured and squeezed. Slowly, passionately, Björn waned. His grunts began to gurgle. Timur regretted this death. Even as he delivered it, he saw himself wiping blood on Anton's shirt.

The Swede's legs began to give way, he grew heavier in Timur's throttling hands. Björn slumped, his eyelids flickered, he dropped the blade. Timur drew a deep breath to hold it, harden himself, and end this.

Something urged between his shoulder blades. The Swede's hands pulsed on Timur's wrists, barely, but battling on.

The prod nudged Timur's spine again.

"This is a gun, Chechen. Let him go."

69

BAT

KILOMETER 4462

B at dragged Björn off the platform.
Timur slouched away to his own cabin. Down the
corridor he supported himself with one hand trailing the wall,
the other pressed against his midriff to stanch his bleeding.
The Chechen's nose was a wreck and one eye would be black.

The Swede died on his berth, gasping, perking blood
bubbles on his lips.

By rising dawn light, Bat cleaned Björn's face with a towel,
brushed away his long hair, and made him look asleep. He
probed the Swede's throat to feel the death; Timur's vise-grip
had flattened the trachea; the airway had not opened enough
for Björn to breathe again, even after Timur turned him loose
at gunpoint. A purple swath banded the Swede's throat,
Timur's handprints, just as Bat had said to the giant.

The conductress entered the cabin without knocking. She
appeared in her uniform and high heels. The train would pull
into Novosibirsk in twenty minutes.

She said, "Goddammit."

"Do you have a first aid kit?"

"Yes."

"Take it to the Chechen. Can you stitch a wound?"

"No."

A second woman's voice said, "I can."

Lara Dill forced her way into the dead Swede's cabin.

Bat said, "No. Stay away from him."

Lara Dill said, "Fuck you." She grabbed the conductress by the sleeve to yank her into the hallway.

Bat sat beside the corpse. The Swede was a big man, death had not diminished him. Bat had only seen the last moments of the struggle. Björn had died hard; the condition of the Chechen confirmed this. The Swede was as far away from his home as Bat was from Mongolia. Were Björn's spirits here, in the middle of Russia? Bat could not summon his own and had little faith he might call another man's.

He lay a hand across the Swede's brow to leave behind what little he could. Bat left the cabin.

The young Englishman was in the passageway, freshly awake and wanting to talk. Gang stood against the windows, golden morning at his back. Bat pushed past them into the Chechen's cabin.

The giant sat, leaning against the bulkhead, boots up on the berth. His jacket and crimsoned shirt lay jumbled on the carpet. Two gashes in his left midriff looked like the mouths of fish; a few centimeters below them was the round keloid of an old bullet hole. Lara Dill sat beside him, a blood-fouled towel across her lap, threading a needle. The conductress and the Russian scientist sat on the opposite berth.

Bat told them both, "Get out."

Anton said, "I'll stay right here."

Bat jerked him to his feet by handfuls of sweater. With the ease of anger he heaved the scientist against the cabin door. The Russian cowed quickly and slipped into the corridor.

Bat said to the conductress, "Go lock the door to the

Swede's cabin. Then bring me all the copies of your keys. Do not keep one."

Natalya cocked her head for Bat to give her a reason.

"The body belongs to me now. It's part of the investigation. Go."

The conductress got on her long legs and did as she was told.

Bat took the berth opposite Lara Dill and the Chechen. The American was breathing fast, controlling herself admirably. She swabbed a cotton ball and a rusty tincture over the first wound, a clean slit. Timur ground his teeth.

With the needle, Lara Dill punctured the flesh below the wound. She pushed up inside the gash until the needle's point poked through the skin above the wound. Expressionless, Lara Dill tightened the thread, and the rip in Timur Makhdi began to close. The Chechen wrinkled his ruined nose, which might also need a stitch.

Lara Dill did not wait for Bat to admonish her for disobeying his order. She said, "There's been enough dying on this train."

Bat nodded and hoped she was correct.

Lara Dill asked the giant, "Why did you do it?"

Gently, Bat said, "You are not the policeman here."

Lara Dill didn't look up from her red, tacky hands.

Bat said to Timur, "Tell me. Why?"

Without taking his eyes from the bulkhead, Timur said, "The Swede was trying to kill me."

Bat calculated this was not true. Björn could have stabbed him in the chest or the neck. He did not. He was trying to slow the giant, not kill him.

Lara Dill threaded another loop through the first wound. Timur made not a sound.

He said, "The Swede attacked me."

This was likely. Björn had a knife. He was prepared.

Bat asked, "Why?"

Lara Dill stopped sewing the giant's flesh. She stared into Timur's profile so intensely it seemed the Chechen could not bear it. He turned to her.

"He didn't say."

She asked, "Do you have any idea?"

"Ask Anton."

Bat extended a hand at the American woman. He did not touch her, the gesture was only a reminder.

"Lara." The giant mustered a smile for her. "Continue sewing, please."

Lara Dill resumed stitching the wounds. The Chechen was so large that the holes in him looked trivial. Timur Makhdi watched her work, motionless as marble. How could pain like this be so tolerable for him? Had he lived with so much hurt that two stab wounds and a needle were only little things?

Bat spoke. "Why should I ask Anton?"

"This must be very upsetting for you, Mongolian. More missing pieces."

"Did Björn tell you Anton sent him?"

The giant chuckled. Lara Dill paused while the man's abdomen shook. The Chechen winced, only a curl of his lip.

"No. But think on it. Anton must believe I know something damaging about him. So he spun a story the Swede believed enough to try to silence me."

"What is that story?"

"That I am a monster."

"Are you?"

"It seems I was to the Swede. I had no other quarrel with him." Timur rested his head against the bulkhead. "Very confusing."

Maxim Maximovich Sprygin also got too close to this story. It got him murdered.

Lara Dill snipped the black thread, finished with the top wound. Timur eased down her hands, gratefully, to let him have an unclouded moment. The stitches were pricking him more than he showed.

Lara said, "You didn't have to kill Björn."

Her friend lay in the next cabin, killed by this Chechen's hands. Her eyes were dry and her fingers steady. Bat wondered the same about Lara Dill, what sort of life she'd led that allowed her to sit beside this beast and not weep, not go for his eyes with the needle.

Timur said, "He stuck a knife in me twice. Was I supposed to interview him about his intentions?"

The conductress returned to hand over her keys to the second-class cabins, then left. Bat asked the Chechen nothing more. He would only get more cryptic answers. The spirits often spoke like this, in feints and dead ends.

Lara Dill stitched up the second gash. Finished, she poured alcohol over the tiny black threads in Timur Makhdi's side, wiped away the last of his blood, then wrapped gauze around his midsection. She brought him tea. Bat watched how icy she became.

Having done all they could, Bat and Lara Dill stood to leave. Timur stopped them.

"You're not going to arrest me?"

Bat said, "No."

"Why not?"

"I cannot arrest you for defending yourself. And I cannot arrest a man for what another man says he might do. That is the Soviets' way. I am not a Soviet. But do not forget, we are in Russia. The KGB is waiting for all of you. The Agency man is still dead. Now the Swede. I warn you both, the Russians will have no such scruples."

Bat and Lara left the giant, shirtless and alone in his cabin.

In the corridor, the quiet Gang had not moved from outside Timur's door. The train slowed, skipping as the brakes chirped and released. Bat checked his watch. Six a.m. local time. Two a.m. on the Trans-Mongolian.

Natalya emerged into the hallway. She shouted down the row of shut doors:

"Novosibirsk. This is Novosibirsk. The train will stop here for fifteen minutes. This is Novosibirsk."

At the far end of the passageway, near the samovar, the young Brit came out of his cabin lugging a leather suitcase.

Over the squeaking of the train, in the juddering corridor, Bat asked, "What are you doing?"

Sinjin said, "I thought since you'd solved the case. You know, Timur. It might be alright for me to keep my appointments."

Bat stepped away from Lara Dill and Gang so he might use his arms. He struck the wall with the back of his fist.

He thundered, "No one leaves the train!"

Bat pounded the window frame.

"I will shoot anyone who tries!"

Natalya stamped toward Sinjin. The Englishman scampered back into his cabin, hauling his luggage fast behind him. He slammed the door just as the conductress reached it.

Bat shouted down the corridor, flooded red with dawn.

"You are all going to *Moscow*."

70

LARA

Kilometer 4512

L ara did not step down to collect soil in Novosibirsk, did not test Bat's temper. She stayed in her cabin with Gang gazing out the window.

The station was the prettiest yet, a turquoise and white expanse of faux columns and stacked windows that gave the old building a palatial air. Hundreds of passengers in swamp waders and knee boots flooded the lower-class cars carrying woven baskets; these were locals bound for a day in the Ural countryside to hunt mushrooms and wildflowers. Sinjin must have been gnashing his teeth.

On the platform a troupe of teenage girls in knee socks and miniskirts waited in a flock. They might have been ballerinas, for when a gypsy-looking woman in gold headdress and a long silk coat stepped off the train, they clapped and broke into little hops higher than Lara expected. The girls handed the woman a bouquet of orange buttercups, called Siberian snow drops.

Novosibirsk was vast, the third largest city in the USSR, a million citizens. In her liaison position at the Moscow embassy,

Lara had twice attended scientific conferences here. Novosibirsk was Siberia's center for metalworking, machine manufacturing, and chemicals, and the nexus for the mining industries sourced in the Kuzbass to the east. Waiting on side rails, hundreds of cargo cars were filled to spilling with coke and coal nuggets.

Police, some with canines, walked among the weekend crowd on the platform. Bat himself marched under the windows of the second-class car. Natalya guarded the steps with her yellow baton, ready to smack someone.

The Trans-Mongolian, motionless and steaming in the station, did little to deflect from Björn's death. The train felt black, like a cortege. How white would Björn, a pale man, be in two days when his corpse reached Moscow? She reeled in her gaze from the window and the living.

Gang asked, "How well did you know him?"

"He worked for the IAEA in Beijing. We did some field work together over the last few years. He was always kind. Very smart. An alcoholic."

"He was a gorgeous man."

"Honestly? He would have been very glad to hear you say that."

When Bat and Natalya climbed aboard and the train heaved, Lara felt safer now that she was moving. The tracks edged close to the Ob River, then crossed it over a nine-span bridge. A crowded excursion boat plied the jade river east, more mushroom hunters. Several cranes and dredgers floated empty on the river, their crews gone for the weekend. Novosibirsk disappeared slowly in a string of warehouses, chemical refineries, coal chutes, factories, spoiled ground, oil-slicked ponds.

The next stop was Omsk, another industrial center. Omsk, like Novosibirsk, was thought to be the heart of Siberia. Ten hours of train travel separated the two cities, showing how huge was that heart.

For the first hour, Lara and Gang sat across from each other, then moved side-by-side, touching while marshes, grass-lands, and croplands slid by. The clouds of yesterday were gone, the air was crisp enough for a chill to drip from the window glass.

The steppe looked to be one immense floodplain. At any moment Lara could count the number of trees on the far horizon. The flat landscape lacked hills, bluffs, rocky outcrop-pings, and stone faces; it was a Gobi of green. The train ran on a five-foot-high embankment to keep the tracks above the annual snow melts and bogs.

After a while, Lara and Gang lay down together. Now that they'd made love they could be curious. They could run their hands over each other, find slowly what they had used quickly, make small gestures like kisses. They clung to each other with so much ensconcing them in this cabin, the speed of the train, Bat's furious threat, the murder of Maxim, the killing of Björn, the danger that a veiled assassin was lurking for them both before Moscow.

A gradual gloom settled over Lara. Gang read it; he lay between her and the bulkhead, a hand on her shoulder, breathing into her hair. He said nothing; Lara took Gang's silence as respect, that she could handle her own melancholy.

When she sat up, so did he. Outside, nothing had changed except the light. Lara was hungry. Breakfast in Moscow wasn't for another two hours. She thought about having sex; Gang read that correctly, too. He raised one brow. She changed her mind and bounced to the opposite berth. Beneath it were the useless ionization chamber and big yellow Geiger counter.

Gang asked, "What?"

"You know what we've got to do, right?"

"I thought I did."

She waved away the notion like smoke. "Forget that."

"Not likely."

"I mean for right now."

"Just tell me."

"We have to find out why Björn went after Timur."

"No." Gang used the same gesture Lara had, to wipe the idea out of the air between them. "No. Let's stay behind a locked door for another day and a half. Keep our noses out of it. We'll make it to Moscow early enough to get the hell out on the next train. Once we're back in China, I can protect us."

"Gang." Lara leaned elbows onto her knees. "You can't go to Moscow."

"I'm not leaving you."

"You heard Bat. He's going to turn us all over to the police or the KGB. You can't be there when that happens."

"I said I'm not leaving you."

"I understand. But I'm a diplomat, I'll be safe. You won't be. You know I'm right. You'll have to go. Soon."

She stopped him from saying no again.

She said, "It's not your choice."

Lara sat back. She removed the mildness from her voice.

"Before you go, I need your help with Timur and Anton."

"Lara."

"I need to know what Anton told Björn. What Timur was stopping Björn from telling anyone else."

Gang shook his head. Not to disagree, but to tell her he feared things wouldn't turn out well.

"Why?"

"Because he was my friend. Because he was killed twenty feet from me. Because I was raised to fucking know why."

Gang surrendered. "Alright."

She said, "Timur knows you killed Maxim. I was in the room when he tried to deflect it onto Anton."

"That's no surprise. Anton knew that could happen."

"Why did Timur try to choke Maxim in the first place?"

"Maxim threatened him."

"But with *what*? Telling the KGB he was a mujahideen in

Afghanistan? Timur admitted that. He did his time in prison, the Soviets let him go. He's not afraid of that anymore."

"Then what?"

Lara hopped beside Gang, to forgive him and bring him along. She pecked a finger on his thigh.

"Whatever it is Timur's protecting, Anton found out. For the first couple days on the train, they got along. Maybe Timur told him."

"Then Anton told Björn."

Lara said, "It was something bad enough to convince Björn that Timur had to be stopped."

Their faces were close. In Gang's eyes were minutes and hours, perhaps the next day or two. Lara wanted years, time to know him, maybe save him. Years were not there in Gang's black eyes.

She asked, "What was so important to Björn that he'd risk his life for it?"

Gang said, "He was a scientist."

Lara had sparred with Björn, watched him trade light blows with Gang.

"He was in the Swedish army."

Then she caught it, like waking.

"Oh my God."

"What?"

"I know."

"Know what?"

"Why Björn attacked Timur."

Lara kissed Gang. She wanted to be certain, no matter what happened next, that got done.

She had the last puzzle piece.

"Sweden."

Gang blinked into his lap and ruefully smiled. "Timur threatened Sweden."

She said, "Chernobyl."

373

71

ANTON

The *Rossiya* looped slowly through Omsk. Anton stood in the corridor windows without seeing much. Another industrial city, more blackened ground and gray structures, venting fires from oil and gas refineries, late blooming trees, bundled-up people, fragile lives. Natalya announced the train's arrival in Omsk without looking at him. The train idled for a quarter hour at another grand and pastel railway station near another cold river. The conductress left the second-class carriage, lowered the steps, then stood like a centurion with a yellow baton at the bottom. Bat made a phone call from a phone on the platform.

After Omsk, the *Rossiya* dodged nothing. The rails were laid due westward across verdant fields and plains, through hamlets and Siberian outposts, smokestacks spiked the distance, sometimes a horse-drawn hay wagon. The next station was Yekaterinburg; the train would pull in after midnight. For now, it bore along with all the heaviness and isolation Anton felt. The killing of Björn did not eclipse Maxim's but was a second moon risen beside it.

In the afternoon, Sinjin left for the dining car and did not invite Anton. The young Brit didn't know who to blame for missing his mushroom outing in the Urals, so he was surly with everyone. Gang and Lara Dill stayed locked in her cabin. Perhaps that was for the best: Anton considered enlisting the American and Gang against Timur, but what could they do? The immense Chechen would just kill them, too, and claim self-defense.

Anton was left with only Bat, but the Mongolian barely showed himself. Bat sat alone either in Maxim's cabin or with Björn's body; the tapping of his little drum reached Anton in the passageway. Bat seemed to have no interest in anything other than solving Maxim's murder and praying over the Swede.

Other trains coursed by, blasting the air, rattling the train like a man shaking Anton by the shoulders out of his reveries.

He determined he was hungry. Anton moved through the hard-class cars, past hundreds of passengers in bunks and crowded cabins, children and gray folks, business sorts and soldiers and sailors drinking or drunk already. Anton couldn't warn them to get off the train, go no closer to Moscow, go the other way. He imagined them all radiation poisoned and dying. In the restaurant car, he bought himself a steak, and one for Timur.

———

Anton rapped on the door, though it was his own cabin. Inside, Timur said, "Come." The door was not locked.

The giant wore no shirt. He sat against the bulkhead, legs spread, boots on the floor, a bloody shirt and jacket between them. A gauze wrap banded his midsection, a red splotch in the bandage looked like the eye of Jupiter.

"I've brought you something to eat."

Anton did not hand the steak to Timur but set the plate on

the fold-down table. Under Timur's quiet eyes, he sat opposite. Anton did not tuck into his own meal but waited for Timur to move, signal some permission for him to remain.

Timur slowly blinked, a small motion that seemed titanic. Not for the first time did Anton think of him as a dragon.

With a grimace, the Chechen sat forward to the plate. Anton had brought no knives, a wrong thing to carry into this cabin. Timur took up the strip of meat with his fingers and bit. Anton did the same.

Chewing, Timur tossed the steak back onto the plate. The meat landed with a dead bounce.

Timur's face showed the battering Björn gave him. His left eye socket was purpling, dried blood ringed one nostril. A freight train coursed in the other direction; the moments of shaking did nothing to disturb Timur. The closer the Chechen got to Chernobyl, the stonier he became.

Once the eastbound train had whooshed past, Timur asked, "What do you want?"

"I have nowhere to rest. I want to be able to sleep in here. I want to know you won't kill me."

"I won't."

"Why won't you?"

"Is that a serious question?"

"Of course it is."

Timur took another bite of steak, then tossed it onto the plate. He licked his fingers. Either he had little appetite or he meant to devour so much more.

"You still do not understand, Antosh."

"Explain it."

"You know what I plan to do."

"Too well. And I beg you not to do it."

"You sent the Swede to kill me. Now you beg?"

"I have nothing left."

"You must know by now my life no longer belongs to me. Anything, *anything* that jeopardizes what I have before me, I

376

cannot allow to stand. Revenge against you does not serve that purpose. Listening to you beg does nothing. Eating this fucking steak would do more."

Timur flicked a thumb at Anton's berth.

"So sleep. I won't hurt you. You did what you had to do."

"I sent a man to his death."

"That gets easier."

Timur swung his legs onto the berth and shifted his torso to rest his back against the wall. The giant showed no hint of pain.

"Besides, Antosh, you have sent men to their deaths. Hundreds so far, I hear."

72

BAT

After dusk, the tracks left the Siberian steppe to climb the Ural range. Deepening darkness, popping stars, the long incline, gave Bat the sense that Maxim's cabin was leaving the earth.

The train crested the mountains in the dark with nothing to see, no towns or outposts, no peaks, only thick growth by starlight. Four hours later, the Trans-Mongolian began its descent. The train took on more downhill speed, Bat heard it in the quickening patter between the wheels and rails. The Russian night was velvet black, without contour. Even the villages that streaked past again were little more than flashes, like sequins.

Bat would not solve the murder. He knew it was Gang but only because the killer could be no one else. He couldn't unravel why or how Gang would kill Maxim Maximovich Sprygin. The puzzle had shown him the solution but would not let him possess it, as if the answer were behind a shop window.

Past midnight, the locomotive tapped the brakes. The train slowed into Yekaterinburg. Bat left Maxim's compartment, then locked it with Natalya's key. He used it to open the Swede's cabin. Bat sat across from the body as the train rounded a bend to enter the outskirts. White stripes from streetlights stroked the corpse like the hands of ghosts.

In the corridor, Natalya did not announce Yekaterinburg or how long the train would idle there. The time was 1 a.m., an hour before midnight in Moscow. Only Bat and Natalya were awake in the squeaking, slacking carriage. Gang slept behind a locked door with Lara. Anton had returned to his cabin with Timur and not surfaced. Sinjin was alone. Bat roomed with the dead.

At the Yekaterinburg railway station, he stepped out onto the platform in a bracing morning. Without a word, Natalya followed, guarding the steps out of the carriage. The expansive stationhouse reeked of arcane grandness, fat ionic columns, gold leaf, it was more imperial palace than public building. Natalya spit on the concrete, she was not an elegant beauty. Yekaterinburg had been the place where the Romanov family was murdered by the communists seventy years before, ending royal rule in Russia. Bat didn't ask Natalya who the spit was for, the monarchs or the Bolsheviks?

He couldn't say how many days he'd been on the train, three or four. He didn't know how far he was from Mongolia, only that to go home he'd have to do all this again.

Inside the building, he found a payphone. The great gilded hall stood mostly vacant, shops shuttered, only some night-owl taxi drivers hunting for patrons and security workers ambling about, everyone had a cigarette pasted on the lips. Bat dialed the Moscow number he'd been given yesterday afternoon in Omsk when he called his sheriff's office back in Choir. He reversed the charges, as instructed.

A raspy voice answered. "*Da.*"

"My name is Bat."

"You're the Mongolian."

"Correct."

"Do you know who this is?"

"I can guess."

"Don't."

Bat wanted no part of another game or riddle, not standing on a windswept train plaza under buzzing electric lights, not with the corpse of Björn and the burden of Maxim riding with him to Moscow.

"What do you want?"

"The murder of the Agency man. Are you still investigating?"

"Yes."

"Good. The murderer is Anton Epstein."

A lifeless hand rested on Bat's shoulder. Not the Swede or Maxim but at last, far from home, an ancestor. The spirit had come along and waited, it might have been able to whisper only once. Bat lowered the receiver from his ear to listen. The spirit spoke clearly.

Don't fuck with these people.

A warm breeze bussed his cheek. Bat nodded to the empty platform, to the flight away of the spirit.

He said to the husky voice on the phone, "The scientist."

"The dissident."

"I understand."

"Arrest him for murder. Bring him to Moscow. You will be met at Yaroslavsky station."

"What about the others?"

"There are no others."

"I understand."

Bat hung up without saying or hearing farewell. He stayed on the platform as long as he could, imprinting what stillness felt like so he could remember it.

When the locomotive made the sound of an anvil ringing,

Bat climbed into the second-class carriage. The conductress stayed on the concrete until the train actually began to move. She walked alongside, then jogged, stretching out her moments off the train. She was athletic swinging aboard.

Bat stood before the passageway windows. The city of the Romanovs' murder passed behind.

He asked Natalya what would be the train's next stop. Perm, she said, four hundred kilometers. Arrival at sunup. She closed herself in her cabin.

Bat stayed in the quiet, dark corridor. He crossed his arms; the oilcloth of his greatcoat crinkled, and he imagined it to be the sound of him hardening into a statue. He stood graven for another hour. The train passed a small monolith lit up beside the tracks, arrows marking directions east and west, the dividing line between Asia and Europe. Bat wanted to be stone and feel nothing, but hurtling away from his home as a pawn now, he could not.

He chose which dead man's cabin to sleep in. With Natalya's key he opened Björn's door and sniffed to see if the corpse had begun to smell. It did not, another consideration from the kind, brave Swede. Bat stretched out on the open berth, forgetting to take off his hat until he lay on it. Should the Swede's spirit be lingering, Bat said, "Goodnight." He added to the Swede's spirit that he was sorry he could find no justice for it. Or for Maxim's.

He tried a long time to sleep but the straight-arrow route of the tracks was done. The western part of Russia grew more heavily populated, the rails twisted and swerved to visit frequent villages. The locomotive mooed every time it crossed a river or highway bridge. More freight trains shot past bound for Asia, rollicking Bat on the berth for seconds that resonated long after they'd ticked away. The cabin swayed, then righted itself. Rest was dangled, then snatched away by some next light, sound, or rattle.

Dawn felt inevitable, one more thing Bat could not prevent. He'd slept but only for stretches cobbled out of an impotent night. He did not rise to Natalya's call in the corridor that the train was pulling into Perm. The train would stay for ten minutes. This was Perm. The last stop before Moscow. Perm.

73

GANG

Kᴉʟᴏᴍᴇᴛᴇʀ 6468

The train went faster in the night, or so it seemed. The rails wriggled left and right; in the sharper curves, sitting at Lara's window, Gang could see the locomotive rushing headlong behind its poor spotlight, and at the same time, see the last carriage behind whipping around to keep up.

At sunup, the Trans-Mongolian eased into the city of Perm, called out by the conductress. Lara didn't stir. A few early risers stepped down from the hard-class cars to buy potatoes from girthy women selling them out of buckets; very few passengers climbed on or off the train at Perm. A string of flatcars piled with timber prevented Gang's view of the city, and just as well. He watched Lara sleep.

Gingerly the train left Perm, tiptoeing out on rails that curled past lumberyards and blast furnaces. The train crossed a steel bridge above the wide river Kama, then turned west, eager to fling itself into the journey's last full day.

The morning sun shined bright and crisp, the sky swept clean. The tracks turned downhill again, departing the Ural foothills. A forest rose up, pine, fir, and larch, on hills like swells. Clearings in the woods opened onto meadows stuffed with violets and yellow kingcups, mist on ponds and mallards paddling inside the mists.

Lara shifted, waking. Eyes closed, she groped behind her. Not finding Gang, she drew a breath that might have been fright. Her eyes burst open. Lara sat up, instantly alert.

She said, "Oh shit."

"Good morning to you, too."

"You're still here."

"Would you like to start over?"

"I slept too long."

"Too long for what?"

She reached, then pulled back her hand.

"Gang, you can't be here. You should have gotten off the train."

"I said I'm not leaving you."

"Shit."

"You can stop saying that."

The tracks trickled down to a plateau of plowed land and pastures. Dirt lanes and tractor ruts made quilts of buckwheat fields and wildflowers. White cook smoke puffed from steep-roofed homes in commune clutches; the sun hadn't climbed enough to shake off the night's chill. Local farmers weren't on Moscow time, so they were having their breakfasts.

Gang sat across from Lara, above the yellow Geiger counter and her forgotten soil kit and case. She hadn't stepped off the train since Novosibirsk.

He said, "There's nothing we can do. Let's make it through one more day. We'll get to Moscow. Then back to Beijing. After that, everything's okay."

"I'm scared."

"You'll be alright."

"I'm scared for both of us."

Lara put hands to her face as if washing from a basin. She pulled tight her skin and swept back her hair.

"There's an assassin out there."

He kept his place opposite her. What he had to say was meant to calm her, but it might not.

"There's one in here, too."

74

TIMUR

The day passed with little change but the light. Timur hardly glanced outside; the Russian palette had winnowed down to repeating patterns of marshes, glades, forests, farmlands, villages that sped by in a twitch, and cattle. Sometimes a crow or two flew alongside the train but could not keep up.

No sound came from the corridor. No one walked the hall, the Mongolian made no more inquisitor visits. The conductress had no more cities to announce before Moscow.

The pain in Timur's side did not worsen or weaken. It tweaked him when he moved, so he did not.

The change that occurred over the hours was in Anton.

He seemed to wane as if he had a leak. Closer to Moscow every minute, the haughty resolve of the scientist six days ago was gone. Left in its wake was a lackey.

He fetched Timur food and tea. Anton freshened the bandage around Timur's waist. When he saw the stab wounds cut by the Swede, he was overcome, for Anton had killed Björn just as surely as Timur. Anton finished the new dressing,

386

then lay on his berth with his back to Timur, sobbing like a child.

Anton stared for hours at great swaths of Russia, so much of it pristine. He and his kind, the scientists and apparatchiks, dreamed of bringing power to this gigantic land, a power over nature, even as that power turned to poison at Chernobyl. Did Anton mourn while he watched Russia go by, or did he plan?

At twilight, Anton said something brittle but defiant.

"I will tell the KGB everything. I will describe you. They will catch you, Timur."

Timur had no worries about the KGB. He carried multiple passports, enough money for bribes, scissors for his hair, straight razor for his beard. He spoke four languages. The mujahideen had contacts in Moscow who would hide him and transport him. No Russian would see his shadow.

Timur did not converse. He'd not set out to ruin Anton, only his country. The two settled into the silent shivering of the train. Anton said nothing else while full darkness fell over the land and train.

A knock came at the door. The Mongolian announced himself. Anton said, "Come in."

75

LARA

L ara and Gang did not make love again. Like a balloon, she wanted to hold one, treasure it, then let it go and watch it go.

The day passed in clumps of hours. A few fell to talk of shallow things, favorite restaurants in Peking, how different Baltimore was since Gang had been there, skipping stones over the deeper waters of the dangers they faced. Gang made her laugh; Lara wasn't shy about being heard by Anton and Timur through one wall, Sinjin through the other. So much hiding, so many secrets on this train, it felt good to let loose.

They didn't know if they would die soon, one of them or both. When they held each other, they held on. For those hours when Lara and Gang said nothing, they let their hands and arms, chests and breaths, speak.

At sunset, Gang took the opposite berth. He leaned in with her to the window to join hands on the little tabletop, watching stars twinkle and the rails snake around hills and follow riverbends. Lara took comfort in the size of the world and the depth of the night. There ought to be enough room for her and Gang.

He left for the diner. He returned with mushroom and potato pierogies, and the news that somewhere on the west-running tracks, the time on the train had finally matched the clock in Moscow.

They ate in the glare of one gooseneck lamp. They finished the pierogies before Lara's teacup had cooled enough to her liking. She reached for the cup. Gang heard something she did not. He lay a hand on Lara's wrist.

Out in the corridor, on the door to Timur's and Anton's cabin, Bat finally knocked.

76

BAT

The first thing Bat noticed was the copper smell of Timur's blood.

A lamp shined across Anton's shoulder on the Chechen, bare-chested and bandaged. Timur glowered from the shadowy side of the cabin. In the time it took Bat to enter, close the door and sit, the train raced through another village. The flickers on Timur looked like lightning.

Bat returned the Chechen his passport. Timur took it. He registered nothing, no pain, no surprise.

Timur said, "So you've solved it."

"In a way."

Timur looked past Bat to Anton. Something pitiless made the giant's black eyes cold as coal, a cold that could burn. In the unsparing glow of the lamp the scientist's face looked puffy. He'd been crying. For how many hours had this Chechen and Russian tortured and suffered each other in their tiny cabin in the stink of Timur's blood? Bat wanted out, and once out, he would not come back in this room, not even in Moscow.

390

Bat took from his greatcoat a pair of handcuffs.

"Anton Epstein, you are under arrest for the murder of Maxim Maximovich Sprygin."

He reached for Anton's arm. The scientist hesitated, but there were no more questions and answers. Anton offered his wrist. Bat cuffed him to the metal frame of the berth.

The scientist said, "I didn't do it."

Bat could sit, talk with these two, try for the last piece of the puzzle. But he wanted no more to do with the Chechen and the Russian, he was done with the deaths of the Agency man and the Swede. Bat would leave the puzzle unfinished on this speeding train through a ruthless Russia. He wanted only to be home. That would begin when he turned for the cabin door. Bat held his breath to breathe no more of this room.

77

GANG

Gang answered the knock. The Mongolian's broad-shouldered coat and brimmed hat filled the doorway. Gang did not invite him in.

Bat handed over Gang's auburn Chinese passport and Lara's black American diplomat's passport.

"You can go."

Gang asked, "Meaning what?"

"In Moscow. Just disappear."

"What happened?"

"Anton confessed."

Gang said, "No he didn't."

"No. He didn't."

Gang started to close the cabin door.

Bat put out a hand to stop him. "He's under arrest. No one speaks to him."

The Mongolian poked in his head to speak to Lara who he could not see behind Gang and the open door.

"Dr. Dill. Be careful. There is nothing I can do for you in Moscow."

From her berth, Lara said, "Thank you, Bat. Go home."

"The same to you."

The Mongolian took a few steps down the corridor. He leaned against the wall beside Timur's and Anton's door. Bat folded his arms and lowered the brim of his hat, on guard until Moscow.

Closing the door, Gang tossed the two passports on the empty berth.

Lara said, "Lay down with me." She turned off the gooseneck lamp. In the sudden dark she waited for him to climb behind her. She snugged against him; they left as little room between them as their bodies might.

Lara had something to say. Gang did not. He waited against her rising and falling ribs. The train raced in and out of hamlets, under highway bridges, clamored over river spans, through intersections where bells clanged and red lights blinked like an ambulance. More trains swooshed by, passenger and freight. In Lara's cabin there was no peace nor rest. Moscow grew one hour closer, then another.

After midnight, Lara stirred. She lifted Gang's arm off her as if peeling away a blanket. Gang knew to move to the opposite berth.

She sat up but clicked on no light. Gang lit the gooseneck behind him. Lara asked him to turn it off.

"No." Not all the terms could be hers.

She said, "We'll be pulling into Moscow at sunup."

"I know."

"The train's going to slow down when we approach the station. When it slows enough, you've got to jump off."

All he could answer, again, was No.

She continued: "You need to do what Bat said. Disappear."

"What about you?"

"I'm going to walk off the train and buy a ticket back to China."

"What if the mob doesn't want you to do that?"

"Then there's no reason for you to be standing there when that happens."

"Yes there is."

Lara reached across the small space, to persuade. When Gang didn't take her hand, Lara pulled back. Then she extended it again, for kindness. Gang nested his hand in hers.

She said, "You saved me once, in Mongolia, when you warned me. You can't save me now. It's Moscow. You've got to protect yourself."

"What if they come after you?"

"Then they're coming after an American diplomat in a public place. That's not so easy to do. If I get on the next train and leave Russia, they might let me go. But you, Gang. I know how the mob works. Moscow isn't that different from Boston. You have to make your way back to China. If they come for you there, at least it's a fair fight."

Lara moved onto the berth that had become his, above the yellow Geiger counter. She climbed behind him and cut off the gooseneck lamp. She lay her head on his pillow and pulled him down facing away. Lara put her nose against his neck and her chest to his spine. She layered an arm over his heart. Another train went by.

In the shuddering loudness, she whispered, "Sleep. I'll wake you."

78

BAT

B at had spent plenty of time on his feet. Five years ago, he walked thirteen hours home when his horse went lame in the Gobi. Seventeen years back, he stood for ten hours beside his bed while his wife bore their daughter, a complicated child from birth. Last spring, he tracked a wounded elk on foot with a bow and arrow from sunup to sunup. As a police chief in a small town, he walked everywhere. Leaning against the wall outside Timur's and Anton's cabin, Bat passed the hours tapping one finger inside a pocket of his greatcoat on his little drum; in the other pocket, he tapped his pistol.

Bat could doze on his feet; every lawman was able to do this. Whenever he closed his eyes, sleep approached like a friend with a gift. Bat turned sleep away. Prayer took on a few of the hours. Longing bore him along for a bit. Anger and submission grappled in his gut for a while. Blank exhaustion handled the rest.

An hour from dawn and Moscow, the last of the open spaces disappeared, no more farms or forests, and with them went darkness. The train no longer coursed through sporadic villages but entered an unbroken phalanx of electric light, streets and alleys, commercial buildings, bridges, and short tunnels, highways burgeoning with sunrise traffic. Bat stepped to the corridor windows to face the arrival of one of the world's great cities, a sight he hoped to never see again.

His hands stayed in his pockets, on his drum and gun, when the train decelerated. The brakes cawed like ravens along the linkage of carriages while the train drained its momentum. Bat spread his boots on the carpet to stay balanced.

Behind him, a cabin door opened. He expected to hear the blonde conductress shout to the second-class car, to the killers and their secret-keepers, that this was Moscow. The journey's final stop. Moscow.

Gang said, "Bat."

Bat turned. The Chinese was there, one stride away. Lara Dill watched from the doorway to her cabin.

Gang looked rested, relaxed, dressed in black head-to-toe. He'd strapped his soft travel bag across his back.

"I figured I'd say goodbye."

The train slowed to the speed of a jog through an industrial zone.

Bat took only one hand from his pocket, off the drum.

"Goodbye."

Gang said, "I thought you should know."

"Know what?"

"Who killed the Agency man."

"It was you."

"Yeah."

"How?"

"Knocked him out first. Then a sleeper hold. Compressed the carotid arteries."

Bat, the old wrestler, said, "Of course."

"Timur and I threw him out the window. Like you thought."

"What of Anton?"

"He had nothing to do with it. Except for shutting his mouth, but Timur threatened him into that. Then he sent Björn against Timur."

"What is Timur going to do?"

"I don't know. Something awful in Ukraine at the reactor fire. You should try to stop him."

"I have orders not to."

"That's too bad."

"Why did you kill the Agency man?"

"Maxim got drunk and started yelling he was going to bring the KGB down on Timur. Timur lost his temper. He would have ripped the guy's head off. It would have been plain murder."

"True. So you did it for him. To leave no trace."

"Yeah."

"Because you can't be investigated or a witness. You are a member of the underworld."

"Lara said you're good."

"She's been helping you."

"Leave her out of it."

The locomotive braked once more to creep into the station yard. Freight cars and flatbeds surrounded the arriving Trans-Mongolian. The day was still too new for the pole lights to shut off.

The time had come for Gang to jump off.

Bat stood alone in Moscow. He had no ancestor, family, tribe, or horse here with him. No desert, no puzzle. What was left? Only himself. And what was he? A lawman.

Bat pulled the handgun from his pocket. He pointed it at Gang's chest.

"You are under arrest for the murder of Maxim Maximovich Sprygin."

79

GANG

KILOMETER 7808

G ang asked, "Am I?"

The Mongolian nodded.

The split-second the brim of Bat's hat dipped, Gang moved. He flattened his back rightward against the windows, out of the path of the pistol's short barrel. With the sliver of a moment before Bat could correct his aim, Gang whipped up his left foot, fast as a lash, to pin Bat's right forearm, wrist, and the gun against the wall. Back-fisting with his right knuckles, Gang thumped Bat on the nose to blind him. In a blink, he twisted the handgun out of the Mongolian's grasp.

Gang said, "Thank you."

He retreated to Lara's doorway while the Mongolian bent at the waist, pinching his nose and sucking air. Gang handed the sidearm, a Tokarev 9mm semi-automatic, to Lara. She dropped the 8-round magazine to check the load, palmed the mag back into the grip, thumbed the safety, then tucked the sidearm into her waistband.

Gang kissed Lara's temple. With his thumb he rubbed it in, to make it stay.

He closed the distance to the Mongolian. Bat straightened, sniffling. His brown face scrunched, tears sheeted his eyes.

Gang said, "Don't try to take it from her."

From her doorway, Lara said, "I will shoot you in the leg and say you assaulted me. I fucking will."

Gang knocked a fist on the Mongolian's thick shoulder as he passed.

"Like I said."

Bat locked onto his wrist. Gang spun on him. He glanced down at the Mongolian's hand. Gang could snap the arm. He brought his eyes level with Bat's. The Mongolian considered, Gang cocked his head, and Bat let him loose.

Gang had no time to look back. A farewell glance at Lara or another warning to Bat would carry him ten yards closer to the station. He shoved out of the second-class car onto the platform; he didn't bother kicking the steps down to clamber off them. He planted a hand on the railing and vaulted into open air.

He landed on his feet in blue gravel, curled into a ball to roll on the rocks, then popped up. Lara clattered past, a hand pressed to the window. Moscow had enough shadows. Gang ran into them.

80

TIMUR

The train squealed to a stop in Moscow.

Timur grunted to lift his arms over his head. He tugged a clean black sweater over the gauze wrap. The blotch in the cotton had gone crusty, the wounds were staying closed. A doctor would be found before the morning was over for a new bandage and some antibiotics.

Deboarding passengers filled the Yaroslavsky station platform. The Trans-Mongolian ended seven days of clacking rails, juddering cabins, vistas of green and stone, factories, farm animals, blue and black skies, everything across eight thousand kilometers. Six hundred passengers left the train in tired strides and lugged baggage, with yawns and a few cries of greeting. Anton, shackled to his bedframe, watched none of it through the window.

Timur patted one pocket to feel his roll of cash, the other for his Russian passport. He put his soft sports bag in his lap.

"Goodbye, Antosh."

The scientist could not cross his arms. He sat back against the bulkhead.

400

"You, Timur Makhdi. You are an apostate from humanity. You may prove to be the worst human being ever born."

Timur leaned forward; the stitches clawed at his midriff. He braced hands on his knees to lessen the pain.

He said, "The worst person ever born is the Russian who killed Marisa. I will kill two hundred million to get to him. I swear to you, it will feel like only one."

Timur gritted his teeth to rise. He stood to his full height, the first time in a day. Anton raised his unchained hand.

"I will curse you with every breath I have left."

Timur said, "That may not be so many."

Anton pointed down at his briefcase.

"But I must ask you for something."

81

LARA

Hundreds left the train. Sinjin sauntered away among them, burdened by a suitcase so large it made him slant to carry it. The conductress Natalya did not vacuum but stood at the bottom of the stairs in her high heels, the blaze yellow baton jammed in the waistband of her gray skirt. She eyed the crowd with disdain and seemed to hate her job.

Lara stayed behind her locked door. Bat's pistol pressed in the small of her back; she was alone for the first time in a week. She had to depart the train, but every person on the platform felt like a threat.

She donned a jacket to cover the Tokarev. Lara decided to take nothing, abandon the soil samples, her clothes, and leave everything behind. She might need her hands free.

A knock on the door shot her to her feet; one hand scrambled behind her back.

The Chechen announced himself.

"May I come in?"

Lara swept the semi-automatic in front of her. She

unlatched the door and stepped back. At the click, Timur pushed open the door. He filled the doorway.

Timur looked ashen. He wore his black plastic jacket, ripped twice in the side. He indicated the pistol in Lara's two-hand grip. The barrel was tipped down, ready to be lifted.

He asked, "Is it your turn now?"

"What do you want?"

The Chechen held out a blue folder.

Lara asked, "Is that Anton's report?"

"He cannot give it to you in person."

Timur tossed the document on Lara's berth. She raised the gun at his heart. The giant did not turn or backstep but stood full and fearless.

"Goodbye, Lara Dill."

She could pull the trigger, likely would have to pull it many times. She hesitated, and this was long enough for Timur to turn out of the doorway. His boots in the corridor ebbed like a fading heartbeat. Lara locked the cabin door.

She watched Timur go out onto the platform. Three bearded men met him. One carried Timur's bag, another moved under Timur's arm to help him walk off. The third walked in front to clear a path through the crowd.

Lara thumbed through Anton's report. In one minute she realized what she had and what she had to do.

Pistol in hand, she opened the door. Lara checked the passageway, then stepped out. Even with the gun, she felt Gang's absence.

In the empty corridor Lara moved to Björn's door. She listened for the rapping of the little drum; when she heard it, she knocked.

Bat opened. He retreated to give her space to enter but she did not. Lara tucked the gun into her waistband.

The Mongolian said, "I'm waiting for the Soviets."

Lara peered inside the cabin. Björn lay covered by a blanket.

She said, "I'm sorry."

Bat seemed not to register sorrow, hers or his own. Perhaps that was what the spirits did for him. His ancestors might carry his sadness and pain away like the man who took Timur's bag, and the other who helped him walk.

"What do you want, Dr. Dill?"

"Björn had a Swiss Army knife."

"The weapon he used against the Chechen."

"I'd like to have it."

"It is evidence."

"The fight was self-defense. You said so yourself."

"Why do you need it? You have my gun."

"Björn was my friend. I want it to remember him."

"Still lying, Doctor?"

The Mongolian dug into a pocket of his greatcoat. He pulled forth an object wrapped in a kerchief.

"Here. Don't tell me. I want no more riddles."

She unrolled the scarlet-handled knife. Timur's brown blood marred the short blade. She folded it away.

Backing into the corridor, Lara said, "Make sure he goes home. You, too."

The Mongolian nodded. He closed the door without wishing her the same.

In her cabin, using the screwdriver head of the Swiss Army knife, Lara set to work gutting the yellow Geiger counter. She emptied it of electronics, saving only the faces of the gauges. In minutes, she folded Anton's report inside, then screwed the box shut.

She opened her cabin door, carrying only the yellow Geiger counter; her other hand stayed on the pistol grip under her jacket. Lara made certain the corridor was vacant; before she walked away, Anton's voice issued from behind his closed door.

"Lara?"

She had nothing to say to him. Björn's death lay at

Anton's feet. He bore some portion of Maxim's killing, too. In Beijing he'd arrived on the train an arrogant man. In Moscow, he yelped like a chained dog. Anton had been naïve from the start. Here at his finish, calling out to Lara, he remained so. He'd given her his report, but she would not use it as he intended.

Leaving the second-class carriage, Lara passed the steaming samovar. She touched it once, quickly not to burn herself, thanking it for never changing. At the bottom of the steel stairs, the conductress was nowhere to be found.

Dawn had slipped into the busyness of early morning. Railway employees in hard hats and blue smocks hiked the rails to check the wheels and couplings for damage and wear. The Trans-Mongolian had crossed four time zones, Asia to Europe, over desert and mountains, steppe and rivers, zoomed past millions of lives and into the wild places where men did not reside. Lara flattened a hand on the train, too, for its constancy.

The station platform was emptied now of passengers coming or going. Lara walked unaccompanied to the great stationhouse. Ahead, four men rounded a corner, all in suits, black shoes, and Macintoshes, making for the resting train. All four eyeballed Lara. They may have been KGB, or rude, or both.

She entered Yaroslavsky station. Foot traffic picked up with Sunday travelers purchasing tickets out of Moscow after the May Day celebration. This told Lara the skies over Russia were still closed. She entered a grand hall of black marble pillars, gold-leaf archways, money exchanges and banks shut in the early hour, and polished stone floors glimmering under skylights. Young people sat on backpacks. A long-haired boy played guitar and sang in English to a girl, they might have been Americans. Older Russians in humble clothes and traveling businessmen quietly entered an Orthodox chapel in the station. She passed a wall of payphones. She might call Rudd to get the latest on the reactor fire, tell him the awful news about Björn, say goodbye. But the doors leading out of Yaroslavsky were right in front of Lara.

She stepped into bright sunshine, into the spring blooms of Komsomolskaya Square in the center of Moscow. Shops and the Moscow Hilton framed the great traffic triangle, a dozen lanes of traffic buzzed east and west. How much radiation were she and the Muscovites breathing right now?

On the brick sidewalk Lara walked to the rail station's drop-off zone. No one paid her more than glancing attention. She stood tall and blatant in Moscow, the capitol of Russia where she'd been warned never to return.

Cars and people went by, minutes of them, tempting the thin hope that she'd survived, that somehow the order to kill her had been rescinded. The mob wouldn't come. She could go back into Yaroslavsky. Buy a ticket out of Russia.

But the mob had to come.

An olive drab Skoda slowed into the pull-over zone. A heavyset woman with a suitcase got out of the passenger side; the man driving left without waving to her. Under the jacket, Lara slid her fingers off the pistol. Another sedan slowed to the curb. Muscovites filled the sidewalk, some close enough for their shadows to cross hers on the bricks. Behind her, she heard the distinct snick of high heels.

A sting bit into Lara's back. A strong hand gripped her shoulder.

Close to her ear, the conductress said, "Hello, Luba."

Before Lara could twitch for the pistol, the sting in her back deepened. Lara grunted. When she twisted her head, her hair fell across her eyes.

From behind, Natalya brushed Lara's face clear.

"Nu, dorogaya."

There, darling.

"You."

"For six goddam days I have been trying to kill you."

The knifepoint burned like a brand under her skin. Lara growled, "Fuck you."

"Speaking of fuck. Who knew Gang would fall into your bed? He is quite something, though."

Lara craned her neck to see Natalya's face, but the conductress crammed her cheek against Lara's ear to stop her.

Lara hissed, "He got away."

The blade scrawled, carving more into Lara's back. The conductress covered Lara's mouth to squelch her yowl.

"Do you know how much money I lost when he jumped from the train?"

Lara searched on rising panic for someone to help her. Traffic whisked by Yaroslavsky station, around Komsomolskaya Square. Pedestrians took no notice; to them, Natalya was just a train conductress hugging a friend from behind. Warmth drizzled down the back of Lara's thigh.

Natalya took her powerful hand off Lara's shoulder. Lara tried to step forward off the knife, but the blade followed. The conductress picked the Tokarev out of Lara's waistband, then drew her backwards into the knifepoint.

Impaled, bleeding, Lara tried to figure how to fight, how to go flailing at death, but pain scattered into her ribs and limbs to confuse her body; she froze and could do nothing more than drop the Geiger counter and arch her spine.

Natalya's whisper cut through Lara's hard breaths.

"A car will pull up. I'm going to stab you and throw your body in the trunk. Then, Luba Mikhailovna, I am going to China."

Blood trickled down Lara's calf. One knee began to buckle. Natalya shifted her grasp under Lara's armpit to hold her up.

Natalya said, "Don't." But said no more.

The woman's chin rammed into Lara's shoulder. Her face slid away, her nose trailed down Lara's back. The pain blinked off. The dagger clattered at Lara's feet, followed by Natalya.

On shaky legs, she turned to Sinjin.

The young Brit held the conductress's yellow wooden baton. He smacked it into a palm, nodding, satisfied with the heft of the rod.

"Lara, dear, would you like to tell me what's going on?"

Lara grabbed Sinjin by one silk lapel to regain her legs.

Sinjin winced. "Or should I not ask?"

"No."

On the sidewalk, Natalya groaned. She stirred as if to rise. Sinjin said, "Excuse me."

He kicked her in the jaw hard enough to make Natalya's blonde hair lift and fall. Walking Muscovites continued on their way, watching but not interfering.

Lara let go of the Englishman to stand on her own.

She asked, "Where?"

"I saw you standing here at the drop-off. I have a taxi waiting and thought we might share. Then this beast of a woman approached you. It wasn't hard to see she had ill intent. And she had this handy little beauty in her waistband."

Sinjin flipped the yellow baton in the air; he caught it with a practiced hand and a fond eye.

"You remember I told you I'd spent four years in the Coldstream Guards?"

Lara nodded.

"Did I mention it was in Northern Ireland?"

Lara shook her head, still scrabbling for language. She wasn't dead, not yet. Realizing that fact consumed most of what she could express.

Sinjin surveyed the sprawled-out Natalya. The knife on the bricks was a star stiletto, a slender four-sided needle. The blade was made for a quick, quiet kill. An assassin's tool. Lara's blood coated the first inch of the tip.

Sinjin said, "Shame I don't have a camera out. The irony of this photo would be fabulous. Are you hurt, Doctor?"

"It's a small hole."

Sinjin collected the spilled stiletto, Tokarev, and Geiger counter. He offered them all to Lara. She took only the Geiger counter.

He asked, "Are you sure?"

"Yes."

"Perhaps take the pistol."

"Keep it."

"I am so terribly curious. A scientist and a diplomat. Guns and knives. Oh, Doctor."

"Can you get her away?"

Sinjin tucked the Tokarev under his jacket. The knife he drove between two bricks, then stepped on it to snap the thin blade. He tossed away the hilt.

"The girl is welcome to my taxi. She'll wake up on a farm. Be back in a jiff."

Sinjin jogged twenty meters to an idling cab. Natalya lay inert, well blacked out. No police wandered in sight, citizens on the sidewalk slowed but did nothing but rubberneck.

Lara touched the wound in her back. She found the pain bearable. The gash would need stitches and a bandage soon. How could Timur endure two such wounds when one almost did her in?

Sinjin's taxi arrived in reverse, backing into its own exhaust. He leaped out to toss his oversized suitcase onto the sidewalk. Together with the dark-skinned driver, some African communist with a happy smile, they bundled the limp Natalya into the rear seat. Sinjin gave the driver a wad of rubles, then stood aside as the cab chugged out of the drop-off lane into morning traffic.

Sinjin clapped, pleased with whatever escapade he told himself he was part of.

"I paid the lovely fellow well enough. I told him to drive out of the city until she wakes, then tell her the fellow who put her in the taxi was a very hirsute Italian."

"Always clever, Sinjin."

"Doctor, what else can I do for you?"

"It's best if you're nowhere near me. Walk off."

"I should like to stay."

"Don't pick mushrooms. Take a train straight back to Beijing."

"The reactor?"

"Or worse."

Sinjin looked defeated at the suggestion of some new debacle. Or maybe it was the idea of another week on a train. He tugged at his bowtie.

"Then I shall hope to see you in Beijing. You'll tell me all about whatever this is."

"I won't."

"No, of course. And I am so sorry about your friend Björn. He was remarkable."

"Thank you. Go."

"I wish you safety, Doctor." He indicated the blood on her fingertips. "Get yourself looked at."

Sinjin trundled his baggage farther down the pull-in zone. A cab found him in moments. Another African driver loaded his bag; Sinjin touched the yellow baton to his brow in salute to Lara. He climbed into the cab and motored away.

Lara bled while she waited, not long.

———

A sturdy GAZ Volga stopped, an improvement over the jalopy of four years ago. The thugs looked to be of a better quality, too.

Three arrived in the black sedan. Two got out slowly, crewcut men younger than Lara, wary of her. One kept his hand inside the zipper of his track coat, the other put both his mitts where Lara could see them.

"Are you alright?"

When she made no reply, he motioned at her feet. Lara looked down; she stood in a small puddle of her blood.

To the one with his hand inside his track coat, she said, "I'm not armed."

He nodded and left his hand hidden.

The rear passenger door was opened. Lara climbed in. Bending over cost her a moment of woozy balance; one of the goons caught her by the arm to ease her onto the backseat. She set the Geiger counter on the floorboard. Her right shoe was soaked and stunk.

Lara said to the driver, another rock-jawed type, "I'm going to bleed on your seat." He turned to smile with gold-trimmed teeth.

The men climbed in, one on each side. The doors swung shut, the Volga merged into traffic. No one slipped a sack over Lara's head, her hands were not tied. They hadn't expected to find her alive. She was bleeding on the seat because she was supposed to be in the trunk.

The flunky on Lara's left leaned away from her, hand still inside his jacket. The one on her right seemed the youngest of the three. He was the biggest, with the kindest face.

She said to him, "Take me to your boss."

He chuckled. "Of course. It is not a long ride."

What he meant to say was that you won't bleed out in the car. You'll get to die somewhere else.

The big one patted his lap. "Please. If you will put your head down."

Lara lowered her ear to his warm thigh. He rested a big paw on her shoulder, surely to hold her down but it felt like care.

She closed her eyes. The Volga motored for minutes on a highway, then into stop-and-start streets. No one asked her how she managed to be alive.

When the car halted, Lara had drifted off from weariness or blood loss, she could not tell. She was helped to a sitting position. The Volga idled in a nondescript alley between high brick walls that might have been factories, warehouses, or tenements.

Every movement echoed: the car doors opening and shutting, Lara's scuffle on cobbles. No trash blew in the alley, Russians were a neat people. The two who'd ridden in the back with Lara took her arms as if she might either collapse or run off. The Volga pulled away.

They ushered Lara past a steel door, up a metal staircase lit by a red Exit sign. She trudged with the Geiger counter up one story. Another door was held open for her. Lara stepped into a long gray corridor of unfinished drywall lit by bald bulbs in the ceiling.

"This way." The big man took her elbow. The other took his hand from his jacket. The floors were concrete without carpet; Lara's right shoe left bloody prints.

The hallway was lengthy and surreal, only the silence was finished. The large thug tugged Lara lightly to a stop outside the only door in any of the doorframes.

"Wait here."

He ducked inside. Lara made no effort to listen to the conversation behind the door but heard it anyway: She's not dead. What do you mean? She's outside in the hall. What the hell happened? I don't know. Why did you bring her here? What else was I supposed to do? Goddammit.

The door opened.

"Please."

The big thug followed Lara into a large gray space. A steel desk sat in front of a wide and curtainless window. The thug directed Lara to a folding chair, the kind in church basements. Lara walked to it, leaving tracks. She sat, holding the Geiger counter in her lap. The desktop was blank except for an old-school rotary phone. To the right of the desk in the unpainted drywall, another door cracked open.

A young man's head peeked out, crewcut like the flunkies. He grimaced, hesitating to enter.

In English, Lara said, "Son of a bitch."

The boy she remembered as Zach said, "Right?"

He opened the door only enough to slide through, then shut it like he was hiding something. In a blue suit and tie, Zach angled toward Lara as though he might touch her to say Hello, then changed course when he saw the red smears on his cement floor. He went straight to the chair behind the desk.

"Are you bleeding?"

"Stupid fucking question, Zach. What are you doing here?"

"Manning the phone." He tapped the rotary phone, making the receiver rattle in the cradle. Zach sucked his teeth. "So. This is awkward."

"Are you in the mob?"

Zach's hands fluttered up. "No, no, Lara." He snorted, a nervous chortle, pointing at the thug in the room. "These guys are the mobsters. Not me. Geez." He smiled without showing teeth. "Been a few years, huh?"

"Surprised to see me?"

Zach shook his head. "Oof. Yeah."

"You're a spy."

"Yep."

"Have you always been a spy? Were you a spy when you were getting my coffee at the embassy?"

The boy dapped the tabletop with a fingertip. "Yep."

"CIA? NSA?"

Zach wagged a finger. Fatso had done the same four years ago, and it got him killed.

Zach said, "See, those questions are what got you here in the first place."

Lara licked dry lips. A lot of her body's moisture was leaking out of the hole in her back. No one had offered her a bandage. That was a bad sign.

"How old are you, Zach? Twenty-eight?"

"Twenty-seven."

"You're the one who flagged my report on the theft of fissile materials."

Zach spread his hands like peacock feathers, into a *ta-da* gesture.

Lara said, "You almost got me killed."

He grimaced again. "Twice now."

"What's going on at Chernobyl?"

"Odd question, considering your circumstances."

"Just tell me. What do you know?"

"Not much. You know the Reds."

Lara twirled a hand as someone with little time.

Zach said, "The Japanese are reporting radioactive rain. President Reagan said the Soviets owe the world an explanation. The fire's out but no one understands what's going on in the melted core under all the shit they dropped on it. There's two dead that we know about, a night shift operator and a firefighter. A few dozen more are sick. A bunch of them are probably going to die, too. Tomorrow your old outfit, the IAEA's arriving in Moscow for a summit."

"Maybe I'll go."

Zach flattened his palms on the desktop. He leaned over them; if he'd been an animal, it was the first position before a pounce.

"Yeah, Doc, I'm not sure that's gonna happen. You see, the mafia."

"Shut up, you little prick."

The boy left his hands on the table but his torso faded back.

"Do what?"

"You're a kid spook and you don't run anything. You answer the fucking phone. The mafia's got nothing to do with this."

Lara pointed at the door in the gray wall.

"I want to talk to whoever that is."

Zach crossed his arms. The US embassy scientist he used to fetch for sat before him bleeding on his bare floor. Maybe he had a crush on her four years ago. Maybe she'd been impolite to him without knowing it. Or he was just one more cookie-cutter kiss-ass amoral government climber. Whatever. Moments ago, he'd had absolute power over her and relished it. Suddenly, he wasn't so sure.

"Why would he talk with you?"

"I've got something to offer."

"What is it?"

In the four years since Lara had last seen him, Zach hadn't changed. He was still skinny, young, and in the way.

"It's something to offer *him*."

She turned to the big mobster standing behind her, hands crossed at his belt. Returning to Russian, she asked, "Do you have a clean handkerchief?"

"Yes."

"Give it to me."

The big man reached into a pocket. Zach raised a hand to stop him, but the thug made a spitting sound and handed over the hanky. Lara pulled up her sweater to reach the small of her back. Clenching her teeth, she poked the cloth into the star-shaped wound. Lights went crazy behind her eyelids, her finger felt like a spear, but she kept upright in the chair. Once the handkerchief filled the hole, Lara cleared her throat and rattled her head like she'd swallowed something strong. Zach glared as if she was showing off. The mobster petted Lara's shoulder, then stepped back into his place should he have to kill her anyway.

She said, "Whew." Lara composed her hair. She gestured at the old rotary on Zach's otherwise empty desk.

"Well. Man the phone."

The dial spun under his finger, *shik*, *shik*, *shik*, three numbers, an intercom extension. With the receiver to his ear, he reverted to the sycophant gopher he'd been in the Moscow embassy.

"Sir? Yes, Sir. She wants to speak with you. No, Sir, I don't know."

Zach covered the receiver with his off hand.

"Where's the operative?"

Lara said, "In a taxi. Waking up."

Zach repeated this into the phone. He said, "I don't know, Sir. She's been stabbed. That's all I can tell. Yes, Sir. She says she has an offer."

Zach listened, focused down at the phone cradle. Then he looked up to Lara.

"Dr. Dill. I regret this very much. You've done nothing wrong. In fact, you've done your job in an exemplary manner. Your country thanks you."

Zach listened again, then spoke. The voice was his but not the eloquence. That belonged to the man behind the door.

"You're a scientist. You understand the nature of nuclear power. Human power is no different. It must be contained and managed. Kept out of the wrong hands."

Zach, the ventriloquist's puppet, paused then spouted more:

"You and I do the same work, Doctor. Yours is the field of radiation. Mine is war. Chernobyl is a demonstration of what happens when atomic power exceeds the wisdom of the hands it is in. Likewise, the Soviet war in Afghanistan, and every war by definition, is a failure of political power. You and I are managers, you of the atom, me of conflict. We're called to service only when there's a fuckup."

Lara slammed a hand on the rotary phone, hanging it up.

She shouted at the door, "Come out here."

Zach returned the receiver to the cradle. Instantly the phone rang. He brought the receiver to his ear, then handed it across the desk to Lara.

A gravelly voice said, "Go ahead, Doctor."

She bit her lip to choose her words carefully. Then Lara decided not to.

"Listen, I could give a shit who you are or who you work for. CIA, NSA, State, Pentagon, it doesn't matter to me. The fact is, you've been stealing nuclear material and giving it to the Russian mob to sell to the Afghans. Aside from how ugly that is, it's fucking dangerous, and I caught you."

"That you did, Doctor."

"You've taken two shots at me. I don't want a third. So I have a deal for you."

"What could that possibly be?" The voice had a twang. It sounded like bourbon and cigars, plainly American.

"You're trying beat the Russians."

"Every way we can, everywhere."

"What if I gave you something that would humiliate the Soviets? In front of the whole world. Something you could hold over some very powerful heads."

"I'd be extremely interested. What would it be?"

"A report that proves the Russians knew the accident at Chernobyl could happen. For years they knew the RBMK reactor had design flaws and did nothing about it. In fact, they made an accident more likely."

"This report exists?"

"I have it. Think about it. Gorbachev's trying to open the Soviet Union to the West. This report will humiliate him."

"You've got my attention. Who wrote it?"

"A senior engineer at the Chernobyl power plant. He was one of the designers of the RBMK. He wrote the report four years ago. The KGB deep-sixed it."

"So how did you obtain such a thing, Dr. Dill?"

"He rewrote it."

"I see. Where did this fall into your hands?"

"The Trans-Mongolian Express."

"Where is it now?"

"Let's strike a deal first."

The voice hummed, then said, "Please give the phone to Zachary."

Lara handed the receiver across the desk. Zach listened, said, "Yes, Sir," then disconnected. He spread both palms on the desk, tipping forward over them, bigheaded again.

"Where is it?"

Lara shook her head. "I'll tell you when you agree to what I want in return."

Zach waved her off.

"I need to have my hands on it first." He tilted his head to indicate the closed door, to say those were his orders from the voice behind it.

Lara asked, "How do I know you'll keep your end of the bargain?"

The big man behind Lara, quiet as the walls, stepped up. Once more he rested a mitt on her shoulder.

"*Ya sama otvezu tebya na voksal.*" I'll drive you to the train station myself.

Lara layered her own hand on top of the mobster's to reinforce, even charm him.

"*Vrach.*" Take me to a doctor first.

Zach glared over Lara's head at the insubordinate mafioso. Because he was gutless, Zach grinned.

"Alright, Lara. Where's the report?"

She leaned down; a pang gnawed in her back as the kerchief shifted. Lara smacked the yellow Geiger counter onto Zach's desktop. He yanked his hands out of the way.

UKRAINE

82

TIMUR

"*Zmei*. Your turn."

Timur laid down his shovel.

A dozen tunnellers leaned against the round wall. They enjoyed it when it came Timur's turn to shove the loaded mining cart. Ordinarily, two men were needed to push the half-tonne of dug-out sand along the rails to the mouth of the tunnel. Timur could do this alone, and when he did, one extra man could rest.

He heaved his bare chest against the trolley to get it rolling. The men whistled, always impressed. Some clapped him on his shoulder and said, "Fucking Zmei."

The tub rolled slowly until it caught momentum and Timur could straighten up to walk it to the tunnel's mouth seventy meters away. In the shaft, he passed diggers, surveyors, radiation monitors, and the crew waiting to assemble the next cement rings to support the tunnel.

Six days ago he arrived in Chernobyl as Carol Nicolescu, a Romanian miner. The diggers worked bare-chested from the heat in the tunnel. The ventilation in the shaft was poor, and there was a small sun dropping down through the sand above their heads. Timur took off his shirt, too. When the men dug alongside him for the first time, when they saw Timur put his back into the work, some called him Zmei, a dragon out of Russian myth who could spit fire and turn himself into a kitchen tool like a broom or a mop to escape detection, and regrow his head if lopped off. No one asked Zmei about himself, his past, or the old bullet hole and two freshly-knit wounds in his side. He did not swill vodka with the diggers on breaks and no one made him a friend.

Nearing the tunnel's mouth, the first gush of free air washed over Timur. Sweat on his back and shaved head cooled him. He pushed the laden trolley into the open night, under the glare of arc lights. Others tipped the tub over to pour out the sand. A bulldozer scraped the sand onto a mounding pile. Timur accepted a ladle of water out of a bucket. The team on break passed around a bottle. The Russian and Ukrainian miners joked and labored, and no one could tell them they might be gradually dying from radiation.

Once the trolley was emptied, Timur goaded it back into the lantern-lit tunnel. Once every three-hour shift, he pushed the cart alone so he could examine the joints of the cement shield rings, search for cracks and seams to sabotage, mistakes by the miners. So far, he'd found nothing he could exploit. The shaft grew daily by twenty meters; the Russians and Ukrainians, even drunk, worked faster than any Afghan.

In four more days, the tunnel would reach directly beneath the ruins of reactor #4. The miners would excavate a greater chamber, then pour a thick concrete pad around liquid nitrogen pipes, a super-coolant buffer laid in the hot core's path. The entire project would be completed in another week.

If Timur could find no way to slow or disrupt the tunnel, he'd have to destroy it.

He'd need dynamite.

———

MAY 13 PRIPYAT
UKRAINE SSR

Pripyat was more than a ghost city. The place was contaminated and would be for twenty-seven thousand years.

At sundown, Timur walked the three kilometers from the miners' tent encampment at Chernobyl to the center of Pripyat. His connection wouldn't arrive for an hour; he poked around the abandoned city. Timur found food rotting in grocery stores, basketballs on a gymnasium floor, blue booklets on schoolhouse desks, keys in automobiles, pots and pans on the curb, and the carcasses of dogs shot by patrols tasked with making sure nothing living was left in Pripyat.

He sat on a park bench between a Ferris wheel, a teacup ride, and a kiosk for flavored ices. Pripyat was dead. Timur would do this to all the Soviet Union, empty it and let it decay for ten thousand years, let the weeds have it, and maybe the dogs. He did not stay long in the park.

Timur walked to the city center, the cinema and the statue of Prometheus. In the softness of sundown, a man waited for him. The man wore all black, his hair was black.

When Timur approached close enough, Gang waved hello.

He said, "Zmei."

Timur did not break stride until he was arm's length from Gang. The Chinese did not retreat.

Timur asked, "Come to kill me?"

"Yep."

"How did you find me? Did Anton tell you?"

423

"Lara figured it out."

"Where is my dynamite?"

"Your mujahideen connection got delayed."

"Who are you working for?"

"The US government. And the Russian mob."

Timur nodded with his lower lip out, impressed.

"And Lara Dill?"

"She swung a deal with them both."

"For what?"

"For her life. My life. And, well, Timur, for yours."

"What did she offer in return?"

"Anton's report."

Timur rested a hand on Gang's shoulder, near the throat, to remind him of its weight.

"And what if I kill you?"

Gang shook a finger between them. "See, there's the thing. You remember Natalya?"

"The conductress."

"Turns out, surprise. She's in the same business I'm in. On the train I thought she had a thing for me, but she was just frisking me. Then in Moscow she tried to kill Lara. I hated her. But now that I'm working with her, she's okay."

"Working with her? How?"

"She's an expert long-distance marksman."

Gang raised his chin above Timur's scarred knuckles. The Chinese scanned the dusk, the vacant buildings of Pripyat, the roof of the movie house.

"So take your hand off me."

Timur lowered his mitt.

"What do you want?"

Gang sat on the low wall surrounding the statue. Wild grass had taken root in the seams between the stones.

"For you to go home."

"No."

Gang knit his fingers between his knees. He shook his head down into the ring of his arms.

"Look, man. You're going to die. I'm going to break your neck tonight, or Natalya will shoot you. Or I'll poison you tomorrow. I don't have any choice here. I'm saving Lara's life and my own. But I'm trying to give you a way out. You can choose to walk away. So walk."

Timur would break the little Chinese's neck; he bristled at the suggestion it might be otherwise. He spit once to clear the taste of it, then sat beside Gang. That might make the conductress, wherever she was hiding, hesitate on the trigger.

"Why do you say this to me?"

"Because Lara made the deal to send me. She thinks I'm a killer."

"You are a killer."

"But what if I don't do it? What if you and I both get out of here? I'm trying to make Lara see me as something else. She's an ex-cop, though, so I don't know if she can do it. But I've had enough, you know? Timur, can't there be enough?"

Two hundred million Russians. That would be enough.

"I will be honest with you, little Chinese man."

"Now would be a really good time for that."

Timur tapped his own heart. "I died in Afghanistan. Again in Siberia. If I die in Ukraine, *feh*." Timur nudged Gang with his elbow. "So try to break my neck. Or signal your sniper woman to shoot me, if she's out there. Better than poisoning."

Gang stood to move away from Timur on the stone wall. "No."

Timur ran a hand over his razor-smooth skull.

Gang said, "Last offer." He dug into a pocket of his black trousers.

"Here's a Chechen passport. There's ten thousand American dollars in there and ten thousand rubles. Go home, Timur. Go get your bicycle shop. Tell your family you're alive.

425

Get back your life, get everything they took from you. If the Russians come to Chechnya, fight them there. But Timur, goddam it, go. Or I have to do what I have to do."

Gang slapped the passport on the wall. Timur rose to face whatever he faced, as he imagined Marisa had done.

Prometheus cast no shadow. The sun was down.

Gang said, "You're not a dragon, Timur. Your head won't grow back if I blow it off."

"My head. Someone else's head. There will always be a head."

Gang inched closer. "Listen, they've got Anton's report. They'll use it against the Soviets, just like you want. There's nothing more you can do."

"Perhaps. But little Chinese man. You wondered, didn't you? For a week on that fucking train you wondered."

"Okay. Sure."

"Let us find out."

Three strides separated him from Gang. Timur covered one of them.

Gang held up a hand. "Hang on. See, there's one problem."

"What."

"Natalya gets paid more if she shoots you."

"Fuck her. She's not even there."

Gang raised a finger over his head. One meter behind Timur, the spot where he'd stood moments ago, a brick in the cinema plaza zinged. A rifle crack followed from somewhere in the warren of Pripyat.

Timur said, "That is not fair."

"Nope."

"I would win."

"Would not."

"You are stupid."

Timur took one of the two strides toward Gang. Either could touch the other. Gang did not retreat.

"Don't die today, Timur. Go home."

Timur tugged at his chin where his beard had been.

He turned to the statue of the god who stole fire. Timur snatched up the passport and flipped through it. The money was there.

"So. You let me live for a woman, eh?"

Gang said, "I've done worse for less."

Timur nodded, his lower lip out. He peeled away the ten thousand rubles and handed them to Gang.

"For Natalya. My apologies."

Timur pocketed the passport and American cash.

Gang asked, "Where are you going?"

"Afghanistan."

"Back to the fight?"

"No." Timur shook his head. "Back to the mountains. The sky. It is a better place to be dead than here."

Timur spit on the Soviet ground. He raised a hand to Natalya somewhere, and walked away.

CHINA

83

LARA

Z ach turned out to be an excellent resource.
The boy was a weasel, but he occupied a knife's edge between the US government and the Moscow mob. Maybe only a weasel could do that. With his help, Lara was able to keep up-to-date on the developments at Chernobyl, even from eight thousand kilometers away.

She hung up on Zach, then typed her notes. She buzzed Rudd to ask for fifteen minutes to give her first report since her return to Beijing. She'd ridden the Trans-Mongolian twice in twenty days. Lara knocked, entered, and sat. Rudd wore a white cable sweater and shorts. Tuesdays were his tennis game.

He said, "I still say you shouldn't be here. Take some more time off."

"Radioactivity never sleeps."

"What have you got?"

She slid two typed sheets across her boss's desktop. "The

highlights. The Soviet government finally declared that vodka's not a cure for radiation poisoning."

"I'll switch to scotch."

"Emissions from the reactor have dropped from eight million to one hundred fifty thousand radionuclides."

"Meaning?"

"That's a lethal dose if you're standing next to it. Bad enough to run from if you're a few miles away. Dispersed into an aerosol and spread over a few million square miles, the effects will be long term and unpredictable."

"How about the surrounding areas?"

"All the schools in Kiev are closed. Every child inside an exclusion zone with a radius of a hundred kilometers from Chernobyl has been relocated. So far, half a million people have been evacuated. A third of them will never go home."

"Deaths so far?"

"A firefighter and an operator confirmed dead. Both were buried in zinc coffins. A few dozen more have been hospitalized. The whole management team at Chernobyl has been arrested."

Lara leaned over her typed pages to tap a bold item.

"Here's the big news. The Soviets announced today they're going to build a gigantic sarcophagus around reactor four to lock it away. They've drafted fifty thousand people to work inside the irradiated zone. This is going to be a health crisis for years."

Lara and her boss spoke for ten minutes on her projections for the effects of latency in the affected areas. Long-term illnesses, birth defects, increasing rates of cancers; the world had never seen this level of ionizing radiation released over such a wide area, not even at Hiroshima and Nagasaki. The Soviets were still downplaying it, but that couldn't last much longer; the international community was increasingly clamoring for information. The Iron Curtain was at risk of being torn down.

Lara stood to return to her office. Before she reached his door, Rudd asked something not noted in her brief.

"What about the reactor core?"

"No one knows for sure. It's quiet."

"So the tunnel?"

"In the end, they didn't need it."

Lara shared with Rudd a moment of staring at nothing. Maybe waste, and sorrow. Then he shook it off, because today was tennis day.

On the way back to her office, Lara paused at a bank of windows. Beijing's afternoon sky was cerulean. Cherry trees past their peak lined the boulevard in front of the embassy. She'd seen the trees bloom before she left but her favorite time was now, when the blossoms faded and became a pink confetti. She would, indeed, take the rest of the day off.

At her desk, in the center of it, a steaming cup of tea waited. It had not been there before, like so much else in her life lately. She touched it but the teacup was too hot to pick up.

A NOTE FROM THE AUTHOR

Dear Reader,

Thank you for reading *Trans-Mongolian Express*, I hope you enjoyed it.

Please leave a review on Amazon and Goodreads and other book review platforms. Your support in this way greatly helps in getting my books out into the world. It will be very much appreciated.

Warmest regards,

David

Richmond, Virginia

ACKNOWLEDGMENTS

Every novel I've written began as an idea in my own head. Every one but this. Jonathan and Michael Adler, sons of the great American novelist Warren Adler, asked me to write *The Trans-Mongolian Express*. I met the brothers while visiting my friend and adopted sibling Dick Robertson in Los Angeles. Initially I was skeptical about creating a novel with roots in someone else's work. But as I developed my own story, dove deeper into the research (the immense train journey across Asia, Chernobyl, nuclear fission, China, Mongolia, the USSR, Chechnya) then invented the cast of characters, I fell in love with writing this work. After so many large-scale historical novels, crafting a thriller-adventure-travelogue-comedy-action-romance-mystery was a marvelous experience. The Adlers have been a joy to work with.

My friend Lindy Bumgarner feeds me, encourages me, and is a model of wisdom and endurance. When I grow tired and frustrated, I watch her and try to be as tough and good.

The kindness and loyalty of dear friend Katharine Sands continues to amaze.

In my hometown of Richmond, VA, I'm honored to be allowed to teach writing to the military veterans of the Mighty Pen Project, the first responders of Frontline Writers, and my creative writing classes at VCU Arts. Each student broadens my world.

Chuck, when you look good, I look good. Dave Aldridge is my spirit animal, Sheila is his keeper. Boss Barotti and

Catherine are the best neighbors I could have. Jim and Jeff are instruments of sanity. Danny and Taylor are models for doing well by being good.

The Virginia War Memorial honors me with their trust. Thank you Pam, Clay, Annie, Dan.

My editor Kevin Smith made this book better than I could have done alone. That was the point.

All artists sit atop a pyramid of friends, supporters and family. When they do not crumble, we do not. To all those who help hold me aloft to do what I do, my thanks and unyielding affection.

David L. Robbins
Richmond, VA Summer 2023

ABOUT THE AUTHOR

David L. Robbins began writing fiction in 1997 with the globally acclaimed novel *War of the Rats*. Since then, he has published seventeen novels, with repeated visits to the *NY Times* bestsellers list. David is also an award-winning screenwriter, essayist and playwright, receiving grants from the National Endowment for the Arts. He has founded five nonprofits to benefit aspiring authors, underserved youth, military veterans, and first responders, all in his hometown of Richmond, Virginia. In 2018, the Virginia Commission for the Arts named David one of Virginia's two *Most Influential Literary Artists* for the last 50 years. David has taught advanced creative writing at Virginia Commonwealth University for almost two decades. Two of his latest novels are *Isaac's Beacon*, set during the creation of the state of Israel, and the sequel, *The Shortest Road*, which invokes the Arab-Israeli War of 1948 and the Palestinian diaspora out of the contested lands of Palestine.

If you wish to contact David, you can do so at his website: davidlrobbinsauthor.com.

Find his books at:

amazon.com/stores/David-L.-Robbins/author/B001HD1YOA

bookbub.com/authors/david-l-robbins

MORE FROM WARREN ADLER

This work was inspired by the novel *Trans-Siberian Express,* written by Warren Adler.

For complete catalogue of Warren Adlers works, including novels, plays, and short stories visit: www.warrenadler.com
Inquiries: Customerservice@warrenadler.com

facebook.com/warrenadler
x.com/warrenadler

ALSO BY DAVID L. ROBBINS

The Promised Land Series

1. Isaac's Beacon

2. The Shortest Road

World War II Series

1. War of the Rats: Stalingrad

2. The End of War: The Race for Berlin

3. Last Citadel: The Battle of Kursk

4. Liberation Road: The Red Ball Express

5. Broken Jewel: Rescue from the Japanese Camps

USAF Pararescue Series

1. The Devil's Waters

2. The Empty Quarter

3. The Devil's Horn

4. The Low Bird

Mikhal Lammeck Series

1. The Assassins Gallery

2. The Betrayal Game

Others

Scorched Earth

The Finger: A Novel of Love & Amputation

ALSO BY WARREN ADLER

FICTION

Banquet Before Dawn

Beneath the Ivory Tower

Blood Ties

Cult

Empty Treasures

Flanagan's Dolls

Funny Boys

Madeline's Miracles

Mother Nile

Mourning Glory

Natural Enemies

Private Lies

Random Hearts

Residue

Target Churchill

The Casanova Embrace

The David Embrace

The Henderson Equation

The Housewife Blues

The Serpent's Bite

The War of the Roses

The War of the Roses: The Children

Trans-Siberian Express

Treadmill

Twilight Child

Undertow

We Are Holding the President Hostage

THE FIONA FITZGERALD MYSTERY SERIES

American Quartet

American Sextet

Death of a Washington Madame

Immaculate Deception

Senator Love

The Ties That Bind

The Witch of Watergate

Washington Masquerade

SHORT STORY COLLECTIONS

Jackson Hole: Uneasy Eden

Never Too Late For Love

New York Echoes

New York Echoes 2

New York Echoes 3

The Sunset Gang

PLAYS

Dead in the Water

Libido

The Sunset Gang: The Musical
The War of the Roses
Windmills